Ruthless People

J.J. McAvoy

Ruthless People
Copyright © by J.J. McAvoy 2014
ISBN-13: 978-1544897820
ISBN-10: 1544897820

NYLA Publishing
350 7th Avenue, Suite 2003, NY 10001, New York.
http://www.nyliterary.com

DEDICATION

This book is dedicated to those who said no, and the people who told me to ignore them.

ONE

"There are four kinds of homicide: felonious, excusable, justifiable, and praiseworthy."

—Ambrose Bierce

LIAM

So, today was the day. I drank straight from the brandy bottle. Fuck the glass. I was too tired to move.

"You plan on sharing?" Natasha asked as she rubbed her body against mine.

Handing her the bottle, I leaned back, watching her pour the liquor down her throat. God, I was going to miss that throat but that was about it.

"This is such a sad day." She frowned when I took the bottle back. If only she would leave after our "meetings." But there was no point kicking her out right this second. Our meetings were officially over, or my mother would demand my balls and my father would hand them up to her.

"What's this girl's name again?" Natasha asked, rolling on top of me.

1

Brushing her blond hair back from her face, I thought of all the things I'd rather be doing instead of talking but had to restrain myself.

"Melody Nicci Giovanni," I said, taking another swig.

She pouted, and it was ugly. Most of her facial expressions were ugly, but I didn't keep her around for her face, or her brain for that matter.

"Arranged marriages are so circa the eighteen hundreds. How can you get married to a girl you've never met before? You don't even know what she looks like. What if she's ugly, or fat?" she asked. It would have been a good point if it didn't matter who my family was and what we did for a living.

"I've explained this Natasha. The Giovannis are one of the most powerful, if not *the* most powerful family in Italy and most of the west coast. My father wants an end to the rivalry between the Irish and the Italians. So, even if she is ugly, or fat, or covered in bloody warts, I will do my duty and marry her." Pushing her off me, I rose to my feet.

Sedric, my father, had spoken of this marriage for the past twelve years. I was only fifteen and wanted to prove myself, so I was willing do anything that needed to be done to make the family proud, like a bloody idiot. I should have just let Declan marry her, but he had already hacked into his first major Swiss bank account, robbing the Russians blind. Neal was too damn old and had already found himself the perfect arm candy. Like

2

all sons, we wanted to impress our fathers. I thought I had no other option, but like I said, I was a bloody idiot.

"You could just marry me. I am one-quarter Italian." Natasha laughed and rolled around in my bed. I was going to have to burn those sheets or maybe get a new bed.

"Not even if hell froze over and my mother was six feet deep," I replied, grabbing a towel.

"And why not?" she yelled, holding the sheet to her chest as if she had any modesty to protect.

I looked her dead in the eyes. "Because you are a floozy, a manky, a whore, a woman of no importance or brains with nothing to note but a good ass and a deep throat."

Walking over to her, I kissed the side of her cheek before holding on to her sweet throat. "But don't be sad. We all have our roles to play, and you have played yours. Your services will no longer be needed."

Letting go of her, I grabbed a few bills from my wallet before throwing them in her direction.

"I am not a prostitute." She held back a sob.

I hated criers. I smirked at that.

"Yet, you're going to take the money anyway."

I headed to the bathroom, and when she didn't reply, I turned back to her one last time.

"Leg it babe, and if you think of taking anything other than the money I just gave you, I will not hesitate to kill you, sweet throat or not." And I meant it. I was a Callahan. Our word was law in Chicago and on most of the east coast. The police didn't even bother with us anymore.

Hearing the bedroom door open and shut, I smiled to myself before jumping in the shower. It would be the last one until I met my future wife.

Did she like showers or baths? I didn't care, but it just proved that I didn't know anything significant about her other than her birthday, February 13, 1990, and a few small facts. Everything else, her father kept buried. There were no pictures of her anywhere—no social media accounts or driver license. Nothing—not even a fucking receipt with her name on it. She was a ghost. If I didn't know better, I would've thought she didn't exist.

It made sense, though. I would do the same if I were to have a daughter. There were some crazy fucks in the world who didn't understand what it meant to be the offspring of a mafia leader. Family was everything. It was the one thing my father had drilled into our heads since we were children.

Rule One: You kill for family. You die for family. Because you can't trust anyone else.

In my awkward years as a preteen, some older fool had thought it would be funny to push me down a flight of stairs at school. That night, Neal and Declan burned his house down, but not before beating him within an inch of his life. When they came back and told father what they had done, he gave them the keys to the Porsche and told me to take notes. And take notes I did, very good notes. It was the reason why I was now my father's right-hand man instead of Neal, despite the fact that he was older. Neal didn't mind though—he was the muscle—while our cousin Declan was more behind the scenes. It worked perfectly.

Rule Two: Take no prisoners and have no regrets about it.

Stepping out of my bathroom, there they stood, my father, brother, and cousin, all dressed in the finest suits money could buy.

"Did you read the files I sent to you, or were you too busy with your whore?" my father asked glowering at the files on my desk.

"He probably stopped when he saw no pictures." Declan grinned from the door as Neal snickered.

"As a matter of fact, I did, but I don't give a shit where she went to school or what her favorite color is. The one thing I needed to know wasn't in that file. For all I know, Melody Giovanni could look like an Italian horse."

Sedric stepped in my path, standing just as tall as I was, preventing me from walking to my closet

"Father—"

"Have you forgotten what is at stake here?"

"How—"

"Do not interrupt me." He sneered then said, "You seem to forget that the only way you are going to be head of this family is through marriage."

"There is nothing there about her I care about."

Grabbing hold of my neck, he glared. "Pick up the damn folder, son."

Pulling out of his grasp, I saw Declan standing by my desk ready to hand me the folder, while Neal just stood a foot behind, ready to crawl up my fathers ass, if necessary.

"I don't need the folder. I fucking read it." "Melody Nicci Giovanni: age twenty-four, born on February 13, in an unknown northern California hospital, only child of Orlando and Aviela Giovanni who both emigrated from Italy as teens. Her mother died when she was young, and since then Orlando has all but locked her away in a tower. She was homeschooled for most of her life, until she went to a small community college in some nowhere prissy town called Cascadia in Oregon. I'm guessing that's where ice skating and glitter was invented." I waved Declan off before walking to my closet.

Wrapping the red tie around my neck, both Declan and Neal snorted at my comment while my father stood waiting for more.

"Other than that, she's a fucking ghost. No photos. No fingerprints. Just fucking breadcrumbs up and down the west coast, while her father killed every rival Italian and Irish family within a hundred-mile ratio, before taking over their streets." By the time we figured out it was them, the west coast was completely cut off to us. None of our production could get in or out without being busted—the son of a bitch—and now they were working their way south, taking over the Mexican cartels.

Italians always had to spread their shit and put their name on everything.

"The first and last time I met Melody, she was skeet shooting while her father and I discussed the possibility of this contract in his office. Not once did that dark little head of hers miss, and she was nine." My father said.

"Am I supposed to be impressed? Nervous? Elated? Thank God, she knows how to shoot skeet. She's still a woman like any other."

He didn't speak but walked across the room just as three noisy women began to pound against the door.

"Liam, hurry up. You have to meet Mr. Giovanni in an hour!" my cousin's wife yelled from the other side of the door.

There had to be a limit to the boundaries an in-law could cross. If Declan didn't care about her so much and she wasn't family, I would be tempted to hurt her.

"Handle your woman," I told him.

Neither of them made any sense to me. Declan was quiet, calm, and paler than snow, while Coraline was loud, outgoing, and well . . . black. My father was pissed she wasn't Irish for about ten seconds before he realized he had no room to talk, seeing as how my mother was a half caste.

"Liam, stop wanking off," Olivia, Neal's ever-so-bold wife said. All three were now infesting my room.

"None of you were invited inside—"

Olivia laughed. "We saw your harlot run out of here like a bat out of hell, so we figured you were getting ready."

Stepping out, Neal and Declan grinned like mad fools at their wives.

"If you care about their lives, you will get them away from me fast," I said through my teeth.

"Are you threatening my daughters?" my mother asked.

"Yes, as always," Coraline said, laughing, before giving her a hug. Of course, my mother returned it, the traitor.

"For the love of God. Get out!" I was going to kill them all.

"Don't raise your voice at me, young man." My mother's green eyes narrowed, causing Neal to laugh outright.

"Tell him, Mom," he said.

I pleaded with her.

"Those damn eyes of yours," she mumbled, and I knew I had won.

Thank fucking Jesus.

"I think we have had our fill for now. Let's let the boy get dressed in peace," she said, and I would have taken offense to the "boy" comment, but I just needed them to leave without resorting to deadly force.

"Let us know if you need help getting dressed, sweetheart," she added as they exited.

Where the fuck was I going, prom?

"I am a grown man, Mother."

Her green eyes narrowed. "Real grown men don't use hookers."

At that, everyone laughed before closing the door, but I could still hear them. This was another reason I needed to get married. You weren't a "real" Irish man until you had wife. Without one, no matter what I did, I would never gain the respect that was owed to me.

I would take this Melody Giovanni and form a woman fit to rule at my side. With her family's power added to my own, I would own it all before I was thirty. The thought of that, and what else the future held, got my cock up. Only a small part of me cared if she was attractive or not. Her last name and her loyalty would get me off just fine. Thankfully, from what I was told, she already knew what her family did. I didn't have time to train her on what to expect or why my clothes may be a little bloody sometimes.

I straightened my tie before reaching for my gun and placing my brass knuckles in my pocket. Opening the door, my father stood waiting— correction, hovering. He looked me up and down before nodding in approval.

Rule Three: Just because you sell drugs for a living isn't an excuse not to dress well.

"Here are the Giovannis' updated finance and business records," he said before handing me a thick folder as we walked.

Him and his damn folders.

"How did we get these?" I said without thinking, and then answered knowingly. "Declan is getting better."

"He broke through the firewall this morning . . . while you were inside Ms. Briar." He glared at me.

"I ended it," I said once we reached the awaiting cars.

My mother smiled, kissing us both on the cheek.

"Hopefully, or I will have to get involved." He kissed my mother back. "Goodbye dear, we will be back in the morning."

"I know the drill. Let me know when you've met her," she said once Neal and Declan entered their own car. We never used one vehicle. My father and I rode separately while Declan and Neal rode together.

Entering my black Audi, I skimmed through the files, knowing that the moment we started to move he would call. When my phone went off, the driver simply connected it to the car Bluetooth.

"Finished?" my father asked me.

I smirk. "The bastard almost tripled his profits in less than a fucking year."

"He's also somehow gotten his drugs into Valero territories—Greece, Russia, and the damn Philippines. He has networks going through most of Eastern Europe, the little fucker," Declan stated through the radio. Apparently we were on a conference call.

We had tried to put our drugs in that side of the world for the last four years, but the Valero guarded it tighter than a father on spring break. There were three families stronger than all the rest. The Callahan, the Giovanni, and the fucking Valero. The Valero were nothing but snakes—no, worms crawling in the dirt eating their own shit. Most of them were Russian, some German, all thieves stealing my property and selling it as their own.

"The man's got fucking horse shoes and a leprechaun up his arse," I said. That's the only way they could have pulled it off without the Valero filling them with bullets.

"Not to mention their numbers are growing. When I was in Mexico, I saw at least twenty of Giovanni's men guarding underground heroin fields," Neal said, a bit too excitedly. "Fucking underground, can you believe it? I wouldn't even begin to understand the amount of science shit they need to make that work. Down there, the name Giovanni sends men running and pleading for their lives."

"*Táimid ag titim ar gcúl.*¹ . . and I do not like to be behind. I will not sit idly by as they surpass us. Do you understand me?" my father replied. "Liam."

"I know," I sighed, *for the last fucking time.*

"Don't fuck it up. With this marriage we can steamroll the Valero and anyone else," my father added *again*.

"Thank God the poor bastard didn't have a son," Declan said.

"Nothing is final yet," my father replied. "Even after Liam marries her, which will take a few days if your mother has her way, they won't just give us everything. It may take months to make sure it is *our* name that strikes fear into the hearts of men."

"Liam, can you do this? You are very vain. What if she is not up to your mighty standards?" Neal's tone was serious, and I wanted to bust a pipe over his face.

"Piss off." I wasn't going to fuck this up. They should know this by now. Orlando Giovanni's daughter was the key to every door. "If she isn't up to par, I will drink until I can't see straight. Or until I can convince her to see Olivia's plastic surgeon." I was only half joking. Ugly people didn't have to stay ugly forever.

"Fuck you," he snapped.

"Great, thanks Liam, now he's going to be bitching the rest of the ride." Declan sighed.

"Look how much I care." I nodded at the driver who ended our call for me.

I needed a moment, but all I could think about was the little Giovanni that was about to be part of my life. Taking the ring out of my jacket pocket, I stared at the massive diamond that would seal our fates. She was Italian, which meant Catholic, just like us, and that meant:

Rule Four: No bloody divorce.

"Let the games begin," I whispered to myself. I was going to make this work or die trying. But, if she was anything like the females I had in the past, she would be dancing in the palm of my hand, and I couldn't wait.

TWO

"Even in killing men, observe the rules of propriety."

—Confucius

MELODY

"Ms. Giovanni, we will be landing in h-half an h-hour," the flight attendant stammered.

Nodding, I simply raised my glass, but the moron was so scared, he couldn't even pour the wine right. I narrowed my eyes at the red stains on my new white Armani jacket before glaring at him. I snatched the bottle from his damn hands.

"I'm so—"

"Don't say sorry," I said in a low hiss. "You aren't even on the threshold of sorry yet."

His eyes widened before taking a step back and backing straight into Fedel, who already had a gun pointed at the back of his skull.

"All we really need is the pilot, ma'am," Fedel said simply.

Stripping off my jacket, I stared at the moron at the end of the nine-millimeter. He was young, only a few years older than I was. What would make him take the job as a steward on my jet? A better question would be, who *cleared* him to be a steward on my fucking jet? Things spoken in here were more sensitive than the damn Watergate tapes.

"Fedel, how did this fool get on my plane?" I asked, only mildly interested as Monte handed me another file.

"His sister racked up quite a large debt. I do believe he is trying to pay it off," he said, waiting for me to give the go-ahead. He was so trigger-happy sometimes.

"Is that why you're here? Your sister is a crack whore?"

He frowned, swallowing the lump in his throat before speaking again. "Crystal meth."

It's too early in the morning for blood. I shook my head at Fedel. He sulked for a moment but did what he was told and lowered his GLOCK.

"*If* you want to pay off your sister's debt, it would be wise for you to stay alive and not spill my Romanée-Conti, or ruin nine-hundred-dollar jackets," I told him before turning back to the file in front of me.

"Yes, M-M-Miss G-Giovanni. It will n-never happen a-again." His voice sounded like a dying dog's. I almost pitied his sister. Was he all she had coming to her aid?

"Count yourself blessed Nelson Reed, 997-00-4279, 1705 Blue Ridge Road," Fedel said, making sure the moron was aware that we not only knew his name, but his social security number and address. Just because we didn't kill him today didn't mean we could not destroy his life tomorrow.

Fedel sighed before taking a seat in front of me. "It was a nice jacket. You should have let me kill him."

"My father wasn't pleased with the bloodstains I left in the last jet." I smirked, lifting the picture of my future husband.

Husband. I cringed at the word.

I wouldn't deny he was attractive—highly attractive, in fact. But I would need more than green eyes, dark brown sex hair, and a charming smile. He wasn't very muscular either, but he looked fast and strong.

"His full name is Liam Alec Callahan, age twenty-seven. He graduated high school at fifteen, Dartmouth at twenty," Fedel said, sorting through the photos.

"Let me guess, top of his class?" I added, waiting for him to pour more wine in my glass.

Fedel did so before nodding. "But of course, nothing less than perfection for the Irish mutt. That doesn't only apply to the schools, but also their fancy half-a-million-dollar suits, luxury cars, vacations houses, parties, and whores."

That got my attention.

"He uses high-end hookers?" It shouldn't surprise me much, all men had their toys. I would have to put an end to it when we were married, but I understood. The marriage contract our fathers signed fifteen years ago stated neither side would tolerate infidelity. It had less to do with romance and more to do with strategic reasoning. Hookers and lovers almost always led to the fall of an empire. The moment you became comfortable with one another, secrets were spilled, and information was stolen in the dead of night. It was just easier to do without it.

"None that we could find. Instead, he just buys them pretty, shiny things like diamond bracelets, expensive purses, or thousand dollar shoes. They all like their shoes," he said mockingly, sliding over photos of all the women Liam had been with. It was quite a list. At least he would be an experienced lover, but that didn't necessarily mean he was good in bed.

"Is he clean?" If he wasn't, we could buy whatever drug was needed. Ninety percent of everything out there had a cure . . . with the right credit card.

"As a damn whistle," Fedel said, almost disappointed. "From his current health records, he is healthier than a racehorse, which is surprising with amount of brandy he drinks. His beverage of choice—Camus Cuvee. He has a damn glass, or even the bottle, to his lips in every photo. He isn't depressed or an alcoholic, he's—"

"Just Irish." I added. They could drink every day, from dusk until dawn, and still walk a straight line.

"Exactly. From what I've gathered, he's the brains and is also highly skilled in hand-to-hand combat, boxing being a pastime of his. It looks like daddy dearest has spent most of his time forging him to take his place."

"Doesn't he have an elder brother?"

"Yes, he does. Meet Neal Aiden Callahan, age thirty-one. Married to Malibu Barbie, aka Olivia Ann Colemen, age twenty-nine, three years ago." He lifted up a photo of the happy couple. Neal was all muscle with brown hair and hazel eyes, while his wife looked like a life-sized Barbie doll. On her wrist was a small tattoo of a Celtic Knot in the shape of an oak tree.

"A Dara knot." I told him looking over the lines.

Fedel's eyebrow rose. "A what?"

I did not repeat myself but explained, "It means internal fortitude; to remain strong regardless of the circumstances around you. It seems Barbie is not very fond of the world she lives in."

"Well she sure likes the money it brings her. She can't bite the hands that give her those nice Jimmy Choo's."

Dropping the photo, I waited for him to go on.

"As for her husband, Neal is also a proud graduate of Dartmouth, by the skin of teeth *as it happens*," Fedel added. "And is also a world-class sniper. When he isn't killing people from hundreds of yards away, he is playing baseball . . . a lot."

"So the brother is an idiot. Olivia's maiden name is Colemen?" I repeated, focusing back on his wife as I took another sip. "As in Senator Daniel Colemen?"

Fedel nodded, lifting up a photo of the man in question. "Yes, Senator Daniel Colemen, a right-wing conservative pushing for a smaller government, and I wonder why? Her mother is an active left-wing liberal blogger, which is why they are divorced and the former Mrs. Colemen is now helping the needy children of Africa as the head of the Callahan's Global Youth Charity. Both know about their daughter's new family and approve."

I grinned at that. "Is it real a charity?"

"Sadly, yes. When they aren't stealing cars for the black-market, organizing several murders-for-hire, or selling heroin, crack, and meth to Suzy down the block, they're attending ballets and charity balls to better their community." He shook his head.

"What about this one?" I asked, pointing to the man beside Liam. He had the same green eyes as Liam, however the man's hair was longer and a lighter shade of brown. I figured the African American woman next to him had to be his wife.

"Ah, Declan Alvin Callahan—"

"Why the fuck do all their middle names start with an *A*?" I asked.

Fedel looked around to see if he had the answer somewhere in his papers. I didn't need to know, but watching him squirm was amusing. First generation Italian, like myself, we looked a lot alike—the same olive skin tone, pitch black hair, and brown eyes. He was my right hand, and in some ways, that made him closer to me than a sibling. Nonetheless, I never wanted him to get too comfortable. No matter how ridiculous my question was, or how pointless it may seem, his job was to get my answer or die trying.

"It seems to be a tradition started in the eighteen-forties after the first Callahans came over from Ireland," he said at last. Nodding, I waited for him to continue.

"Declan Alvin Callahan, age twenty-nine, married to Coraline Wilson, age twenty-five. He is the son of Sedric's older brother, who was set up by the Valero twenty years ago, and killed by Chicago PD in the crossfire. Since then, Sedric has raised Declan almost as his own. Coraline, the wife, is the daughter of Adam Wilson, big shot bank owner. From what we can tell, Declan was the one who hacked the system this morning and stole that twenty-seven million from the Russians a few years back. Most of them still don't know he did it. Those who did were killed off, most likely by Neal."

What a lovely family.

"Coraline. I've seen her face before," I stated, staring at the photo of Declan Callahan's wife.

"Maybe that's because if Robin Hood and Mother Teresa had a daughter it would be her."

I tried not to smile. "Explain."

He left a spread of photos across the table. In each one Coraline was either feeding the homeless, giving blood, rebuilding homes, and so on.

"She spends more time giving away all her shit than anyone in the family. Last year alone she spent almost nine million on charities and performed over two thousand hours of community service. It's like she's—"

"Guilty," I stated. Giving was normal. Giving to make yourself look like a better person was normal, but this went way beyond that.

That might be a problem. Both women seem to love the lifestyle and hate the life . . . just great.

Lifting the last set of photos, I knew who they were—the world knew.

"Sedric A. Callahan, who is named after the first Callahan, age fifty-four, and his wife, Evelyn Callahan, age fifty-one, make sure their kids breed well," he stated, placing the file down.

"Now Fedel, it's wrong to judge." I grinned. The truth of the matter is that I was slightly impressed, and it took a lot to impress me.

I could tell Liam's green eyes came from his mother, while his darker features came from his father. They were all quite good looking, and from what I could tell, all was God-given with the exception of Malibu Barbie. It was good, but I could tell she's had work done. Nevertheless, they all looked Hallmark ready. It was almost sickening.

"Ma'am, why in the hell is Sedric stepping back and allowing his second son to take over? It makes no sense. I've checked into his health records, and he's fine."

I took my time drinking in the warmth of the wine as I stared at the photos. Fedel was right. People like us didn't just step down. We didn't retire. We died and then someone tried to replace us. But I think I knew Sedric a little bit better, after all my father spoke often of him.

"All I know is he didn't want to lead but had no other choice after his brother's death. Now he's washing the blood off his hands on to his sons."

He frowned shaking his head at the photo. "The Irish and their fucking drama."

"My father lost his elder brother as well, Fedel. We Italians have drama."

"Yea, well they still need you more than you need them."

"Are the wives involved in business?" I asked, ignoring him. Evelyn, looked too sweet to be packing with her sandy brown hair curled gracefully under a large sun hat, but then again, it was my grandmother who had taught me how to fire my first gun. I was only seven, and I had never been without one since.

Fedel huffed. "No. They prefer to keep their heads above ground, planning parties, making sure everyone attends Mass on Sundays, going to charities and monthly dinner parties. They all know and accept it with open arms, but they aren't on the same level as you, ma'am."

Smirking, I shifted my gaze to him. "And what level am I on?"

Fedel adjusted his tie before sitting straighter, his face void of all emotion, eyes almost black.

"You, ma'am, are ruthless, and not a soul on this planet would dare cross you. You would put a bullet in our heads if we were ever disloyal to you or the family. You are the Boss," he replied.

When I glanced at the men surrounding me, they nodded, not making eye contact, but aware that I was looking.

It made me proud. It had taken a lot of blood, sweat, and no tears to make sure that they, and everyone else, knew that I was the Boss. I may be pretty, I may be young, but I was a Giovanni. Giovannis were—and always would be—beautiful, but lethal when crossed.

Nodding, I leaned back in my seat, finishing my wine as we descended. I was the head of the Giovanni Empire now, a fact that no one other than my men and my father were aware of. The world still believed he was Boss, but since the age of eighteen, everything—the drugs, the hits, the money—had been run through me because my father was dying. The great Orlando "Iron Hands" Giovanni was dying of stage four colon cancer.

Ninety percent of everything out there had a cure, if you had the right credit card. Cancer, however, was a self-righteous bitch that fell into the ten percent that couldn't be bought.

The irony was, most people in our world thought that sons were the only way to keep our underground empire growing. My father didn't. He felt he was blessed. The men in our family all seemed to die of the same cancer, but the women were made of tougher stuff. My grandmother lived until she was one hundred and four before she passed away, in her sleep, with a gun under her pillow. The reason my mother died was because of a plane crash.

I was six when I figured out what my family was. I was brighter than most kids my age, and at seven years old, I was learning to shoot my first gun. By eleven, I was being homeschooled in college algebra, drug cartels, and at my father's insistence, hand-to-hand combat. By seventeen, I knew the business like the back of my hand. Fedel was right. I would put a bullet in his head in a blink of an eye if he gave me a reason, and I liked Fedel.

"Ms. Giovanni, we are now in Chicago," the pilot informed me as I rose from my seat.

Monte, my body guard and third in command opened the plane door, stepping out first, followed by two other men carrying my things. The moron, Nelson, stood at the front of the plane trying his best not to make eye contact with any of us as we reached him.

"Ha-ave a g-good day, Ms. Gio-van-ni."

Handing him my jacket, he stared at me wide eyed. "Take it to your sister and let her know how close you came to dying today, and while you are at it, go find your balls before I see you again."

With that I walked out and found a shiny black limo waiting for me. Stopping next to Monte, I tried not to roll my eyes.

Where am I going, prom?

"Monte, see if you can get me a car, in white . . . and soon." I sighed. I did not want to be driven. I wanted to drive. I needed to drive. It was one of my four *S*'s. Swimming, shooting, sex, and speed were the only four things that could help clear my mind.

"Yes, ma'am," he said, pulling out his phone, already speaking to someone. If Fedel was my right hand, then Monte was my left. He was never taken by surprise. He didn't need to be acknowledged or even seen, and only spoke when necessary. Unlike Fedel and me, he was the only half-Italian. His blond hair made him stick out like Donatella Versace at a Walmart. His fix? He just shaved most of it all off.

Fedel stood beside me and handed me my personal phone. There was only one person who had the number.

"*Ciao, padre,* calling to make sure I got on the plane?" I asked, while Monte and Fedel arranged for a new car.

He laughed before coughing. "*Il mia bambina dolce.* I would never doubt you. After all, you were the one who renewed the contract."

The contract stated I would willingly marry Liam Alec Callahan and would merge our families. Orlando and Sedric had signed the contract fifteen years ago when they first created it. Then it needed to be signed by Liam and me on our eighteenth birthdays, and one last time during the first year of the marriage.

"I did. Has he?" I asked, just as a white Aston Martin pulled up in front of me. Smirking, I turned toward Monte and Fedel and nodded, *that was much better.*

"No, not yet. But he, his father, and brothers will be arriving any moment to do so." He practically coughed up a lung, but I was used to it.

Taking the keys from Monte, I slid in and pointed for him to get in, too. He'd done well. He could ride alongside me.

"So I am guessing that means he hasn't seen the change yet." This was going to be interesting.

"You mean, where you demand to be kept informed and in agreement with his future decisions involving the business?" Orlando laughed. "It will be quite interesting to see his reaction. This isn't the normal position wives play."

I snorted, pressing my foot on the gas, a row of black sedans followed behind me as I pulled out of the airport.

"It's nonnegotiable. If he wants a stake in my empire, then I need to make sure he doesn't destroy it. His brother hacked our records this morning. They are aware of how much we are worth. He's going sign, and he is going accept that I'm not normal. I don't expect normal," I said, flying down the back roads that would lead to our Chicago home, despite the fact that we never spent time in Chicago. Now I was stuck here.

"You *allowed* them to hack into our records." I smiled.

Monte looked at me while shaking his head, but chuckled as well. He knew what I was talking about even if he couldn't hear the whole conversation.

Declan was good—great, even. He was one of three people who could crack my level one firewalls—the second was dead—and the third was me. If Callahan didn't accept, which would make him an idiot, then I would have Declan buried right next to number two. I hated hackers who were against me.

"My dear, if you were not my daughter, I would fear you." I could hear the smile in his voice over the phone.

"It's because I *am* your daughter that you should fear me." In his day, Orlando could make grown men cry and beg for a bullet. If Orlando got his hands on them, pain was guaranteed.

"You are one of the best who has ever been. But don't count Liam Callahan out. It may surprise you, but he is just as, if not more, ruthless than you are." He was right. Liam Callahan was a name many feared. He was known as the "Boogeyman of the East," and I was the unknown "Wicked Witch of the West."

"Ma'am." Monte cleared his throat, holding my work phone.

"I will see you soon. *Addio*," I said to my father before hanging up.

Monte placed the phone on Bluetooth.

"Make my motherfucking day," I said, breaking the speed limit as I turned the corner.

"With pleasure, ma'am," Fedel replied. "Ryan Ross, Amory Valero's right-hand man, fucked up big and drove drunk. Guess who picked him up?"

"Fedel . . ." I said, my tone laced with anger. He knew better than to ever play guess-who with me.

"As luck would have it, Brooks was the one who pulled him over and brought him to us. He's waiting in the room under the house, so drugged up he can't see straight . . . but he's still not talking."

"Goodbye, Fedel," I said as Monte ended the call.

"Motherfucking day made, ma'am?"

I just nodded, driving closer and closer to my future husband, my empire, and some new intel. "Yes, Monte, motherfucking day made."

THREE

"Murder is born of love, and love attains the greatest intensity in murder."

—Octave Mirbeau

LIAM

"Someone is just a tad bit presumptuous." Declan snickered into phone. "She's already packed, Liam."

And sure enough, when my car pulled up to the Italian-styled mansion, I watched as some of Giovanni's men placed suitcases, what I figured were Melody's things, into a white suburban near the far side of the house. When they noticed us, they finished as fast they could and disappeared behind the tree sculptures that lined the back. They were all the size of Neal and I couldn't help wonder how they would fit in with our people. This would be the biggest merger the mafia world had ever seen. The Irish and the Italian were like the English and the French—we had been fighting for generations.

"She is just like the rest of them," I said into the Bluetooth. "In love with Daddy's credit card. But from the looks of it, she is no worse than Coraline."

"Or your mother," Declan said as the cars came to a stop. He couldn't deny his wife was a savage when it came to spending money. She held onto her plastic card with the *Jaws of Life*, and Declan, being the whipped bastard he was, couldn't bring himself to stop her. It would have been great if she actually spent the money on herself or the family, but no, she had to sprinkle it throughout the whole city, drawing unneeded attention at times. Neal's wife, Olivia, was the complete opposite. She would walk right past a starving child and buy herself another pair of shoes. I, just like the rest of them, would have to allow Melody to shop herself crazy as long as I got what I needed.

Hanging up, I tried to resist the urge to grin like a fool. Just from getting out of my Audi, I could feel the tides turn in my favor.

"Liam," my father said, stepping in line beside me. "You take the lead on this. I'll not interfere with whatever happens from this moment on. If you do this, you will have successfully cleared all obstacles in our way, and I will allow you to take my place as *Ceann na Conairte*. However, until that contract is signed, they are still the enemy. Should you fail, seek comfort in your mother, for you won't find any in me."

I wouldn't fucking think of it, I thought bitterly. Outwardly, I nodded and put my business face on.

Declan and Neal mimicked my expression. We had talked about the different scenarios this could come down to and were prepared for them all. Neal had four of his snipers outside, and Declan had jammed all frequencies that were not our own. We also had a car positioned less than a block away with men just waiting for the chance to clip the Giovannis' wings. They were the enemy until the contract declared otherwise. I was more than ready to get the papers signed and continue my blood ascension to *Ceann na Conairte.*

"Incoming," Neal declared from my left, just as the doors to the mansion opened, revealing an older, jaded-looking man with a scar that ran from his forehead to his chin.

"Welcome, Callahans, to the Giovanni Villa. Mr. Giovanni is already waiting and told me to skip the formalities for the time being. I shall escort you to his office." The older man bowed as though he had come out of *Downton* fucking *Abbey.* I knew Declan would have a laugh about that later, but for now, we were working.

I nodded, not wanting to waste time with formalities either. We all knew why we were here, and there was no need to bullshit. Usually, my father walked ahead of us, but since I was point man today, I followed the old man inside first. The house was beautiful, rich, and very fucking Italian with vintage ceramic tiles, one too many statues, and the overwhelming scent of roses. It felt more like a museum to ancient Rome than a home.

Finally, the old man stopped and didn't bother to knock before opening a door for us. Stepping in, for the first time in my twenty-seven years I was shocked. It didn't show on my face, but internally, I was shocked.

"If it isn't my favorite Irish crime family," Orlando said, coughing and in a wheelchair. The man known as "Iron Hands" was gone. The Giovanni study was filled with ancient scrolls, floor-to-ceiling walls of books, with the exception of one large window, and nineteenth-century handcrafted furniture. However, nothing in here was more priceless than the sight of this old crippled man.

His hairless face broke out into a smirk. "Sedric, you trained them well. They didn't even flinch."

"I am insulted you are just figuring this out now," my father said and with just a sidelong glance I could tell what he was thinking. He was as shocked as we were. He just hid it well.

In the mafia world, Orlando "Iron Hands" Giovanni was the stuff of legends. The things he had done could not be said out loud without making many people sick, or causing them to piss themselves in fear. He was one of the very few men my father respected, and in some way, dreaded. They both had a healthy fear of each other, but the man in front of me now looked like he hadn't been in the same room with "Iron Hands" for years.

This explained why he wanted this merger finalized, I thought.

"Please, have a seat. The contract is on the desk," he said to us.

I knew my family wouldn't make a move. Only the *Ceann na Conairte* was able to sit down with the enemy, so I unbuttoned my jacket as the rest of them flanked the sides of my chair.

"We've already read the contract. We simply wish to see your daughter sign it," I told him. In fact, I had read it so many damn times, I knew it line by fucking line.

"Read it again, she has already signed," he said through a barking cough.

Tempted to lose my cool, I glared at Declan, telling him with my eyes to read it. He could read just as fast as I could, and I did not want Orlando see me bend to his games. I would play nice for now, but I was not above beating a man in a wheelchair.

"Liam," Declan snapped, handing me back the paper.

It took me a moment to read over the two lines that had been changed.

"You're kidding." I snickered, handing it up to Neal and my father. "You are asking that she basically babysit how I run my company?"

Orlando's brown eyes narrowed. The fact that he no longer had eyebrows only made him look more ill.

"We prefer the term *empire*," he stated.

"Of course you do." *Fucking Italians and their empires.* "Orlando—and I will call you *Orlando*, not out of disrespect, but because I know that by the end of tonight I will have a ring on your daughter's finger—your daughter will want for nothing. She will be able to buy the sun twice over if she wanted. She will be taken care of and treated like every other Callahan woman, which is like bloody royalty. In my care, your *empire* will be treated with the same care and reverence."

Orlando leered before crossing his weak arms. "Pretty words, boy. And I will call you *boy* because even if you were royalty, you would still never be good enough for my daughter. I did not ask her to babysit you. Melody is smart and will be more than useful. I have no doubt that the empire will be just fine. As your brother saw when he hacked our records."

Out of the corner of my eye, I saw Declan stiffen beside me. No one ever knew he hacked into their files. It was then that I realized we had been set up. Orlando wanted us to see how much we would lose if we didn't give in.

"Orlando—"

"Don't try to sweet-talk me. I'm Italian, we wrote the book on it. So take the deal or walk away.

That's my only offer. And in case you hadn't noticed, I don't have time to waste."

The old motherfucker cut me off.

I slid my left hand down and felt the brass knuckles in the pocket of my pants. I wanted bash his face in. The vein at the side of my neck pulsed thickly, as it always did when I became bloodthirsty. My vision began to cloud over with rage. I knew, without a doubt, my father was waiting to see what I would do. Whatever choice I made, he would back me up here and bitch at me at home. I would not let anyone show me up, much less an old-timer halfway to his grave already. Not here, not now, and not ever. The room was silent as I stood up, walked over to his stocked bar, and poured myself a glass of brandy. He wanted to play hardball? So could I.

"How much does she even know about the company, excuse me, I mean the *empire,* as you people call it?" I asked him as I poured.

"Enough."

Leering, I turned back to him. "Enough? That's all you can give me? Orlando, meet me halfway here. You and I both know she may be smart, but no father would ever allow his little princess to see the things we see, or do the things we do."

"She's a quick learner. Considering the women you've been with, is that not enough?" He had a point.

Turning to my brother, I drank some more before leaning on Orlando's desk. It would be mine soon enough.

"Neal, dear brother, what do you think?" I asked, taking Orlando's the pen and point it at him.

"As long as she fulfills her other duties, why not? Anything she doesn't know, you can teach her. It may help bind you both together." I almost wanted to applaud him. I laughed at the thought.

Sometimes, Neal was just so wise.

"And Declan, dear cousin, what do you think about this rude, last-minute shift in the contract?"

Declan grinned. "Worse comes to worse, you have to waste five minutes explaining things to her. Plus, I kind of like the idea. Maybe if the women knew how hard it was to make a few million, they wouldn't spend it so quickly."

We all laughed and turned to Orlando who smirked at me with those damn chapped lips of his. I wasn't sure if it was because he agreed or because all the cancer drugs were messing with his brain. Orlando Giovanni was harder to read than most.

"Well then, Orlando, I do believe I'll be marrying your daughter," I said with no emotion in my voice. Declan handed me the contract again.

Before the pen touched the paper, I stared at the meticulous script that spelled out Melody Nicci Giovanni.

I wanted to see her first, but I signed anyway. My father had always told me to pick my battles so that I could have energy to survive the war. There was too much riding on this for me to refuse just because I would have to get an okay from a little princess. Besides we were married, I would keep her too busy to care.

"You aren't going to seek counsel from your father?" Orlando asked as I signed away my soul.

"His bride, his choice," my father said, speaking for the first time, and with just as much emotion as I had. None.

"My choice it is," I repeated, handing the sickly man, my future father-in-law, the papers. We shook hands, and I tried to force myself not to snap his in half. "I would like to see whom I have chosen."

"But of course," he said, ringing a bell that echoed throughout the room. Finishing the last of his horrible brandy, I waited.

When the door opened, I felt my cock try to detach itself. The girl who walked in was an ugly duckling with thick and messy dark brown hair, dark glasses, and goddamn braces.

Fuck it all to the seven levels of hell! my mind screamed.

"Just think, underground heroin fields. When would you like that plastic surgeon's number?" Neal murmured beside me. I could hear the laughter being held back in his voice. He cared about those damn underground heroin fields so much, you would think he did fucking heroin himself.

"Ms. Bianchi, where is my daughter?" Orlando asked, and my blood pressure dropped while my cock rose in hope. I could have sworn I heard the old man snicker.

"Closest fucking call of your life," Declan uttered, as we waited for the ugly duckling's reply. The timid girl glanced at us, but did not answer. Instead, she kept her eyes glued to the floor. If she didn't speak up soon, I would twist her ugly little head off.

"It's fine, Adriana. The man before you is Melody's fiancé. You may speak freely," Orlando told her while I was losing my goddamn patience.

Bowing at us first, she rose and gave me her full attention, standing with so much pride it almost distracted from her appearance . . . almost.

"Good morning, sir. The Boss is in a meeting in the basement," she said, making us all freeze. Everyone in our world knew that fucking word.

"Is this some sort of joke?"

"Who do you think has been running things while I die, gentlemen?" He snickered, before turning away from us. "If you don't believe me, you are free to go to the basement. But be forewarned, you won't meet a woman who needs to be taught anything. *Benvenuti nella famiglia,*¹ Callahans."

Flaming, I turned back to my father who was still staring at the sick man in the chair.

"Did you know this?" I glared at him, only to have him glare right back. Most days, I knew my place under my father, but the tides were shifting. I was rising, and I needed to know if he had held information from me.

"No, Liam, I was not aware. It seems to have been a well-kept secret, but does explain the recent growth of the Giovanni Empire," he replied, seeming somewhat baffled by the thought of it as well.

"No fucking way a girl has been behind all this," Neal said like a child.

"Take us to her then," I commanded the girl, and she nodded. I would see this Melody and find out if she was truly the *Boss* they had dared to call her.

"Sedric, may I share words with you for a moment?"

My father nodded, no longer caring what I chose to do.

One last time I turned to Orlando, who didn't even bother looking back as we left. It must have been a grim day for him. He would lose a company and a daughter. I didn't pity him, though—he'd be dead soon enough.

The ugly duckling didn't speak, or even bother breathing, until we reached the end of the hall that was guarded by two of Giovanni's men. From the corner of my eye, I saw both Declan and Neal slowly reach for their guns. In Declan's left hand, his cellphone was ready to call in more guns if this was a trick. But my instincts and common sense told me that Orlando really was dying and he wanted to marry off his daughter first. What I didn't know was what to believe about said daughter.

"Sir." The men glanced at me before opening the door, only to reveal an elevator with Fedel Morris inside. He was the bastard son of Gino Morris, one of the fucking mutts who had the balls to break into our safe house and kill fifteen of our men sixteen years ago. It was the reason my father pushed for this goddamn contract.

"This is as far as I can go, sir. It was a pleasure to be of service," Adriana said to us, giving me a short bow again before stepping back.

"Mr. Callahan," the mutt said with forced respect, making space for us in the elevator.

The moment we were all inside, Neal took a step next to him, clearly itching for an excuse to pull the trigger. He knew Neal was there but did not say a word or even flinch when Declan reloaded loudly.

All any of us could hear when we stepped out of the elevator was a man gasping for air as water splashed around him. We were a level up from where they were waterboarding the man. The basement was just one giant gym with a boxing ring in the corner. They had cleared everything on the ground floor to make room for their prisoner. As I stepped up to the rail, a few eyes fell on me. The men gave me a short nod as if they understood the shift happening within their company. Each one of them looked just as deadly as our men, and they all stood silently, allowing the man's underwater screams to echo around the space.

"Enough," a gentle voice called out, and each man stood straighter when the most beautiful woman I had ever seen stepped forward. Even from where I stood, I could tell she was perfection. From her wavy, black hair, flawless olive skin, and deep brown eyes, to her perfect hourglass figure. The knee-length white dress she wore hugged each one of her toned curves and, God, her tight ass—fuck. Her lips demanded to be kissed, and my cock demanded I have my way with her right then and there.

"Melody Nicci Giovanni, head of the Giovanni family and the Boss," Fedel informed us.

Neal stepped up to see the goddess below.

"Holy shitcock, motherfucking damn," he said, his mouth dropping open.

"Neal," I said, without emotion. The last thing I wanted the Italians to believe was that we were impressed.

Nodding, Neal returned to the same cold monster I needed at my side. Declan met my gaze, telling me he was on the same wavelength as Neal.

If it weren't for the obnoxiously loud gasping coming from the man below us, all three of us would have forgotten he was there. But when I looked closer, I realized who it was they were waterboarding.

Ryan Ross. *How the fuck did they get him?*

"Ryan, as much as I would like to draw this out, I am late for a meeting with my fiancé, and I hate being late," Melody stated, as a blonde man stepped forward, holding her jewelry on a white fucking pillow.

"To hell with you and your fiancé. You no good Italian cunt bitc—" Before he could finish, one of the men who had held him down smashed his fist several times into his face.

"It's Boss or Ms. Giovanni," the man said, spitting on him. "Nothing more. Nothing less."

Melody frowned and even that made me hard. She had beautiful lips.

"I didn't want to do this," she said, putting her earrings in before being handed a gun.

Spitting the blood from his mouth, Ryan smiled. "Do it. I'd rather die than talk to you, bitch."

"Who said this was for you?" Melody smiled back as two men dragged a sobbing female forward and placed her on a chair in front of the scum. Ryan's eyes widened as he looked at her.

"The Valero don't know about your special friend, do they? They aren't big on you fucking women outside the ones they offer you. You tried really hard to keep her a secret," she said, walking behind him. It made my blood boil at how close she was to him.

"Did you know she's pregnant?" Melody asked, causing the girl to hold on to her flat stomach and sob even louder. "Two lives saved if you just tell me what I want to know." She loaded the gun.

He didn't say a word, even as the girl begged him.

"So this is your answer then, Ryan?" Melody asked slowly. "I will kill her."

He still did not speak.

Sighing, she fired not once, not twice, but repeatedly, only stopping when the girl's lifeless body fell from the chair. She didn't even flinch. Instead, she walked toward the girl and emptied the rest of her clip into the body. When she was done, she turned back to the now blood-spattered Ryan who sat wide-eyed and shaken. This must have happened often, because her men went to work, carrying the body and cleaning up the blood on the ground, which hadn't touched her. They brought a new blood-free chair for her to sit on and handed her a pair of heels. All of which happened in a matter of seconds. They moved like the military.

"Does it make me a hypocrite if I still consider myself pro-life?" She didn't even blink as she stepped into her white shoes.

"She's just as fucking merciless as you are," Neal uttered in disbelief.

In a single moment, though, she had gone against everything I ever believed. This was not the role I wanted my future wife to play. She was too beautiful for the blood and the darkness. She should be upstairs, flipping through catalogs and painting her pretty little nails, or waiting in our bed for me to have her. This could not stand, and this would not be her role. I was to become the Boss and the *Ceann na Conairte*. She was to stand at my side so the Italians would fall in line.

Not that I could deny how sexy I found it. My mind hated this . . . saw the danger in this . . . but my body lusted after it painfully. My cock throbbed for her.

Declan snickered to my right. "Right now, you *wish* the biggest thing you had to deal with was a charity junkie for a wife."

I couldn't agree more. I would have to fix this situation and fast.

"Everyone out!" I roared, making every last one of the inhabitants of the room look at me as though I had lost my mind.

The eyes that shined with the most rage were those of my beautiful, soon-to-be wife. Oh well, this would be her first lesson. There was one Boss, only one *Ceann na Conairte*, and it was not her.

FOUR

"Every murder turns on a bright hot light, and a lot of people...have to walk out of the shadows."

—Albert Maltz

ORLANDO

"Thank you for lying to him. I know it is not your forte." I coughed. I was always bloody coughing. I wanted nothing more than to rip my damn throat from my neck.

"Yes, well," Sedric said, handing me a glass of brandy. "One day he may thank me for keeping the identify of your daughter secret."

With shaky hands, I held on to the glass before tossing the contents down my throat. It helped the hacking this damn cancer caused, but not by much.

"She's your daughter now." I hated saying it. I couldn't even meet his gaze. I just stared at the empty glass. My own hands looked so foreign to me.

When had I become this man? This broken and tired old man who was frustrated at watching the sun come up in the morning and seeing the moon fill the night sky? When had I become tired of

45

living? In my youth, all I did was live, some say a little too much, but I knew this was to be my future.

Even now it wasn't enough. I wanted to live more. I wanted more. It was the curse of being a Giovanni. We wanted it all, even if we didn't know it yet. I rode like lightning and—

"Orlando?"

Snapping out of my trance, I stared at the gracefully graying man before me with slight envy. Even now, he did not look a day over thirty-something. The Callahans, I swear, had found the Fountain of Youth.

"My apologizes. What did you say?" I frowned, trying to sit up, but my body was my prison and I couldn't.

Walking over to me, Sedric slowly lifted me up with one hand. "I said, she would forever be your daughter. I wish to know why you didn't tell me about the cancer. I wouldn't have used it against you."

"Liar." He couldn't help himself, a small grin spread across his face. "I didn't wish for anyone to know, Mel included. But that damn girl was too bloody smart for her own good and blackmailed the doctors into telling her." Snickering, I grabbed the bottle off my desk, spilling a few drops on my hands.

Sedric nodded, staring out the window as he drank. "When I first found out about her, I was shocked and angry that you would allow your daughter to get tied into the life we have chosen. I had to see it with my own eyes, and watching her chop off two men's hands down in Mexico sure did the trick."

"So you saw her on a good day."

His eyebrow rose, and all I could do was snort.

"I didn't *allow* Mel to do anything. She doesn't ask for permission. She takes what she wants. By the time you've figured out what happened, it's too late to stop her. I didn't even realize it when she started taking over. One moment she was helping me balance cocaine and clean guns, the next she was telling me not to worry because she already knew what to do. I tried to fight her, but the damn girl's plans always worked so well. I was left speechless."

"Your empire may have needed us once upon a time, but not now. I must admit, she has done well, frighteningly well, in fact. You could have terminated the contract," he said, and he was right, I could have. Any self-respecting Boss would never have shared his or her throne with another, and yet here we were.

"If Mel was a man, no one would dare deny she has the capability to be the best there ever was. But there will always be a fool who thinks she can be run over, and she would never stop fighting. If someone backed her into a corner, she would either fight or tear down the wall and attack them from behind." I chuckled. It was one of the things I loved about her. That fire in her eyes reminded me so much of her mother.

"My son is not going to just let her rule. In fact, I fear the years of peace we've enjoyed inside my house will be on hiatus." Sedric grinned and I knew he was looking forward to it. Behind his polished accent and polite demeanor, he enjoyed chaos. I had an old bullet wound in my arm to prove it.

"But"—he turned back to me—"that is not your only reason, Orlando. If you minded her fighting, you would have locked her away from it all the moment she was born. The fighting does not bother you. What does?"

Damn Irish bastard, I thought as I glared at him.

"The difference between a female and male Boss is that the female sells not only her soul, but her heart. Mel hasn't felt anything but rage in years. She is walled-off and will stay that way if she does not marry. Even if she were to hate him, at least I know she will never be alone. She will still have a family." Everyone she has ever loved has died, and I was well on my way, too. In return, Mel died a long time ago.

Sedric frowned, shaking his head. "It is odd. You believe that Melody needs Liam to end the loneliness, and I believe Liam needs Melody to not fear being alone. He has all the makings of a *Ceann na Conairte.* I knew it the very first day he was born. Neal was . . . not mentally strong enough. He doesn't have it. But Liam? He was born for it. It is in his DNA. Even as a child he loved to leave his mark on everything."

"But?" I coughed.

"But behind Liam's façade, he craves to be loved, and he hates to be alone." He frowned, hating that he had to admit the truth, and that was the truth. "He is not focused as he should be and is too compassionate sometimes. I blame his mother for that."

"And compassion is only for the family," I said.

He nodded. "He is merciless in many ways. But to be the *Ceann na Conairte*, you must not show mercy to anyone but your family. You are cold. You are distant. You enjoy the blood, the death. Liam kills, but he does not relish in it as he should. If he did, the Valero would fear him as they fear you, or should I say, the woman now acting as you."

"I must ask you for something, Sedric," I added, wishing more than anything to never have to speak the words that were about to break free from my lips.

"Whatever it is, say it, and I will have it done," he said, only making the ache in my heart burn more.

Swallowing my pride I nodded. "I wish for you to walk Mel down the aisle."

There was a pause, and he searched my eyes. "Are you sure?"

I nodded. My *bambina dolce* deserved to walk down the aisle and be proud. She would argue about how proud she was of me already. How she didn't care that I would cough throughout the ceremony, or that I needed to be pushed down the aisle, or the fact that more people would be focused on me rather than her. But I cared, and I did not want that. If I went and our enemies saw how weak I was, they would try to use that against her, against her empire.

"I will call Evelyn, and she will have everything ready in three days. You can watch from a secret room. No one will see you," he said with a grateful nod. Offering any more than that, and he might as well carve out my heart.

"Do you not feel like we are Pandora just as she is about to open her box?" I grinned at him. "They will bring chaos like we never could, and we did it simply with the hope of bettering them for the future."

Sedric chortled before finishing off his brandy. "Yes, in a twisted sort of way."

"We do live in a twisted world," I replied as the door opened to reveal Adriana once again.

"Yes?"

"Mr. Giovanni, Mr. Callahan. I am sorry to intrude, but I was told to come get you both," she said with her head down.

"Why is that?" Sedric asked with a coldness in his voice that he hadn't had since our conversation started.

"The Boss and Mr. Callahan apparently cleared the room in the basement so they could be alone and no one was to enter. But, a few minutes later, a gun went off."

FIVE

"It's a pity you didn't know when you started your game of murder, that I was playing, too."

—Robb White

MELODY

Who in the fuck is asking to die?

I glared toward the back of the room, searching for the face behind the voice that had dared interrupt me.

My blood boiled.

Liam, soon-to-be-fucking-dead, Callahan was walking down the stairs—*my* fucking stairs—with his sex hair high and his green eyes sharper than razor blades. He was beautiful, and I almost regretted the fact that I would have to put a bullet in his head and then smash it through a fucking wall.

"So, this is the man behind the bitch?" Ryan laughed.

Before I could even stop myself, I brought the butt of my gun across his face and did not stop smashing it until I heard a sick pop. I beat him into unconsciousness and left him slumped in his chair, his eyes swollen shut.

Wiping the blood from my face, I took a deep breath and held the gun up for Monte before I turned back to face the fuckable idiot.

"You overstep, Callahan."

He looked me up and down with both disgust and lust. "Do I? I believe you're mistaken, love. After all, I just signed a very powerful document making all of this mine."

"Did your father pay for your Dartmouth diploma? Because you don't seem to be good at reading." I glared at him, trying not to let the thick waves of lust that radiated off him bother me. "That paper says you work *with* me after our marriage, Callahan, and we are not married yet so you're still a fucking guest in *my* fucking house."

He smirked and it was sexy, dangerously so, and I wanted to kill him for it. "Be a good fiancée and tell your pets to leave, or I will put them down, sweetheart." His green eyes assessed at me as though I was his shiny new toy.

Do not kill. Do not kill. Melody, stay calm and do not kill him.

I wasn't going to lose my cool in front of my men. Glancing across the room, each of them stood with their hands tensed at their sides, waiting for me to give the word. Just a tip of my head would signal them to put as many fucking bullets as possible into the motherfucker in front of me.

"Monte, Fedel, take Mr. Ross and wake him up. If he doesn't cooperate, please show him the live feed we have of his brother, whom he also failed to hide, and the bomb in his house." I never broke eye contact with Liam. "The rest of you, leave."

I could hear their feet as they followed my orders and ran like roaches in the daylight. The only men who didn't move were the two I recognized as Liam's brother and cousin.

"That applies to you two as well."

They grinned and looked to Liam.

He raised an eyebrow at me. "They stay here."

Taking a step forward, I stopped when he was a little more than an inch away from me. I could feel his breath on the tip of my nose, and smiled sweetly.

"Only if they're in body bags," I said, stepping around Liam and scowling at the two men who had yet to leave. "You have two seconds."

They shifted their eyes toward the man standing behind me once more before heading toward the door. The moment it shut, I spun around, fist flying toward his head. It met his palm.

Grabbing my fist, he flung me into the chair Ryan had occupied. He cupped my cheek with one hand, and with the other, he held both my wrists tight.

"First, your joke?" he said, panting in my face like a lion eager for the chance to jump his prey. "Not funny."

"Second." He brushed his thumb over my lips. "The moment the ink touched that fucking paper, you were mine. Mine to fuck. Mine to fucking command, and mine to put in your fucking place."

"Third." He kissed me brutally before pulling away. "All this is over. You sit at my side and you stay beautiful, like a lady."

I stared at him wide-eyed. "Is that all, master?"

He grinned, but before he could speak again, I pulled my head back and smashed it against his fucking nose. His head went back and his grip on me loosened. I brought my knees back just far enough to kick in him in the crotch, causing him to release me completely.

"You fucking—" he started, but I didn't let him finish speaking before sideswiping his legs out from under him. With my now-ruined white Gucci heels on his neck, I glared down at him.

"First," I said, pressing into his neck, "get used to this position, because you're my bitch, not the other way around."

"Second, do not ever put your fucking lips on me without my permission!"

He twisted my foot and brought me down to the ground, pinning me there with the weight of his body, before I could get to my third point

Fury burned in his eyes as he breathed roughly through his nose. "My mother told me never to hit a woman, but you are pushing my limits."

"Funny, my father told me the same thing. Would you like me to apologize?" I pushed my thumbs to his eyes, forcing his hands to let go of my throat.

We fought and struggled on the ground like savage animals before he picked me up and threw me into the nearest wall. I grabbed a chair and smashed it against his side. It went on and on, each of us trying our best to kill the other without actually killing each other.

When I landed a kick to his side, he fucking grabbed me like a ragdoll and flung me across the room. It was nothing. Instead of letting myself feel the pain, I jumped back up. My heels were now long gone, and the dress I had changed into just to meet him was torn up the sides. His suit jacket had been lost in the heat of the battle, his shirt was ripped, and his tie was barely hanging around his neck. His hair was even more disheveled, and eyes were wilder than the fucking jungle.

When my fist collided with his cheek, he drew his gun and aimed it directly at my face. He stalled when he got a good look at me. Panting like the beast he was, the lust in his eyes returned in full force.

Without a second thought, he pushed me up against the wall before attacking me with kisses. His mouth was everywhere, from my neck down to the front of my chest, back to the sides of my face, before it met mine again. He gripped my ass with one hand and my breast with the other, the one that still held his gun. I felt his hard-on pushing against my waist, trying its best to find its way inside me. His actions were barbaric, almost animalistic, like a man dying of thirst, and the only source of water was my skin.

I loved every moment of it.

But I would not let him win. I would not bow down to him. Not today. Not tomorrow. Not ever.

He was so busy trying to figure out how to get the zipper of my dress down that taking the gun from him was like taking candy from a baby. Frantically rubbing himself against me even harder, closer, he almost just let me have the firearm.

With one great push, I forced his body to separate from mine, which surprisingly missed his warmth already. He stared at me with desperation. I pointed the gun and pulled the trigger, causing his leg to buckle. He started in shock as the bullet went through his thigh, then roared in pain as he fell down on one knee.

That's right, hail to the Boss.

"Third, if you ever interrupt me again, Liam Alec Callahan, may God have mercy on your soul when I send you meet to him." I kissed him on the cheek and removing the clip from the gun, along with the bullet in the chamber, before walking toward the door.

When I opened it, my men were there with guns drawn on Declan and Neal, who mirrored their poses. It explained why neither of them had come in. They couldn't check the door without putting their backs to the enemy.

My men all looked me up and down with proud grins on their faces.

"What would you like us to do with them, ma'am?" one of them, Antonio Franco, asked, grinning wider than the rest of them. Antonio hated the Callahans as much as Fedel did. He wasn't as close to me as Monte or Fedel, but he was as loyal as they come. He and his father had worked for Orlando long before I took over. Getting him to fall in line had meant getting the older ones—the ones who were still bitter that I, a female, and a young one at that, was now Boss—to fall in line.

I turned to my family-in-law and smiled before reaching out to shake their hands. "I apologize for not being properly introduced. As you know, I'm Melody Nicci Giovanni, but you may call me Mel."

They didn't shake back. Instead they glared, their guns still raised.

"Oh, right, your brother." I pretended to forget. "He is a little beat up and will need a doctor. But don't worry—the shot was clean through and through. He'll be walking in a few hours. You may check on him, and I will have Adriana show you to your rooms."

I nodded to my men, directing them to drop their weapons—they frowned but complied—before following me toward the elevator. It opened to reveal not only my father, but also the eldest Mr. Callahan. Making me realize, once again, the Callahans were blessed with almost a little too much pretty for my liking.

My father looked me up and down before shaking his head and sighing while Sedric just stared with no expression on his face.

"Did my son do this to you?" he asked, looking at my slightly bruised arms and legs, cut lips, and messed up hair.

"It was a small disagreement." I smiled. "And I shot him for it. If he weren't my future husband, it would have been worse. I do hope we can be introduced properly later, Mr. Callahan, as I find your past work fascinating."

And with that I stepped into the elevator as it reopened. It was only when the doors were closing that I saw Liam's brother and cousin rush back into the room to collect him. I withheld my laughter.

"I'm shocked you didn't shoot him in the kneecap for that shit, ma'am," Antonio said as we made our way up.

I smiled. "How would I look with a handicapped husband, Antonio?"

The moment we reached the top floor, I headed straight into my room. I had it conjoined with my father's once he became worse. I almost sighed at the feeling of the soft carpet on my bare feet. This room, my room, was my sanctuary. The day I took over, I had it remodeled to a more eighteenth-century Roman décor—paintings included.

Changing into a white and gold bathing suit, I headed toward the swimming pool. I felt dirty and downright tired, but the last thing I wanted was for the bruises on my skin to linger more than a few hours. The way to avoid that was to take a swim in ice water. It would sting at first, but a few hours later my skin, and my mind, would be good as new—clear. God knew it was fucked up now.

I could still feel his hands all over me, demanding and possessive. His lips as they bit into my neck, my ear, and at last my lips. He wasn't just a good kisser, he was a sensual kisser. He wanted to make sure, with just one kiss, that I was wet for him and willing to give in. Had I been anyone else, it would have worked.

There was no doubt in my mind that he knew what to do and how to do it. He was a force, and I wouldn't have minded, *if* he hadn't come into my house and tried to make me into his little Stepford wife.

In the pool, I shivered, but I needed to try to escape him. I couldn't, though. He was there pushing his way to the front of my mind. I hated him. I loathed him. I lusted after him, and it made me angry with myself. Even in the cold water, as I swam I felt him pressing against me. I felt the electricity of his hands, his sensual tongue. I couldn't deny that I wanted him.

I would have to figure out how to have him and, at the same time, make him understand that I was not surrendering to his will. Not even close. It was my choice. It was going to be animalistic and wild and a way for me to wind down.

When I finally came back up for air, there he was, the object of all my anger, rage, and lust sitting poolside in a fresh suit with a bandage over his leg—a leg that was resting on *my* pool chair. Rising out of the water, I reached for my towel while his eyes raked over my body.

"See something you like?" I asked, squeezing the cold water from my hair.

He frowned. "Sadly, yes, but it's an illusion. The moment you get close, it turns into a ruthless savage and shoots you in the thigh with your own gun."

"If I turned into a ruthless savage, it was only because another ruthless savage stepped into my arena. If you came for an apology, look elsewhere. Now, get the fuck up," I said.

Glaring, he got up. The moment I sat down, he grabbed my hand and I saw in his eyes that he felt whatever spark it was that coursed through us. He leaned in, catching my gaze in his own. He stopped just inches from my face before I heard a click near my wrist. Looking down, I saw that he had handcuffed my wrist and my ankle to the chair.

"After that display earlier, I believe you need a time out." He chuckled, kissing my forehead like I was some pet or child. "You were swimming so long you missed dinner, so I did you a favor and brought you some." He pointed to the dish that was only attainable with my free hand. "I will come to get you in the morning."

"What makes you think I can't pick a lock you son of a bitch?" I sneered, pulling on the damn handcuffs.

"I filled the locks with cement. You can't pick it love, believe me, I've used them before," he said, brushing the side of my face. "If you ever hold a weapon to me again, Melody, I will handcuff you fucking upside down and underwater."

He kissed me again, this time on the mouth, and with my free hand, I slapped him across the fucking face. His head snapped to the side before he turned back to me and winked. Smug, sexy bastard. With his free hand, he slid an obnoxiously large diamond engagement ring onto my finger. He let go and grabbed a few more towels, dropped them over me, and walked toward the exit.

"Say you're sorry and I will free you now, love, and then we can start anew."

He was trying to break me, the fucker.

"Fuck you and the Audi you drove up in."

Frustrated, he ran his hands through his hair before shaking his head. "We will talk later, then. Eat. I wouldn't want to bring you home to my mother sick. I will make sure the room stays warm. I sent everyone else to bed for the night. Goodnight, wife."

"Fuck you, fiancé," I said, leaning back in the chair.

I was fine until he turned off the lights and shut the door. He didn't know. No one knew except for my father. I had an irrational fear of the dark. Even though there was still the dimmest light from the pool illuminating the small area, I could still feel the fear creeping up my spine.

There was no way in hell I was spending the night here. Sighing, I tried to calm myself before pulling the chair and myself to the edge of the water before jumping in.

I was going to get out of this tonight, even if I had to break my hand to do so. Hopefully, the chair would break against the walls first.

Either way, he would not win.

SIX

"Murderers are not monsters, they're men. And that's the most frightening thing about them."

—Alice Sebold

LIAM

"Have I taught you nothing?" my father asked, his voice a pitch above a whisper as I read the files on the desk before me.

"No father, actually, you have taught me quite a lot," I replied before I took another drink of Orlando's horrible brandy. "Why do you ask?"

"Do not be coy with me boy. What happened between you and Melody today was unacceptable. You beat your wife—"

"She is not my wife yet," I said, smashing my hand against the oak desk and rising from the chair. "This woman, this Melody Giovanni, is insane, borderline demented, and she took a swing at me. It escalated, and then she . . . she shot me through the fucking leg!"

Sedric glared, his eyes blazing as he stepped forward. "As she should have. You had no right to

64

interrupt her. If the tables were reversed, what would you have done?"

I would have killed the person slowly.

"You cannot possibly be on her side. You should be on my side." I almost wanted to laugh at the thought. "Imagine if it had been Mom, or Coraline, or Olivia. What would you have said to them if you saw them act as Melody did?"

"What are you? Four? I am on the side of the family, as you should be. It was not your mother, or Coraline, or Olivia. It was Melody. Melody, who will become your wife in less than seventy-two hours. Make peace with her."

Seventy-two hours? "Why in the hell are we getting married in three days?"

"So you don't kill each other before the week is out. The press has been notified, and by morning, the world will know. Every gossip column, every news outlet, and every damn mafia member in the world will know the Giovannis and the Callahans are one. This means you two will have to pretend so fucking well, you fool yourselves that this isn't just some arranged marriage, or so help me God, I will set you both on fire." The fact that my father, Sedric Callahan, had just raised his voice and cursed in the same breath was proof enough he was serious. He had set a man on fire before . . . two actually.

Taking a seat once again, I turned and stared at the roaring fire that lit Orlando's office. This day had not gone how I planned, and while my bones were aching for sleep, my mind could not stop racing.

"Son, do I approve of what Melody does? No. I do not, and that is because of the simple fact that I was raised differently. And by a man much more controlling than myself. The strongest survive, however, and the key to survival is to evolve with your environment. We have made so many strides. No longer are we just uneducated thugs with guns. We have evolved, the mafia has evolved, and now it's your turn. Melody Giovanni is your evolution, embrace it and make peace."

It was only when the door shut after him that I allowed myself to relax. I filled my mouth with the horrible brown liquid in my hands, but even that didn't help my mind drift from the beautiful, dark-eyed woman who was to become my wife.

Our moment in the basement made my blood boil and other parts of me ache. She did not fight like a woman, but like a trained man, and the way she had looked—like a lioness about to rip apart her prey—made me want her even more. I almost had her on that damn wall, and she had wanted it. I had felt her nipples respond to me as they pressed against my chest through the thin material of her dress. Her eyes were begging, and her lips had parted for me as she held back moans of pleasure. Even her olive skin warmed beneath my hands. I would have taken her against that wall many times over and given her the pleasure we both hungered for, but instead, the wench shot me. She fucking shot me.

I'd been so shocked and horny that my mind couldn't even comprehend what had happened. My thigh was burning like fire when she kissed my cheek and walked away. With that one shot, she had proven that breaking her was not possible. She would never convert to what I needed her to be. She was a ruthless savage, and if you cannot break a ruthless savage, you need to figure out how to tame them.

I needed to make Melody understand that she was not above me. That she did not give the orders. That she did not move mountains or cause tornados to rip through the sky.

I did.

I had worked too long and too hard to let anyone stop me, least of all her. I would have rather died than give up my fucking claim to this family. When I found out what my father did for a living, I saw how people created paths for him as he walked in crowded buildings. I watched as governors, senators, bankers, and fucking judges alike kissed his feet. I knew what I wanted to do. Some people, like Neal and Declan, were simply born into the family, but I knew I was born to *rule* the mafia. It was beyond my fucking calling, it was in my blood. It was what pushed me daily, and the only person who ever stood in the way of that was my father.

I should have taken over on my twenty-first birthday. I looked forward to that day, but not so I could drink legally—I had been drinking since I was fifteen—but because I had wanted to hear him say it. I had wanted to hear my father tell the world that I was to take over the company, but instead, all he did was give me an island and pat me on the back. His explanation was that *it is not the time.* He was the damn *Ceann na Conairte.* He made the fucking time, and the rest of us followed it. Melody was eighteen and legal at that point, so it wasn't as though he was waiting for her. But each year after that, I waited, killing anyone who dared to get in my way, and now to have to deal with my wife-to-be? It was fucking bullshit, and I never saw it coming.

"Today has been interesting, dear cousin," Declan stated, walking in and heading straight to the bar. Forget crack, we Callahans were addicted to brandy and drank it like it was water.

"*Interesting* does not even begin to cover what happened today," I said. "My fiancée shot me with my own gun."

Declan grinned, the little fucker, before taking a seat on the couch. "How did she manage to disarm the greatness that is Liam Callahan? I have seen you draw, load, and shoot your gun in three seconds flat."

I frowned, knowing that he knew and simply wanted to hear me say it. Sometimes I wished he would go fuck himself.

"She looks like a sweet little lamb from afar, but when you get close, you find out she skinned and ate the damn thing just to use it as a coat. She's a beast." I glared at the fire, remembering similar flames in her eyes as she shot me. It was like she had figured out how to make hell reflect in her gaze.

"I like lamb," Declan said.

"Shut up, you dick." I threw my glass at his head, but he dodged it, allowing it to shatter against the wall.

He only laughed. "Does this pent up frustration I feel radiating off you have anything to do with the fact that you want her so badly? That's how she got the gun. You were feeling her up and—"

"And she took it from me and shot me like a dog. Yes, cousin, that's how it happened." I did not want him thinking about her firm ass in my hand or the bullet hole, which was now in my leg.

"And yet, you still want her, you sick fuck." He drank. "I don't blame you, though, she is—"

"Finish that sentence and it will be your last one. Cousin or not." Already I was reaching for my loaded gun.

Raising his hands, glass still in his left, he nodded with a grin. "You are possessive. I wonder what your future wife thinks about that."

"I don't give a flying fuck what she thinks about it, and what would Coraline have to say about your words over Melody?" I asked, knowing full well how pussy whipped he was.

"She would be pissed off, so much so that I hope she shoots me in the thigh. We've never had that kind of foreplay before."

I cringed at the thought of it. "And I'm the sick fucker?"

"No more than you," he replied, stretching. "Where is the queen anyway? She wasn't at lunch or dinner. I think I've seen everyone but her since then."

Walking over to the bar, I grabbed another glass.

"Oh, sweet Mary, mother of shit, what did you do?" Declan asked, rising from the chair.

"My mother would have your tongue for speaking like that," I replied, knocking back a glass before pouring another.

"Not before taking yours for what happened today. I should have known you would retaliate."

Rolling my eyes at him, I walked over to the desk and gathered my files. "I handcuffed her to one of the chairs in the pool house and left her some dinner. I'll get her in the morning."

"You can't be serious, Liam," he said, causing me to turn to him. He should have known better than to doubt me.

"Okay, you're serious." He frowned. "But you can't leave her there all night. If this was how she was with a good night's sleep, imagine how irritated she is going to be in the morning. Do you want her to be like that for your mother?"

He had a point, but I was fucking pissed.

"I'm not going to do it." If I released her, it would be as though I was saying she was right. That she was Boss. I wasn't going to bow down to her.

"You hard headed son of a—"

"Mr. Callahan." Adriana, the ugly duckling, came in, already dressed in an ancient nightgown as though she had come out of the fucking middle ages.

Declan held back his laugh by filling his mouth with brandy, while I just turned to the poor, time-confused girl in front me.

"Yes, ugl . . . Adriana?" I asked.

She glared at me as though she knew what I almost said. "The Boss wanted me to ask you what time you will be departing in the morning?"

Declan spit out the drink in his mouth, coughing like a dying man before laughing hysterically.

I stared at her for a moment before stomping out of the room without answering. I had made sure all her men had been far away. There was no way she should have fucking been able to get out of those cuffs. They were designed by me and made with reinforced steel. Bursting into the indoor pool house, I froze.

"Oh, my dear cousin, you have met your equal, and it is funny as shit to watch," Declan muttered, standing right beside me as I stared at the broken chair, now resting in its watery grave.

It looked as though a monster had ripped its legs and arms off. Seeing as how I only handcuffed her to one of each, it baffled me. The food was still uneaten and the towels all rested at the bottom of the pool as well.

"I'm going to bed," I told the grinning fool who was my cousin.

"Sleep with one eye open, cousin, and your hand on your gun. She may just kill you tonight," Declan said as I walked back to the room I was given for the night.

When I entered, there sat my reinforced steel cuffs in tiny pieces all over my now shot up bed. On top of that, a fucking note by hers truly, in her precise handwriting, with a bullet taped to it.

I came to visit you honey, so we could finish what we started in the basement, but you and your cousin were busy giggling like schoolgirls. Oh well, I hope you have a good night. About the bed, well ... you can understand right, sweetheart?

Checkmate.

Melody Giovanni

I could hear her laughter ringing in my fucking ears. *Checkmate?* She thought this was checkmate?

We hadn't even started playing yet. Beaming, I jumped on the bullet-infested bed, kicking up feathers, before pulling out my phone and dialing quickly.

"Hello, mother? I'm sorry it's late."

"I was beginning to think you had forgotten about me. I miss you all. The house is to quiet I can't think. Oh how is Melody? Is she beautiful? I met Orlando once and he was looker. I'm sure—"

"Yes, I have missed you as well. Yes, Melody is . . . she is one of a kind Mom, one of a kind. I was calling to see if you wouldn't mind having a welcoming party for her. Just to show her how happy I am to have her in my life."

"Really? Someone sounds smitten. The whole family?"

I wanted to roll my eyes. "Yes, the whole family. Can you do it? She is almost as maniacal as Olivia."

"Are you sure she isn't tired. I thought she just came into town today."

"She won't be tired at all."

"Sure! I'm so excited. I'll get right on it."

When she hung up, I grinned. My mother would do what she always did for celebrations. She would go over the top. I knew now that Melody could lie down with the lowest and roll in the dirt like a motherfucking pro. But she wouldn't be able to contain herself with the family. They shit rainbows and unicorns, and while she was distracted, it would give me time to work on a new lead I had on the Valero.

I was planning something huge for those motherfuckers, and I was going to use information I had acquired from Orlando's files to do it. The Giovannis' contacts were now my contacts. I almost wanted to say checkmate fucking now. But I wondered how she would feel when I used her work and multiplied the destruction by twenty. She was playing childish games, and I was no child. This wasn't about who could outdo whom, this was me proving a point. I would kill two birds with one stone. The Valero would never see it coming, and I would make my mark as the new *Ceann na Conairte* and Boss.

Sleep tight, my little Giovanni, for tomorrow, you will dance like my very own puppet on strings, I thought, lifting my hand behind my head and grinning.

SEVEN

"We kill everybody, my dear. Some with bullets, some with words, and everybody with our deeds. We drive people into their graves, and neither see it nor feel it."

—Maxim Gorky

MELODY

"Which one, ma'am?" Adriana held up two teal dresses for me to wear for my first day with the bloody Irish clan, but I really didn't care what I wore as long as I got through the damn day.

"Dr. Anderson, what do you think?" I asked the older man bandaging my wrist. Dr. Anderson was the only doctor I trusted enough to touch me. After all, he was the one who had delivered me, and he had seen more than enough of my injuries to not even bother asking.

He looked up, pushing his thick glasses up his nose before finishing his work on my wrist. "The long-sleeved one would be best to hide your wound. It won't hide the one on your ankle but that one is not as bad as your wrist."

He was right. I had used so much force to pull the plastic arm off the chair that it had cut deeply into my wrist. The idiot had made his cuffs with reinforced steel, which made it easy to break the chair, but it still hurt like a bitch and would scar.

Adriana looked at me waiting. "White heels, ma'am?"

I nodded, rubbing my wrist once the doctor let go. I had to fight the urge to throw this damn ugly ring down the drain every time I looked at my hand.

Fedel held the door open for Dr. Anderson, but not before handing him an envelope with more than enough money to make sure he wouldn't have to work for a while.

"Ma'am, after the announcement of your and Mr. Callahan's wedding this morning, I have a few magazines, charities, and interviewers looking to have a moment with you," Fedel told me with a phone in his hands.

After rising from my chair, Adriana handed me the dress as I walked behind the screen.

"Fedel, do I look like Martha fucking Stewart?"

"No, ma'am. I would never think you would be foolish enough to end up in jail." He cleared his throat, and I laughed. Stepping out from behind the screen, I let Adriana drop the white heels at my feet.

"Then tell them to go fuck themselves."

"That would not be wise, *mio bambino dolce*." My father coughed as he was wheeled in by his nurse.

Walking over to him, I kissed him on the cheek.

"Why can't I tell them to fuck themselves?" I asked him as Adriana handed me my bracelets.

"Because, to the rest of the world, you are the fiancée to one of the most powerful men in this country—the prince of Chicago. You aren't the Boss to them. They want a Kate Middleton or a first lady, someone to kiss babies and write big checks on behalf of your fiancé," my father snapped at me, causing me to stop and just stare into his dying eyes.

"Fedel. Adriana. Leave." In seconds they, along with my father's nurse, were gone. "You're still mad that I shot him."

He frowned at me. "I do not have time to hold on to anger. And yet, here you are, forcing me to waste time to discipline you."

Shaking my head, I smiled. "You should be proud I didn't kill him. He is a spoiled brat who thinks he was born in the nineteen-twenties when women served their husbands and bowed down to their will. I'm not now, nor shall I ever be, any man's arm candy."

"Melody." He sighed, using my full name like when he was annoyed or pissed. "You are as hard-headed as your mother."

"Thank you. I will take that as a complement." I turned away from him.

"It was not one," he hissed. "Have you forgotten why you wear the white shoes?" My whole body froze for a moment, and a chill ran up my spine.

"That was a low blow, Orlando." I sneered at him and took off the damn white shoes before walking into my closet. Most of my things had already been taken out and were en route to Callahan Manor. I had left some of the things I would need in my closet here. One never knows when I would need a personal moment away from the leprechaun.

My father wheeled in behind me. "I will not go to my grave knowing that this marriage is condemned and that, yet again, two people who are made for each other will not swallow their pride, lower their swords, and act as fucking equals! You, Melody Nicci Giovanni, will not walk the same path your mother and I did. You will support your husband, guide him when needed, and stand by his side and his side alone. You will be a damn Callahan, and you will make sure both families, past and present, rise!" he yelled, not once coughing or even so much as blinking for that matter. Had I closed my eyes, he would have sounded like the Orlando I used to know.

"What happened with you and Mom is not the same," I replied, slipping on the tan shoes, while in the back of my mind a voice told me to change back.

"But the outcome will be if you do not take my advice. Make peace with him Melody. Remember how long it took me to adjust to you as Boss? Prove it to him. Prove it to them all, and do it without making your husband the fool so I can rest in peace." The tenseness in his voice dropped before he coughed again, returning to the sick man that he was now.

I hated the thought of having to prove myself. I had done that for years—proving to every man we interrogated, every boss I took down, every crackhead with a big mouth, and even with my men. I thought I was done with that phase of my rule, and yet here I was again.

"Don't think too long about it, we're not all still in our twenties." Orlando smiled at me, and even though he was only a shadow of the man I used to know, that smile always made me smile.

Walking behind him, I pulled his wheelchair back before exiting my closet for the last time.

"Fine, I will try, but if he treats me like a doormat or worse, Martha Stewart, I am shooting him in the other thigh." I was only half-joking.

"That is all I ask," he said as he was wheeled out of my bedroom. Adriana and Fedel's backs straightened as they followed us down the hall.

"Fedel, are the houses finished?" I asked him, walking slower than needed, but I was in no rush to get to my destination.

"Yes, ma'am, they are. Most of our equipment and technology has been moved into the basement, and the men were moved last night. However, they want to stay away from the Irish for as long as possible."

"So would I." I muttered.

When I had found out whom I was to marry years ago, I had slowly but surely bought, bribed, and taken "government-protected" lands just far enough away from the Callahan Manor to give my men a place for their families that was nearer to where I would be staying. The houses were not anything close to Callahan Manor or my home here, but they were nice, common family homes that would typically be found in the suburbs of Chicago. We had started building three years ago, a task I left to Antonio and Fedel to complete.

"Are you ready?" Orlando asked me.

My father's right-hand man since he was a teen, Fiorello, stood at the door waiting for us to answer before opening. He was the only one, with the exception of a cook and a nurse, who my father wanted to stay with him here. Fiorello had been tortured by the Valero once upon a time, for dirt on my father, which left him with the scar that now graced his face. He fought his way out and came back, asking only for a doctor and a large glass of red wine. I knew my father was going to be fine. I just wasn't sure if I was.

Nodding, I signaled for Fiorello to open the door. Beside me, Orlando's nurse took her place at his wheelchair. The moment the door opened, I was met with four pairs of eyes staring at me, each more beautiful than the last until they fell on Liam, whose green eyes were glued to my legs. His gaze lingered a little on the bruise at my ankle before wandering up the rest of my body meeting mine. His lips were turned in a frown, but in his eyes were filled with lust.

"Ma'am." Monte walked over to me, handing me an iPad. He must have put all the information on Ryan Ross here. I took it from him before walking toward my new *famiglia*, or *teaghlach* as it was called in Irish.

"Good morning, am I late?" I asked as kindly and brightly as possible.

"No, ma'am, just thinking you're beautiful this morning," Declan replied trying to take my hand to kiss it but I pulled back.

His cousin did not seem to get it because Neal opened his arms as if he were about give me a hug. "Save your fancy words, she looks fucking hot. Simple."

"Let me make this clear to the both of you. Touch me and I will strap you down then take every last bone out of your bodies. Understood?" I asked him with a smile. His arms dropped and Declan kept his hand in his pocket.

"Beautiful." I added.

"Stupid *Irish* brut," Fedel hissed lowly in Italian.

"*Senza rispetto*," Monte said softly. He was all about respect.

"Enough you fools. We are going to be late. Your mother says it's mayhem outside the manor. Let's go," Sedric told them before winking at me. The old pervert.

They walked toward their cars, leaving me alone with Liam and his brand new black, Audi. He said nothing, opening the door for me and then closing it when I took a seat. He didn't say anything when he took his seat beside me either, and I didn't need him to. In fact, I had work to do.

According to the files on my tablet, Amory Valero had gotten out of prison, a secret the Valero were trying to hide from the world until they released the savage for their own personal use. Apparently, from what Ryan spilled to Monte and Fedel, they wanted Amory in Brazil to attempt to steal my fucking cocaine. They must have been *on* fucking cocaine to think that it was going to work. But this was what the Valero did, it was what they were good at . . . the fucking thieves. For years, they had stolen whatever they could from my family. The leader, Amory's father, Vance, was all but run out of Italy by my father. Instead of withering into nothing, however, he resorted to the black market. If it was worth a penny, Vance stole it, flipped it, and bought himself more men. If I could, I would hang him by his balls.

"What is that?" Liam's green eyes narrowed as he tried to read the encrypted files all while the driver in front pretended not to even be in the car.

None of your business, you motherfucking Irish asshole.

"Work," I replied instead, trying my best not to speak my mind. I knew needed to listen to Orlando, but the look of anger and disgust in Liam's eyes made me want to shoot him in the dick.

He tried to pull himself back. "You should relax today. It's a day for family."

"Thanks, but I'm fine." I smiled. "I slept like a fucking baby."

Because I got out of the chair you fucking chained me to like a dog, you bitch ass motherfucking cock.

He glared at that. "So did I, in fact. The bed was not what I am used to, but I am not one to complain."

Unless you don't get what you want. Then you just cry like a newborn baby who had his ass slapped.

I smiled again before looking back at the information in front of me.

"You should know that my mother is not fond of cursing, especially in women. To her, women who have to curse are classless, brainless, and foul." He stretched every word out as I crossed my legs, my beautiful sexy legs. He could not look away.

I grinned. "You don't fucking say? Well damn, ain't that a mother-shit-fucking bitch? Don't worry, Callahan, I am not going to cock it up. In fact, I am going to try my absofuckinlute best not to curse in front of Mama Callahan."

His eyes blazed. "Stop the car," he told the driver, who stomped on the brakes.

Liam grabbed the iPad from my hand, a bottle of brandy, and then stepped out of the car and poured it all over the poor device before dropping his lighter, flame blazing, on top of it. It went up so quickly that I could hear the glass cracking. Stepping back in the car, he ran his hands through his hair before adjusting his jacket and tie.

"Go on," he told the driver.

Remember Orlando.

"A tad bit immature, don't you think?" I asked, not bothering to look over for fear that I might smack the shit out of his face.

"You don't fucking say?" He repeated my words. "But it was either the tablet or you, and since there are dozens of photographers and reporters all waiting to see a happy couple, I figure killing you wouldn't go over well."

"You better hope it burns thoroughly," I said, breathing through my nose.

He sighed. "Knowing you, love, I wouldn't doubt if it had a self-destruct switch."

"Do I look like James fucking Bond?" I smiled. It was a compliment, and he didn't even know it.

He glared, realizing his slip only a moment later. "No. More like a black widow."

"Even better." I laughed, looking out my window. It did have a self-destruct switch, but he didn't need to know that.

Leaning back, I allowed myself to drift, trying to forget about the beautiful asshole beside me and the world he was taking me to. Gone was the underground secret life, where no one knew who Melody Giovanni was, and I could just be Mel, the fucking Boss. Gone were my days of absolute freedom. Marriage was a horrible, horrible idea, and I should have said no to my father, but the bastard had me locked into it. I had to think on the bright side—no more wasted money or blood as we try to get our drugs from South America into Miami and then the rest of America. No more wars in the middle of downtown Boston or San Francisco. The amount of money I . . . we . . . would make now was so fucking ridiculous it would make Bill fucking Gates shit bricks.

When Liam's hand took mine, I jumped, pulling a knife from my thigh before either of us could even blink. He stared at me wide-eyed, then smirked at the large blade in my grip before looking at my thigh. I could see the question perfectly—how the fuck did I have it so well hidden?

"It's time," he said, nodding out the window at all the cameras waiting just outside a pair of black iron gates with a *C* in the center. I hadn't even noticed that we had arrived, and now all the Callahans and media were waiting on us.

Sliding the hem of my dress up, I slid the knife back into its holster only to find Liam trying to burn a hole in me with his gaze.

"I killed the last man who looked at me like that," I said, waiting to see the disgust at my words, but only saw more lust. He was getting excited, and the last thing we needed was that in print. "For the love of God, control yourself Callahan. Your mother, the woman who whipped your ass as a child, is waiting for you."

That did it.

"Try not to be a bitch," he snapped as he tapped on the window, signaling the driver to open the door.

The moment it did, camera flashes assaulted us. Liam pulled me closer to him, his arm around my waist, and I used the opportunity to try to fix his sex hair. He kissed my cheek when I was done, causing reporters to throw as many questions as possible at us. I wanted to flip them off, but Liam squeezed my hand, and I smiled squeezing back. To them we looked like lovesick fools. If they only knew.

A stunningly beautiful woman, who could only be Liam's mother, stepped forward from the clan behind her. "Liam, put some room between you and the poor girl, we are Catholic for goodness sake."

She pulled me into a tight hug, and I knew where Neal got it from. *These people needed to stop touching me.*

"Mrs. Callahan, it's such a pleasure to meet you. Liam could not stop ranting and raving about you," I said as politely as possible.

"Please call me Evelyn, my sweetheart." She smiled brighter than the sun. "You have no idea how long I have waited to meet you, and no wonder your father hid you away, you are so beautiful, Melody."

I dropped my head for effect before smiling. "Thank you Mrs . . . Evelyn, but please just call me Mel. My name doesn't fit my personality at all. I can't carry a note."

Nodding in pleasure as she pulled me forward. From the corner of my eye, I saw the shocked look on Liam's face.

Just because I hated the fucking role didn't mean I couldn't play it.

He wasn't the only one surprised. Declan and Neal looked at me in confusion, before looking at each other to make sure they weren't insane. Sedric just nodded at me with approval, looking a tab bit impressed.

"Mel, these are my other two daughters, Olivia, Neal's wife." The Malibu Barbie, with her long gold hair and bright blue eyes glared at me but shook my hand, giving it a tight squeeze.

"Wow, you're so beautiful," I said, smiling.

Her eyes lit up like she had found the true meaning of Christmas. "Thanks," she said.

Next was Coraline, the rather tall, chocolate-skinned woman with a wide smile on her face.

"Hi. I'm Coraline. I'm glad to finally met you." She couldn't contain herself from pulling me into yet another hug.

What the hell was up with these damn people?

"Oh my, Italian silk, very nice." She grinned when she pulled back saying, "Oh, my God, and the shoes! There is walk-heel-ton for charity next Saturday, you should join me."

She wants me to ruin my shoes for charity?

"Hi, Coraline." I smiled at her. "Everyone is so nice. Thank you for welcoming me into your home. You have no idea how nervous I've been."

I heard Neal hold back a cough.

Coraline grabbed on to my free arm, while Olivia just smiled, clearly finding no threat in me whatsoever. *Just like the rest of them.*

"Come, Melody, we will make sure the rest of the family doesn't overwhelm you too much." Evelyn smiled, leading me to the manor. It was the exact opposite of my home, sadly. Callahan Manor was a modern day fortress. Beyond the cream marble floors that stretched for as far as the eye could see, the double grand stair cases framed with black iron, and the engraved wooden French doors, there was nothing but forty-six thousand square feet of illegal activity. There were no statues, barely any plants, and only modern paintings. Everything was simple, crisp, and clean.

I wanted to puke. For eighty-five million, I expected more.

"I'm sorry." I paused, her words only now catching up to me. "The *rest* of the family?"

"Liam wanted to make sure you weren't overwhelmed by too many new faces at your wedding on Sunday. So he thought it would be best to have you meet everyone now." Olivia smiled. They all smiled, as if they were talking about five or ten people.

But I knew the Callahan Clan considered between ninety to hundred people their family. My Italian line was mostly gone. I didn't deal with that many people anywhere, with the exception of my men.

Turning around, Liam was grinning like a fucking cat with a ball of yarn, and I knew then that I should have killed him in my basement. He winked, and I was tempted to lose my cool, but I wouldn't give him the pleasure.

"If they are as welcoming I think, I can make it, but please don't leave me completely alone. I really wouldn't want to insult anyone."

Coraline smiled. *Again with the fucking smiles.* "Mel, you are family. We wouldn't throw you to the wolves without giving you a spear."

Please give me a fucking spear. I knew whose heart I wanted to throw it through.

Allowing them to pull me away farther down the boring halls and out a set of large French doors, which opened to a large grass lawn, now covered in white tents. At least a hundred people sat drinking, laughing, and stuffing their faces with food. Music roared from an old Irish band staged by the trees, and when I said old, I meant old. With full-length white beards, they played their handcrafted instruments for the crowd.

For the love of God.

"Don't be nervous," Evelyn said. "You're young and beautiful. They already love you. And those who don't will have to because you are Liam's."

I'm my fucking own, I wanted to yell at her. And I wasn't nervous. I was pissed. I wanted to play whack-a-mole with all these motherfuckers heads. But instead, I just smiled and walked outside.

"Everyone this is Melody, Liam's fiancée!" Coraline yelled at the top of her lungs.

They all stopped their dancing, singing, and drinking, as if they wanted the world to know it wasn't just a fucking Irish stereotype, to stare at me. Then they raised their mugs and screamed:

"Cheers!"

I don't need this shit.

But I had a part to play so I grinned. "*Sláinte!*"

Everyone shouted with joy, and I was motherfucking-in with the Irish clan. At least the drunk ones with dicks. The girls would be harder. I could already tell from their glares. Maybe I could tell them they were pretty and try not hold their faces underwater.

"Hi, Melody!" A group of young kids ran up to me, speaking with strong Irish accents. If I didn't know better, I would have thought they were drunk as well. But even the Irish couldn't be that crazy.

Crouching down to them, I smiled. *"Dia duit, mo pretties beag."*[2]

Their grins almost split their faces as they began to speak in full-on Irish. Liam must have followed me, because he was being congratulated by some other male drunks. He looked surprised that I knew Irish. But he was a chauvinistic pig, who thought all I did was paint my toenails and shop. Of course I spoke Irish. My father had me learn the moment the contract was formed.

As the children pulled me toward a corner of the massive garden, each dancing around me, I pretended not to notice the women glaring at me. I would speak with them later, but now I needed to make myself look like a fucking saint. I took my shoes off and danced along with the kids, singing their Irish songs and even spinning some of them around. It made even me laugh. Don't get me wrong, I liked kids . . . kind of, sort of. I was just sure they were annoying as fuck if you spent too much time with them. But I needed them today, so I danced.

When I finally stopped, Coraline handed me glass of water. I wanted wine. *My* wine.

"They all love you." Coraline grinned. "A few men even cursed Liam for finding you first."

Just smile and drink Mel.

"Oh, we are going to have a garden party for you tomorrow, for all us girls." Evelyn's eyes shined with joy. "Everyone is dying to meet you."

I would rather have everyone just dying.

"I can't wait," I said, but they didn't even notice I was lying.

Glancing around, I realized then that all the Callahan men were gone.

"Where is Liam?" I was ready to break the glass in my hands.

Olivia and Coraline frowned, but Evelyn held her strong demeanor. She turned her back to the guests to stand in front me.

"Melody, do not worry. I know you are aware of what our men do. But believe that they are safe. They often use parties like this one to cover up something else. We try not to get involved and to know as little as possible. My son would never want to endanger your well-being." Evelyn's face became serious before relaxing into a carefree smile once again.

I nodded, trying my best to stay calm, but as my gaze landed on Fedel and Monte near the doors, looking scared for their lives, I knew that someone was going to die tonight.

"Excuse me."

Fedel and Monte stiffened, waiting until I was before them to speak.

"Flight 735 just exploded over the Atlantic ocean. Death toll is one hundred ninety-two. Eighty-seven of them Valero who were smuggling drugs in the seats," Fedel said.

The glass shattered in my hand, but I didn't feel it. Even as the blood dripped from my fingers, I couldn't feel it. Walking calmly into the house, I moved straight to the foyer. I had gotten blue prints to this whole place years ago and noticed there was space left out. It didn't take genius to realize they were hiding something behind a fake wall, and that the rather larger Jackson Pollock hanging on the faux wall really had to be a door.

Bloody hand raised, I waited for Fedel to hand me a gun.

"We are outnumbered, ma'am," he said instead, and I simply shifted my gaze to him. Today was not the fucking day.

Monte handed me the semi-automatic he always had strapped to his leg.

"Fedel, stay out here, I wouldn't want you to get hurt," I snapped before shooting right through the wall. Neither Monte nor I stopped, not even when the painting, tattered and unrecognizable, crumbled to ground. The wall blew apart bit by fucking bit until the door bounced open.

When it released, I stepped in. There stood the rats, all drawn and panicked with the news playing in the background. My eyes met Declan's, who looked white as a sheet, then Neal, who was trying his best to stop the bleeding in his arm. Next was Sedric, who didn't seem surprised it was me. In fact, he was the only one wearing a bullet-proof jacket underneath his suit. If he hadn't been, the bullet hole in his tie would have killed him. The biggest rat of them all, who must have had a fucking guardian angel in his pocket because he was perfectly fine, was furious.

"Tell me it wasn't fucking you, and you still get to come to the motherfucking wedding sweetheart," I said still calm as ever, ready to start shooting again.

I should have worn the white heels.

EIGHT

"The facts of a person's life will, like murder, come out."

—Norman Sherry

LIAM

"Your fiancée is . . ." Neal stopped talking, taking her in through the window as she laughed and danced with the children. A part of me wanted to run over there and save their lives. The beautiful woman with the kind smile, laugh and blushing face was just an illusion. They were dancing with a fucking lion, a snake in the grass.

"She is a master of fucking disguise," I hissed angrily. I would have enjoyed watching her dance and smile and sing off-key if I hadn't known better. If there wasn't a bullet hole in my fucking thigh, I would have been tempted to think myself lucky.

The woman before us now was the woman I was expecting, the one I wanted, and it pissed me off to no end, because she didn't exist. This party was supposed to make her uncomfortable, but she was playing every last one of our family like fools.

95

"She has them all eating right out of her hands. She's a master," Neal said looking at her in wonder and awe.

"Neal, I will shoot you in front of Olivia and then give her the gun to shoot you again if you don't stop staring at my fiancée like she is the fucking Virgin Mary." I knocked back the brandy in my hand. I hated her for this. For, once again, making me realize she could play this game, the game of murder and lies, like a motherfucking pro.

"Don't take your anger out on me. You're the one who fucked it up. If you had just—"

"Shut the fuck up Neal, or I swear to God!" I gripped the glass in my hand so damn tight, it almost broke. "Go do your bloody job. I want that plane in ashes in three minutes."

He didn't say anything more, but left to meet with Declan along with the rest of our men while I watched my soon-to-be wife walk on fucking water.

The moment we had stepped out of the car, she had transformed into this delicate little bird. The Melody I met the day before, and the Mel she announced herself as to my mother, were two very different women. But she drew them in like moths to a flame. She was so fucking beautiful and nonthreatening when she met everyone, that for a split second I forgot.

Had she been this way when I first met her, I would have dazzled and charmed her while we were making love on my bed. I would have taken pleasure in making her whole body blush, keeping her safely tucked away.

If only my life was that fucking easy.

"Sir, we're ready," one of my men, Eric Reese, called from behind me. Eric wasn't family, but pretty damn close. He was one of the few of my men with more than half a brain, and full loyalty. The rest were in this out of fear, or for the money.

Nodding, I walked through the door that lead to the secret office my father had built into the walls to make sure no one would "accidentally" find it. The room was filled with monitors and maps, all focused on where the inbound airplane would be.

"Are you sure you want to do this Liam?" my father asked as he stared at the dot indicating the plane's current position. It would be crossing into American waters soon.

"It's fucking brilliant," Declan said, waiting excitedly. "The Valero will never see it coming."

"I wish I could see Vance's fucking face man." Neal grinned. "This is going to set him back a fortune."

Eric nodded. "You should send him a wedding invite, just to sweeten the pot, mate."

They were all right, and yet my father still did not seem to approve. Well, fuck him then. Vance Valero had no idea anyone knew about his secret plane, and still allowed a few unlucky everyday folks board it. He must have figured no one would be ruthless enough to kill a few innocents to get to his men onboard. After today, though, it going to cause him regret. Not only would he lose men, but he would also lose half a million dollars in cocaine and heroin. That would be a bitch.

The moment I saw the plane appear on one of the video monitors I gave the go ahead. "Do it."

Declan smirked, but before he could push the button, Neal beat him to it like they were fucking kids.

"I'm the fucking oldest, cousin," he said, before grinning like a mad fool. A moment later, there was red, orange and yellow flames filling the sky. Metal ripped from metal, ashes fell into the sea and all I could do was revel in the greatness of it all.

Sitting back in the chair my father had once claimed, I allowed myself to dream of the future for one moment. The men in the room roared in victory over our accomplishment. The Valero had been fucked by me today. This, plus our wedding announcement, would make it clear that Liam Callahan had arrived, and I planned to make them eat shit for the rest of their lives. I would control the east and the west and, once that was done, all of fucking Europe. Who said you couldn't have it all?

Even Melody, through all her bitching and shooting, had come in handy. Finding the flight plans was almost too easy. She had been keeping notes on it for months and never did anything. Some fucking Boss.

She could have cut Vance off at the knees, but instead, she did nothing just to save a few people's lives. She didn't understand. We ran the fucking Mafia, we spared no one, we took what we wanted, when we wanted it, and we killed to get the job done. All those people were in the wrong place at the wrong time, and I would make sure to have my mother . . . or maybe make Melody, open a charity in their names. Right now I—

Bullets exploded through one of the walls before I could even finish my thought. They pelted us like rain, destroying anything and everything in their way.

"Fuck!" Neal screamed in pain as blood poured from his arm.

"Open the fucking door and blow the motherfucker away!"

Declan froze just as a bullet went right past his head and embedded itself into the monitor behind him. My father fell back as a bullet connected with his chest and Eric held on to his wrist. The rest of the men in the room scrambled to follow orders but froze when the door opened.

"Tell me it wasn't fucking you, and you still get to come to the motherfucking wedding, sweetheart," Melody screeched, looking me dead in the eyes.

Kill her. Put a bullet through her pretty fucking head and toss her off a motherfucking bridge, my mind yelled as I glared down the barrel of my fiancée's semi-automatic.

I tried to stay calm. I even prayed for the strength not to lose it, but all I could see was red. Glancing over to Eric, who stood closest to her, he took charge and put a gun to the side of her head, causing her to lower her gun.

"You little bitch, have you lost your fucking mind?"

"Carrot top," she said, still staring into my eyes. "You better pull the trigger now. You will regret it if you don't."

He glanced at me, but in a split second, Melody swung around and used the butt of her gun to bash his face in, knocked him off his feet, and held her gun to his balls.

"I said you would regret it," she hissed. She pulled back and hammered into his jewels with the butt of her gun.

My father frowned, stepping forward as I reached for my gun. There comes a time when enough was fucking enough. "Ms. Giovanni, I would ask that you not to kill anyone in my house."

Monte, I believe the man's name was, walked forward pointing his firearm at Eric as Melody turned to my father, gun held right at his face.

"Sedric, I like you. I really do," she said with no emotion in her voice. "But step out of the way or I will kill you before I kill your son."

"His mother is fond of him, and I am fond of his mother, Ms. Giovanni." The motherfucker smiled, as though this bitch had not just insulted us, as if she hadn't almost killed family. "Melody, I understand your anger, and you are justified in it—"

"The fuck she is!" I shouted, holding my gun up as well. Never in my life did I ever want to put someone down so fucking badly.

"Liam Callahan. For the next forty-eight hours I still rule. Stand down!" Once again, the blood in my veins was demanding blood to be spilled, and so I shot right past her head and at Monte's arm.

Melody eyes glowed with rage, but before her bullet could hit me, my father went for her hand. He twisted her wrist and struggled with her until the gun was out of her grip and he had her arm behind her back.

"Melody, listen to me," my father said while she snarled like a damn lion. "As the head of the Callahan family, I apologize for my son's idiotic move today and the memories it must have recalled of the damage that was done to you. But, I need you to breathe and walk away from this now. Not as a woman, but as a Boss, to regroup and think. If you found this room, you must know where Liam's is. He will be there momentarily, and you can speak Boss to *Ceann na Conairte*."

When she nodded, he let her go, and she left with Monte, who held on to his arm, and Fedel, who hadn't moved from the destroyed wall. When she was gone, my father didn't even have to speak, he glared at our guys and they left faster than she had—leaving me with the man who had just spit all over my victory. Once again, all I could see was red, and for the first time in my twenty-four years of life, I wanted my father's blood.

"You embarrassed me! This relationship, this marriage will not work. I will burn the fucking contract so I can put a bullet in her myself."

He stepped forward, his eyes darker than a brewing storm. "*You* embarrassed yourself today. Did you not think that a woman, a Boss, like Melody, could have easily bombed the fucking plane? Yes, I knew where you got the intel from, you fucking idiot. I checked their files, too, while you were busy chaining your fiancée to a pool chair."

"But she didn't do it, probably because she was weak and didn't want to kill innocents," I snapped back, trying my best not to point a gun in his face.

He pointed at the crumbling wall, which now exposed us. "Did that look like weakness to you, or are you so blinded by the thought of power that you have forgotten everything I have taught you?"

I sighed deeply, dropping the gun on the table before I pulled the trigger. "Everything I did today, you would have done as well."

"Yes, but I would have made sure it didn't hurt my wife first. Congratulations, you have proven to Vance and his brothers that you are just as merciless as they are. You won the pride of your men, and you pulled off a job no one will tie to you," he snapped angrily. "But if you had heeded my words and tried to make peace with Melody instead, you would have used your access to the Giovanni files and did your homework on what happened to Melody and her mother to bring you both together in the first place."

I froze, not understanding what Aviela Giovanni had to do with this. She had died years ago.

"Think about it, then go back to her and grovel." With those words, he left the room.

Taking a seat at one of the only computers not blown to the heavens, I pulled up the very files he was bitching about, and my blood froze.

MARCH 19: FLIGHT 307 CRASHES INTO THE ATLANTIC OCEAN; ONE SURVIVOR, SIX-YEAR-OLD MELODY NICCI GIOVANNI.

"Fuck," I murmured to myself as I read the title, but it only got worse.

NOTES:

According to young Melody's memory, there were four men on the plane who stood up mid-flight and started shooting and demanding Aviela Giovanni, wife to the Boss, to show herself. Mrs. Giovanni, with the help of her bodyguard, placed Melody into one of the overhead compartments right before they were both shot and killed. The men, who were later identified by the *V* tattoo on their arms, were Valero. After the death of Mrs. Giovanni, they proceeded to kill everyone on the plane. It was due to her tears and whimpering that the men found her. Landing the plane on the surface of the sea, they filled the chambers with smoke before dragging young Melody onto an awaiting boat.

Melody explained that, because she was praying, they decided they would let God decide her fate and threw her back into the ocean holding on to a piece of wreckage. As they drove away, they told her that if she survived to join the Valero when she was older.

The Boss found his daughter the next morning clinging on to one of the broken wings of the plane. The plane was torched beyond recognition, and the body of Mrs. Giovanni was never recovered.

Melody was alive, but suffered from hypothermia, and developed extreme Achluophobia, which she still has not recovered from. With therapy, it might lessen with time.

COVER-UP:PLANE CRASH DUE TO ENGINE FAILURE.

"Fuck." I sighed running my hands through my hair. "Fuck. Fuck. Fuck. Mother of fucking fuck."

My mind was so messed up. I couldn't think straight, all I could see was a younger version of my fiancée, clinging to a wing in the middle of the fucking Atlantic Ocean.

In the dark. Just how I fucking left her. "Fuck."

My father was right. I truly needed to grovel, but even that wouldn't change things. It wouldn't be enough. Nothing would be enough, and I had nothing left to give.

I had no idea I was even moving until I found myself standing outside my bedroom, dreading the thought of going in. My bedroom was my sanctuary, and now, it was going to be place of my death. But, I needed to man up and deal with the consequences of my actions.

Inside, she stood at the foot of my bed, dressed in gray with a gun and a knife strapped to her thigh. She seemed to be taking it all in, from the dark reds and gold of my bed and walls, to the wooden floors, large windows, lion-skin rug, piano in the corner, and flat screen plastered on the wall. She turned around slowly, and I really wished I could hear her thoughts. It wasn't a woman friendly room. However it was wasn't meant to be.

"We had a machine onboard recording their conversations. It's now somewhere in the ocean. A team and I will be getting it back," she told me as she tried to leave the room, but I grabbed hold of her arm first.

"I can go," I said as she glared up at me. "I should go because it's my fault. I'm sorry. For everything, I . . ."

"Look who finally did a background check. If you want to come, I can't stop you." She ripped her arm from my grasp. "You are everything I thought you would be—a child in a grown man's body. You're brash and wild, and you don't seem to get the gravity of our situation. You don't impress me, Liam Callahan. So get that poor little girl out of your head, because I am not *her*."

Closing the small space between us, I glared down into her brown eyes, wanting to rip them from her oval-shaped face.

"I am brash? I am wild? So says the woman who blasted her way into a private meeting nearly killing her future in-laws. You do not know me, Giovanni. Do not be fooled by my wit or charm. It has taken all my strength not to kill you."

"What wit? What charm? You're nothing but talk, and I do not need to know you, Callahan. I just need to marry you." With that she held her head high and left.

I would not bow down. She would not bow down.

The gravity of our situation was starting to eat away at me. I needed this to work. The Irish needed this to fucking work. But how the hell was I going to handle a lifetime of her—a hot-blooded Italian Boss?

Step one, accept she was a damn boss.

Step two, hide all the knives, guns, and maybe the pillows, too.

NINE

"One murder makes a villain, millions a hero. Numbers sanctify, my good fellow."

—Monsieur Verdoux

MELODY

There was something about Liam Callahan. He was immature, rowdy, and impatient. Those were just the kinder things I could think of, and yet I knew he smelled like cinnamon, spices, and apples. I had taken the time to reflect on his scent, even enjoyed it. *Ugh.* On top of that, I enjoyed how he looked up close. The way he flexed his muscles out of habit and cracked his knuckles when he was tense. I had noticed that in just two days. I had a whole arsenal of men under my control and many were attractive in some way, shape, or form, and yet there was something about Liam Callahan.

When he stepped out of his room, he was dressed in dark pants paired with a black and green vest with the letter *C* on the breast. He looked surprised to see me, as if he wasn't sure why I was here. On his arms were bruises and marks from our fight.

The idiot should have treated them, but instead, he had to be a man's man and leave them.

"Took you long enough, Callahan. Did you need to fix your hair?"

He glared at me before smirking. "It's called sex hair for a reason. That's the only way I fix it. You done being a bitch?"

Fedel came down the hall, before I could respond.

"Ma'am, the helicopter is ready. Monte is fine, and we are ready to aid," he said, waiting for orders.

"I already contacted Monte, and he'll tell you what to do." His eyes widened, knowing what I meant. He just lost his title as right-hand man, the fucker. "Next time, Fedel, when I tell you to fall on your sword, do it without hesitation. You waste my time and insult my intelligence with a statement like, 'we're outnumbered.' That is all."

He nodded and left quickly, leaving Mr. Sex Hair and me alone. Liam stared at Fedel's with narrowed eyes then turning his glower on me.

I cut in before he could speak again. "The helicopter is lifting us to Delaware. The flight is an hour. From there, we are taking a speedboat north. The GPS is picking up the signal fifteen clicks from shore. However, the Valero are already aware of your stunt and will most likely have men in the water trying to recoup any lost drugs." Stepping forward, I made sure he understood I was not playing. "First, you see what I'm doing, telling you every detail of this? Yeah, that is what you should have done. Second, this is my operation now. My men. So if you fuck up, I will slit your throat and then fill you with bull—"

His eyes lit up like fire before he grabbed me and threw me against the wall. "Every moment you waste roaring at me, is a moment against us, Captain Bitch-a-Lot. As smart as your plan is, it would be better to have snipers in the air. Something I thought of before I even stepped out here."

I just grinned. Even with his arm on my neck, he thought he was so fucking smart. "You are so right. Which is why I already have Neal and Antonio locked, loaded, and waiting. Anything else you assume I didn't think of? When will you get that while you've been number two for daddy, I've been number one?"

He said nothing, just glared.

"You should release me, Captain Dipshit or lose your arm. Your choice."

I didn't wait, I broke free. I was tiny compared to him, so all I needed to do was drop down and roll out of his grip. He had so much to learn, and this was his time to do it.

Due to the fact that I had shot up Sedric's house, the party they had thrown in my honor had ended and everyone departed.

Outside were four motorcycles, two of which were taken by Declan and Monte. The other two for Liam and me—mine white, and his green and black. He looked at me as if I was a china doll, and all I could do was roll my eyes before jumping on my bike and taking off as soon as one of their people opened the gate. Only a second had gone by before I saw him skyrocket past me, almost cutting me off, the sour brat, so I sped up beside him. We raced through the backstreets of Chicago, the lights from the buildings up above us all blending together in a single streak. No matter how much gas I gave while weaving in and out of traffic and intersections, he was always winning. I could only get in front of him for a second before he would shoot past me out of nowhere. It was as if he was toying with me.

By the time we got to the silver, luxury-style helicopter parked privately at the airstrip, Declan and Monte were right behind us. Liam was already off his bike, arms crossed with a grin on his face, as if he had waited hours—the asshole.

Saying nothing to him, I walked right onboard to find Antonio and Neal salivating over sniper rifles like kids on Christmas morning.

At least I don't have to worry about Irish and Italian feuding between them.

"I'm glad to see your loyalty is *still* so easily bought, brother." Liam glared at him as he took a seat.

Or not.

Neal froze, and I saw a speck of anguish go through his eyes. Liam must have seen it as well, because he didn't stop whatever mental assault he was delivering. It was like he could see into his brother's soul.

Can all siblings do this?

"Jinx," I said as loudly as possible.

Liam, Declan, and Neal all looked around to find the person behind the name, but no one came. A second later, the helicopter's engine kicked on and a soft voice broke out over our headphones. "*Benvenuto a bordo,*⁸ ma'am. I will have us to Delaware in forty."

Monte sat before me in the seat Fedel normally would be in and turned to Liam, who also sat across from me. "Jinx is our master aviator. If it goes in the sky, he can fly it."

"That's his name?" Neal asked, "Jinx? I feel safer already."

Monte sneered. "If he's good enough for the Boss, he's good enough for you *cane*."

Antonio snickered.

"Cane? What the fuck did you just call me?

So much for no feuding.

"It means dog." Liam glared at me.

Was he waiting for me to do something? His brother started it. Rolling my eyes, I looked to Monte who muttered something under his breath. Neal hunched over like a *cane* and focused in on his rifle.

I knew Antonio could shoot to kill in any sort of condition. The wind and darkness of the evening wouldn't be an issue. It wasn't the first time he had done it in such conditions. However, I was testing Neal, and if he didn't pass, this would be the last time he worked closely with me. At least until he became better. I already had an idea of Declan's skills. Seeing as he was the one who had "hacked" into my computers. I made it easy for him, but he still did it quicker than I expected.

"You will be monitoring the GPS," Liam stated, finally catching up.

Monte nodded, and Liam turned to me.

"Declan can hack into the surrounding frequencies and keep track. The area should be filled with paramedics, cops, and the coast guard," Liam said, and in his eyes he was daring me to agree, now of all times.

Seeing as he was being a good little boy, I would let him have his moment of dominance. Monte looked at me, and I nodded. I had planned to have Declan on the sea with me since he was great with hand-to-hand combat as well and we may need it, but sure, Liam could pretend he helped. Once finished, Monte stood up quickly to get out of the negative bubble created by Liam and me.

He did not say a word, but I could see Liam's mind racing, and I could tell he didn't like me being here. I almost wanted to tell him to get the fuck over it, but the helicopter was tense enough. Declan and Monte were focused on the four sets of laptops between them, while Antonio and Neal both kept checking their rifles. They seemed close already since Neal threw him a pack of chewing tobacco and Antonio accepted it like it was gold. One moment they were fighting, the next they are trading toys.

Finally, when my eyes fell back on Liam, I found him watching me. He didn't look away like most people would when caught staring. Instead, he just stared harder, as if I were a book he was trying to read, but it was in a language he didn't understand.

"Yes?"

He shook his head. "We're here."

And sure enough, the helicopter began its illegal descent on the beach.

"Sir, ma'am," Declan said, looking between us both. "We have a problem."

"What?" Liam and I asked at the same time.

Monte clicked away at his computer. "The Valero have just gotten the recorder and are heading further out to sea. They have a boat waiting."

Taking a deep breath, I pushed the button overhead. "Jinx, take us . . ." I looked over at Declan and Monte for the coordinates.

"38.09, -72.50," they both said, quickly.

Liam nodded, looking over at Antonio and Neal as the helicopter pulled up. "They'll bring it to us. Melody and I will wait on their boat. You guys will shoot from the door."

They nodded while Liam stood up and looked over to me. He was doing so well until he opened his mouth again. "Or you can shoot and Neal and I can go."

Standing up, I glared right back at him. "Give me a rifle and the bullet goes in your spine," I told him as I waited by the helicopter door. Jinx was going to have to circle around continuously. Liam stood in front of me, hand on the door handle and just stared at me, once again. Always with the staring, the creeper. For a moment, in the midst of the storm that was in his eyes, I saw worry. He was fucking worried about me, the fucker. This was not my first—nor would it be my last—jump out of an aircraft. He needed to grab his balls and take a shot of testosterone, because I wasn't worried for shit. I just wanted this over so I could drink myself to sleep.

Monte walked over to hand us parachutes, but we both shook our heads. They would only slow us down enough to be shot. We need to drop down quick and hard.

"Jinx, take us as low as possible," I said.

Our stomachs dipped as we felt the helicopter drop. Somehow, knowing before Jinx even had to speak, Liam opened the door and in the darkness of the night, we could both see the yacht waiting below. He looked back at me, but I ignored him and pushed off the wall to jump. The moment the cold breeze hit my skin, I braced myself for the impact of the deck. When my body landed, I rolled as bullets came flying my way.

Grabbing onto my gun, I turned and shot one right between his eyes just as Liam dropped onto the shoulders of another. There were screams and curses in Russian as Liam dove right beside me.

"Come here often?" he said, chuckling as adrenaline clearly pumped through his veins. I supposed he was no longer seeing me as a china doll in that moment, but as another person on his side. *Finally*, the dipshit.

"Not really." I tried not to smirk back as more Russians came shooting at us. "The hospitality here is fucking shit."

"You should write a strongly worded letter."

Rolling my eyes, I turned and shot a man on the top deck in the kneecap. "This is more eco-friendly. Save the trees, and all that shit."

He grinned and then shot the man now screaming in pain in the head. "I was never good at recycling."

Two more men came forward, one right behind Liam, and another behind me. We both raised our hands as they yell at us.

"*Kto vy? Vy lokhi!*"⁹ they shouted at us.

Liam smiled at me—he truly smiled for once—obviously enjoying this. "*Ya*, Liam Kallahan. *Eto moy zhenikh, vy tozhe mertv.*"¹⁰

Just as the man finished, bullets went into the side of their heads, courtesy of Antonio and Neal, before the helicopter spun out of view once again. A second later, Liam's phone rang and he placed it on speaker.

"They are four miles away and will be there shortly," Declan said. Liam said nothing before hanging up as I reached down to grab their guns.

"Yarygin or Stechkin Pistol?" I asked him, causing him to frown.

"The Russians can't make guns for shit," he said in disgust, and he had a point.

Smiling, we began to throw the few bodies overboard as we waited for our friends. It only took a second, and by that time, we had thrown the overweight, drunken Russians off.

The boat was silent except for another crew as they made their ways back on deck. They stumbled and laughed liked fools.

"*Vse chertovski narkotiki ushli. Chert by pobral etikh vlagalishcha v ad. Valero sobirayetsya ubit' nas.*"[11]

One of the men asked where their brothers where Liam was already on his feet.

"Dead." Liam said as he shot one right in the nose and I shot the other in the eye. He screamed in pain as I walked over, patting him down for the mini-equipment. Once I had it, I shot him once more for the heck of it.

"I'll call the guys," I said, handing it to Liam, but once I turned around, I found myself looking down the barrel of a gun. It was the man whom Liam landed on, and he had his gun pointed right at me. Liam pulled me out of the way and shot the fucker in the face, but not before taking one in the arm.

"Fuck it all to hell," he said, pulling back his wounded limb.

He must have left his guardian angel at home.

"Jinx, head in, we'll meet you onshore. We're fine . . . for the most part," I said before hanging up and grabbing his arm.

He pulled away. "I'm fine, just wish I didn't kill the fucker so I could torture him."

"You have a bullet in your arm." I glared at him. "A Russian bullet, which you, yourself said was shit. I am going to take it out."

"I said I was fucking fine, Melody!"

Angry, I holstered my weapon before I shot him in the other arm, and grabbed on to his wounded arm again, causing him to hiss out in pain.

"You are not fine." I pressed down harder. "Now stop bitching and let me fix it, you asshole."

I didn't allow him to speak before pulling him inside the cabin and pushing him onto the nearest bed. They must have been ready to eat because alcohol and an array of meat, bread, and apples awaited them. Getting a napkin and a knife, I poured the alcohol over it and his wound before giving him the rest to drink. *Hopefully, the liquor would keep him quiet.*

He smirked at me before taking the bottle to his lips. "I think I like you as a nurse."

Glaring at him, I dug the knife into his bullet wound. "You really shouldn't say stupid things to a woman with weapons."

He hissed and roared in pain like a fucking baby until I got the bullet out and used the napkin as a bandage.

"Drink and shut up, I'll be right back," I said to him before going back on deck.

I made sure to drag and throw the bodies off the boat before setting course back to the mainland. I also called Monte to let him and Liam's brothers know what happened. It took me about an hour and a half. By the time I went back to Liam, he was frozen on the bed, listening to the audio from the plane he had destroyed.

All either of us could hear were screams, crying, and prayers. They brought back memories I would rather forget. Walking over, I pushed stop and he, was pulled out of his trance.

"I thought you were going to set the boat on autopilot," he said, proving just how out of it he was.

Grabbing another napkin, I took the old blood-soaked one off and redid the bandage.

"Do not take a bullet for me again."

He snorted before pulling away. "No good deed goes unpunished. The correct words you are looking for are 'thank you.'"

I pulled tighter, and he winced, the baby. "Thank you, but don't do it again. The last thing I need is for any of my men to think I can't handle myself."

"You are so fucking ridiculous. Why must you always try to prove that you're a cold-hearted bitch?"

"Because a *cold-hearted bitch* is what I need to be," I snapped back, rising in front of him. "You can fuck up as many times you want, but at the end of the day, no one will doubt you. I, on the other hand, make one mistake and it's over. Some cocky asshole like you will come over and claim I'm too soft, or that I don't have the balls. I've worked too hard to backtrack now."

He said nothing. He knew I was right. I didn't have time to waste, proving and reproving who I was.

"And in a way, they would be right, because I should have blown that plane up myself," I confessed, grabbing the wine from the table and leaning against it. "If I had, I would get the credit—"

"You want credit?" He eyed me up and down, his green eyes picking up only the dimmest light of the cabin we now shared. "You want credit for the mass murder I committed."

"Don't say it like that. We are not serial killers. We do not kill for the fun of it or chaos. It is just business. Every last person we kill is for family. If we do not kill them, they kill us. It is the way of the world. It is self-defense. It is survival. If it were your life for theirs, they would kill you in a second to save themselves or their family. *Everyone* is ruthless. They just don't know it. You do. I do. And that is why we are on top and will remain so."

"And you feel nothing."

"And I feel nothing," I repeated.

He looked me in the eyes, and I hoped to God he understood, because I didn't know how else to explain it. It was that kind of thinking that made it easy for me to sleep at night.

"Neither do I," he said, and I believed him.

I tried to move, but he grabbed on to my sides and held me in place. There was that look in his eyes—the hunger, the lust, and the caged animal dying to get out. Pulling me even closer, he pressed himself against me.

"L—" His lips were on mine and he was pulling at my clothes. With his one good arm, he cupped my ass and the other one cupped my breast as he rubbed himself against me. His lips hummed against my neck before he lifted me up, throwing me on the bed.

He stopped for only a second to look me over, and the storm in his eyes raged worse than I had ever seen. "This is your one and only chance to tell me to stop."

TEN

"It takes two to make a murder. There are born victims, born to have their throats cut, as the cutthroats are born to be hanged."

—Aldous Huxley

LIAM

She leered, and I could see the lust growing in her eyes until it reflected my own.

"You better not rip my clothes." Her brown eyes narrowed at me and with that, every chain, lock, and bolt in my mind broke loose.

I grabbed her by the ankle and spread her legs until she was no less than an inch from me taking her. I could feel her become wet just from the sheer closeness of our bodies. Brushing my hand on the side of her face, then against her lips, I grabbed on to her hair and pulled it back, allowing me to latch on to her neck. Neither of us needed to speak. We knew what we wanted, and there were not enough words in the human language that could express what my tongue physically could, as I bit, licked, and sucked on her neck. I felt like a fucking animal, but I could not stop myself, and by God's name, when she unzipped my vest and rubbed her cool hands all over my torso, I became ravenous.

Pushing her back, I pulled off her top as quickly as possible, trying my best to do as she asked and not rip the damn thing off her. However, it didn't work, and I heard a small tear before the top was in shreds.

"Damn it, Liam!" she yelled at me, and I stopped, pushing up to stare into her deep, dark eyes, my breath on her lips.

"Say it again," I muttered as I grabbed her breast through her bra. I would have preferred a laced one instead of a sports bra, but a breast was a fucking breast.

"Say what?"

Leaning in, I kissed her lips quickly before biting her bottom one. I then kissed her cheek, before I finally got to her ear and nibbled the lobe. I was losing my mind, I could feel it, all I wanted to do was devour each and every fucking part of her.

"My name," I whispered in her ear, and she shivered with pleasure. "Say my name again. Not in anger, or disgust, but as you did just now. As if I am the only man in the world who can satisfy you."

Because I was. I kissed down her neck once more. However, she grabbed me by the hair and brought me back to eye level. She said not a word, just gazing up at me for a moment, before kissing me almost desperately. For once, she fucking kissed me first, and I couldn't help but think it was better than fucking heaven, until she flipped me onto my back.

She straddled my waist and stared down at me before pulling her bra off. She kissed up my chest slowly, grinding herself against my cock as it begged for release. When she reached my neck, my hands went straight to her hair and hers went to my pants. *Thank fucking Christ.*

Flipping her over, I pinned her hands above her head and stared down at what was now mine. Her cheeks were flushed, her nipples erect, and I bent down to suck on them, as if they were begging me to do so. She moaned loudly as she tried to wriggle her hands free.

"Liam," said, arching toward me.

"Again," I demanded as I moved to the next one, my tongue circling around her areola, not sucking on her nipple until she did as I said. But my girl never just gave in to me. Transferring both her hands to my right one, my left traveled into her pants, not stopping until it reached its target. I could feel her, and that eclipsed the pain from my arm. She was dripping from me. The moment I cupped her, my girl's back rose off the fucking bed.

"You fucking bastard." She moaned, trying to rub her legs together and force friction that I would not let her have.

"Again," I demanded once more, my lips traveling from her breast down to her waist slowly. I kissed every part of her, as I barely rubbed her wet pussy. She wanted more, and so did I, but she had do what I wanted.

But, once again, my girl wanted to make my life as difficult as possible, leaving me no other choice but to release my hold on her hands so I could pull her pants off completely. The moment my eyes saw the spring of honey begging for my tongue, I latched on, sucking and lapping up all the juices she had provided for me.

She gasped, gripping on to my hair as she rubbed herself against my face. "Liam."

I pulled away, only for a moment. "Again."

She refused and so my finger found its way into her, and she gasped out in ecstasy. In and out, as fast and as deep as possible, I pounded my fingers into her as she ground onto my hand, wanting the satisfaction only my cock would give, but trying her best to make do with the three fingers I had inside her. Just as she was reaching her climax, I stopped. Her eyes narrowed at me as she breathed deeply.

"You fucker."

"Not yet," I whispered, stepping back to release my cock from the confines of my pants. She stared at it, and I let her, just for a moment, before pulling her back to me. Before she even had time to think, I thrust deeply within her. Her back arched, as she shouted in Italian.

I pulled her even closer to me and went even deeper still, if such a thing could be possible. Wincing at how slowly I moved, I watched her tremble as my cock filled her.

"Say my name," I told her, almost stopping altogether as my cock throbbed. I was hoping and praying she would give in so I could have my way with her.

She didn't, so I thrust forward quickly. "Melody, for the love of God, just say my name."

Instead, she slipped slightly away from me before wrapping her arms around my neck. "Mel, just Mel," she panted.

Holding on to her waist, I eased back slowly before thrusting again. "Say it, Mel."

She kissed up my neck, then my ear before stopping at my lips, staring me deeply in the eyes. Hers were so dark I could see myself in them. Her breath was almost on my tongue, and I just needed to hear it.

"Liam," she hissed and kissed me deeply.

My name was the key to opening the deepest levels of possession possible. I pushed her onto her back, causing both of us to cry out and hiss as my cock slammed into her over and over again. She moved in rhythm with me, every thrust, not missing a beat. She cried out my name over and over again.

Grabbing her breast, I fucked her deeper, not even stopping when she screamed out her release . . . I wasn't even close to finished, she would come at least once more before I released in her.

Pulling out of her, we both cried out in protest until I flipped her over and took her, holding her waist and shoulder as I forced myself deeper.

"Fuck, Liam! Harder," she begged. "Faster."

And at both wishes, I complied, until I couldn't hold myself back anymore, just as she couldn't, and we came together.

"*Mo Mel álainn.*"[12] I gasped before pulling out of her and falling onto the bed.

Flipping onto her back, she tried to control her breathing before speaking. "You can only call me Mel during sex."

"Why is that?" I raised my eyebrow at her.

"You haven't earned it."

I couldn't have this. After what had just happened between us, everything had changed, whether she knew it or not, and it started with me. Grabbing on to her, I rolled over her, allowing her space so my weight would do no harm. She looked at me surprised, but said nothing.

"What happened tonight will be repeated," I told her calmly, still trying to catch my breath. "You are mine, as I am yours. But for this to work, you need to stop seeing me as a goddamned enemy and more like your husband."

Her eyes narrowed. "My husband you say? So I'm supposed to sit back polish your shoes and make dinner in between fucks?"

"Mel," I replied, moving down until I was at her entrance again. "I get it," I said to her before I thrust forward and buried myself into the tight place that was quickly becoming my new home.

"Do you?" she hissed, trying to stay focused as I inserted myself deeper.

"Yes," I whispered going for her neck again.

"You are not a housewife," I said, pulling out only to slam myself in again.

"You do not want to be my arm candy." *Slam,* she reached up for my hair.

"You are a cold-blooded murderer." *Slam,* she moaned as sweat dripped from my chin onto her chest.

"You are a Boss." *Slam.*

"You are my evolution." *Slam,* this time, she grabbed on to my ass, trying to pull me closer.

"I'm willing to try to disregard my chauvinistic ways." *Slam.*

"To treat you as an equal, but you must fucking do the same for me, Mel." And with that, I thrust into her repeatedly, her body molded with mine, her breasts pushed against my chest. She was so fucking tight I couldn't keep my eyes open.

Her nails dug into my back and her legs wrapped around my waist, pulling me closer to her. Her hands weaved into mine as we entangled ourselves, rising to the highest of climaxes and crashing together.

Gasping for breath, I held her tightly, my arms wrapped around her while I used her breast as a pillow. We were both silent, allowing our breathing to fill the cabin, and neither of us let go of the other.

"You see me as Boss?"

"Yes, and it annoys me, because I want that title," I replied honestly, causing her to pull my hair.

"No matter how many times we fuck Callahan, I will never just bow down to you. I will never let you rule me. I will not be your bitch to screw and command. I don't think you can handle that."

Maybe it was the sex talking, or maybe my father's words were finally beginning to sink in and I was starting to see a new way of getting what I wanted. All of what I wanted.

Rolling off her, I looked up at the wooden ceiling, not speaking for a moment as I gathered my thoughts.

"In many ways, I can't," I told her. "In my mind, there will always be a chauvinist, but I will fight it. You and I both know that once we're married our companies will be one. Which means there will be only one head, for a divided house cannot stand."

"Thank you, Abraham Lincoln. But I am not giving up my claim as Boss," she replied, and I knew she wouldn't. She wouldn't "bow" to me. The only way for this to work other than the one thing I hated to do most—share.

It was so simple. It made logical sense, but I was a greedy motherfucker, and in many ways, so was she. We were too fucking alike.

"There is one head. But also a brain within it. Everything we choose for the company will be thought of together in our bed and then we bring it to the men. We rule as one together."

She said nothing, and I allowed her to think it over as I breathed in the smell of sex, *our* sex. The best fucking sex I had ever had. Sex I never wanted to stop having.

"We won't always agree on everything," she whispered, and she was right.

"Everything we don't agree on, we fuck out." I enjoyed the thought. "This is, after all, the longest interaction we have ever had and you haven't shot me once."

"Not yet," she said, sitting up. I loved how she didn't care if I saw her naked in the light. She didn't reach to cover herself. She just allowed me the pleasure of looking at her. My hands reached up to mess with a few strands of her hair.

"What do you say, my Mel? We end our war and join brains and bodies to destroy any against us. We become one ruthless person instead of two."

"You can just do that?" she asked, eyeing me skeptically. "You can just share, like that. You don't seem like the type."

"Because I'm not. But when I thought of what my life would be like when I married, I thought of a woman, who handles what I do and allowed me the pleasure of confessing my sins as I took her mercilessly," I replied, looking up at such a woman. "And now I have a woman who takes part in them as well. Who enjoys it. Who does not shy away from it. If I can't share it with her, who can I share it with?"

"My father was right, you are a sweet talker." She frowned, and I hated the look of it, so I brushed my finger over her lips.

I stared at her. "I mean it, Mel. Join me and set the world on fire and I won't take your title, no matter how much I once wished to. I wish for less fighting and more of this."

I grabbed her face with one hand and her breast with the other.

"You are using sex to cloud my judgment, Callahan."

"I'm simply showing you another way, because I'm tired of being at war with an opponent I can't kill," I whispered to her. "You stand at my side. I stand at yours, and together we rule the East and the West, so much so that they'll rename cities after us."

"The Valero." She bit her lip as I pinched her nipples. Leaning forward, I took one of them into my mouth and pulled her close to me.

"We put a bullet in each one of their heads and then fuck in their beds," I replied as she pushed me onto my back and grabbed hold of my cock. I felt it jump alive in her hands.

She bent down and licked the tip of it. "Are you lying to me, Callahan?"

She took me in her mouth and I moaned incoherently, words I weren't even sure were English. I could barely even think straight, her mouth was that heavenly. Forget Natasha, and any of the other bitches I had been with. Had I known this was what waited for me, I would have come here fucking first.

"Well Callahan?" She ran her teeth along my length, and I shivered.

"Fuck no, Mel. I'm not fucking lying." My hands went to her hair.

"You and I work as one?" she asked me before sucking down harder, making me almost come in her mouth.

My head went back, and I tried to hide how blissful this felt. "Jesus yes. Fuck yes. You and me, no one else. We will . . . fuck, baby. Ohhh! Yes! We'll rule as one."

"Even now, as I'm sucking your cock, you will see me as an equal." She used her hands when she spoke, before her magical mouth enveloped me once more.

What was her question?

"Yes. Fuck yes. Even as you fucking suck me off, I still won't see you below me, just as you won't when I'm eating you out." I moaned, thrusting into her mouth, she just took it, and my hands went to the sides of her head, as I fucked her mouth like I fucked her pussy—hard and fast.

When I came, she sucked it all down her throat and wiped her mouth.

"Well, I guess I can handle that, but if you fuck me over, Callahan, I will kill you."

"Let's get dressed and get this marriage over with, so I can fuck you with a ring on both our fingers."

She rose before me and lifted her torn top, groaning. "You are such an ass."

"I would say sorry, but I wouldn't mean it," I said, rising from the bed as well.

We stood there, staring at each other, both naked and both desperately in need of each other.

"One last fuck before we get married?" That look in her eyes made me shiver.

All I could do was smirk before pushing her against the wall.

"You and I, what a pair we make," I said, spreading her legs once again and one of the many more times that will happen in the future, I hoped.

"You and I against the world then?" she asked me as I pushed inside her.

"With this fuck, we start a new chapter in our life," I hissed as I slammed into her. "May we forever be rulers, may our enemies tremble at our feet, may we never forget our great love that is the family. Which we will rule with an iron fist."

"May we be ruthless and have no regrets," she added gripping onto my back. "May we take what we want, when we want it, with the world at our feet."

I smiled as I fucked her against the wall. We moved in sync. It was like our bodies were also agreeing to our package of glory, death, and blood.

"Mrs. Callahan, we shall have the world soon," I said, never wanting to stop my hunt to go deeper within her. The tides were changing, and we must adapt to survive during drastic changes, and Mel was that drastic change. What we had was much bigger than the two of us, but as she moaned out my name, I couldn't be more grateful. She would help me fill the sky with the Valero blood. Once we did, we would rule.

That thought added to the pleasure, and it was the best fuck of my life.

ELEVEN

"I love the old way best, the simple way of poison, where we too are strong as men"

—Euripides

MELODY

"After hours of rescue missions and millions of prayers, we have yet to find any survivors of Flight 735. Our hearts go out to all the families affected by this great tragedy, which was caused by a simple and unpredictable engine failure. The Callahan family has created a charity in honor of the victims and has already donated fifteen million dollars on behalf of Melody and Liam who, as we all know, are getting married this evening. Their wedding has been the talk of the town since we broke the story to you only three days ago. Apparently, the couple had been seeing each other in secret for quite some time now. The rumors of who are to attend this wedding range from U.S. senators to the very top of the A-list . . ."

"Ma'am would you like me to turn it off?" Adriana asked as she fixed my hair. Taking a sip of my wine, I shook my head at her before looking into the mirror.

"Adriana, I do not want an up-do." Screw tradition, I liked my hair down.

"Are you sure?" Evelyn smiled kindly as she walked into my room.

Tying the robe around myself just a little tighter, I smiled before standing up. Adriana left us quickly to get the dress that hung in the deepest, darkest part of my closet.

"I prefer it down," I stated when Evelyn walked up to me looking me up and down then nodding. Reaching over she pulled the pin out of my hair and took a simple step back.

"Well, I must say you do look even more beautiful with it down."

"Thank you, Evelyn."

"Mel, please look at me," she asked, and when I did her palm came right across my face so quickly I never saw it coming.

Shocked, I touched the side of my cheek, unsure if I was dreaming or not.

"What the fuck!"

She didn't even flinch. "So, I'm guessing this is the real Melody Giovanni, the girl who had the balls to step into my house, destroy my Jackson Pollock, and then shoot my fucking husband?"

Now I was starting to get angry. Standing straighter, I glared into her eyes. She got one slap and that was it, the next time she raised her arm at me I was going to break it. Before she could move, Adriana stood behind her with a gun to her skull.

I grinned, wiping my cut lip thanks to her fucking ring. "Evelyn, *you* should know better."

Evelyn glared back not even a little bit scared. "I come to you as a mother coming to a daughter. Had it been any of my sons who had put a bullet in Sedric, I would have taken them out of this world so quickly they wouldn't even know it was me. I may not walk the same line you do, nor do I wish to, but you should know that when it comes to my husband, I will not hesitate to kill anyone. You crossed the line."

Look who has a spine. Nodding over to Adriana, she took a step back and walked over to the bed pulling out my dress.

"Noted," I said, not even a least bit threatened. I was too amused for that. "Sedric is off limits. He wasn't my target anyway; your idiot son was."

She glared once again before smirking. "It took me a long time to shift Sedric's view on women when I first met him and again when he first learned about you."

What?

"Sedric found out about me the same time Liam did." *Didn't he?*

Evelyn beamed. "Like I said, I may not choose to walk the same path as you, but that doesn't mean I'm naïve to the inner workings of this family. Everything Sedric has ever done he has told me.

The moment he knew what you were, he believed you were the best thing for my *idiot* son, as you so elegantly put it. He kept it a secret from him to let him deal with the information as he saw fit. I will commend you on your acting and will expect it whenever you are in public with me. What you and Liam do is none of my concern. I just wanted to make sure you knew where you stand."

"And where is that?" I wanted to bust her smug face in. It reminded me of Liam for fuck sake.

Evelyn pulled out a small box setting it on the table. "Today, you become my daughter; I will love you, stand by you, and when necessary put you in check. You may very well have the world in your hands, but you are still young and that makes you just as stupid as my son is at times. I like you, Mel, so I hope the next time we speak in confidence it is more civil."

I said nothing as she looked over to the bed and grabbed my new white shoes.

"Christian Louboutin." She smiled before turning back to look at me. "When we go to Paris in the spring you, Coraline, Olivia, and I must go shopping. You have impeccable taste."

"That would be Adriana, but I shall take the invitation all the same," I replied, and she nodded before walking to the door.

"Well, I will leave you to it. The girls and I will come back later if you don't mind." It didn't seem like a question, but I nodded anyway.

When she left, I smiled as I finished the rest of my wine. I was starting to like Evelyn.

My moment of peace didn't last long, however, before Liam walked in dressed in nothing but silk pajama bottoms as if we weren't getting married in a few hours.

"What is with you people and not knocking?" I glared at his chest before pouring myself more wine. I would have to make sure it was close by if I was going to make it through the rest of the day.

"What did my mother want?"

"The better question is what do you want?" I asked him, stepping forward. He towered over me, and the fact that I was in my underwear beneath the robe was not lost on either of us.

"Adriana, leave us." She froze, looking to me.

Rolling my eyes, I nodded, and she stepped outside, the moment she did he kissed me, opening up my robe so he could cup my ass. Pushing him away, I slapped him across the face.

"Just because we fucked already doesn't mean we need to jump each other every time we make eye contact," I snapped at him. Despite the fact that he did look rather sexy, I didn't want him getting used to the idea that my body was his to do anything he wished with when he was horny.

"Maybe if we did, you would be kinder." I just snorted and turned away from him to the items on the bed.

"Callahan, seriously what is it you want? We have the wedding of the decade to go to soon," I replied, stepping into my shoes.

"Those shoes make it hard not to have you right now," he said, staring at my legs. "However, I will take pleasure in that later tonight. I just wanted to let you know Vance and his son, Amory, will be attending."

What the fuck?

"You do know this would be a perfect moment for him to strike back at you for what you did to the plane." I crossed my arms over my chest, and his eyes went to my breasts. Jeez, you would think we hadn't had sex all night. If it weren't for Sedric's call, we'd both still be on that boat.

Stepping forward, he let his hands trace up and down my sides. "Well love, as our new personal contract states, we now work together. My plans were to either beef up security and enjoy the evening, or take a moment out of our night and poison the bastard right then and there."

I frowned at the thought. "First, do not call me *love*. Second, when Vance falls, I want him to watch his empire burn around him and know that he was outsmarted, outgunned, and fucked over. Drowning in the soup seems . . ."

"Too easy." He agreed. "Then the first option it is. I'm shocked, *Mrs. Callahan*, did we just agree on something? Can it really be this easy?"

He cupped my breasts, and I gripped his dick tight enough to cause him pain. "If that's all, *sweetheart*, I would like to spend my last few moments as a Giovanni by myself."

"Bitch."

"You, too."

"I should have—" He stopped himself before stepping up behind me. "You look beautiful. See you at the altar, and try not to flinch at the holy water."

"I won't, if you won't," I replied as he kissed me where my shoulder met my neck.

He said nothing else before leaving, allowing Adriana to come back in. I sat down again, and she finished making the waves in my hair as I stared into my own reflection. His kiss brought back all his touches of the night before. He was amazing and had stamina that was unheard of. My body cried out for his, and my mind both hated and loved that. I loved being dominated in such a beastly sexual way, how his hands, lips, and tongue all grabbed on to me. He was the best partner I had ever had, but I didn't want him to know that. I didn't want his head to become any bigger than it already was.

I also didn't want him to think that just because he was a great fuck, that he held the key to making me bend. He said he understood, but the Boss in me told me that everyone lies. People lied about how much they drank, how much they were in debt, how many people they had killed—people were liars. I always thought I was good at reading liars. I could see it in their eyes, and if I did, I would kill them. However, with Liam, I was lost. It was like I was blind. He seemed honest, but he was just like me—a master liar.

"Adriana, what do you think of Liam Callahan?"

She froze, not sure what to say.

"Adriana, you can speak freely. I'm sure you've dug up more dirt since we've been here."

She nodded. "Liam Callahan is cocky, arrogant, controlling, manipulative, hotheaded, and attractive. What makes it worse is that he knows it. He has bloodlust. He stares at people with such rage, it is as though he wishes for them to mess up so he can put a bullet in them. However, the moment he looks at you, it's gone. He is content, which is far from the man I saw three days ago. He seemed a rather isolated and lonely person. From what I've gathered, he was a very ill child, to the point he was crippled. Add that to his high intelligence, and it made him a prime candidate for bullies throughout his early life. He keeps it private and is embarrassed about it, seeing as he is a Callahan. He was admitted to a hospital for almost year, and from there, gradually became better. He trusts very few people, which includes his family. He's searching for something."

I stared at her through the mirror, eyebrow raised, before grinning. This was Adriana's talent. She was a profiler. A very good profiler. Everyone overlooked her, thinking she was just my personal maid. However, I kept Adriana close because she was my second pair of eyes. She saw people as if they were an open book and could collect information because no one noticed her. She wasn't a fan of the blood, or the violence, and I wouldn't force her to be. She proved her worth often in times like this.

"So you think I should trust him."

"Only you know, ma'am. You are a better judge of character than I. I think he wants you to care about him as much as his mother cares for his father. I don't think he is out to hurt you—yet. But he is still a Callahan, and the Irish are tricky. He is going to be your husband, and you are not cringing at the thought of it, ma'am."

She was right, and I didn't know how to process that.

"It has been a long three days." I sighed, standing up and allowing my robe to fall. She nodded, grabbing my dress and holding it for me to step into.

"You look beautiful," Coraline said, beaming when she, Olivia, and Evelyn stepped in. Olivia looked sour, and I wouldn't have been surprised that she figured out I was the one who put a hole in her husband's arm.

"It's very simple," Olivia said fingering the tattoo on her wrist, looking my dress up and down. If I weren't in all white and about to enter the house of God, I would have bashed her head in.

"Some people have to try harder than others. Others can make simple look elegant."

"Agreed," Evelyn said. Apparently, she and I had come to a new agreement.

"Did you give her the bracelet?" Coraline asked even though Evelyn was already walking toward the desk to pick up the small box.

She opened it, and my eyes widened ever so slightly. The vintage bracelet, made of all pearls and pendant with the letter *C* embedded in it. It had to be from the early 1900s, at least.

"Something old. All the Callahan woman wear it during their wedding. It was the gift given to the wife of the first Boss." She smiled and placed it on my wrist.

"Thank you," I replied, and for the first time it hit me. I was getting married today.

"We should get going. Sedric is waiting," Olivia said, frowning and clearly pissed that the moment was happening between everyone but her. The bitch.

"Sedric?" I asked her and one met my gaze. "Why is Sedric waiting? Where is my father?"

LIAM

So what happened on the boat, Lamb?" Neal asked me for the billionth time as we waited in St. Peter's Cathedral.

"Mind your own fucking business. And if you call me Lamb again, Neal, I will kill you, then bury you under the church."

He smirked. "You're excited. You didn't even describe how you would kill me. That boat ride must have—"

Before he finished, I punched him in the fucking nose.

"For the love of motherfucking fuck!"

"Last chance brother or you're going to piss me off," I replied, fixing my tie.

"Liam, calm down before you get blood on your suit. I'm sure Melody wouldn't mind, but the press . . ." Declan sighed, throwing a cold beer at Neal who held it on his nose.

Neal mumbled something under his breath and left.

"One day you two will have to work out your issues," Declan said to me.

One day maybe, but not fucking today.

Saying nothing, I took a deep breath and walked out the door that lead to the front of the Cathedral. Looking outside, I noticed my mother had made sure to invite every last motherfucker with a net worth over a hundred million. They all looked like tourists, excited to be on the guest list. My eyes met Vance's, and I could feel the blood in my veins begin to run hotter. He smirked, nodding at me as though he was fucking proud, the bastard. Next to him sat Amory. The golden-locks-wannabe was all but sucking on Natasha's neck. It had seemed Deep Throat had switched ships. She winked at me, and I wanted to puke.

"How is security?"

Declan snickered. "They would have a better chance getting to the president than any one of us today."

"If this doesn't go off perfectly, shoot him for good measure." I wanted to be the one to take Vance's life, but if it needed to be done today, then I didn't care who did it.

"Just worry about Melody and pray she doesn't run away."

"No, she wouldn't run." Running wasn't in her nature. "She would come if only to kill me."

Before he could reply, music rang throughout the church and the door opened slowly making my heart rate quicken. A vision in white stood beside my father with a bouquet of blood-red roses in her hands. She didn't bother with a veil to cover her face, and for that, I was fucking glad. She was beautiful, deadly, stunning, and all mine.

When she reached me, she stopped and kissed my father on the cheek before taking my hand. However, when I looked in her eyes I saw a twinge of sadness, and it pained me to my core. I squeezed her hand, not to hurt her, but to tell her I saw and I didn't like it. I wanted her to be happy. I would let her pick anyone in the church and kill them if it made her smile.

"Dearly beloved, we are gathered here today in the face of not only God, but the world, to join together Liam Alec Callahan and Melody Nicci Giovanni in holy matrimony."

Everything he said after that faded when she squeezed my hand back.

She glanced up at me, and the lioness in her eyes wasn't gone, but simply asleep. Something was wrong, and I hated that I couldn't figure it out.

"Liam Alec Callahan, do you take Melody Nicci Giovanni to be your wife, to have and to hold from this day forward, for better or for worse, for richer or for poorer, in sickness and in health, to love and to cherish? Do you promise to be faithful to her until death do you part?"

"I do, always," I said without any hesitation, and she snickered at me, shaking her head as I placed the wedding band on her finger.

"Melody Nicci Giovanni, do you take Liam Alec Callahan to be your husband, to have and to hold from this day forward, for better or for worse, for richer or for poorer, in sickness and in health, to love and to cherish? Do you promise to be faithful to him until death do you part?"

"I do, always," she replied, and I felt overflowing relief and joy as she slid my ring into place.

"May these rings be blessed so he who gives it and she who wears it may abide in peace and continue in love until life's end," he said as we stared at each other. "You may now seal the promises you have made to each other with a kiss."

In that moment it didn't feel like our lips met. It was though our souls did.

Mel, *my Mel,* wiped the lipstick from my lips.

"Ladies and gentlemen, I now present to you the loving couple, Mr. and Mrs. Liam Callahan," the priest said while Mel rolled her eyes at me. Apparently, Mrs. Liam Callahan didn't sit well with her, but too fucking bad.

Everyone rose from his or her seat, clapping and cheering as we walked down the aisle hand in hand. We stopped at the top of the stairs to take photos for every damn magazine in the world, when my father leaned in beside me.

"I believed both of your emotions, so will the world," he whispered with a smirk as we smiled. "But was it true. Do you believe it? Did it take only Russian blood and a boat ride?"

I said nothing before stepping into the Rolls Royce.

"What's wrong?"

"Nothing."

Sighing, I leaned in and held the side of her face so she would have to look me in the eye. "Wife, what is wrong?"

She stared before sighing as well. "Husband, my father refused to walk me down the aisle. He's gotten worse."

With that she ripped her head from my hand and glared out the window. I felt like a bloody moron. I was so focused on her, I didn't even think about the person walking her down the aisle. Melody Gio . . . Callahan had the ability to make me forget anyone else existed when she was near.

"After we do our time at the reception, if you want, we could sneak out and go see him."

She looked at me, and her eyes narrowed. "Is this you trying to be sweet? Because I'm fine and would prefer to deal with *asshole* Callahan. You know, the son of a bitch I fought in my basement who thought his balls were bigger than they actually are?"

And there was the lioness again.

"I'm putting in effort, maybe you should fucking try it, Melody. I'm planning on going to war with the entire world. I don't need one with the woman sleeping beside me."

Neither of us spoke after that, she knew just how to fucking kill the mood.

Not looking at me she took my hand into hers and squeezing it before letting go. "I've never been . . . nice. I'm not used to being anything other than a Giovanni. Affection and tenderness are not our strong suits. So I do not know how to reciprocate that. *Bitch* is standard mode for me, and I will work on it."

"I don't mind you being a bitch to anyone else, as long as it is not me," I whispered, taking her hand

and kissing it quickly. Part of me was starting to enjoy her ripping out other people's hearts. It was her thing, and she was good at it.

She laughed, and I enjoyed the sound. "You do know that we have known each other for only seventy-two hours."

"Holy fuck, I feel like I've known you for decades." If not longer.

"Really?" she asked. "What is my favorite color?"

Fuck.

MELODY

When we got to the reception, which was being held outside at Callahan Manor, there were more photographers, who Evelyn allowed to take photos from a distance. My face felt as though it would break from all the forced smiling.

"Call them off, or I'm calling snipers," I said to Liam.

He leaned down to kiss my cheek. "I would, gladly, but my mother and father want good press."

I glared at him, pinching his arm until he pulled me away from the cameras and headed toward the sea of guests. There were more damn photos and fake congratulations there, until I saw Vance and Amory making their way through all the drinking and celebrating in the courtyard. Our guests danced underneath the steams of lights, blissfully unaware that two of the most deadly men in the country were about to collide with another deadly pair.

Both Vance and Amory were as slick as eels with their dark eyes and oily skin. Amory stood at the same stunted height as his father, even though Vance was rather stout and Amory was sickly thin. They shared many of the same traits—blond hair, though Vance's was graying, a strong chin, and small ears.

"Remember, the Valero do not know I took over for my father," I whispered, making sure it seemed as though I was nothing more than an excited bride. Behind Liam, I saw Neal and Declan step closer to us. Monte and Fedel were near the entrance focused on me. With a glance, Fedel let me know Antonio and three other snipers were in the windows of the manor, waiting.

"Oh, and you should know, Vance tried to arrange a marriage with Amory and me, years ago." His eyes widened before narrowing into dangerous slits of green.

"Mr. and Mrs. Callahan!" Vance said as he reached us. "Congratulations. I must say this was a huge surprise. Melody what a fine young woman you have become, hasn't she Amory?"

"I'm sorry, do I know you?" I asked innocently, squeezing Liam's hand. He needed to step up and be calm. Amory looked at me with pure lust, however, making me want to cut his eyes out, and doing nothing to help Liam calm down.

He sneered, shaking Vance's hand, which had been extended for me. "This is Vance Valero, love. The owner of the company that keeps stealing many of our *products*."

Vance glared dangerously, as did Amory before he smiled at me. "I do not wish to bore your beautiful little head with such youthful fiction. Your father and I were quite close. I was hoping to speak with him, however, he seems to be absent from this joyful occasion."

I tried not gag. "Liam and I wanted to get married. My father spoke of some new huge business venture in Austria that he needed to get a jumpstart on. I will let him know you spoke of him."

Amory's eyes widened before he grinned and reached out for my hand, but Liam took it instead. "I'm sorry gentlemen, but my wife and I must be making the rounds. Please enjoy yourselves."

"Yes, please do," I added, smiling as though I was naïve to the tension between them. "Evelyn has worked so hard on this day. We are lucky to afford such a lifestyle. One day you could be sitting on the top of the world, then the next it could be sitting on you, my father says."

"Your father has always been wise." Amory winked at me before glaring at Liam. "But we are all human and make mistakes."

Fuck you, you no good motherfucking asshole.

When we walked away, Liam pulled us onto the dance floor under the purple and red fabric draping.

"What the fuck is going on in Austria? I know that is the last place your father is."

"Calm the fuck down. Nothing is in Austria, but Amory doesn't know that. He is a leech, and I have no doubt he will be on the next plane tonight trying to steal from us." Plus, if we divided him and Vance, it would be easier to break them.

His hands wandered down my spine. "You want them to think you don't know anything."

"It's easier to kill a deer if they think you are a rabbit rather than a wolf. Amory was so busy staring at my breasts, he couldn't even speak."

"I noticed. I should just kill the motherfucker now and save myself the annoyance. He is lucky I didn't rip his eyes out, and believe me I would have."

The darkness in his voice made me shiver in pleasure. I allowed him to spin me before bringing me in close. "You need to clear your mind and take a deep breath. We were able to flip Ryan Ross. He reports directly to Monte now, then to me. It's how I knew Vance knew about the plane. He wants to do something bigger. He wants us to relax before he attacks. But mostly, he wants to hurt you."

"And how the fuck is Vance going to hurt me?"

"Me," I answered. "He will want to use Amory as a way to gain intel. Amory will probably flirt with me and try to gain my trust. It wouldn't be the first time he went after a married woman."

"You aren't making my desire to kill the fool lessen." He stopped to look me in the eyes. "In fact, I want to kill him more."

"Then I get to kill Vance." He wasn't going to get to kill them both.

"I kill Vance. You get the brothers and Amory."

"Deal. But the only way for that to happen is to give Amory a little wiggle room and some rope to hang himself with."

"So more parties and balls. My mother will like it. However, I will cut off the motherfuckers' fingers if they touch you. But until then, Valero has a shipment of prized cars coming in two weeks to Italy. Vance loves his cars."

The bastard was getting excited just thinking about it.

"You hit his drugs, and now you want to take his toys? Husband, that is quite cruel."

He raised an eyebrow at me. "Do you have any other ideas?"

"No." I grinned. "But after we steal them, we should set them on fire."

"And I'm cruel?" He kissed my cheek, and I froze for a moment, realizing that we had once again just worked together with ease. It was like our minds fed off each other.

"We will talk about this later. Apparently, it's time to cut the cake," I told him, noticing Evelyn waving. I had almost forgotten that this was our wedding with thoughts of theft and blood in the air.

"Yes. Later," he replied, looking at me with lust once again.

LIAM

It felt like hours after we cut the cake that we were able to sneak off. Orlando was in one of the rooms in the eastern part of the manor. The moment we arrived, Mel went to sit beside him. He was breathing only through tubes and machines, which all looked painful.

"*Ciao, mi bambino dolce.*"[13]

Mel kissed his hands. "*Ciao, mio dolce padre.*"[14]

"*Sei bellissima*, Melody. *Mi dispiace che non ero abbastanza forte per voi.*"[15]

"*Tu sei, e sarai sempre abbastanza forte.*"[16]

I felt bad for intruding on their moment. I wasn't sure what they were saying but it seemed to be too personal for me to just be standing there. However, I couldn't bring myself to leave Mel's side.

Orlando looked up to me breathing heavily, waiting for me to take his hand. When I did, he squeezed it.

"*Sii buona con lei,*[17] Liam," he said to me before turning to Mel. "*Sii buono con lui,*[18] Mel."

"*Lo farò,*"[19] she said, and I repeated it, even though I didn't know what it was she said. It just felt right. When I did, he kissed both our hands before giving them back to each other.

Mel closed her eyes, taking a deep breath and standing up. I watched as she pulled a needle from the nightstand, and realized what she was about to do. Reaching out, I grabbed her hand, and for the first time I saw the true depths of her strength and how much she hated it. She would put her father to sleep to give him peace, and it would kill her slowly every day of forever. Yet, she would still do it.

"I have to do this," she whispered to me, as I tried to pull the needle from her.

Shaking my head, I snatched it from her hand. "You will hate yourself, and I would rather you hate me."

In her eyes there was a fight, because she was Mel, and my Mel would always fight me. But I would win this battle. Stepping in front of her, I pulled the cap off with my teeth before going for his arm. Mel wrapped her hands around my waist and placed her head on my back, not watching.

Good. I didn't want her to see this.

I did it as quickly as possible and turned off the machines, before turning and holding her.

MELODY

I just listened in Liam's arms, not crying or depressed but somewhat relieved that someone else had fulfilled my father's wish. Something I had dreaded since he first asked. We stood there holding each other for God knows how long before Liam spoke.

"Wife, Mel, my Melody. Let's go to bed," he whispered, and I nodded. He lifted me up bridal style, and a part of me wanted to fight him but not now. Not tonight. Not our wedding night. Not my father's last night. I knew I would fight him on a million things soon, but not tonight.

TWELVE

"Cruel with guilt, and daring with despair, the midnight murderer bursts the faithless bar; Invades the sacred hour of silent rest and leaves, unseen, a dagger in your breast."

—Samuel Johnson

LIAM

"Is that all, sir?" Dylan questioned softly, placing the tray of food and the files I requested on the top of my desk. He knew just as well as anyone that if he woke my wife, I would snap his neck.

"Tell Patrick I want to know of Amory's whereabouts in the next few hours."

The moment the door closed I turned to Mel, only to find her sitting up and staring back at me. Her face was void and her eyes clear as day. It was almost haunting.

"I'm sorry, I didn't mean to wake you," I said, leaving distance between us as I tried to read her mood.

She frowned, noticing that she was still in her dress, before standing up and turning around. "Help me out of it."

Without saying a word, I unhooked the tiny part at the top and unzipped it slowly, trying my best not to get excited, but it didn't work.

Her fucking father just died, calm down.

Seeing her in nothing but white lace almost killed me.

Fuck it all to hell.

"Let me get you—" She stopped me with her lips, and I gave in, gladly pulling her body to mine and gripping her ass. I loved her ass. I loved how it felt like it was made for my hands only.

When her tiny hands pulled away my tie and ripped at my shirt, I had to push her away.

"Mel, we can wait. I can wait." I gasped, breathing deeply to control my raging cock.

"Well, this isn't about you. This is about me, and I can't wait. I don't want to think. I just want you inside me now."

Fuck.

This time when she kissed me, I picked her up and laid her back down on the bed kissing a path from her lips to her neck. She moaned, pushing up against me with her hands in my hair while I worked my way down to her breast.

"I will buy you new ones," I told her as ripped the bra from her, allowing her breasts to bounce in freedom, and pulled her underwear off. She glared at me but only for a moment before closing her eyes as I pinched her nipples.

"Harder," she asked. So I did, pulling on them before taking them into my mouth. She was already rocking against me, and I knew she wanted me inside her, but I wouldn't give in just yet.

My hands traveled down to cup her, and she arched up in pleasure.

"Just fuck me already, Liam." She moaned, grinding herself into my hands.

"No," I replied, placing three fingers in her. I watched, enjoying how she looked as she met her pleasure with my hands. I moved my fingers faster and deeper into her wet core. Each time she let out small moans of pleasure, and one of her hands went to my chest while the other pinched her breast. Watching her, this hungry for my cock, made my desire for her grow even more. I made sure to take mental pictures of this.

"Liam, your cock."

"No." I snickered, fucking her with my fingers even more, until she was so close that I pulled out of her.

She stared at me furious and wide-eyed. She looked enraged, and all I could do was lick my fingers of her juices.

She watched me for a moment before tackling me. I stared up at her in amusement, holding on to her thighs as she ripped my pants to get at my dick. She didn't have to wait because the moment she pulled my pants from me it sprung up before us. This was why I chose to go without boxers. She glared at me, grabbing onto me, and I bucked up at her unable to control myself in her hands.

"You want this just as bad as I do," she said, and I was almost tempted to tell her no fucking duh.

However, when she eased her way onto me, I couldn't even think straight. My hips began to move, pushing my cock entirely in her.

She was moving too slowly, watching me struggle to fight back the urge to ram my way in her until she couldn't walk.

"How quickly the tables can turn," she whispered. I gasped when she leaned down to kiss my chest.

Grabbing on to her waist and hair, I held her on top of me before sitting up. I was done playing around. I just wanted to fuck her so deep that she wouldn't be able to see straight.

"And how quickly they change back." Gripping her waist, I forced her to move along with me, fucking her as we sat in the middle of my bed.

She looked me in the eyes as I looked into hers. Our lips were only inches apart, breathing each other in as she rode me. Reaching up, I brushed the side of her face and pulled her hair, along with her head, back so I could kiss her neck. Then I pushed her down onto the bed and rammed myself harder.

She moaned, and I smiled. "Fucking Jesus, Liam."

Leaning down, I kissed the side of her face before whispering, "Not even he can save you from this now."

Holding onto her wrist with one hand and gripping her thigh with the other, I fucked her pussy hard, ramming farther and farther inside her as she trembled in pleasure.

"Fuck, Mel," I yelled as I felt her walls tighten around me. But even then I didn't stop. I wanted to fuck her pretty little brain out, so I let go of her hands and grabbed on to her hips. I fucked her like she was a bitch in heat. I went quickly. I went deeply. I went in and out so many times I couldn't even see straight, and she was screaming my name while clawing at my back. She had come twice already, and I would keep making her come until she was filled with only me.

Slowing my thrusts down only slightly, my head went back as I released in her just as she came for the third time. Drained, I forced myself to hover over her, not wanting to crush her. However, she surprised me and pulled me on top of her. So I just laid there on her breast, leaving small kisses on her neck.

"Thank you."

"You never have to thank me for sex." In fact, she could have it anytime she fucking wanted.

"Not only for the sex, Liam." Stopping my kisses, I sat up to stare in her eyes, but she refused to look at me.

"My dear wife, you do not have to thank me for that either." I kissed her cheek before finally pulling out of her. I was going to bring up condoms later, and hopefully, she didn't want them either.

We didn't speak for a moment as I lay next to her. Instead, the smell of sex and our breathing was the only thing to fill the room.

"What do you want from me, Liam?"

I wasn't sure how to say it without . . . without sounding like a pansy. But I knew if I lied she would know, and the last thing our relationship could handle was a lie, whether it was big or small.

"I want you to love me," I said softly. "But if not, then I want it to be the closest thing to you loving me. I want your loyalty. I want your honesty. I want you by my side and no one else's. I want your body. I want your mind. I want to know your hopes and dreams so I could one day make them reality."

I paused, knowing the sicker, inner-darkness part of me was about to speak. But that was who I was, and I wanted her to know it. I hadn't even realized I wanted it until now.

"I want you to be willing to kill for me. I want you to be the same killer I am and not flinch away from the blood. I want you to revel in the blood alongside me. I want you to help me take down every fucker who stands in the way of a Callahan."

She was silent, and so was I as we lay there.

"The second part of that I can do with ease," she finally replied. "The first, the love. I haven't loved anything in a long time. I cared for Orlando deeply, but we were never close. I spent most of my life training. He was working. I wouldn't know where to start with love."

It wasn't a no. It was just a how, and I would have to show her. I took her hand, kissing it before sitting up.

"We will start with getting to know each other," I replied, loving how she looked in my bed . . . our bed.

"Know each other?"

"Like what the fuck is your favorite color, and other not important, but important things like that."

"It's teal. I do not know why, but it's teal."

Smiling, I got up, naked as the day I was born, and grabbed the plate of food, the wine, and the files, and placed them before us on the bed.

She picked up the wine and smirked. "You know my favorite wine."

"I do," I replied, uncorking it and not telling her how I knew. She didn't need a cup and drank straight from the bottle before handing it to me. I drank as well, laughing in my mind at how far I had come. Had it been any other female, I would have seen them as less of a woman. But with Mel, it only made her sexier to me. Everything she did made her sexier.

"What's your favorite color?" she asked, taking a bite of sandwich.

"I don't have one."

She shook her head at me.

"Favorite movie?" I asked her.

"*Shawshank Redemption*," she said.

"Seriously?"

"Yes, seriously. What's yours then?" she asked.

"*Goodfellas*," I said, winking and causing her to roll her pretty brown eyes at me.

"Of course."

"I'm also a huge superhero nerd."

She looked me over before nodding. "I can see that."

"Shut up," I said as she laughed. It wasn't forced, or harsh, but soft like bells chiming in the wind.

She brought her legs in, and I noticed she was still wearing her white heels, which meant a few things. One, I fucked her in her heels and that was fucking hot. Two, she looked fucking sexy sitting on my bed naked with only heels on, and third, she almost always wore white shoes. I would make a note of that for whenever I bought her something, but still.

"Why do you wear white heels all the time? Is it an Italian fashion statement or something?"

She froze for a moment, before her shoulders dropped and her eyes glazed over.

"Orlando and my mother, Aviela, fought often when I was a child. I was young, but even I knew something was wrong. On the outside they put on a show of this happy, well-off couple, but really, my mom was living in a different wing of the house. She even spent most of her time in Italy. Sometimes, after her fights with my father, I wouldn't see her for weeks. When they were young and fell for each other hard, my father didn't want to lose her, so he only told her about what he did for a living after they were married." She frowned, drinking from the bottle again.

"Shit." There was no way a relationship in our lives could work if we didn't make it clear who we were from the get go.

"Yep." She shook her head. "From what I gathered, my mom was a hippie. She hated violence, and like all hippies, she protested. My grandparents wouldn't let her get a divorce, and so she wore white gloves. Basically, she was telling Orlando every time he saw her that her hands were clean. She told him if he could go a week without killing, she would take them off and he could touch her. But it never happened. My father turned to whores, pretending they were her, and she fell in love with her bodyguard. However, she was pregnant with me, and my father told me that she miscarried once while they were dating, so she didn't want to risk anything the second time around. They tried to stick it out for my sake, but Orlando finally gave up trying to win her over and they agreed to let me spend holidays with him. It was like that until the plane crash."

"And so you wear the white shoes . . ."

"Because my hands aren't clean, but . . ." She half smiled. "When I see them, I think of her and I don't feel like I never had a mother. I just see a woman with white gloves."

"That's . . ."

"Really weird I know. That's something no one knew about me but Orlando, but you asked."

I cupped the side of her face. "It is odd, but it makes sense to me. I didn't realize it was so deep. I wouldn't have asked."

"No, you would have most likely looked into it behind my back." She shook her head. "I'd rather get all the skeletons out now while we are both civil and sexually satisfied."

I smirked at that. "I'm not sexually satisfied yet."

She rolled her eyes at me. "Relax, tiger. Tell me about you."

Grabbing the wine, I took a deep breath before knocking back a drink. She went deep into her past and shared something no one alive knew, with the exception being me. She trusted me. I would have to trust her. I just didn't know how to start.

"You don't have to."

"I want to, Mel," I said softly. "I want to, and I will. I haven't traveled this deep in me for a long time."

"Is it about your childhood?" she asked, and I shouldn't have been surprised, but I was. "I don't know anything other than that you were sick once and tormented for it."

I started slowly. "I was born a twin. Evelyn was on her way to a fundraiser with my brother when one of Vance's people drove them off the road and into a tree. The driver was able to get Neal out, but Evelyn went into labor and couldn't move. When the paramedics came and got her she, was already pushing my sister out. But she never cried, or even took a breath, and when they got to the hospital I was stuck. They had to pull, and because of that my shoulder was broken. My heart and lungs weren't fully developed yet, and I barely even cried. It was more like I was gasping for air. They didn't think I was going to make it, but I did. However my growth, weight, and speech were stunted, and on top of it I was blessed with clubfeet."

For some odd reason, even though I didn't remember it, I always felt a pain in my shoulder when I thought about it.

"Evelyn went into a deep depression, and as much as she *loved* me, she couldn't look at me without seeing her dead baby girl in her hands, so she stayed away. In all honesty, my earliest memory of her isn't until I was maybe twelve. It was my father who spent most of his time with me at the hospital. Over the years, he read articles from the paper and would tell me how important my future was while the doctors did tests and I went through treatment. I remember him losing his shit at doctors once . . . or twice. All that reading and teaching he did stuck with me, though. By the time I could finally leave the hospital and go to school, I was well beyond any twelve-year-old. One moment I was at Saint John's Hospital, the next I was Northside College Preparatory High School with Neal, who had a reputation as a badass." I laughed at the memory. Students almost shit themselves when Neal was pissed at them.

"He was captain of the football team, a wrestler, and played hockey and every other sport that let him destroy guys for fun. So naturally, I looked up to him, but in school he stayed away from me. I, shaky legs and all, tried out for the football team only to have balls thrown at my back. The coach took pity on me and made me the water boy. One day, some of Neal's friends pushed me down a flight of stairs before putting me in a locker with their dirty clothes. Neal didn't know I was there. He just walked in when his friends were pissing on my clothes and told them to chill out, that I was my father's *favorite* and he would have to deal with my *mental* shit later. I didn't say anything because I couldn't. I hadn't taken my medication that morning and ended up having a seizure in the fucking locker." I almost wanted to laugh because it was so fucked up.

"I was shaking so badly that the locker shook with me in it, and the coach found me. I ended up in the hospital with my mom crying and praying over me. I had been in a coma for a week, and she promised God she would be a better mother if he just made me healthy. They ran tests, gave me drugs. Declan, who had spent most of his time to himself after his parents died, came to me and told me they burned down the house of the fucker who put me in the locker. Neal and I don't take trips down memory lane. I think I got better in spite of him."

I had almost forgotten she was sitting across from me when she handed me the bottle of wine again.

It wasn't better than brandy, but it was good enough.

"Okay, you win most depressing childhood. You should have cut his dick off and shoved it down his throat." I coughed as I took a drink, before smiling at her.

"I was twelve."

She shrugged. "I don't give a fuck. Neal's dick and the fucker's dick, or anyone else who was there, would have to live with it, the assholes."

She didn't know it, but for someone who didn't know how to love, she was sure doing a good job.

"Noted." She was the best thing in my life, and it only took three fucking days. She made me excited for the future.

"Now I don't feel bad for shooting Neal," she replied, falling back on the bed, and I allowed my eyes to wander up her legs, then her thighs and her stomach before reaching her breasts.

"Did you ever feel bad?" I asked her, pushing the tray of wine and food off the bed and onto the floor. It shattered, and I knew it would make a huge mess, but I didn't give a fuck. I just wanted my wife.

She watched me as I rose above her.

"What were the files for?"

I had forgotten all about them. Grabbing her back, I pulled her up against me. "First pleasure, then work."

"I think it's the other way around," she replied, wrapping her legs around my waist.

"We make our own rules from now on, Mrs. Callahan." I kissed her forehead, cupping her ass and thrusting into her tight pussy. Her lips went straight to my neck.

"Rule number one. After, or during, our meetings and chats we make sure to fuck each other's brains out." I slammed into her. "Agreed?"

She gripped on to my shoulders and moaned. "Agreed," she said, before pushing me back and holding me there.

"Rule two. We never use a fucking condom. Agreed?" She hissed at me, and I almost came. She was fucking perfect.

"Fuck yes."

I flipped her over and pulled out of her, grabbed the lube on the bedside table, and squeezed a generous amount before burying myself in her tight ass.

"Rule three." I moaned out loudly, unable to think when she raised onto her knees, pushing her ass against me with her hands wrapped around my neck.

"Rule three. We trust no one but each other," she said to me, and I could no longer control my need. Grabbing onto her ass as I did her waist earlier in the evening, I slammed myself into her. Pushing her back down, I pulled on her hair as though it were reins.

"Agreed."

"Fuck, Liam." She moaned as she came, and when she did I pulled out of her, allowing my seed to slip onto her back.

It was sick how much I enjoyed it. She was mine. She was all fucking mine.

Rising, she turned to me and slapped me in the face, something I was starting to fucking enjoy even as it burned. It was one of the many things that made Mel different.

"Now I have to take a shower," she hissed at me, getting up, and I looked to her proud and in lust. She had found the monster inside me and fed it. Sadly, I didn't think it would ever have enough of her.

She headed over to my bathroom and stopped to look back me. "Are you tired already Mr. Callahan? I still have more rules."

She's fucking perfect.

I almost groaned. We were going to break each other, and it only made me more excited. Jumping up, my cock standing alert and searing for her, I let her lead me into the waiting shower.

She's fucking perfect. Even as she pushed me down onto my knees and forced my face into her pussy, I would happily drink her in.

MELODY

I said nothing, choosing one of his clean shirts to wear as he spoke with a dark-haired man at the door.

Taking a seat on his bed, I watched him carefully as two maids ran in quickly to clean up the mess we had made with the wine and food. Neither of them dared to look up. Instead, they worked as quickly as possible.

I wasn't sure what was going on between Liam and me, but the untrusting part of my mind was telling me to put on the damn breaks. We had only known each other for three, now four days, seeing as how it was still very early in the day. Neither of us was tired, which was odd because we had done nothing but have mind-blowing sex for hours. The only time we had spoken was when we had confessed some of our darkest secrets. He put me on edge because he made me trust him. He told me the truth, and then stepped up in the one thing I knew I did not have the strength to do.

Orlando had wanted to make sure he died after my wedding because he didn't want me to feel alone. I tried to tell him I wasn't lonely, but he always told me the path of a Boss was a dark and lonely one. I never had friends. I never socialized with anyone other than my men and the servants at our home. I always kept myself busy learning languages, studying, and training. I never thought too much about it. Not until now. Not until Orlando, the only family I had, had died. It hit me like a tsunami. I did not have anyone. And then there was Liam.

For the first time I understood why Orlando had pushed me so hard into accepting him, because even though I didn't trust Liam yet, the promise of future trust was there. He was now the only family I had. A fact that confused me.

I felt like I could trust him. I wanted to trust him. I wanted to be what he needed, because now I needed somebody. I never realized how much Orlando filled that role for me. Over the last four years since I had become Boss, he was the one person I vented to. The one person I used as a whiteboard for all my plans, telling him each and every step just because I needed to get it out of my head. I told him when I was stressed, when I just wanted to murder someone, and when I did murder someone. Orlando was my true right-hand, and now

Liam was taking his place. Not in a creepy *Liam is my daddy* type way, but more like Liam was now the only person I could freely speak with.

Everyone else was under me, everyone else I didn't respect. Orlando had been it. Now Liam was.

"You were right," Liam replied, his voice serious as he took a seat in front of me. The maids were gone. I hated that he was in pajama bottoms. I missed staring at his ass.

"I know." I smirked. "But about what?"

Rolling his eyes at me, he handed me the file before heading to his desk. He grabbed his brandy and poured us both a cup. Looking over the flight transcript, I grinned.

"Amory is on his way to Austria," I read aloud, taking the glass he offered.

"Yes, and I was thinking about using it as a cover." He frowned, drinking slowly. I waited for him to go on, but he didn't.

"Well?" I asked, annoyed that I had to waste words.

He eyed me carefully as though I were a child before he spoke, and it pissed me off. "Orlando didn't want the world knowing he was sick. I was thinking of causing a fake accident and let rumor spread it was Amory."

He stopped, and in my mind I thought it was perfect. But he misread my facial expression.

"I don't mean to use your father's death as a chess piece, nor do I want to—"

"Liam, shut the hell up. I'm not a child whose feelings will get hurt. Yes, I care for Orlando, but he is dead. I knew it was coming for years. It sucks, but don't treat me as if I'm glass. My father would have loved to be used to screw the Valero. So let's do what we do best—a game of chess."

I was not going to be seen as emotional because my daddy was dead. Nor would I let Liam forget who I was, even though our relationship was changing. I was still a fucking Boss, and I still had work to do.

He raised an eyebrow to at me before leaning back and smirking. "Glass you are not, wife. Very well. We will allow Amory to think he killed Orlando. The bastard will be so full of himself he'll take bigger risks, thinking he took out the great Iron Hands. When he goes to Morocco in the next couple of weeks, we will go to Italy and burn down some cars."

"Vance will be forced to react and bark orders at Amory, who will tell Ryan, and when we know, we will keep bleeding him dry," I replied.

"Death by a thousand cuts."

"And then cut off his head," I said, raising my glass before knocking it back.

He handed me another file, this one full of pictures of all his men.

The first was of a hazel-eyed, dark-haired man in his early thirties. "Patrick Darragh, is like my malware. He can make sure nothing that we don't want in the press gets in the press, and he can also get anything on air in seconds."

"The next is Dylan Cormac," he said as I looked at the green-eyed man. "He is my weapons expert. If you want it, he can get it, no matter what it is."

I filed through all the photos quickly. "You fucking Irish breed like rabbits."

"Speaking of, how many kids do you want?"

I glared at him, not sure if I should shoot him or not. "You will find out when I'm okay with the idea of being barefoot and pregnant."

"Why do I have a feeling that that isn't a measurable amount of time?"

"How about we get to know each other, and in a few years, we can discuss this topic again," I said, and he grinned, the fucker. I knew he just couldn't wait until I was round and fat, unable to drink, and stuck in bed while he fucked over the world. Hell to the fucking no to that.

"Was that Rule Four?"

"I guess so."

THIRTEEN

"Murder is not the crime of criminals, but that of law-abiding citizens."

—Emmanuel Teney

LIAM

"The plan was flawless," I said, pinching the bridge of my nose. "Every last detail was planned out for you, you no good brainless cocksuckers. We all but drew you a fucking map! So *where the fuck did I lose you!*"

I threw a gun at Neal, Antonio, Eric, and Jinx's faces. Those idiotic muscle-head fuckers messed up, and I was tempted to kill them all.

"Sir, we had Amory on the Port Lincoln, but he had already been in Austria for days and knew something was up. We set the trip wires and even gave him time to leave, but the *Italian* here didn't give us a heads up he was circling back," Eric said, looking at Antonio who was ready to throw a punch at his fucking face.

"You know what, you Irish son of a bitch—"

"Enough!" I stepped forward, my voice still echoing off the rafters. "Will one of you explain to me how we lost some of our own fucking men? Did you push the idiot button?"

"Amory found the trip wires and reconfigured them onto the safe house," Neal answered, looking me dead in the eye, and I wanted to bash his fucking skull in. We lost five of our men—three Irish, two Italian—all blown to bits because of their fucking dumb shit.

"Is this your first time on a mission? You embarrassed the family." I moved toward Neal. "You embarrassed *me*, and now you stand before me with your cocks in your hands unsure of what to do with yourselves."

Sighing, I turned back around to find my wife sitting in my leather chair behind the oak desk, simply staring at the fucked-up men behind me. She was stunning dressed in a beautiful blue, lace dress with her white shoes. But I knew she was just as pissed as I was. In the last nine days, we had fought and fucked hard, and I was starting to read her as well as she could read me. Unfortunately, our men were like cavemen and had no idea how to fucking work together, and now I had five dead on my hands.

We stood in my basement with all our men around us, but no one was speaking. Not a single one of them. Mel pulled out a gun and placed it on the table with a single bullet before looking me in the eyes. She wanted blood, and so did I.

"Who was the biggest fuck up?" she asked softly. I noticed she never really yelled at the men when she was pissed off. In fact, her voice became softer, as though she wanted to haunt those around her.

No one spoke up, so I walked up beside her, leaning against the table. "She asked a question. We want an answer, or we will kill you all and start over. How much do we pay them, love?"

She glared at me, and I knew she hated when I called her that in public, but I didn't care.

"Five million a year? I could go to the ghetto and get men to replace them in five minutes with the offer of 500k," she said offhandedly as she spun the gun on the table.

Nodding, I looked back at the men. "So again, we ask, who fucked up the most?"

Eric stepped forward. "It was Ian."

And the moment he said it, Mel lifted the gun and shot him right in the kneecap, the poor fuck. I didn't even know the gun was loaded, seeing as how there was one bullet still on the table.

Mel hissed at him. "Since when do you give up your brother, you fucker?" And she had a point. Even when we commanded them, they weren't supposed to give that information up unless someone was betraying us.

Eric yelled like a dying pig as Ian stepped forward. Pushing off the desk, I extended my hand for Mel as she rose from the chair.

"This bullet is for you, Ian," I told him as he eyed the gun and bullet. Eric's bitching was all that could be heard as we waited.

"Five dead because of you. Take your own life," I said as Mel and I walked to the elevators.

"If he doesn't," Mel added as we stepped into the waiting elevator, "the rest of you put the idiot out of his misery. That's an order."

She must have timed it perfectly because the doors closed right on cue.

"I like Eric," I told her as we rode up to the main floor. My mother was throwing one of her many end-of-the-summer charity bullshits, and we all had to attend, of course.

"Next time he will hopefully keep his mouth shut." She smirked, obviously enjoying shooting him way too much.

"Touché, but we can use this fuck up to lay the cover-up. For all anyone knows, one of the five really could have been Orlando. We can release a statement tomorrow," I said stopping the elevator and pushing her against the wall. I wanted her. I needed her, and if I didn't have her right then, I would have to wait hours.

"Calm the fuck down, Liam." She glared at me. "Whenever you see blood you get excited."

"Whenever I see *you* spill blood I get excited. There is a difference," I said, correcting her as I leaned against her.

"We have an interview we're late for," she said, as I grabbed the back of her neck, allowing my hands to wander up and bury themselves in her hair.

"Then we can have a quickie," I lied, nothing ever came quick for either of us, and she knew it.

She pushed me off her as she began brushing off her dress and released the elevator to get it to start moving again. "You're quickly becoming a sex addict."

"Only for you." I winked, fixing my tie as the doors opened. And there waiting for us was my mother, tapping her pumps against the floor.

"You both are late. I have *Time Magazine* waiting to take a photo of the happy couple without the happy couple," she said, her voice clipped.

"Evelyn, *Time Magazine* will wait for as long as we want them to wait seeing as they're the only ones we're talking to," Mel replied.

I watched in amusement as they spoke with their eyes. However, it faded when my mother slapped me in the arm without warning.

"The elevator Liam, honestly?" She huffed at me, while I stared at her in confusion. Mel and my mother seemed to speak a language with their eyes that no one else seemed to understand.

"I don't know what's wrong with him, Evelyn." Mel smirked, before winking back at me.

"Let's fix your hair before the whole world knows about it." She sighed, taking Mel from my side. I hated to say it, but it ticked me off. Over the last few days, Mel and I had spent most of our time together. Sometimes we talked, most of the time we fucked, and the rest of the time we just laid next to each other. It was like we were both allowing our bodies, minds, and souls to just get used to one another, and I loved every moment of it, which was why I hated when she was taken away from me.

"I know that look." My father smirked, as he stepped next to me.

"What look?" I hissed, as I leaned against the wall waiting for my wife to come back. My *wife*. It made me smirk.

"That look." The old fool grinned. "I know it, because it comes across my face from time to time. It's lust, it's desire, it's hope and love all wrapped into one. It took you a little over a week. It only took me forty-eight hours."

I hate him sometimes. "It's too soon for love, father."

He snorted. My father, Sedric Callahan, snorted. "If Shakespeare had said that the world would have never known Romeo and Juliet. Do you still hate her?"

"I never said that," I interrupted quickly. "I've been waiting for someone like her for a long time and didn't even know it. However, I can't let her know that I . . . I can lust after her, I can be loyal, and I can care, but I can't love her yet. She doesn't get love. So I will wait for her to feel something."

"And if she doesn't?"

I straightened up off the wall once I saw them heading toward us. "I'll still be right here."

"Who are you and what have you done with my son?" His old eyes gleamed at me.

"Do not even start, Father."

"What are you both whispering about?" My mother eyed us carefully when she finally reached us.

My father smirked, kissing her cheek. "World domination." She rolled her eyes at him while Mel just raised an eyebrow at me.

"You had your chance and failed. Time to step aside and let the new blood step up," my mother said. My father pretended to be hurt, before pulling her into his arms. That was what I wanted to do with Mel, but she would most likely shoot me for showing public displays of affection . . . or any type of display.

As if to prove my thoughts, Mel stared at them in confusion before meeting my gaze as if to tell me, *your family is so odd.*

"Don't you have an interview, oh new king and queen?" my father asked us with a smirk. He had officially given up his title on the night of our wedding, and since then I . . . Mel and I ruled, and he was more relaxed, happy even. He had been waiting a long time to step down, and here I thought this whole time that he just didn't want to give up his title, but he did. He just wanted to make sure he would never have to step back in again.

After offering my arm to Mel, we both headed toward the living room, and I laughed when I saw her working on relaxing her face.

"Shut up. God knows how long we will have to smile for these people," Mel retorted as I stopped at the door.

"Just be like Evelyn."

"Be like your mother? You're a sick fuck, Liam Callahan." She winked, making me want to both strangle and kiss her.

"Be unlike yourself," I replied through my teeth, before opening the door.

When I did, she stepped forward. "We're so sorry we are late. Tearing Liam away from his work can be difficult. He's shy about these things," she said kindly, as the crew smiled at her.

It never failed to amaze me how quickly she could switch on and off. She had the ability to disarm people so easily.

"Oh, don't be, Mrs. Callahan. We are just so glad you could make time for us. I'm Jan, and this is my crew. We were just making sure the lighting and whatnot was okay." The woman grinned, obviously already figuring out that she was getting the interview of a lifetime. Walking up beside my wife, I wrapped my arm around her waist.

"Do you need anything? I'm sure we could have someone come to help out," I said softly overusing my Irish accent. She froze, staring into my eyes. Without fail it happened to every fucking woman I met except Mel. The one person I wished it did happen with.

"Liam, stop before you give the poor woman a heart attack." Mel smiled up at me, but all I saw were knives in her eyes before she turned back to Jan. "Please don't mind him. He doesn't know the full extent of his Irish charm."

I rolled my eyes and kissed her cheek affectionately. I felt her stiffen just slightly, but she didn't break out of character. "All I needed it for was to catch you."

I still needed it to catch her.

"This is going to be a great interview. I can feel it. Are you both ready?" Jan asked. Nodding we walked over to the chairs that were staged for us. I waited for Mel to sit down first before taking mine right next to her. The moment I did, she leaned in like a fucking pro and placed her hand on my knee. For someone who had never done an interview before she was doing well. Crossing all the *t*'s and dotting her *i*'s. But that was my wife, a master manipulator.

"First of all, it's my pleasure to be sitting across from America's Royal Couple," Jan said to us, leaning forward.

Mel looked at me, and I knew that if Jan wasn't careful, my wife would kill her.

"*America's Royal Couple?*" she smiled before letting out a small fake laugh.

"Yes, Mrs. Callahan, all of America loves you, and I have to say I personally loved your wedding dress. After your wedding, orders came flying in all over the country," Jan said, gushing.

"Oh, my God, really?" Mel blushed, looking innocent and doe-eyed while she held on to my knee with a grip from hell. "That is so odd to me. Suddenly, everyone cares about my clothing and hair. I feel like a celebrity or something."

"Believe me when I say there are no bigger celebrities than you two. My friends are even trying to figure out the secret behind the Liam Callahan sex hair," she continued, and it took all I had not to groan instead of smile for the fucking camera.

"Honestly, I do nothing," I said, laughing.

"Because he is Liam Callahan and is naturally sexy," Mel continued, before sticking her tongue out. So I leaned in and kissed her lips.

"See why I can never win a fight?" Mel frowned back at Jan, before grinning again. "He just kisses me, or worse takes off his shirt, and I'm completely dumbfounded."

If only that was fucking true.

"Yes, because *I'm Liam Callahan and naturally sexy*," I said, throwing her words back at her before turning to Jan. "Do you think we can get that on a bumper sticker?"

Mel hit me, laughing softly, and I disliked it simply because it wasn't her. This bubbly, preppy faker was not my wife. It was odd, because I had wanted her to be like this before we met. However, my Mel, both in private and with our men, was stronger, ruthless, and sexy. This Mel was cute, but it wasn't her, and I wanted her to be who she truly was when she was with me.

"So the very first question the world wants to know is . . . where did you two meet?" Jan asked.

MELODY

I groaned as we walked into the study. "Thank motherfucking God."

Liam handed me a glass of brandy, reminding me, once again, that I needed to have someone set up my wine in here. "I'm surprised you didn't kill her when she asked if you were pregnant," he said, watching me carefully as I drank.

"Me, too. Apparently, marriage has made me soft," I replied, turning back to the paperwork on the desk before us.

He wrapped his arms around me slowly, and I felt my body automatically begin to relax into him. I wasn't sure when it started, or if it was due to all the sex, but it did that now. My body now knew his touch and was accepting of it, in fact, it enjoyed it. I enjoyed it.

What the fuck was happening to me?

"Liam, we need to make sure everyone believes Amory killed my father and prepare for Italy," I murmured, but he just kissed along my shoulder and neck. "I'm serious. Cork your cock, and let's finish this before Evelyn drags us out for the dinner."

He groaned, pulling away, and my body instantly missed his warmth. Drinking some more, he sat down, looking at the file after I pushed it toward him.

"Six of Vance's most prized cars will be en route from Suvereto to Lucignano. It's about one hundred and four miles, but they will take the back roads because it's safer and the roads are clear of police. I don't care if they are Vance's men or not, they are still men," I replied, showing him the map.

He looked at me with an eyebrow raised and with a twinge of lust as always. He was such a fucking sex addict.

"What is that supposed to mean?"

"It means if they have dicks, they are male. If they are male, and you put them behind the wheel of a multimillion dollar sports car, they will break the speed limit. They will race each other, because males have to prove they are better in everything." I rolled my eyes.

He glared up at me as he gripped my arm. "You know I hate it when you refer to any other man's dick but mine."

"Get over it, it's not like I'm sucking it," I said, glaring at his hand. He had one second to let go before I cut it off.

"Fuck, Mel. Why must you always try to piss me off?" His eyes narrowed before he finally let me go.

"The *American Royal Couple*, remember? That means I embody freedom of fucking speech."

Before he could reply, there was a knock on the door.

"Great. It's your mother." I sighed and prepared myself to be civil.

Rolling his eyes, Liam turned toward the door. "Enter."

However, the person who entered was not Evelyn, but Declan, whose eyes were dark and his jaw set.

"The new Chicago Police Superintendent is here and wishes to speak with you," he said, glowering. I looked back to Liam who was now sitting up straight in his chair scowling at the door with the promise of death and blood in his eyes. This Liam I found to be the sexiest of all.

"Bring him through," he said softly.

Declan stepped aside, allowing a middle-aged man, though younger than I would think a

Superintendent would be, to step forward. Beside him, another man around his age entered. They both looked unafraid, which meant they were either naïve or stupid.

"Thank you, Declan," Liam called out. Declan eyed the officers, his jaw grinding, before walking out and shutting the door behind him.

"Superintendent Andrew Patterson is it? What brings you to my neck of the woods?" Liam asked as I took a seat on the desk crossing my legs.

"Yes it is, Mr. Callahan," he said before glancing at me. "We came to talk to you privately."

Privately? This mother-fuckering bitch.

"I think I'll stay," I said as kindly as possible, before Liam could speak.

Liam snickered, leaning back in his chair. "Well, you heard the lady."

"As you know, Mr. Callahan, in fact, I'll call you Liam, I'm the new Superintendent because the former decided to retire early. I was chosen by the good people of Chicago to make this city safe. Something it hasn't been in a long fucking time. I know who you are. I know what you do, and I'm here to warn you that your days of walking all over the law are over. I won't stop until you and the rest of your kind are where you belong. Behind bars reaching for soap."

Liam laughed, looking at me. "Sweetheart, we really have to start voting. Look what happens when we don't. Some idiot gets a badge and a gun and tries to pick a fight."

"It's not too late," I said, smiling as I moved beside him. "He won't *stop*. So all we have to do is kill him and then make sure to fill out the next ballot."

The darker skinned officer beside the fool stepped forward. "Is that a threat, Mrs. Callahan?"

I smiled. "With my hand on the fucking bible, you very stupid man."

Superintendent Patterson looked at me, shocked. "Maybe you didn't hear me—"

"No, we heard you clearly," Liam snapped, his eyes narrowing dangerously. "But it's time for you to hear me. You think you can run this city? *My* fucking city? I fucking own it. I fucking bought it! I fucking fought over it! No crackhead bitch over on the corner of Jump Street, and damn well no 5-0 with his Smokey the Bear looking sidekick, will ever tell me differently. I own Chicago! Which means I fucking own *you*!"

Patterson stepped forward. "You may think you walk on water, but you are just a man, Liam Callahan, nothing more, and I'm not afraid of you. I will use every measure of the law and every man I have to put you down like the fucking dog you are!"

I had to hand it to him, the man had balls. He was a fucking idiot, but he had balls.

"You think you will," I replied, as Liam breathed through his nostrils and stood up. "You think you have every cop, but you don't. You never will. What happens if someone were to pop off their families? They aren't all like you Superintendent Patterson. You lost your wife, your child, and your fucking house." He looked at me surprised, as if I wouldn't do a background check on the new head of the police department. "You lost it all, and now you think you have nothing to lose. Well, believe me, you do. You are not the first man who thought he could control this city through law and order. You are *replaceable.*"

Liam moved from around the desk to meet his gaze. "You think you can change the world? You think you can change my fucking city? Here is a reality check for you. One cop down a day, one family member a day how do you think your *men* will like that? This town will bleed. I will make it rain blood and tears. It will taint your hands so badly you will never be able to wash it off. Those men will hate you. I wouldn't be surprised if they put a bullet in your skull themselves."

Liam took another step right in front of the fucker's face.

"I will unleash hell on these streets like you have never seen, and when a mother comes to you with a picture of her dead son, when your people are so afraid that they sleep in bullet-proof vests and they turn to you, tell them it's because you thought you could step up to me. Tell them it was because you were an idiot and stepped into the wrong *house* one Saturday," Liam said, and I couldn't deny how sexy I found him at that very second.

Walking over to the door, I held it open. "You've been uninvited, which means get the fuck out of my house before I use my second amendment rights and blow you the fuck away."

They left quickly after that, and when they did, I let the door slam behind them before I walked over to Liam and kissed him deeply. He lifted me up and carried me to the desk laying me out on it. He spread my legs with his knee as his hands traveled up my stomach and then to my breasts while he kissed the side of my face.

But before he could rip my shirt off, I grabbed a gold-plated letter opener and held it to his neck. He froze, staring at me in shock and confusion.

"Remember how close you came today to having me in this office," I said, pressing the opener just a little bit harder into his neck. "Then remember you do not own Chicago. *We* own Chicago, which you forgot in the heat of your roaring. We! Next time you forget, I will cut you from the tip of your pretty chin to your heart. Now *off*."

He glared into my eyes, grabbing my wrists and squeezing until the letter opener fell from my grasp. His hands went to my neck, and I saw the very monster I lusted over staring at me back in the eyes. Even then, I still found it sexy.

"I've told you once—but I will tell you again seeing as how you are my wife, *whom I trust and care for* in too many twisted ways to describe—do not ever hold a weapon to me."

He kissed my lips hard again before letting go of me and stepping back. I began fixing my dress, as he went straight for the brandy.

"We are going to have to kill the Vance mission," I replied, walking up to him to fix his tie.

He looked angry, frustrated, and bloodthirsty. "And why the fuck is that? That bitch and his sidekick have nothing to do with Italy."

"Liam," I hissed pulling on his tie. "We are about to go to war. We will not be stuck in the middle of Vance and the Chicago PD. Especially when our men are acting like children and fucking up every time we look away. They hate each other."

"Hate is a strong word."

"Since I've gotten here, has there been one night where either of our men haven't insulted or tried to kill each other?"

His pink lips parted for a quick second before closing again.

"Exactly."

"We Irish have been fighting you Italians for generations. Of course they are not going to stop just because you're sprawled out in my bed."

The grin on his face, like an obese cat after a meal, made my blood run hot. When was he going to get it?

"You are a fucking . . . it is this thing you Irish do that pisses us off. You don't think before you speak. *Sei in ottone, idioti maleducati, egoisti e cazzo, razza di mangiare, dormire, uccidere e gobba come cani!*"

"I'm sorry you lost me after speak."

Talking a deep breath I took a few steps away from him, trying my best not to just . . . ah. "How can someone with your IQ not have taken the initiative to learn Italian?"

"Have you seen the *Sleeping Dictionary?*"

"The what?"

"In the movie this Englishman goes to a foreign country in the nineteen thirties to help colonialize the area. But he doesn't know the language so they give him this beautiful village girl whom he sleeps with and shares words until he knows the language."

I . . . I couldn't even. He had to be a masochist or just enjoyed fucking with me. I didn't have the energy for this.

"Let me guess, the movie was written and directed by men. *Voi tutti mi fai schifo.*"[20]

The corners of his jaw turned up as his shoulders relaxed leaning on the front of his desk.

"So, dear wife, what shall we do about *our* men?"

"Tonight we go to dinner and tomorrow we prepare for camp," I said with a smile of my own.

He stared at me as though I had lost my fucking mind. "Camp?"

"When I took over as Boss my men didn't trust me. They didn't think I could lead them and when I brought in new people, they didn't trust them either. I bought a stretch of forest near Cascadia, Oregon and made it into sort of a camp. It's their moment to let their guard down, because the place is like a fucking fort. The hackers all spend time playing with the newest toys I provide them. All I ask is that they don't get on any FBI lists. The very fact that I have to tell them that is beyond me. The woods are filled with targets to challenge snipers. The gym is for the hand-to-hand knife nuts, and there are seven chefs there around the fucking clock to feed them. They kill things together, they eat together, and they sleep in the same houses. By the end of the week, they are brothers." It was genius on my part, and I could see it in his eyes as well.

"One week? That's it, and then we will be the Brady Bunch?"

"Well, they won't be trying to kill each other as often. That's a start."

He shrugged. "Well, wife, to camp we go then."

I grinned almost wanting to take more pride in his words. "No women allowed other than Adriana and me."

"What the fuck is with this Adriana?"

"She is part of the crew, Liam, and if you saw past the physical looks, you would know that. She is a trained marksman, expert profiler, and a damn good personal dresser," I added, pushing away from him to grab my phone off the desk.

"I still want to take out Vance's cars." He frowned. *Men and their cars.*

"We can, and we will." I smirked, already loving the plan forming in my head. "Except this time we will have to steal it from Vance's estate before he gets there."

He looked at me, grinning like a mad fool, and stepped forward brushing the side of my cheek.

"Fucking perfect," he said to me before kissing me once again, and I knew this time there was no stopping him.

FOURTEEN

"If the desire to kill and the opportunity to kill came always together, who would escape hanging?"

—Mark Twain

LIAM

"You destroyed my underwear," she hissed at me as she put her white shoes back on.

Straightening my tie, I tried not to smile, but I couldn't help it. "Next time, don't wear any at all and we won't have this problem."

My beautiful wife stalked up to me, slowly glaring at me with daggers in her eyes, and yet, it only made me want her more. I wanted to reach out and touch her.

What the fuck is wrong with me? No matter how many times I had her, it only made me want her even more.

"I don't have a problem with that," she said, glaring. "I'm not the one who has to sit through dinner thinking about how I have nothing under this dress, about how you could easily slip your hand underneath it and reach in me. But I think I will sit opposite you tonight."

She backed away so quickly it felt like I'd been awakened with cold water from the loss of her warmth. That, and the fact that all the blood in my body was rushing to another part of my anatomy. Damn her.

"You're going to sit next to me," I demanded as she walked toward the door and, my eyes went straight to her ass.

"No, I'm not. I would rather shoot you, but since I can't, I will sexually frustrate you instead. Do not rip my clothing," she snapped, leaving me aching for her.

"Bitch is going to kill me," I muttered, trying my best to calm myself down.

Staring at the file on the desk, I wanted nothing more than to destroy Vance now. I wanted to stare into his eyes as I lit his world on fire. However, I would wait. First I . . . we needed to fix the idiots under us.

The moment I stepped out of the study, Declan was already waiting.

"How long have you been out here?"

He smirked. "Long enough. I apologize because I would have waited, had I realized. She told me to calm down, it was just fucking sex. That woman scares and bewilders me all at the same time."

Just fucking sex.

I frowned. "Try being married to her. One minute she kisses you and the next she has a letter opener to your throat."

Declan's eyes widened at me before he broke out laughing. "One day she may just kill you Liam, I swear it."

"One day, she just may." I sighed. Truthfully, I wasn't even sure if she liked me for any other reason than the fact that we were married. I was 'just sex' to her, and it shouldn't have bothered me as much as it did, but I couldn't shake the feeling that she wasn't going to change . . . that she would never care.

"So, I'm guessing you both handled the Superintendent? Or is there something I can do?" he asked, right as we stopped outside the door. I could see it in his eyes. His own bloodlust.

Declan wasn't as much of a killer as Neal or myself. He had always been, and would always be, the man behind the computer, where I needed him to be. But when it came to the police, Declan wanted blood. It was, after all, an officer who had taken both his parents. He hated them and the code they lived by.

"If things get messy, you can personally clean it up, Declan," I answered. "But until then, just keep a watch on our Superintendent. If he buys a home near anything Callahan, let me know."

He nodded, and the dark look in his eyes disappeared the moment he stepped into the dining room. He stopped for a moment, noticing my wife sitting in his position next to Coraline. He raised an eyebrow at me before smirking as if he already knew the reason why. Saying nothing, I walked over to my Mel, kissing her on the cheek softly. She flinched as if I had slapped her instead.

"Evening, wife," I said, trying to be polite while being just loud enough for everyone to hear. I knew full well it would tick her off as I took my seat across from her and to the right of my father. But I didn't care.

She was pushing me and I was close to snapping.

Sedric was and would always sit at the head of the table. I didn't care. It was a prop chair. It held no real power other than carving a turkey. I sat at the true head of the table. My mother sat on the opposite side and as always, they were speaking another language with their eyes. I tried to focus my attention on Mel. However, she seemed lost in her own mind. A mind I would give anything to read.

"Mel, is there a reason why you are not sitting next to Liam?" my mother asked kindly as I reached for my glass of brandy.

Mel frowned. "I swear he's trying to get me pregnant. He can't keep his hands to himself. It's kind of annoying, actually."

I felt the liquid rush back up my throat as I coughed. I glared at her. Of course she would bring up sex at the dinner table, of fucking course. She was *my* Mel and didn't give a damn about decorum. She lived to make me fear for my life, horny, or uncomfortable.

"What's wrong with getting pregnant?" Olivia asked, glaring as she drank her wine while the servants brought our food.

"Nothing," Mel said, glaring back. "Nothing at all, especially when you do nothing else other than make yourself look pretty and shop."

Declan kicked my foot, but I said nothing, simply cutting into my steak. This was not my battle, and I was definitely not taking a bullet for Olivia.

"You think you're better than us?" Olivia snapped, causing Melody to laugh and me to stuff my mouth with meat.

"Barbie, I know I'm better than you," Melody said, sipping her red wine. It was basically a food group for her. "All my parts are original and not made in China."

It took all my might not to laugh, but I did grin like a fool, and in the corner of my eye, I could see my father smiling as well behind his glass.

"You bitch," Olivia spat, rising from her seat.

Glaring over at her, I met Neal's eyes. "Control her, Neal, or else she will need new parts. No one calls my wife a bitch . . . with the exception of me."

"No one calls me a bitch, period. You aren't special, Liam," Mel said, and it felt like she had stabbed me.

"Maybe you should tell her we don't attack family," Neal said as Olivia sat back down.

"Yeah, we simply fail to defend them," I replied, knowing full well it would shut him up. However, he simply turned to me.

"How long are we going to do this Liam? It's been almost two decades!"

"When I said I would never forgive you"—I took another bite—"I meant not in ten, twenty, or even eighty years. We share DNA, nothing more."

"Liam!" Evelyn shouted. "I'm not sure what happened between you two, but Neal is right. It's time to make peace."

"Neal, would you like to tell our mother what happened between us?" I asked him, waiting. The coward had never told either of our parents what he had done to me as a child. Part of me believed Sedric knew, even though he had never let on.

Neal nodded slowly to himself before standing up and walking to the door.

"Neal," Melody said, calling after him. His back straightened before he turned to her.

"Pack your bag. I have something planned for the week. We leave tomorrow after mass," she said, not bothering to look at him.

He left quickly, causing Olivia to stand up as well.

"Are you happy?" Olivia asked.

I turned to Mel. "Well, love, are you happy?"

"No." She frowned at my use of *love.* "I would be happier if you passed the peas," she said, pretending not to even notice Olivia.

Coraline, who had kept her head down and mouth shut this whole time, surprisingly reached over and handed them to her. I looked over to Declan to find him glaring at her, and I knew that look. Coraline had most likely gone through another credit card saving the hungry children of *fill in the blank* . . . it had only been two weeks. People were going to start questioning where all this money was coming from. At least we looked good. He was pissed. Maybe I would let him kill the police officer just to release some stress.

"You all sicken me," Olivia hissed.

"You're still here?" Mel asked, acting confused as she added peas to her plate. Olivia stormed out, and I was fucking grateful. I was already in a small battle with my wife, the police, and Vance. The last thing I needed was Olivia and Neal drama.

"What are you two planning?" my father asked, simply.

"Camp," Mel and I said at the same time.

"Camp?" Coraline's head popped up. If I remembered correctly, Coraline actually liked the outdoors.

"No women," I said without thinking, causing her to look at Mel. Mel eyes narrowed.

"Only those who are part of the job, Cora."

Coraline looked surprised at the nickname, as did everyone else. "Cora?" she asked.

"I'm still working on a nickname for you." Mel smiled. It wasn't real, but it was better than the glare she gave Olivia. I could see the mischief she was spinning in her eyes, and I wasn't sure whether to be afraid or groan in awe of her.

"So this camp?" Evelyn asked, unsure. If it was criminal, she didn't want to know, but she was interested.

"Basically, it's bonding for the men, or I plan on killing them all." Mel smiled, which only made her threat more deadly and sexy. The fact that I knew she would made me want her, made me want to give her the gun and pull the trigger alongside her. However, she just rolled her eyes at my lust.

"Camp," Sedric repeated. "Maybe I should—"

"Sorry, Sedric, but that invitation isn't for you either. You are the past, and as much as I respect it, and you, my men need to walk forward as one." My jaw almost came off as I stared between Mel and my father, who glared at her with fire in his eyes. However, they were no match for hers and only made her seem even stronger. Sedric shook his head and sighed.

She said *my* not *ours.*

Declan leaned into me. "When she wakes up in the morning, the devil curses."

"We both do," I muttered. *How the fuck did she do it? How the fuck was she able to call forth hell and heaven in her eyes?* I was in awe of her so often it pissed me off. I could hear Orlando's words in the back of my mind. *You won't find a woman who needs to be taught anything.* He was right. She could rule without me. She wanted to rule without me. She didn't need me, and it ticked me off. She ticked me off, and once again, because of her, I always needed to think. She confused the fuck out of my goddamn emotions and me. I felt like a teenager again—unsure if I wanted to fuck her or punch a wall.

"Well then, daughter, I wouldn't want to get in your way. After all, you will rule the world one day," Sedric joked, though I'm sure he partially believed it.

She smirked. "One day soon, hopefully. I have placed all the pieces in order. Nothing will stand in my way. I've worked too hard for that."

"Don't overwork." Evelyn frowned. "I still think you and Liam should have taken a honeymoon."

"That would have been pointless. Liam and I got married for the company. A honeymoon would have wasted time." She frowned at the idea of it. She frowned at the idea of *me*.

Running my hands through my hair, I sighed before rising from my seat.

"I'm not feeling well. Goodnight," I told them all, walking away. I needed to remember I was just a piece to her.

MELODY

I watched him leave in shock. He looked like he was so lost in his thoughts that he made himself sick. I wasn't sure if I should stay or follow after him. What did wives do in these situations? Maybe he needed a moment. Evelyn met my eyes, and I could almost feel her pushing me to the door. Sighing, I stood and wished them all a good night before walking out as well. What the hell was I supposed to say to him?

Honey, are you okay? Fuck no.

Liam, what the fuck was that? Then we would fight.

Liam, are you okay? He would try to have sex.

"Melody?"

Turning around quickly, I came face to face with Cora.

"Yes?" I shouted, causing her to jump. She was so sweet, I almost felt sorry for her, but she needed a spine and quickly.

"Umm . . . I was wondering . . . umm . . ."

"Ahh, I hate when people waste words. What's wrong with you?" The Coraline I met was living high off glue and unicorns. This one seemed liked she had been roundhouse kicked off cloud nine.

She took a deep breath and stood straighter, which was still quite short.

"I'm losing Declan," she stated directly.

"That sucks," I replied. "Evelyn is the other way for couples counseling."

She glared at me before shaking her head. "I don't need Evelyn's help, I need yours. Ever since you came, Declan has been looking at me differently . . . like an annoyance."

"That could be the constant giving, you're rarely with him. So again, Evelyn . . ."

"Mel—and I am going to call you Mel because we are family and you can't kill me."

"Are you sure?" Declan was going to have to get a new wife if she didn't get to the point soon.

"Only in this family would charity work be deemed a flaw." She sighed. "But they notice me. They see me. Every time I write a check, help rebuild a house or a community center, you should see their faces. It's like I'm an angel to them, I'm important, needed. Do you know what that feels like? How it feels to be praised like that?"

She didn't give me a chance to speak before laughing to herself. "Of course you do, you're the great Melody Giovanni."

"Cora get to your point."

"I love Declan, and I don't want to lose him. But I see the way he looks at you," she muttered, and I really hoped this conversation wasn't going where I thought.

"There is nothing—"

"No, I know," she said quickly, her eyes wide. "I know Declan would never cheat on me even if . . . I want him to look at me the way those kids do when I hand over a check. I want him to light up like he once did. So I need to be more like you. I need you to help me be more like you."

"Not gonna happen," I replied. "There is only one Melody Giovanni, and there will be no second edition."

"Mel. I don't want to be you. I want to be *like* you. I want to be able to shoot a gun. I want to learn how to fight. I've always wanted to learn, but it was never our *place*. But then you came in shattering glass ceilings and literally breaking down walls. I want to see if you could train me. I don't need to become the best, but I want to be able to feel in control, and I want Declan to see me more than just a—"

"A good old housewife," I finished for her.

She frowned, her nose flaring. "Yeah. I want to get into the ring and show him there is so much more to me."

"Why not ask him yourself?" Declan was a great fighter, he and Liam boxed every morning.

"Because he has stopped seeing me. Everyone has stopped seeing me! I know what that means for our future. If I don't do this, Declan and I will only grow further apart and he will resent me. I would rather die than have that happen." She looked so scared that I almost wanted to help her.

"Cora, you have to train for yourself, not Declan, or any man for that matter," I replied, and she looked at me as though I was the one who was crazy.

"Declan *is* me, Mel. We have always been in sync, and then somewhere down the line, the music changed for one of us, and now I'm looking for the right station to get back to him. He would do the same for me. He *has* done the same for me. It's what married couples do. So, please, help me," she begged, and I wasn't sure what to say.

"I'm busy, Cora." The look of disappointment in her eyes bothered me. "However, Adriana can stay behind and work with you while we are gone for the week. Then after that, I will see. Be prepared for months of bruises and pain."

Coraline grinned, pulling me into a large hug.

"Thank you!"

"You're touching me."

"Sorry," she said, letting go quickly. "Thank you."

"Yeah, goodnight," I told her before leaving. Coraline was good at getting what she wanted from me, and the last thing I wanted was to agree to anything else.

When I entered Liam's and my room, I could hear him in the shower. Stepping toward the door, I watched him as he stood under the stream of water. The drops rolled off every part of his body. He was so beautiful. He looked like a statue chiseled out of finest stone.

"Is there something you needed, Melody?" he asked me, not bothering to look up.

Melody? He hadn't called me that since the first time we had sex, and for some reason, hearing him call me that now bothered me.

"What's wrong with you?"

"Nothing, Melody. I will be out in a moment," he replied, emotionless, but even I could hear the lie in that.

He was ticking me off. We do not lie to each other. Taking off my shoes, I walked straight into the shower, not even bothering to take off my dress. Flinching at the coolness of the water, I glared into his eyes, grabbing the side of his face.

"What the fuck is wrong with you?"

"Mel—"

"Call me Melody again and I will knee you in the balls." I was not going to let him lie to me.

He brushed back my wet hair before pulling it and my head back. Pushing me against the wall, I glared into his eyes, they no longer seemed green, instead they were filled with fire burning with passion and rage.

He snapped at me. "You do not own me. You do not own us. I am not your pawn."

"I never called you a pawn!"

"In my mind, I thought I was getting closer to you. But then tonight I realized all you do is play everyone around you, including me. I bend at your will. Since when did I start bending? You do not own me! I'm not another piece, I am your husband."

"Stop bitching at me. You're mad over my words? Why are you so fucking emotional?"

"Because I'm human, and therefore I have emotions!" His volume made my eyes widen. "Do you even like me, Melody? As just Liam?"

Where the fuck was this coming from?

He smirked sadly, shaking his head as he turned off the water. Stepping forward, he kissed my forehead. "The fact that you can't answer that question is enough."

"You make it seem like we were high school sweethearts who eloped. This is business, Liam. I told you I could rule beside you, but I can't handle your emotional shit."

He knew this! Why the fuck was he being such an idiot?

"I made a mistake. I thought you didn't understand love. But you do. You love the blood and the power, as do I. However, I was making room for you, and it has made me soft. You're surpassing me because you don't give a fuck. You wouldn't take a bullet for me or even shed a tear if I died. I'm the guy to staunch your need and then you're off. I'm just sex. This whole night was nothing but Melody. This whole marriage has been about Melody. I won't waste my time. You want business? You will get business," he answered, leaving me standing in the shower. I was shocked and confused.

Did I even like Liam?

He was amazing in bed and beautiful, funny . . . sometimes. I didn't hate him.

When I stepped into the room, it was pitch black, making the hair on the back of my neck rise as I made it onto the bed.

He turned off his light. He never turned off the light. Ever since he found out about my . . . fear. The nights we didn't have sex—which were rare— he read until I fell asleep and each night he said *goodnight, love.* He tried not to make it obvious, but I knew the reason. If he was going to be cold, I was going to be colder. He was such a dick. But part of me felt like he was right. I hadn't really put in much effort since our second night together when I'd told him about the white shoes. He had looked so happy then, as if knowing that little detail about me was going to make his day.

So what if I had called him a pawn or a piece tonight? We were both pawns. We both knew that when we got married. Why was he trying to complicate the relationship? We fucked. We worked. Simple. But now that motherfucking asshole had to make sure I *cared.*

Groaning in frustration, I sat up quickly. He was awake, staring up at me with no emotion. I wanted to scream at him! Because of his fucking shit, I couldn't sleep.

"Let me guess, you need to have the last insult?" he asked, sitting up to prepare himself.

I raised my arms ready to strangle him, but pulled back. I was going to kill him. I wasn't clear about the reason yet, but I was going to kill him. There was so much I wanted to yell at him, but nothing was coming out.

"What the fuck do you want from me, Liam?"

"Go to sleep, Melody. You're going to wake the house."

"I don't give a fuck," I snapped. "What happened? One moment we are fine and the next you're . . . what the fuck Liam?"

He yawned and it ticked me off to no end. "I'm going to war, Melody. Everyone is coming for me . . . coming for my family, but the most dangerous woman in the world is sleeping next to me. I care for her, but she doesn't give a shit about me or anything."

"That's why I'm the most dangerous woman in the world!"

He smirked. "It's also why you're alone. You can trust me in work, but with you personally, you won't let me get close."

"I don't know you!" I yelled. "How long have we been married? Ten fucking days, Liam? Who falls in love in ten fucking days? Who feels anything in ten fucking days! That isn't normal!"

"I do." He glared at the ceiling. "We aren't normal. Normal people don't shoot other people almost daily. Normal people don't sell drugs nor are they at risk of dying every day. I don't have any time to waste going through the motions. Either I like it or I don't. Either I'm in or I'm out. I do not walk in the middle."

"Not everyone is like you."

"You're like me," he whispered. "But you would rather lock everything out. Joy, pain, love. You work on anger and lust."

"I don't hate you, Liam. Goodnight." I frowned, turning onto my side.

LIAM

And just like that, I wanted to smirk. I knew I had her. Step one, smother her with love. Step two, take that love away. Step three, drag the raw emotions out of her kicking and screaming. The moment I left the dining hall, I knew it was time for step two. I planned step three for the morning, but she just had to talk it out now.

I knew who she was, and most of the time I loved it. But I didn't have time to take down her walls, brick by brick. I needed to find a weak point and then blow it up. I would keep going, keep being cold to her until she admitted the truth to herself. We weren't just sex anymore. Even now as she drifted to sleep, I could feel her leaning back for my warmth. She cared. She wanted to care more, but she was afraid.

Waiting until she was deeply asleep and muttering to herself, I reached over and hugged her against me. She smelled amazing. Kissing her lips softly, I watched as she rolled into my arms.

She wanted this. She wanted me. I was going to break her out of bitch mode . . . for me. I enjoyed her bitching at Olivia.

"My sweet Mel. You're going to admit you love me, even if you have to pull your hair out to say it," I whispered, kissing her forehead.

After all, everything between us was a game of chess, and the key to winning when the game changes is to switch tactics. I had, and now checkmate was only one more play away.

All I had to do was complete Step four and she would have to say it. Once she did, we could be what we needed to be. However, I was going to need help, and sadly, that meant Neal.

FIFTEEN

"If there is no struggle, there is no progress."
—Frederick Douglass

CORALINE

I watched him through the mirror as we both prepared for church. Like always, Declan was calm, collected, and deep in thought as he changed into the clothes I picked out for him. He seemed to be on autopilot. Truthfully, I think he had been on autopilot for a long time.

"I love you, Declan." I smiled at him, causing him to stop and look at me oddly.

He walked over and kissed my cheek. "Me, too."

On the outside I kept a smile plastered on my face even though I felt like screaming. He didn't say it back. He used to say, "I love you more." But that seemed like ages ago. Part of it was my fault—my habit. However, he was to blame as well. He stopped talking to me. He stopped making me part of his life. I just stood on the sidelines now, waiting for whenever he was drunk enough to want to have sex.

I brushed my hair and stared at myself, taking a deep breath before standing up.

"Are you ready?" he asked, trying to tie his tie. Even with my heels, I had to stand on my tiptoes to help him.

"Yeah." I smiled for him again. I always smiled for him.

Nodding, he took my hand and led me out. With each passing moment, it became clearer and clearer what I needed, and it was Mel's help.

DECLAN

I was going to hell. The moment I saw Melody step outside, I knew I was going to hell. I was breaking so many sins at once, and on a Sunday no less. One, I lusted after my cousin's wife. Two, I was jealous of the type of relationship they had. And three, my sweet wife was standing right beside me all the while, unaware.

I cared for Coraline deeply. Looking at her, I couldn't help feeling like a complete ass. She was so loyal and beautiful. However, she wasn't the same full-of-life Coraline I remembered. She was so strong when I first met her, she would laugh so hard she would cry. Now . . . now I didn't know what had fucking happened. Maybe she was scared of me. Maybe she had seen too many bloody shirts. Either way, she stopped being my Coraline a long time ago. Now I looked at Melody, wishing to God I could have one night, and it made me hate myself.

Liam was only now starting to understand how lucky he was. Melody was passionate. She enjoyed the job. She fucking wanted to be more involved in the job. Liam didn't understand. Every time Neal and I tried to confess to Coraline or Olivia our *sins*, they would look at us as if we were monsters. We *were* monsters. We knew that. But our wives shouldn't think of us that way. Melody was the opposite. During the wedding, she had congratulated Neal for passing her test.

She watched him put a bullet in a motherfucking Russian's head from a helicopter and came over to say good job, and meant it.

"Declan?"

Smiling, I took Coraline's hand, walking her to the car door before opening it for her. She looked at me oddly but I kissed her cheek. She smiled back like always as we took our seats. She held my hand as I looked out the window.

I wasn't going to cheat on Coraline. I would never cheat on Coraline . . . physically. In my mind, I already had. This morning in the shower as I stroked myself, I already had. All I thought about was Melody's wet—

"Declan!" Coraline giggled, looking down at my erection in my pants.

"Fucking shit." I tried to adjust myself.

She stopped me and began to unzip me, but I grabbed her wrist.

"You don't—"

"I want to," she said, pulling me out of my pants. I jerked in her hands.

"Coraline—"

"Shh, baby," she whispered before taking me in her mouth.

Instinctively, my head went back, and I heard the driver change the music to something louder. I trusted Sal. He wouldn't dare speak a word.

I shivered when her tongue licked me. In my mind—because I was a fucking bastard—all I could see was Melody. In my mind, it was Melody kissing my cock, and it made me want to fuck her mouth. The moment Coraline . . . Melody took me into her mouth I grabbed her head. She sucked faster and faster as I thrust my dick into her mouth. Her beautiful brown eyes looked up seeing me coated in lust. I fucked the shit out of her mouth, groaning madly until I came deeply at the back of throat.

When Melody released me, I grinned like an idiot, enjoying how she looked as she licked me clean.

"Better?" the voice of Coraline asked, making me see clearly again.

I was going to hell. Damn it.

"Thank you, sweetheart." I kissed her forehead as I put my dick back in my pants. What the fuck was wrong with me?

Melody was not my wife. Coraline was my wife, and Coraline was great. Fuck me, I was going to hell.

Taking Coraline's hand, I tried not to think. I tried really hard not to think of her. I was going to figure out something to make Coraline and me better because she deserved better than this. I, as her husband, owed her better than this. I would be better than this.

I took her hand and kissed it.

"Ready?" I asked her. She nodded, stepping out of the car.

I would be better . . . for her.

SIXTEEN

"It is only if the murderer is a good man that he can be regarded as monstrous."

—Graham Greene

MELODY

"I know you're awake," he said coldly, as he stepped in from the bathroom. Opening my eyes, I watched as he tied his tie.

"I wasn't hiding the fact that I was. Is there a meeting I do not know of?" I replied, sitting up. It was six thirty-two in the morning. Why the fuck was he getting dressed at the ass-crack of dawn?

He sighed, bored, before turning around. "Yes. However, you do not need to concern yourself with it seeing as it is a personal one. The moment the conversation shifts to shooting puppies in the street, I will call you."

Kill him. Cut his fucking balls off and shove them down his throat.

I could feel my eyebrow twitch at the tone of his voice. He was talking to me as if I was a fucking child.

"You—"

"As much as I enjoy our verbal assaults, Melody, I really do have to get going," he said, walking toward the door. "I will meet you in the car for church. If you feel like ranting then, by all means, scream your head off."

I didn't even think. One moment I was trying to breathe, next thing I knew, my hand was under the pillow and I was firing at him. However, nothing happened. Instead, Liam shook his head.

"Gun under the pillow? I hope you didn't think I was just going to leave it loaded," he asked, ice dripping from his voice.

"You touched my gun!"

"I've touched more than your gun. Get over it," he said, closing the door as he left.

The blood in my veins was boiling so badly, my skin was turning red.

Grabbing my phone, I tried not to yell when I heard the other voice on the line.

"Fedel, are you ready to redeem yourself?" I asked. I could almost hear him jumping out of bed.

"Yes, ma'am, anything," he replied right away.

"Liam has a breakfast this morning. I want every goddamn detail. He sneezes, I want to know about it."

"Of course, where is he?"

"I don't fucking know! Do your job!" I screamed before hurling the phone at the wall, shattering it and the mirror it hit. Running my hands through my hair, I tried my best to breathe, but I was pissed off. I wanted to kill him. I wanted to kill something! But I couldn't—not now at least—so I stood still, breathing slowly, shutting out the world around me. I didn't allow myself to think, just breathe. I wasn't sure how long I stood still. All I knew was that my boiling blood was becoming cold.

"Ma'am." Blinking, I came face to face with Adriana. "I'm sorry, ma'am, but you've been like this for an hour and you need to get ready for mass."

I stared at her before turning to the clock, and sure enough it was seven forty-seven. Nodding, I walked into the bathroom.

"Adriana, I need a new phone," I said before stripping down and heading into the shower. As much as I enjoyed the warmth of the water as it beat against my skin, I needed to get a move on.

My father always said, never keep God waiting. When I stepped out, Adriana was already waiting with a towel.

"Adriana, you will not be going to Camp with us," I told her as I dried out my hair.

"Did I do something to upset you?"

"No, I simply have another assignment for you," I replied, dropping the towel and reaching for my underwear. "While we are gone, you are to train Coraline Callahan in hand-to-hand combat. She wants to learn how to shoot as well, but she will fail at it. Teach her the basics on knives. She may be good at that."

Adriana handed me a blue dress with a white bow on the front to step into.

"How far am I to go, ma'am?" she asked. I knew she was worried about Declan.

Placing my earrings on, I thought for a moment. "Make sure any scars or bruises are not visible and that she treats them quickly. Give her safety knives first."

She placed my shoes before me and nodded. "Is that all, ma'am?"

"Yes, and don't go soft on her. Make sure she understands it only gets worse after Day One before it gets better," I replied, stepping into my shoes before sitting down so she could place a little bit of make up on my face.

Before she could reply, there was a knock at the door.

"Enter," I called out. Fedel walked in quickly with a camera in his hands.

"Good morning—"

"Did he see you?" I asked, stretching my hand out for the camera.

"No."

As I looked through the pictures, I felt my anger return. He sat across from a blonde bimbo, leaning in close to her stupid fucking face.

"Her name is Natasha Briar. She attended the wedding with Amory. She came after Declan and

Neal met him for breakfast. They spoke for a few moments, and when he headed toward the back, she followed. Twelve minutes later, he headed back into his car, where he then went to a boxing club in south end."

Do not overreact, my mind screamed as my throat closed up.

Standing, I placed the camera down and grabbed my sunglasses along with my purse before walking out of the room. I wasn't going to think or say anything until later. Right now, I just needed to breathe and stay calm. I would kill him, but not on a Sunday. I didn't kill anyone on Sundays, even if I really wanted to. Stepping outside the doors, I watched as everyone spoke among themselves. I wasn't sure how far away the location of Liam's breakfast was, but he was back and speaking quickly to Neal. He stopped when his eyes caught mine.

Evelyn smiled. "You look beautiful, dear."

"Thank you, Evelyn, as do you," I said as I walked toward Liam's Audi. His driver held the door open, and I sat inside.

When Liam stepped in, newly showered and dressed, he didn't bother looking at me. Instead, he focused on his phone. In my mind, all I saw were the photos, and it made me want to stuff the phone down his throat.

"Remember to pretend as if you care about anything. There is always a chance for a photo of us to be taken."

Fuck you.

Nodding, I looked out the window to see the same church we had gotten married in, only a block away. I did my best not to think about my wedding. It only reminded me of my father. When he took my hand, but I flinched away, and he smiled sadly, shaking his head before tightening his grip.

"Do what you do best and lie," he whispered as he helped me out of the car. Sure enough, there were a few photographers. You would think they would have more respect. We were going to church for God's sake.

Sighing, I took off my sunglasses the moment we stepped inside, looking around again at the beautiful and grand cathedral that mirrored many of the ones I loved in Europe.

"You really do look beautiful, Mel." Coraline smiled at me, but I could tell she was more excited about her future than she was about me.

"Thank you, Cora," I said, smiling back. Olivia gave me a glare before taking Neal's hand and walking deeper into the church.

I bit my tongue to keep from saying something rude in God's house. However, when my eyes met that of a blonde in a pink, too-short-for-church dress, I felt the floodgates open and a smile spread over my lips. She walked into the bathroom, and no one else seemed to notice her. Not even Liam as he spoke with Neal, again.

Looking up, I smiled. *Thank you, Jesus, for this gift.* "You all go in. I will meet you in a moment."

Liam eyed me carefully. "We should go in together. My mother wouldn't have it any other way."

"Then your mother will just have to deal with it. I'm heading to the ladies room. I'll be right back."

I sighed loudly. He had to fight me on everything. Coraline stepped forward, but I glared at her before she could dare volunteer to join me. I handed Liam my purse and turned away from him. He rolled his eyes before walking in after Neal and Olivia.

My pulse quickened when I stepped into the bathroom, pushing the wooden door open. There, of course, stood Natasha, adding more lipstick to her Botox-filled lips. The way she looked at me when in the door closed behind me told me all I needed to know. She had no idea what type of person I was.

I smiled at her, washing my hands. "Hi."

She smirked. "Well, if isn't the infamous Mrs. Callahan."

"Do I know you?" I asked innocently.

She whipped her golden hair over her shoulder twice, and I wanted nothing more than to rip it from her head.

"You should," she said, giving me a fake frown. "Look, I'm not trying to hurt you and you seem sweet . . . a little too sweet, actually. But you need to know. Liam and I were something before you got married. I know this is just some arranged marriage. He told me so. It won't last, sweetheart. Like I said, you're sweet, but Liam doesn't need sweet. He needs a real woman."

"And you're that *real woman?*"

She smiled. "He doesn't know it yet, but yes, I am. I know how to give him pleasure like no one else. He came every time my mouth was on him. He *begged* at night for me. He made me come over and over again. We went at it like animals. But then he would make sweet, slow, and passionate lov—"

Before she could finish, I grabbed her by her stupid blond hair and slammed her face against the mirror. She screamed, letting out a cry of pain as the glass shattered around her head. It almost looked like a spider web . . . a bloody spider web. Pushing her face harder against the broken glass made her cry out again.

"Please . . ."

"I think you have said enough," I whispered, moving slower to her. Blood poured from the side of her face as I met her eyes. She whimpered, struggling against me, but I held her still, pulling on her hair. Tears spilled from her eyes as she opened her mouth to scream.

"You scream, I will bash your skull in, you hear me?" I glared at her, and her eyes widened in fear.

"I'm—"

"Shut the fuck up, you five cent bitch," I said before she dared to lie and tell me how sorry she was. "My husband is off the market. You should be ashamed of yourself. We're in God's house . . . the very church we were married in, and you are thinking of trying to have an affair. You are a disgusting little whore. How many daddy issues could you possibly have?"

"I'm s-sorry. I j-j-just . . . I just love him," she sobbed. She was an idiot, for sure. I wanted to take her head and bash it in further, but I didn't kill on Sundays.

Peeling her face from the mirror and grabbing another fistful of hair, I pulled her into the bathroom stall. She fought against me, but it made me pull harder, throwing her against the stall before punching her in the nose. She gasped out, sliding down onto the floor and gripping her bloody nose as she sobbed. Kneeling in front of her, I made sure she could see me clearly.

"What were you doing with my husband this morning?"

"Fuck you, you scary bitch."

"Natasha." I sighed. "I'm going to ask again nicely. What were you doing with my husband this morning?"

"Sucking his sweet dick."

"Wrong answer."

Grabbing her head, I shoved it into the toilet. Her arms swung around like a mad woman, but I pinned them down quickly with my other hand. She screamed into the bowl before I let her out.

Giving her a moment to cough up water, I smiled.

"Now, Natasha, were you really sucking my husband off this morning or are you trying to piss me off?" I asked her, sweetly.

"Please . . ."

I dumped her head back into the water again, and this time, she struggled hard but sadly for her, I had pinned down men twice her size. When she stopped struggling, I let her go and she ripped her head from the toilet falling back onto her ass as she coughed and cried.

"Natasha . . ."

"I knew Liam liked to eat at Remy's on Sundays, so I waited for him. When I came up to him, he told me to leave or he would drag me out himself. I-I lied about having information about Vance and Amory. I told him I could only tell him if he followed me out back. I made up some story and somehow he knew. He tried to leave, but I tried to kiss him and he grabbed me by my neck. He called me a whore and yelled at me to stay away or next time he would kill me. He said the only reason he wasn't doing it now was because it was Sunday."

Liam's words from the night before came to mind. *You are like me.*

"Why did you come here then Natasha?" I asked, stepping up slightly. She slid across the small space on the floor to get away from me.

Tears streamed from her eyes as she shook, covered in toilet bowl water and blood.

"I love him," she sobbed. "Please don't kill me."

"Find a new man to love, Natasha. If you come around him again, I will snap your neck and bury you under this church," I warned, kicking her in ribs once before stepping over her and walking out of the stall.

I looked myself over in the cracked mirror—her blood still dripping from it—and fixed my hair before washing my hands once more.

"It was nice meeting you Natasha. Let's not do this again," I said and left.

Walking through the grand entrance, I dipped my finger into the blessed water before making the sign of the cross over myself. Moving quickly into the front aisle where the rest of the Callahans were standing and singing, I stood by Liam who stopped, glancing over at me. I smiled and took the book from him.

"I, the Lord of sea and sky, I have heard my people cry. All who dwell in dark and sin . . ." He wouldn't sing so I nudged him. He just shook his head picking up where I left off.

Well, I feel so much better.

LIAM

"Peace be with you," we all said.

"Go in peace, the Mass has ended," the priest replied before leaving. Soon after, everyone started to take their exit as well, however, I grabbed Mel before she could move.

She turned to me, eyebrow raised, as if she had no idea why I was holding on to her. Maybe she really didn't think I would notice.

"What?"

"You have blood on your shoe," I said, waiting for an explanation.

She looked down and frowned, pulling away from me and taking a seat. She looked completely at ease as she took a cleaning pen from her purse, bleaching it clean before grabbing hand sanitizer.

"Better?" she asked me with a smile. For the love of God, she had no shame, and it made her even sexier.

I needed to stay emotionless though.

"Yes, now, how did it get there?"

She frowned. "Liam, please don't make me lie in church."

"You've got to . . . then don't lie Melody." She was going to drive me mad.

"I had to settle something, and it's done," she replied, standing up and bowing toward the altar, then leaving.

"Of all the women in the world." I looked up at the crucifix before taking a deep breath and followed after her. I would find out soon. Right now, I just needed to make sure Step Four worked out.

We were leaving for camp tonight. After that, she and I would bond and get back to killing those who were less important.

Neal came up quickly, looking over at me and turning his back to the rest of the family.

"Liam, are you sure?" he asked me for the sixtieth time.

"Yes, Neal," I sighed. "For the last goddamn time. While we are at camp, you are going to shoot me and you're going to make sure it's a good, but not fatal shot. That's the only way I will let the past go."

"I could kill you," he hissed at me as we walked to our cars.

"If you do, I will haunt you for the rest of your life." I smirked. "You won't kill me, Neal. You want my forgiveness too much to kill me."

"This is cold Liam. If she finds out . . ."

I watched her as she spoke with Coraline and our priest. I couldn't help but think how beautiful she was. "She won't find out. If she does, she will be mad but will get over it. She loves me, and she's alone. I simply have to remind her that I'm all she has. Remember what happened last time my plans didn't work?"

He looked at me confused. "No."

"Exactly." I smirked, because my plans always worked.

"Okay, I will do it. You want it on the second day?"

I nodded, stepping forward then stopping and glaring into his eyes.

"You tell anyone of this, Neal, even your wife, I won't just hate you. I will kill you and her, I swear to God, I will," I whispered so softly I wasn't sure if he could actually hear me. The fear in his eyes told me all I needed to know.

Turning away, I walked over to my beautiful wife. The bow on her dress made me smile. She was a gift—my gift—and I couldn't wait to unwrap her. I couldn't wait for camp.

MELODY

"Liam, my young boy," Father Thomas called out behind me as Liam approached.

Liam took his hand. "It was a wonderful service, Father Thomas."

"You would say that even if it bored you to tears," Father Thomas said, winking at me. "I must say, you have chosen well, another woman of God in the Callahan family. It is why God blesses you all so greatly. You all honor him every Sunday without fail."

If only you knew what I did in your bathroom, I thought to myself.

"Thank you, Father."

He took my hand, and Liam held on to my waist.

"I see a child in the near future, my dear child. God will bless you with such, as well," he whispered for only Liam and me to hear. My nostrils flared and my eyes narrowed, but Liam gave me a light squeeze.

Smiling at him, I pulled away, hoping Liam would say something, but he was still sitting on his mountain of ice.

"Thank you so much, but we must be going, Thomas," I replied, pulling Liam toward the car.

"I need your phone," I said once we were inside.

He looked at my oddly. "Why?"

"Because mine is broken." I sighed. "Are you saying no? You don't want me to see you're past whores' names?"

He glared at me, handing me the phone. "No. There are no whores in my phone. I simply wanted to know who my wife needed to speak with so badly."

"My doctor." I frowned as I dialed. "Everyone seems to think that a baby is popping out of me soon. Why, I'm not sure. However, it's not happening and I'm going to make sure my birth control is working as well as possible. Anything else you would like to know?"

"Olivia has had a hard time conceiving, it was leaked to the press a year ago. Declan doesn't think he or Coraline are ready to be a parents, mostly because he and Coraline are always too busy. You're new and young—no one doubts you will be able to have children. That's why they bring it up," he said plainly, leaning back and watching the city outside pass us by. He wouldn't even look at me. I didn't care, not now at least. I had my blood fix this morning. It was the breakfast of champions. I could take on the world and Liam.

I couldn't wait for camp.

SEVENTEEN

"Murder, like talent, seems occasionally to run in families."

—George Henry

MELODY

"They're excited," Sedric replied as we all stood in front of the jets, which were fueled to take us straight to Cascadia. The men were all beside themselves as they grabbed their gear and walked onto the planes. Those who weren't flying with us had driven, leaving late last night with Monte so they could be there by the time we landed.

"How could any place named Candia be exciting?" Olivia frowned, her hands across her chest as if she were a child. It was kind of funny. I didn't know Barbie's could bend their arms.

"Cascadia," Coraline corrected while Adriana stood beside her. I was curious to see what would happen in the week I was gone.

"Whatever, my point is the same." Olivia rolled her eyes.

Evelyn smiled, clapping her hands. "Well, I'm excited for you boys. I always wanted to send you all to camp. Take pictures!"

"Honestly, mother, it's not that type of camp." Liam smirked, kissing her on the cheek before grabbing his bag.

"Actually it is," I replied, as Fedel handed me my new smartphone. "I'm simply going as a chaperone to make sure they don't lose complete control."

"A chaperone?" Declan smirked. "What do you think will happen?"

Turning to Fedel, I raised my eyebrows. He was trying really hard not to smile and even coughed.

"Well don't be shy," I told him.

"Last year, some of the knife nuts captured five or six skunks and placed them in the sniper cabins," he snickered quickly before returning solemn.

"And?"

He dropped his head down. "And then the snipers covered their cabins in honey and fire ants."

"Then the hackers were hacked and their computers were filled with gay porn. They also replaced their normal mice with dildo shaped ones. The hackers then gave them laxatives. Which lead to the things I do not even want to begin to explain. If I hadn't stepped in, one of them probably would have died," I said as I checked my messages. Looking up, I saw Evelyn's red face still processing everything she just heard.

"Holy Jesus fuck, what's on the menu this year?" Neal asked, wide-eyed. I could see the excitement building in his eyes.

Fedel grinned. "You Irish better watch your backs."

"*Non vedo l'ora di prendere questi cani verso il basso.*" Antonio laughed alongside Fedel.

Declan stepped forward. "If you're going to trash talk us, do it in English or Irish so everyone can hear or *beidh mé briseadh do liathróidí.*"

"Just in case you don't know, he said he will break your balls." Neal laughed.

Antonio held up his hands, not even least bit afraid. "You Irish and your balls. All I said is I can't wait."

"Enough," Liam snapped at them.

A whole week of this . . . how fun.

Sedric looked desperate, and I would be, too, if I had to spend time with the women. "Mel, are you—"

"No, Sedric," Evelyn and I said at the same time. She looked at me and grinned as if we had an alliance.

"This sounds so stupid," Olivia declared with her nose so high a bird could nest in it. "Neal—"

"Neal works for me . . . *us,*" I said as Liam glared at me. "This is part of the job. Don't like it, too bad. But if you're really worried, I will personally make sure he doesn't become someone's butt pirate."

Their jaws dropped, and Liam opened his mouth but closed it quickly, chuckling to himself. Smiling,

I glanced once more at Adriana before turning toward the plane. In an hour, we would be at camp and I wouldn't have to deal with being a Callahan for a week.

The moment I stepped onto the plane, they all stopped speaking and looked at me.

"Continue." I didn't have anything to say to them. Sitting down, I noticed Eric had a leg brace on. He met my gaze, and I simply grinned, forcing him to look away.

Fedel walked up to me—not sitting, seeing as how he had lost that right—with a file I hadn't seen before. I almost wanted to smile at him. Information was the key to my good graces.

"Yes, Fedel?" I asked as Nelson, the stuttering fool, handed me a glass of wine before going to serve the rest of the plane.

"I know you don't like apologies—"

"And yet here you are wasting words, Fedel."

He nodded. "I have kept watch on Vance and found something, but I haven't been able to confirm it yet."

I hated unconfirmed information because it often led to dead ends. However, he knew that, so whatever it was had to big enough for us to pay attention to whether it was true or not. Glancing around the plane, I only saw Neal.

"Wait until Liam takes a seat, and then join us," I replied. I watched as shock flashed through his eyes before he nodded.

He wouldn't have to wait long seeing as how a second later, Liam stepped onboard with Declan right behind him. Liam looked almost annoyed when he looked at me, and it was ticking me off. I wanted to shoot him in the fucking face, the emotional bitching bastard. I hadn't done anything. He wanted to be Mr. Cold and act like a dick then I would let him. The cabin went silent again for him.

"If anyone plays a prank on me, I will cut your hand off and make you eat it. Feel free to spread that around, because I'm not joking." He didn't even have to state it. The amount of poison and ice in his voice promised more than the loss of a hand.

They all nodded before continuing to speak among themselves. Liam walked back to where I was, stopping to stare—glare—at Fedel.

"Didn't you fire him?" he asked me.

"Leaders don't fire people. It sets a bad precedent." I smirked. "Instead, we kill them."

In that moment, I saw his lips twitch up into a smile before it was gone again. He nodded, placing his bag in the overhead compartment before sitting down.

"Why isn't he dead then?" he asked, pulling out the brandy from his coat pocket. He was such a drunk.

"He may have information on Vance," I replied, taking a drink of my wine. Liam glanced up, waiting for Fedel to speak, but before he could, Jinx started the jet.

"Well sit down, Fedel," Liam stated.

He was more than happy to, and I respected that he was working hard to make sure I didn't ever have to put him in his place again.

"You said he might have something?" Liam asked, and Fedel pulled out what looked to be letters in code and some in Russian.

"I haven't been able to decrypt them all," Fedel replied quickly. "However, from what I can tell, this is Vance's Step Two."

"You skipped a step?" I asked, picking up the papers.

"It wasn't clear until now. Step One was getting started with Alexei Rozhkov," Fedel replied, pulling out the photo of the old Russian mob boss with a scar across his neck. Some brave soul had snuck into his bedroom and slit his throat but the bastard still lived.

He was one of the most powerful men, alongside Orlando and Sedric. *Was* being the key word.

"Did your people kill him?" I looked to Liam.

Liam shook his head. "Father had been hacking away at him for years. Then when Declan stole the rest of his fortune, the man was basically crippled. He couldn't afford the high quality smack anymore. No junky would even blink at his shit. His men left him, he lost his houses, friends, everything, and my father wanted to kill him, but I thought it would best to make him live in the slums he created. All he had was some precious fourteen-million dollar red diamond, which I thought was just a rumor until we heard someone stole it."

Fedel looked at me, snickering as I just drank my sweet red wine. The whole cabin became silent as Liam and his men's eyes slowly fell on me. My people boasted with pride, but Liam stared at me in shock.

What the fuck were they shocked for? As if stealing a rock was the worst thing I had ever done.

"You stole it," Declan said, slowly rolling it around his tongue, and Neal looked jealous.

"I needed a new coaster?" I replied. It wasn't a big deal to me. Liam didn't speak, he simply leaned back into his chair and frowned out the window.

"How old were you?" Neal asked, leaning back as well, as if I was about to give him a fucking bedtime story.

"It was the weekend before my eighteenth birthday. I wanted to get myself something nice, pretty, and shiny. So I did a little digging, found his not-so-secret safe house in northern Russia, and thought why not? I haven't pissed off any Russians yet, and stole it." It wasn't the easiest thing in the world, but I did it.

"She was in and out in eight minutes," Fedel added. "Three minutes to break in, two minutes to kill two of his men, a minute and nineteen seconds to grab the jewel, and then forty-two seconds to get out."

"What happened to the last minute and forty-one seconds?" Declan asked, but his mind seemed to be racing.

"The last minute and forty-one seconds to send the house up in flames," Jinx added over the intercom, making me smile.

Jinx didn't often show his face—he preferred to keep hidden from everyone—but that didn't mean he wasn't always listening. Plus, he would know. He was the one who picked me up.

LIAM

Are you fucking kidding me! Seriously! At seventeen, I was a sophomore in college still trying to get rid of my acne and my awkward bullshit, while she was blowing up houses and stealing a rare jewel in the bloody motherland.

Pinching the bridge of my nose, I turned to Fedel. "What does this have to do with Vance?"

The idiot was so busy getting high off his past memories he almost forgot why we were talking about this.

Declan pulled out a photo of a red-haired woman. "Meet the woman formerly known as Saige Rozhkov."

"He had a daughter?" I replied but the closer I stared, the more I saw the resemblance.

"Formerly?" Mel asked him as she glared at the redheaded woman in the photo.

"By the end of tonight, she will be Saige Valero," he replied, and both Mel and I put our drinks down.

"What the fuck?" Mel and I said together.

"From what I've learned, the man who slit old Rozhkov's throat was Vance when he was on his rise to power. He wanted Saige to marry Amory. However, the old man wouldn't have it. That's when he went to Orlando, but he was rejected again. So Vance took a step back, and I guess allowed both your families to destroy Rozhkov. But since you let him live, Vance went back and killed him, but not before torturing every last secret out of him. Even though Alexei was destroyed, he still had the names. As both of you know, old names come with old favors. He pulled every last one of them after the fall of Rozhkov," Fedel explained quickly as he looked through more papers.

"Then why does he need this Saige?" I asked. He had the power already. The girl seemed to be useless.

"Because they're foreigners," Mel whispered, and I could see her connecting the dots in her mind. "Vance and his brothers came from Italy where my father all but banished them. The Russians hate outsiders. This Saige is a pawn. Something to make his men stand straighter behind him."

Made sense. "Does she know?"

He nodded and frowned. "She's the one who sold out her father's location to Vance. She apparently misses the power—these encrypted letters are hers. I thought they were ranting's of a mad woman at first—"

"Today *is the day*," I read the letter aloud, which had the worst grammar, even in Russian. "Today *is the day I take my rightful place on the throne. My father was fool and lost everything. He didn't know how to play the game. But I do. I have spent years planning my revenge and now with the power of the Amory. With the power of the Valero, I shall be queen. I will cover the earth with the blood of my enemies. Starting with Irish Cunt and Italian whore.*

"And this is why we do not keep journals. It's dated for today," I added as I handed it to her. I knew she couldn't read it, but she looked ready to rip it from my hands.

"So she's batshit crazy. Give me a location and I will kill her now whether it's true or not." Mel's eyes narrowed in on the paper. If she wasn't careful, she would set it on fire.

Fedel frowned. "I don't have one. These letters were taken from her personal tablet. However, they are bouncing from eight different countries. We see everything she types but have no idea where she is."

"What makes you think this is real? She cannot honestly be stupid enough to be writing her innermost thoughts and plans," I asked him. He said he hadn't verified it yet, and despite how true it may have seemed, it could have been a lie.

"As requested, a notice was put out about the death of Orlando. Because of that, Amory went back to Russia. However, it wasn't just him who came home—all the Valero did. Most of them spread out through Moscow. But all within walking distance to the Black Hotel where there is no one else staying but a Mrs. S.," Fedel explained, and all I wanted to do was bash his head in. The downside to ruling an empire was the lack of fucking vacation days. I was looking forward to this camp.

"Tell me about Mrs. S. personally," Mel demanded softly as she stared at the photo of her.

"Saige Rozhkov, age twenty-six, born in Stavropol, Russia to a prostitute of a mother. Her father basically wanted nothing to do with her, from what I could find. He had two other sons, and I guess she wasn't cool with being treated as a second-class citizen, so she killed both boys at sixteen. She got her father's attention, and he made her his heir. She has been a black widow of sorts. However, she doesn't need to marry them to suck the life out of them. She's trained herself in hand-to-hand combat, taught herself how to fly almost anything, and she can speak Italian, French, English, Spanish, Hebrew, and Russian. She's cold, and she's merciless," Fedel finished, and at the end of his little biography, he looked straight to Mel.

On the outside she looked cool, calm, and collected, but on the inside I could see the lioness trying to claw its way out of its cage.

"Fedel, leave us."

I stared in her eyes, scanning them quickly before standing. She finished off the rest of her drink before rising along with me. We both walked into the private room at the back of the plane without speaking.

The moment I closed the door, she took a deep breath and tried to stand still for a second but couldn't.

"I want her head on a plate."

I wasn't sure why, but I chuckled. "Is this jealously? Are you mad that this woman is on the same level as you are?"

A knife flew at my face giving me only a second to react. I moved out of the way before it embedded itself in the door.

"*No one* is on the same level as me."

"She killed her brothers."

"Half-brothers don't count. I would kill them too if they stood in my way," she replied.

"She betrayed her father."

She glared at me, her eyes searching my face. "Her father was an honorless, spineless bitch. I would have killed him first."

Brushing her hair back, I brought my lips closer to hers. "Then why are you so angry?"

"Because I read the rest of the letter."

I stared at her, confused. "You don't know Russian."

"I may not be able to speak it, but I can read most of it just fine. My IQ may not be the same as yours, but I handle myself." She took a deep breath. "I believe she said I a classless, emotionless, cunt-faced daughter of a whore. She knew that my parents were separated, and she also knew that my mother was having an affair with her bodyguard, Roger. That I should have burned with her in the plane. The only way she could have known that is if she was with Amory and Vance. So I want her head on a fucking plate!"

Every time I thought I knew her, I figured out something new. When I gave her that letter, I honestly didn't think she would be able to read it. I had read ahead and stopped when I noticed where the letter was going.

"Then her head on a plate you shall have. However, it will be next week. The men need this. We will keep Fedel and Declan on top of everything they do. But we can't go after them with our men acting like children remember."

She nodded, and I turned to leave when she grabbed my arm. Facing her, I watched as she opened and shut her mouth twice before dropping her hand and stepping back.

"I don't know how to do this, Liam," she replied, crossing her arms. "I don't know how to be open. I'm not that type of person."

"Bullshit." I laughed, causing her to look me in the eye. "You don't want to know. You can speak God knows how many languages. You are an expert fighter, shooter, and a master manipulator. If there is something you wanted or needed to be able to do, you would force yourself to learn. You would commit to it through blood and sweat. You would do that for everything but me. So don't try that card with me. I do not accept that excuse. I know you too fucking well for that shit."

"I am trying! You are closer to me than anyone else, Liam!"

"That would be enough, if everyone else wasn't dead." She froze at my words.

I stepped in her face again and kissed her forehead. "I. Am. All. You. Have. Just as you are all I have—fuck Declan, Neal, Olivia, Coraline, even my parents. My family and loyalty start with you and you alone. The sooner you fucking realize that, the sooner we can get back to losing ourselves within each other and actually killing all those who stand against us."

She said nothing, looking away from me, and I turned to leave. She didn't stop me, because she was my Mel and hardheaded as fuck. I could say it to her a thousand times, but she needed to realize it herself. Tomorrow she would, and it couldn't come fast enough. Then I would fuck her senseless for all the frustration she had caused me.

MELODY

Once he left, I laid back on the bed, trying not to think, but failing miserably.

I. Am. All. You. Have. His voice replayed in my mind even as I tried to push it out. I didn't understand why he couldn't just be happy with sex. I was willing to have sex. I *wanted* to have sex. However, instead of a quickie, I was laying on a bed alone. My mind felt so clouded. He was making it that way. I should have been thinking of ways to kill Amory and Saige, but instead, I was thinking of him, stupid fucking sexy Irish man.

I rose from the bed, fixing myself before walking out. I didn't bother looking at Liam. Instead, I grabbed my things and walked off the plane. The moment I stepped out, I took a deep breath and smiled. I loved Cascadia. It was small, it was quiet, and it was green. I had hated it at first, but now the trees gave me peace. Nature was the only thing that made sense.

In front of the plane were Jeeps waiting to take us to the camp. I walked straight to Monte, and he already knew not to ask. Instead, he threw me the keys. Before driving off, I glanced back at Liam who glared at me. However, in the rearview mirror, I watched as he ran faster than any fucking man I had ever seen and jumped onto the back of the truck with ease.

He smirked at me before turning back to the rest of the men, fist in the air. They applauded him like he was something special.

"Camp Callahan begins now!"

Never mind, he was special . . . a stupid, *special* kid. I was tempted to turn sharply and send him into one of the tress, but he climbed into the front with me.

"If I wanted you to ride with me, I would have waited for you," I said as he looked out at the small town we drove through.

"Why Cascadia?" he asked me, ignoring my comment completely. When I didn't answer, he said, "This is a good time to be open, Melody, or does that only happen after sex?"

Stomping on the pedal, I drove us even farther, taking a path onto an abandoned road in the middle of the forest.

"I went to community college here. It's small, rainy, and unknown. Cascadia is the place you go when you don't want to be found," I replied, turning left near the riverbank.

"You went to community college?" he asked, surprised, but of course he was. He was a rich kid from Chicago. I was a rich, too, but I was never really a kid.

"Yes, and I'm damn proud. Just because we have money doesn't mean I wanted to waste it at some big fancy university, studying for a *career* that isn't really an option. Nor did I want to deal with all the fake people who walked through the halls. I met Adriana here actually." It was freshman year, and she looked so nervous. However, I saw what she could do one night after a few guys were just a little bit too rough.

"You didn't want to go to school with two-faced people because you wanted to be the only one in the room," he stated, causing me to stomp on the brakes, and he jerked forward.

"You don't make me want to try. Do I lust after you? Yes. Any straight female would. Do I find you attractive and smart? Yes, and yes, again. But you are so very cocky, arrogant, possessive, and chauvinistic. You think you see me as an equal, but you don't. You are pushy, annoying, and childish way too often. You piss me off! I signed that contract. I was going to try, but then you came at me like an animal. You disrespected me. You tried to make a fool of me. You insulted me, and now you think you can demand my love. You think you can force me to love you because my father is dead? Because you're being a dick? I don't give a motherfuck. I really don't. So fuck you, Liam Callahan. I. Am. All. *I*. Have. That is how it has been and always will be."

He stared at me wide-eyed as I unbuckled my seatbelt and stepped out into the forest. Grabbing my bag from behind my seat, I walked up the side of the hill by myself. I knew the forest well enough.

LIAM

I watched her walk away in shock, right before the pain kicked in. All I could see was red when I jumped out of the truck. I didn't stop moving until I was right behind her. Grabbing onto her arm, I pulled her back and shoved her against the tree.

"We have already established that I am cocky, arrogant, possessive, and chauvinistic!" I yelled in her face. "And yes, I am pushy, annoying and childish often. But it is because I'm sick of being alone!"

I stopped, blinking a few times before stepping away from her. I hadn't meant to say that. Fuck. I really hadn't planned on saying that. I wanted to grab all the words and shove them back into my mouth, however it was too late. What was said could not be unsaid.

"Li—"

"I'm sick of being alone, and I know you are, too, even if you don't admit it to yourself. I just want to skip this part." I sighed, looking at her once more before walking into the forest.

I had no idea where I was going, but I just needed to get away from her. If I didn't, I would say something else, which would be just as dumb. Somehow, my walking led me to a clearing of lavender flowers. They looked so soft that I took my jacket off and just lay down. Was every day of my life going to be a battle? Sighing, I took a deep breath, allowing myself to look up at the darkening sky. Being a city rat, I had never seen so many stars shine from the sky. I wasn't sure what it was, but all of a sudden, I was drifting off.

I would head to the camp in the morning. Right now, I wanted to sleep in this moment of peace. Making sure my gun and knife were easy to grab, I allowed myself to relax.

MELODY

"Did he ever make it back?" I asked Monte as I looked out of the cabin window. The sun was starting to rise, and I hadn't moved since I realized he hadn't made it to camp. That had to be at least nine hours ago.

"No, ma'am. Are you sure you don't want anyone to search for him?"

I'm sick of being alone! His words echoed in my mind, and all through the night, I couldn't make it shut up. I had this weird feeling that something was going to happen. My gut told me something was going to happen, but I just wasn't sure what that was yet.

"Ma'am?" Monte asked me again.

"No, we had an argument. He will find his way."

"Should I let the men know?" he asked me, and I turned to him, glaring into his eyes. The men were settling fine.

They were already doing what they were supposed to be doing—relaxing, eating, practicing.

They didn't need Mel and Liam drama right now.

"Ma'am, he's back." Monte pointed, and I followed his hand to the man fighting to get flowers off him as he broke through the tress. The idiot fell asleep in the forest. But then again, it was Cascadia. He was fine, nothing ever happened here. Rolling my eyes at him, I turned away from him just as a gunshot rang through the air. I had heard guns go off all night and in the morning, however, this one made me freeze. Every hair at the back of my neck rose.

LIAM

Fuck my back hurts. I groaned as I walked toward the noise. Part of me was so confused and tired that I really wished I had remained sleeping. Had it not been for the damn sun, I could have slept there all day.

Stepping into the campsite, I glanced around at the cabins scattered deep within the forest. My Mel sure knew how to pick a vacation spot. A few men smirked at me, and it was then that I realized I was covered in flowers. Sighing, I brushed myself off quickly before attempting to walk forward. The key word being *attempting*.

It happened so quickly I didn't even have time to blink. My body was thrown back at the force of the bullet that collided with my chest. I couldn't scream. I couldn't even breathe. All I felt was the pain.

Goddamn it, Neal!

My body began to shake as chaos erupted around me. Eric was beside me in a moment before a scream rippled through the air.

"Liam!"

That was the voice of an angel. My angel. She pushed Eric away from me before falling to her knees beside me. She looked so beautiful. I reached up to touch her face, but when I did, all I could see was the blood on my hands. My blood on my hands.

Mel grabbed the side of my face with one hand and gripped tightly to my hands with the other.

"You're going to be okay," she whispered. "I swear. You're going to be okay."

She was starting to blur as the pain took over. In the back of my mind, I could feel them ripping my shirt. But in the front of my mind, all I could see was her. She was worried, scared, and caring as she held onto me. I smiled at her and she smiled at me.

"You're not alone, Liam," she whispered, and I knew that the pain, the burning in my chest, was worth it. This was so fucking worth it.

I took a small amount of pleasure in the panic in her eyes as mine closed. Half of me felt so bad for causing her pain. The other half knew that we, as humans, sometimes learned the best lessons from pain.

Checkmate.

EIGHTEEN

"There is no greater blessing than a family hand that lifts you from a fall; but there is no lower curse than a family hand that strikes you when you're down."

—Wes Fessler

NEAL

I cleaned my rifle for what had to be the fifteenth motherfucking time as I waited for the sun to come up. I wouldn't be able to sleep until this was over. Truthfully, I hadn't slept well in over a decade. Every night since high school, I woke up in the same cold sweat, and every night I would believe it was just a dream until I saw the tattoo on my arm. It was nothing special or fancy. It was just the number *224*. The locker I found Liam in. It would forever be burned into my skin and in my mind.

Every night I saw him, this small nerd with messy brown hair and glasses shaking in a locker. He was beaten up badly. He had even pissed himself he was shaking so hard. I was momentarily frozen in shock. I screamed for help over and over again, even when Coach D was already there trying to help him. I just kept screaming until my voice went silent. He stepped in and did what I had failed to do. In that one moment, it was like a sheet was lifted from my fucking face and I realized I was an idiot. I was jealous of Liam. Our father had poured his love into him since the moment he was born. The sun and moon revolved around Liam. Was he all right? Did he take his pills? How far did he walk today? Did you see how fast he read that book? Did you know he understands your homework Neal? Liam this. Liam that. Whenever I needed to speak with our father, he was in Liam's room. Whenever I need help, he was busy with Liam. Always fucking *Liam*. I was jealous. He lost his twin, had his shoulder broken, his feet crippled, and small dying lungs, all within hours of just being born, and I was jealous of him.

It didn't make sense anymore, but back then with a child's understanding, that's what I thought. Whenever our mother saw him, she would break down. She would sob and sob then lock herself away for months. I blamed Liam for that. What made it worse was that I truthfully hated myself. I hated myself for not protecting our mother. I was young. I couldn't do anything, but it didn't help. It was just easier to blame it all on Liam because it started when he came. So when he was being bullied, teased, or flat-out embarrassed, I looked away. I always looked away until I saw him shaking in that locker, and then I couldn't look away any longer.

Declan stepped in, knocking back a beer. "This is such a stupid plan."

"It's my only chance, Declan," I said with a sigh, cleaning the barrel once again. I didn't want the bullet to back-jam. If it did, then it would come out with more force. It would definitely kill him.

"There has to be another way. This is going to backfire on you both."

"There is no other way! He is my brother. I want my brother back, Declan. You have no idea. You both have always been close. I want to be able to sit with him, drink, and joke and laugh like you both do. I want to go on hunting trips, to fighting clubs. I fucking want to be part of the family again. I want a seat at the damn table, because if I don't get one soon, Liam will cut me out permanently. Do you know what happens to people Liam cuts out?" I snapped, throwing the gun on the table as I took a deep breath.

"Neal—"

"He eithers kills them or he leaves them to die, family or no family. The only thing holding him back is our mother, and how much longer do you think that will last? I may one day wake up and find my wife and myself in chains or in hell thanks to him. I cannot let that happen."

"Are you doing this because you fear he will one day turn on you or because you truly want his love,"

Declan said, as he placed his beer down to clean my gun. "He's been a crappy brother as well. You messed up, but you were young. We were all young."

"You don't see what I see at night, Declan," I replied, taking the gun from him. "You don't understand how disgusted I feel with myself whenever I wake up in the morning."

"I'm starting to."

"Why, because you're lusting over Melody?"

"How—"

"Because every last man with a working dick is lusting over her. It's hard not to when she shoots people in a tight dress and heels, and fucking loves it. We all want that from our women, but Liam got it. Always Liam. However, I have enough bad blood to last me a lifetime. Last thing I need is Melody added to the mix." Plus, that woman scared me almost as much as Olivia did.

"You're going to shoot her husband, she's added to the mix."

He had a point.

"Yeah, well I need to work on Liam." At the first sign of light, I lifted the clear bullet.

"What is this?" Declan grabbed hold of one.

"I call them blanks, I made them for Liam. They will hurt like a bitch and may cause bleeding, but it shouldn't kill him. I got it from paintballs." It wouldn't take long at all.

"When this goes to hell, and it will go to hell, remember to tell Melody I had no idea about this."

This couldn't fail. I would do anything Liam needed for this not to fail. It was crazy but that was who Liam was, ninety-eight percent of everything he did was crazy, but it worked. He gave me his word that he would finally let the past remain in the past. Maybe then I would finally be able breathe again, to sleep again, to be at peace again.

Declan didn't understand. Olivia didn't understand. No one understood what I felt. How deep the guilt had embedded into my soul. Father had told me repeatedly that family was everything. That we lived and died for family, but then Liam happened and I swear Sedric knew what I had done. He looked me dead in the eye and waited for me to confess my sin, but I couldn't speak. For the last twelve years I couldn't speak. What is the point of being strong on the outside when you are weak on the inside?

That was why I needed to do this. Not just for Liam but for myself . . . for Olivia. So I could finally be the man she needed. Instead, she was the woman who held on to me each and every fucking night as I tried to get the image of the little boy in the locker out of my mind.

She wanted kids, but she wasn't the problem. I was. Apparently, my own body had begun to betray me. The doctors called it "stress," stupid motherfuckers. It was my body's way of telling me I was not ready to be a father, not when I couldn't even hold my shit together.

Sighing, I dropped my head against my rifle.

"May my aim be true in its intent," I whispered to myself before tucking the cross around my neck into my shirt.

Walking toward my window, I waited. I would wait all day if I had to. But sure enough he walked out from the trees.

"Forgive me," I whispered as I pulled the trigger.

NINETEEN

"He who makes a beast of himself gets rid of the pain of being a man."

—Samuel Johnson

CORALINE

Day 1

"Ahh!" I screamed at the top of my lungs as a rush of freezing cold water was poured all over me and my bed. Jumping out of bed I came face-to-face with . . . Adriana I believe? She looked like I was an annoying brat.

"You're late." She stared, placing the bucket on ground.

"It's six in the morning!" I yelled at her, shivering horribly. Why in the world couldn't she just shake me like a normal person?

"Training starts an hour before sunrise. The sun is up, which means you're late." She walked to my closet and pulled out two random items of clothing that didn't even match, then threw them at me.

"I didn't"

"Strip."

"What?" She wanted me to change in front of her?

She rolled her eyes and pointed to my pajamas. "Take off your clothes and get changed, so you can start the training you begged the Boss for."

"Okay let me just go to the bathroom."

"Why? Do you have special lady parts that I don't have?" She glared at me.

"I don't remember you being this mouthy to Mel."

"What was that?' she asked, making me jump.

"Nothing, these clothes don't match," I replied walking over to my closet.

Adriana followed of course. "Does it matter what clothes you bleed in?"

"Bleed in?"

"There is a reason why people say they worked through blood, sweat, and tears." She rolled her eyes making me feel like an idiot, and I wasn't doing this to feel even worse about myself.

"Look I'm new at this whole—"

"Being strong? Being confident? Being a fucking Callahan? Yeah, I'm getting that. Which is why I'm annoyed, because this isn't you. Or at least is shouldn't be you. Aren't black women supposed to be strong?"

"You don't know me, you racist bitch!" I yelled at her. Yes, I was supposed to be the "typical" black woman, the one who takes no shit and is ready to fight at every moment. God forbid there be a black woman who was shy, who hated confrontation, who didn't fit the stereotype.

She smirked, pushing her glasses up her small nose. "Nope, I don't know you, but do you know you? Is this meek, small woman in front of me the real Coraline or is it the face you put on because you're scared to deal with your shit?"

I wasn't sure how to respond to that.

"Think about why you asked to do this. You could have chosen any other way to remake yourself—to better yourself. You could have gone back to school, lost five pounds, wrote a self-help book. But instead, you wanted to learn how to fight. People who choose that option are born differently than the rest of the world." She stepped right up to my face, and I felt the need to back away.

"There is a drive, a hunger within you Coraline. You're trying to break out of your shell but are scared to do so. You're scared because all you know how to do is hide behind sick children and big fat checks. You hide behind everything, even your clothes. It's why you can't take them off in front of others. Let me get guess, you and Declan have sex in the dark? You hide and wait under the covers—"

"Shut the fuck up!" I yelled, my fist flying at her fast, however, she caught it easily and smiled.

"There's the real Coraline breaking out. Maybe you aren't hopeless. We will try again tomorrow, and you better not be late." She glared before walking away from me.

When she left, I felt myself fall and I just lay down in my closet. Who was the real Coraline Wilson Callahan? I wasn't sure. My whole life was unsure, with the exception of Declan. He was the silver lining in my life. Neither of my parents really wanted anything to do with me, seeing as how they weren't really my parents. They were my very bitter aunt and uncle. After my real parents died, they took me in, hoping they could get the money that was left to me.

They didn't care about me, and they were pissed when they found out only I could withdraw anything and not until my sixteenth birthday. They never said a kind word to me as a child, and then on my sixteenth birthday, they were taking me on shopping trips—more like I was taking them. But they were happy and they treated me better, so I kept buying. Now here I was at twenty-two, still trying to buy affection. But it didn't work so well when everyone around you had just as much money, if not more.

I didn't know who the real me was. But I knew I wanted to kill this Coraline. Not all of her, just most of her. I wanted to be who I was when I first met Declan, free, alive, happy. I wasn't sure when I lost it. I think it was just a few months after we got married. I saw a darker side of him, and I got nervous, I became afraid and walled myself off from him.

The more blood I saw, the more wounds he came back with, the more I walked away, which was stupid, because he confessed on our third date who he was and what he did. He told me he loved me enough to let me walk away. He said that if he went on one more date he wouldn't be able to handle it if I left him. I didn't want to leave him, so I stayed, and then I kicked him in the gut for it later. I accepted this life, and I didn't want it to rule me. I wanted to walk on the same water Mel and Evelyn did. Evelyn would walk through fire for Sedric, she would kill for him, and I wanted to be that way. I wanted to be a real Callahan woman.

Day 2

I walked straight into Adriana's room to find her placing knives on her bed. She looked up at me then to the time and smiled.

"Four-thirty in the morning. I'm impressed. Ready for the blood, sweat, and tears?" she asked.

"Yes."

TWENTY

"Maybe this is why so many serial killers work in pairs. It's nice not to feel alone in a world full of victims or enemies. It just seems natural. You and me against the world . . ."

—Chuck Palahniuk

MELODY

I couldn't stop shaking, me, motherfucking, Melody Giovanni, now fucking Callahan, the girl who did not blink when she sold her first ounce of coke at sixteen in a back alleyway. I was the girl who murdered a cartel member at seventeen because he stole a pound of weed from us. However, here I was, and I could not stop shaking. I did not shake. I did not bend. I did not fucking flinch at the sight of blood, drugs, or at the sound of a fucking bullet! Yet here I was, watching as one of Cascadia's doctors looked over Liam, and I was bloody shaking! What the hell was wrong with me?

I was trying my best not to scream at the fool hovering over Liam, who hadn't moved in nine hours. If it weren't for his chest rising and falling, I would have thought he was . . .

This stupid doctor had five seconds to give me an update or I was going to reach up and pull his tongue out of his ass!

"Mrs. Callahan—"

"You're wasting words," I hissed. "How is he?"

"He's fine. Luckily, the bullet wasn't lethal. In fact, I'm not sure exactly what it was. He has two bruised ribs, but they will heal. He is on medication for the pain, but other than that he is fine and should get back to moving around in a couple of days," he replied, stepping back when I moved to the edge of the bed.

Liam looked so . . . peaceful. There wasn't a wrinkle or any discomfort in his face. I felt the urge to run my hands through his hair. Part of me wanted to lay with him. A big part of me wanted to lay with to him. It was like my mind knew that was the only way the shaking would stop. However, I couldn't. Instead, I turned around and walked out the door. Knowing he was okay, knowing he would be fine meant that I could do what I had been itching to do from the moment Fedel came to me.

I stepped outside, allowing my eyes to roam the yard of men who were all waiting for the same update I had been. My gaze stopped at the fool's, and it was like the lion was out of the cage.

"*Neal!*" I roared, causing every man in his right fucking mind to part like the fucking Red Sea as I walked to him. He didn't move, he didn't even look surprised, but in a moment, he was going to look like he was in a hell of a lot of pain.

But I couldn't get to him, though, Declan blocked my path and grabbed my arm.

Who did this motherfucking bitch think he was?

"Melody—"

Before he could finish, I punched him straight in the throat, kicked his back legs so they buckled, and brought him to his knees. Grabbing his hair, I yanked it back and pressed my knife to his neck.

"I will end you Declan Callahan, if you ever stand in my way again." I pressed the blade even harder against his Adam's apple.

"You aren't thinking clearly—"

He didn't seem to get that I wasn't fucking joking. Pulling the knife from his neck, I stabbed his shoulder. His eyes widened as I backed away, allowing him to fall to his ass before letting out a roar of pain.

"Have you lost your fucking mind?" Neal yelled at me, rushing toward Declan. However, I stood in front of him.

"Yes, because if I was fucking sane right now, if I was Melody Giovanni instead of Callahan, I would have fucking killed him for stepping in my way! But I can't kill Liam's cousin and his brother in the same day," I yelled, and he looked me over, unsure of what to do or even say. I would help him find his tongue.

"Did you shoot Liam?" I knew the answer, but I wanted to hear him say it.

"Melody—"

"Did you fucking shoot my husband, Neal?"

"Yes."

I felt a moment of peace before I found myself lunging at his neck. He saw it coming and grabbed hold of my arms and lifted me as if I was a fucking newborn.

"Melody, it was an accident!" He yelled, but look at what long legs I have . . . only to strangle him with.

I wrapped them around his neck like a python, and squeezed until he had to let my arms go to grab hold of my legs. When he did, I flipped off him and kneed him in the crotch. He bent down and the stupid, tall, bear-like motherfucker gasped in pain.

"You, Neal Callahan, are the accident!" My fist smashed into his face.

His head jerked, and I felt the pain in my hand, but I didn't stop. "You, Neal Callahan, are scum. You do not deserve my respect." Another punch in the fucking nose.

"You do not deserve your last name."

At that, he grabbed my fist, stopping it before spitting the blood from his mouth and rising to his feet. He glared into my eyes, and his own were burning. "Watch yourself, sister, or you may get hurt."

He did his best to tower over me as if he was trying to say something with his size.

"What? Because you chew on steroids for breakfast I should be afraid of you?" I spun into him so quickly he didn't have time to comprehend what I was doing until it was too late. It was one of the few things I had learned from my failed attempts at dance lessons as a child. Let your partner lead. It was probably why I failed at it. I did the leading. However, it worked for Neal, who was too big to stop me from spinning into him and grabbing his gun before spinning out.

With my left finger, I pulled the fucking trigger. Sadly, it wasn't a gun but a Taser. However, it worked, and eighty-thousand volts sent him straight to his ass, shaking like a fish out of water.

"A Taser? Really? What are you, a mall cop?"

I sighed, looking down at him. But the big bad wolf couldn't speak.

Bending on one knee, I leaned in so he could see my eyes. "If you ever cause harm to Liam again I will cut you in half and stuff you inside a locker."

Standing back up, I turned to look over the rest of the men. Mine were all smiling, while the rest looked proud. I guess they didn't like their boss being shot either.

"He's fine, just needs rest. Continue on pretending like you are not trying to kill each other. I'll see you all later," I told them, and my eyes met Declan's. He was being held up by none other than

Eric, who I was starting to dislike. Declan looked pale and in need of a drink. He would be fine. If not, well then boo fucking hoo.

"I'll send for the doctor," I said in a mocking tone, then walked past them and into the cabin.

The doctor looked at me, unsure of what to do or where to go.

"Fedel will handle your payment after you look over Neal and Declan," I told him, taking off my boots. My hand was sore, but I would deal with that later.

He must have noticed because he stepped forward, but I glared at him. There was only one doctor I trusted, and it wasn't him. Getting the message, he left quickly, leaving me alone with the handsome, sleeping asshole who was my husband. Once again, I found myself staring at him. He looked beautiful, and I gave in to my need, allowing my good hand to run through his hair. When he let out a small moan, I stopped. Even in his sleep he was a horn dog. He was definitely all right.

Smiling to myself like an idiot, I stripped down as I walked toward the bathroom, grabbing myself a bottle of brandy as I did.

Turning on the shower, I waited until the water was hot, which would take a moment. It was one of the downsides with camp. Drinking from the bottle, I allowed myself a second to stare in the mirror. Most people hated to look at themselves. They always found a flaw within the person they looked at.

However, I never had that problem. I knew I was attractive, and I knew I was smart. I wasn't looking hard enough, though, not until Liam shoved a metaphorical mirror so close to my face that my nose was touching the glass. It was only then I truly saw that, in many ways, he was right. I was alone, and I was lonely. I had always accepted that, and I made sure never to think about it. It wasn't until we were in the forest that I actually understood. Losing Orlando hurt underneath everything, even when I saw that coming. Liam though . . . that bullet, I didn't see it coming, and in a moment, he could have been gone.

No one to fight, laugh, or rule with. I frowned to myself, taking another sip of the brandy before placing it on the counter. It also meant no one to sleep next to and no one to talk to. I could speak to others. However, I could only talk to Liam, because somehow he . . . I didn't know. I could just talk with him, and in a second, stupid fucking Neal almost took him away. "Where is the brandy?"

I jumped at the sound of his voice. The mirror was so foggy I hadn't even noticed when he walked in.

Turning to him, my eyes went straight to the bandage that was wrapped over his shoulder and around his waist. When I did glance up, he was looking me over as if I was water and he was a man in the desert.

I hadn't realized until then that I was standing completely naked while he stood in pajama pants.

"Li—"

His lips were on mine, before I could get the words out. My hand went to his hair, kissing him just as hard as he was kissing me. He tasted like honey, and I didn't want to let go of him. But I had to.

Breaking away, I took a deep breath, preparing to speak when his lips went to my neck.

"Liam we need to—"

He gripped my nipple, and I felt a moan ripple out of my throat. When his tongue began to trail down from my neck toward my breasts, I began pulling on this hair.

"Jesus! Fuck, Liam! Stop!" I yelled, and he froze, slowly ripping himself from me to look down at me. In his eyes I saw confusion, frustration . . . and hurt.

Letting me go completely, he took a step back, shaking his head. "Sorry. I just came in search of the brandy."

He frowned, reaching around me, but I grabbed it first.

"You shouldn't mix alcohol and pain killers," I said quickly. He glared at me before spotting my hands. I wasn't sure why I only then noticed the dry blood that was still on them . . . Neal's blood, maybe a little of Declan's as well.

Don't ask, Liam.

"What the fuck happened to your hand?"

Damn it, just listen to me once.

"Neal was the one who shot you," I replied, waiting to see how he would react, but he didn't look surprised.

"That doesn't explain your hand."

"I said your idiot brother shot you, and all you care about is my hand?" He should be out there kicking his brother's ass.

"Yes, because you're my wife." He sighed. "I will deal with Neal when I'm not on drugs."

Turning away from him, I took off my ring to wash my hands. "I handled it."

"You killed Neal?" he whispered, stepping up right behind me. Warmth radiated off him like waves. I felt myself leaning into him, closing my eyes, and relaxing as I rested my head on his chest. That is, until I remembered he had a bullet wound and stood straighter.

"No, I didn't." I should have. "I tasered him after beating into his face and stabbing Declan."

I prepared myself for his bitching, but when I turned to him, he was smiling. He must have been on some really good drugs.

"Let me get this straight. You stabbed Declan. And attacked and tasered Neal while I was out?" he asked, and I nodded. He was going to find out anyway.

"You show affection in the oddest ways," he said, kissing my forehead and grabbing the brandy.

But once again, I took it from him, placing it on the counter again. "Not with pills."

"You've got to be kidding me! Give me the bottle, Melody." He groaned, reaching for it.

But I poked his wound, causing him to hiss and flinch back. "No, means no, Liam."

"This is the worst thing you've ever done to me." He frowned like a six-year-old boy.

"I shot you, stabbed your brother, tasered your cousin, and almost cracked open your ex-girlfriend's skull—"

"My ex-girlfriend?"

"Shit. I didn't mean to say that." I bit my lip. "Natasha and I met in the bathroom at church. She said some things, and I put her head through the glass. So, no, withholding brandy isn't the worst thing I've ever done to you."

Once again, his lips found mine, but only for a second before he broke away.

"In my eyes it is," he whispered. "I have two pleasures in this world. One is you, Melody Callahan, and the second brandy. Withholding them both is just plain cruel and borderline inhumane."

And just like that, something clicked in my mind. Here I was standing naked in front of him, not only in body, but with my "sins" as well, and he didn't care. He saw the deepest and dirtiest parts of my soul and mind but didn't care. In fact, he wanted to stay in the darkness with me. Just him, me, and the fucking brandy.

"They're both just temporary holds. You can have them once you're feeling better," I whispered back, kissing his lips softly before pulling away.

His eyes widened as my words set in. Grabbing hold of my waist, he pulled me closer to him. Bringing his lips to my ear, his hard-on pressed against my stomach.

"I won't feel better if I don't have you now," he replied, biting my neck and making me want him even more.

I moaned, rubbing against him. "Liam, you're hurt."

Pulling me away from the sink, he pushed me against the bathroom door. "Mel, I plan on fucking your brains out." He pulled the drawstring on his pants. His dick was pointed right at me, and I closed my legs trying to think clearly.

"You want me to fuck you against this door." He whispered staring into my eyes. He held me prisoner with almost no effort at all.

Think Melody.

"I want to hear you scream my name." He rubbed against me as he spoke. "You want me inside of you. I can feel it," he added, licking up my neck while using his good arm to grab my ass.

"You're going to be so sore in the morning," I choked out as he sucked away. The warmth of the steam along with his body made me feel like I was on fire. I couldn't even think. All I could do was feel him, and he felt amazing.

"If I do my job, you will be, too." He smirked. "So just stop fighting this once and let me have you, wife."

I couldn't speak because he didn't wait for a reply. Instead, he plunged so deeply into me that my head went back. Moaning, I grabbed his neck, wrapping my legs around his waist as held me against the door, going deeper and deeper with each thrust.

"I'll take that as a yes." He moaned, pulling out once more only to slam back within me. "I've wanted to fuck you against the door for a long time." He smiled at me while he rammed into me over and over again.

I couldn't even make a sentence. I couldn't speak. I could barely see because my eyes rolled back.

"I wanted it to be hard," he added, pulling my hands from his neck and holding them above my head.

"I wanted it to be rough," he said, and it was like he let the animal out of the cage as he thrust into my body repeatedly, giving me no time to think or even move. All I could do was accept and moan like a bitch . . . his bitch.

He let go of my hands to grab my waist, and I let out a scream of pure pleasure as I came against the force of his cock. He didn't let up, fucking me harder and harder until he thrust so deeply my voice cracked as he came. When he let go of me, I felt my legs release him. But I was too weak to stand and slid to the floor. I took in the warm air greedily but when I looked up, all I saw was his erection.

How is that humanly possible? I thought as I stared at him in shock. He had stamina like I had never seen. Looking down at me, he stroked himself, which in return only made me want him again.

LIAM

Sitting up, I grabbed the bottle of pain meds, taking two with a glass of water and not brandy like I should have. Mel could have her way for now. Looking down at the sleeping beauty beside me, I waited for the guilt to kick in. However, it was nowhere to be found. I had tricked her, and I didn't fucking regret it because I now had what I wanted. I had her. I felt it, the shift in her, as we had our way with one another. We went from the bathroom, to the shower, to the bed, where she helped me redress my wound before we fucked again. My shoulder, like she had said, hurt like a bitch, but it was worth it because I had her. I did what I needed to do to get my wife, and there was no fucking taking it back.

She knew now. She knew I was hers and she was mine, and now we could move the fuck forward. It felt like the longest war but it was over now, and we were both victors. One day, when we were about to die of old age, I would tell her. But for now, I would shut this away and never speak of it again. All I had to do was make sure my brother and cousin kept their mouths shut. If they didn't, I would kill them . . . and I meant it.

Trying my best to ignore the pain, I lifted myself from the bed, grabbing a pair of jeans and a jacket. I had thought I was quiet, however Mel sat up, rubbing her eyes as she tried to focus on me. Fuck, she was beautiful.

"Where are you going?" She yawned, and it was cute.

"I'm going to have some words with my brother." I grinned. Walking over to her side, I kissed her cheek, and she accepted it without a glare or flinch.

The pain was worth it.

"Come back to bed. We can kill him when the sun is up." She smiled, pulling on my jacket, and I was tempted, but I needed to make sure this didn't blow up in my face. I didn't want to lose her.

"I will be right back." I kissed her lips. I couldn't stop kissing her. "I'm not going to kill him. My mother is fond of him. However, I will express how I feel in other ways."

She rolled her eyes at me before falling back on the bed. "Fine, but if you change your mind, Cascadia is the best place to hide a body. So much forest, and so few witnesses."

God, I loved her.

"I'll keep that in mind." I laughed, walking out the door. The moment I did, I was hit with fresh air. I had to give it to her; the camp location was beautifully hidden in the midst of the forest. It was large enough to fit all our men, with ten or eleven houses and one dining hall at the far end.

Seeing me, Eric limped over. The poor fuck.

"Neal and Declan are in the dining hall," he stated. Nodding, I walked slower so he could walk beside me.

"How is your leg?" I asked, trying my best not to smirk. Melody and her handiwork.

"Doctor said it will be like this for another four or five months. I think your wife hates me, sir."

I couldn't help it. I laughed even though the pain ached in my chest.

"Don't take it personally. She hates everyone equally. At least she didn't stab you."

"The men were thinking of starting an injured by BM club," he said, and I stopped.

"BM?" What the fuck were they calling my wife?

"Bloody Melody," he answered quickly.

It fit. The moment she found out, though, they were all going to prove that name right. Shaking my head at him, I continued forward.

"None of you call me anything do you?" If they did, I would kill them myself.

Eric tensed, and I didn't even bother pushing. When I stepped into the dining hall, everyone shut up immediately. My eyes narrowed in on Declan, who was hunched over a bowl of food and looking a little pale. Next to him was Neal, who appeared to be in much better shape, even with a broken nose, a black eye, a spilt lip, and what looked to be a choke hold bruise on his neck. He would live.

"Don't you just love my wife?" I asked them loudly, causing the men to either laugh or grin like fools.

Antonio stood up with a mug filled with what had to be alcohol. *"Lunga vita alla Regina!"*

"Fada beo an Banríon!" My men yelled back in Irish.

Long live the queen, indeed.

They had been here, what, two days? Maybe three if I'd slept for as long as I thought, yet here they were, drinking and laughing at one another.

Grinning along with them, I nodded over at Neal and Declan who were both glaring at me. Rising, they followed as I walked from the dining hall to the shade of the trees. Declan moved slower than usual, as did Neal.

"So how are you?" I asked them, trying not to laugh.

Declan stepped forward, nose flared and eyes wide. He was pissed.

"You fucking two-bit asshole of a dick! You are fucked in the head. Your wife stabbed me! She fucking stabbed me, Liam! Have you ever been stabbed? This bitch"—he pointed to Neal—"was the one who fucking shot you, and he only gets tasered! All I did was try to calm her down. What kind of bullshit is that?"

I laughed. I couldn't help it. Even though it hurt like a son of a bitch all I could do was laugh. It was so fucking funny. I hadn't ever laughed like this before my Mel came along.

"Why did you even try in the first place? She shot me in the thigh when she was calm. I'm surprised she didn't do more."

Declan shook his head, and I could see the rage building in his eyes. "I fucking hate you all!"

With that he walked away. Slowly, the big baby.

Neal stood still, not saying a thing and waiting for me to live up to my side of the deal. Part of me had hoped he would fail so I could hate him, but it was time to move forward. He did what I asked. Sighing, I reached out for his hand.

"There will be times where I'm still going to be an asshole to you," I said when he took my hand. "However, I promise to move forward, brother. I will not hold the past against you any longer. I will no longer hate you for it. I still dislike your wife, but I don't hate you."

"Can you just do that? Can you let go of the hate?"

"Automatically, no. However, you're the reason why my wife and I had mind-blowing sex last night and will continue to. That's enough to make me at least want to have a beer with you. After now, we never speak of this moment again, and let Declan know." I had told him the truth, and he looked . . . lighter, like someone had taken the world off his shoulders for once.

"Thank you, Liam."

"Well, the first few beers are on you. That shit hurt!" I winced and grabbed my chest before walking away.

Walking back to our cabin, I found myself feeling lighter as well. Things in my personal life were finally making sense. All I had to do was kill Vance, Saige, Amory, the police, and then take over the rest of the country, plus Europe. All of which was possible thanks to my wife. Thanks to my Mel.

As if she could read my mind, the moment I walked in I found my beautiful wife dressed in my shirt, sitting on our bed with files and a laptop around her.

"The life of a mafia couple." I smirked, taking off my jacket slowly while trying not to wince at the pain.

"It's a bloody but necessary one," she said, handing me a file as I lay back down.

"They are calling you Bloody Melody now." I smirked at her, flipping through what looked to be more coded letters from Saige.

She stopped and frowned. "That doesn't strike enough fear into the hearts of men and woman everywhere."

"Oh, it does. They fear and respect you. Maybe more than me." I pouted, and she smiled, bending down to kiss my lips.

"You could blow up the police commissioner's house for trying to break into our downtown factory."

She smiled, causing me to rise up quickly. Maybe a little bit too quickly but I ignored the pain.

"What the fuck?" I shouted, searching for the file she was talking about, but she simply handed me the laptop.

"That is our meth lab in Orland Park, isn't it?" she asked, even though we both knew it was.

"How the fuck did he get in there?" I snapped, watching as the idiot and his men broke into the factory. So much for personal rights.

Mel picked up Saige's coded letters. "Apparently Vance is tipping them off as a way to keep us distracted."

Taking the letters, I raked through them quickly.

"This could be a trap. Saige could be writing these as bullets for us to pick up and shoot ourselves with." I didn't know this Saige well enough yet. But from what I did know, she was a snake in the grass and someone needed to cut off her head before she fed and grew.

"I thought the same thing and had Fedel contact Ryan after we first got off the jet. Apparently, Saige forgets things constantly and needs to write everything down. Amory has her computer coded weekly so no one can hack in. Ryan is a big help with that. But I'm not ruling out anything yet. Right now we do still have a police rat outside our door," she replied looking at the computer screen.

"Declan put a bomb under his house," I said, reminding myself. Mel flipped the channel to the small and modest family home in the Chicago suburbs. He must have kept it even after he lost his family. It was kind of sad.

She handed me a cell phone, and I smiled. Pressing send and watching the house go up in flames was like watching fireworks during New Years. Now it wasn't so sad anymore.

Flipping back to the factory, I dialed the site number and pressed send once more for the heck of it, and Mel turned to me wide-eyed.

"What the fuck did you just do?" she gasped, staring at the screen.

"Too many people knew about the place. We were having meth-heads show up at the door. I had everything moved from there a month ago." The commissioner would have found nothing anyway.

Mel smiled, but in a flash it was out as we spotted the commissioner's stupid, Smokey the Bear sidekick helping his boss out.

"Some rats just don't know when to die."

Kissing her neck, I pulled her toward me. "In due time, love. In due time. We will make them all suffer."

"And then we kill them?"

I grinned. "Then we will kill them. One by one, until all that's left are bloodstains."

As she relaxed into me, we watched the police officers who weren't so lucky get burned alive. I counted six running around like chickens with their heads cut off. However, I wasn't sure if there were any still inside the burning building.

"He's going to try to pin this on us." Mel smirked, drinking my brandy.

"I hope he does. Now I have a reason to go annoy Judge Randal." What's the point of having a judge on the payroll if you never get to use him?

"And Senator Colemen," she added and looked to me. "You know, I've never killed someone in pajamas before."

"Neither have I. May we always remember our first," I replied, taking her lips with mine. This was how it should have been from the start. She and I setting the world on fire together.

TWENTY-ONE

"It is not easy to find happiness in ourselves, and it is not possible to find it elsewhere."

—Agnes Repplier

CORALINE

Day 3

"I can't do this!" I choked out before puking into the bowl once again.

"Cora, you're doing well, and I'm not going to be the one to tell the Boss you gave up after only three days," Adriana said, holding my hair back.

Pushing her away, I backed up against the tub. "My skin is so beaten up, it changed colors. I can barely stand. I can't do this. I can't. I'm in so much pain all the time, Adriana. Please, let me give up."

Adriana sighed, kneeling in front me. She took my hands and pulled me to my feet.

"You are stronger than you think, Cora. In three days, you have come so far. Yes, I know you are in pain. But you aren't the same Cora. So suck it up, get dressed, and go to dinner so we can get to work tonight," she demanded, handing me an outfit to wear.

Grabbing the clothes, I glared at her. "I hate you."

"No, you don't." She smirked, before leaving.

It hurt like a bitch getting into those clothes. My arms felt like they were being burned off. If I hadn't just thrown up everything in my stomach then I would have just gone to bed, but I was so damn hungry. Washing out my mouth, I rinsed before heading down the stairs slowly.

"Coraline?" I jumped at her voice.

Not Olivia.

"Yes, Olivia?" I turned to her when we reached the dining hall.

She looked me up and down but didn't say anything. Stepping into the dining room, both Evelyn and Sedric stopped speaking and just stared at me.

How did Mel handle all the staring? Whenever people stared at her, she simply walked prouder.

Taking a deep breath, I walked slowly to my seat. Placing the napkin in my lap, I grabbed some food and pretended they weren't there.

"Okay, Coraline, enough. What is happening to you? Are you all right? I'm worried," Evelyn asked, causing me to jump.

"Nothing, I'm fine," I replied, filling my plate.

"The way you wince when you breathe means you, at the very least, have a bruised rib. Not to mention the busted lip you're hiding under makeup. But those are only the wounds we can see. I'm willing to bet Declan's life on it, so tell me the truth, Coraline," Sedric demanded as he cut into his lamb.

"I'm taking a self-defense class," I answered, waiting for them to flip out. However, only Olivia seemed shocked.

"Why in God's name are you taking a self-defense class?" It seemed like a stupid question.

"Because I would like to defend myself?"

"This is about Melody isn't it?" she snapped. "She is killing this family and tearing us apart from the inside out."

It's not like we were perfect before.

"What would Declan think Coraline? What if you were to get hurt? You have no idea what you're doing. You aren't some—"

"Shut up!" I yelled, standing up angrily. "What I want to do with my life and my body is none of your damn business. The only person's opinion that matters is Declan's. We get it, you're bitter that Mel stole your thunder and that the magazines no longer give a shit about you. But it doesn't mean you have to take it out on me. Go look up baby names or something, and leave me the hell alone."

When I was done, I blinked a few times, unsure of where that came from. Taking a seat again, I kept my head down and finished eating.

"Sorry for cursing, Evelyn."

"Not at all. It seems like you have been holding that in for a while." She laughed when I looked up.

Sedric frowned. "Who is giving you these lessons? Are they trustworthy?"

"Adriana, Mel's—"

"The slave girl who follows Melody around like a lost dog?" Olivia snorted, drinking her wine.

"Olivia, that is enough," Sedric snapped, and she stood up straight immediately. "Coraline, when do you train again?"

"Tomorrow at five," I answered, smiling at Olivia.

"Very well, I shall see you both then."

Shit.

Day 5

"Do it," I told Adriana as I sat in front of the mirror.

"Are you sure Cora?" Evelyn asked, looking at my hair.

"It is just hair. It will grow back, right? Adriana almost ripped my ponytail out during our fight yesterday," I said. After everything, Evelyn and Sedric were both watching as if it were some damn sport. Sedric didn't really speak. However, he would frown every time my body collided with the floor.

Adriana demanded I learn how to use my size to an advantage, so everything I learned had been quick jabs and kicks. She made me jump up and down for an hour straight before having me kick her hands. But I could barely even stand up, let alone kick. When I puked, she gave me water, some bread, and a six-minute break before putting me to work again.

"Here I go," Adriana said, and I closed my eyes. All I heard were the scissors snipping away at my hair.

"Evelyn, your nephew will still love me if I'm bald right?" I joked.

"Um—"

"Evelyn!" My eyes flew open, and I stared at my reflection. I looked so different. Not bad different, just different.

Evelyn gasped. "Adriana, you must cut my hair from now on." She messed with some of the edges of my hair until she met my eyes in the mirror. "You look beautiful, and Declan, will fall in love with you all over again."

God, I hoped so.

"Now you, Adriana." I smiled, standing up as I pulled her down.

"Cor . . ."

"Nope, we're doing this, and if you don't, I will cut your hair while you sleep," I threatened, causing her to roll her eyes.

"I don't sleep," she joked.

"Why doesn't that shock me?" I smiled, grabbing the flat iron.

"I think we may have some contacts. Let me see if there are any for your prescription," Evelyn said quickly, walking out of the room.

"Sexy Adriana is under here somewhere." I grinned. "This is going to be like one of those teen movies."

Day 7

I pressed my dress down for what had to be the ninth time since we stepped out of the car. I felt like I was going to jump out of my skin. I was so excited to see him. However, the first person to step out of the jet was one of the men I didn't recognize, followed by Mel. She looked me over as she made her way toward me.

However, I couldn't pay attention because there was my Declan. His eyebrows squished together as he looked at my hair.

"Do you like it?" I asked him as I brushed the back down a little.

He reached over and played with a little before looking back to me. "I'm kind of shocked, but you look cute."

Cute, not beautiful, but I would take that for now. It was better than nothing.

TWENTY-TWO

"It is surely easier to confess a murder over a cup of coffee than in front of a jury."
—Friedrich Dürrenmatt

LIAM

"That's right, you little shit, come closer," she said as she eyed the deer standing a few dozen feet away.

"Relax your arm and breathe," I told her, resting my head right beside hers.

"My arm is relaxed, and you're doing enough breathing for the both of us," she replied like the smartass she was.

Backing away from her, I rolled my eyes. "Well then, go ahead, kill Bambi."

She released the arrow and just like I figured, it went right past the deer's head, causing it to run away in fear. She watched it disappear into the forest in silent rage before turning back to me. Handing me the bow and arrows, she pulled out a gun, and I tried not to laugh.

"I could kill it so much better with this!" she yelled, and it was cute, especially since I knew I wasn't the source of her rage.

"That's not the point." I lifted the bow to the sky, pulling it back and releasing the arrow. It went straight through a bird's heart. Mel simply rolled her eyes, pointing to the sky and shot three times.

"Three birds for me, one for you. What's the point again?" She smiled, looking down at the . . . fuck.

"We just killed Mockingbirds." I frowned, kneeling down to stare at the four birds now half-blown to pieces on the ground.

"Please, tell me you're joking."

Smiling at her once more, I stood and released another arrow into the tree, watching another one of the beautiful birds fall to its death.

"Show off."

"I found the one weapon my wife can't use." I grinned as she glared at me. "I think I'll show it off as much as possible."

"I'm a people hunter! Who hunts people with arrows?" she snapped, and I opened my mouth to speak but she glared.

"If you say the Green Arrow I will shoot you in the other thigh," she added, and all I could do was smirk at her.

"All people are animals, love. They freeze when they are afraid. They cry out in pain as they die. A hunter is a hunter, and if you can kill a deer, you can kill a person. It's that simple," I replied. "Plus, I wasn't going to say the Green Arrow, maybe Hawkeye or Katniss Everdeen, but definitely not the Green Arrow."

Her eyes became wide, and she turned away from me, heading back to camp. It wasn't hard catching up to her.

"You are such a child," she said, but I could see the smallest grin on her lips.

"Yeah, yeah," I said, taking her hand and pulling her to me. She looked at her hands and then to me. I knew she was somewhat uncomfortable, but she didn't pull away.

"What? Aren't you going to ask me to go steady first?"

"Maybe if we were in the nineteen fifties."

"Have you ever been on a date?" I asked her, causing us to stop.

"I don't date, and you better not try any of that romantic shit on me either," she said.

"Girls like romantic shit." I smiled. She always made me smile, and I wasn't sure if I could bring myself to hide it from her or the world.

"I'm not 'girls.' I'm Melody."

"We can compromise," I said, leaning against one of the tress.

She crossed her arms and stood straighter. "Or I could shoot you."

"Violence is not the answer, love. Well violence against me isn't the answer," I replied, thinking quickly. "We can have private dates. You and I in our bedroom, where only I can see you being kind."

Before she could speak, I pulled her toward me and pressed her up against the tree, kissing her ruthlessly, only to break away.

"On special occasions, we can kill the cops or anyone else who gets in our way in our pajamas again. We can watch as they bleed out and burn, drink wine and have each other over and over again. After all, we are both people hunters," I whispered into the distance between our lips.

She kissed me, pressing her whole body against mine and broke away with a grin. "You sure know how to charm a woman."

Her words made me so hard I lifted her up and pinned her against the bark. *God, I loved my wife.*

"Sir, ma'am," a voice called out from behind us, and right then and there, I wanted to snap his neck. The darkness in Mel's eyes told me she wanted him dead as well.

Breaking away from me, she turned to Fedel who stood with his back turned. "*What!*"

He didn't turnaround. "The jet has been fueled and will be ready to depart. Neither of your phones were working, but your father, sir, has tried to reach you. The police commissioner is giving a statement to the press about the fire in an hour. They also came by the house this morning."

That bitch came to my motherfucking house again? He was just asking to fucking die!

"Are the men ready?" Mel asked, adjusting her clothing, but she didn't need to—she always looked the same—beautiful, deadly, and fuckable.

"Yes, ma'am. Monte and all the others who drove left last night," he answered quickly. He was definitely more afraid of Mel than he was of me. I was going to have to balance that scale as well.

"Leave us," I demanded, and he was gone. Turning to my wife, I tried to breathe calmly, however I wanted the cop fucker dead.

"I'm going to kill him," I told her. "I'll find out—"

"It won't work. You have to break him." She sighed, stepping in front of me. "Killing him is only half the battle. He is becoming a model for the rest of the force. He is becoming a hero. He is going to give some uplifting speech and try and reinstate a hope for better future. It's time we do what we promised to do if he didn't back down."

"We make Chicago bleed," I said, and she nodded.

"When the crime is in the ghettos, no one gives a shit. When the crime makes its way to the suburbs, people demand better from their police officers."

"They begin to distrust them. When they do, we will step forward and remind them why they love the Callahans."

"I will have Declan and Monte hack the records and find all the police officers who have families." She smiled, but it wasn't enough. I wanted the city and the state to cry out in agony.

"Not just the police," I added as we headed back to camp. "I want the names of every judge, politician, and businessman who does not support our family. You step in front of us, we blow a hole through you and every last person who ever knew you."

There would be blood, and lots of it.

MELODY

"People of Chicago, I come to you now because I know you are afraid. I'm from Chicago. I know this city like the back of my hand, and I know that we can get back to the glory days. It's why the Chicago PD is working overtime to make our cities safe. If you see anything, we will protect you if you come forward. It's time we take our city back from those who believe we have given up. From those who think we are just going to allow them to keep—"

"His voice makes me want to shoot myself." I groaned muting the computer in front us. "Maybe we should kill him now. Don't we have snipers in the area?"

Liam drank my wine as he relaxed as well. "You and I both know that would be a bad idea. Tomorrow begins the reign of terror, just hold off another twelve hours."

Sighing, I looked to the computer screen where the idiot was still speaking.

"Does he really believe anyone is going to talk?"

"They would have to be pure idiots," Liam said. However, Fedel stood up and placed another file in front us.

"What is this?" I asked, but the moment I opened it, a grin spread across my face as I handed it to Liam, waiting to see how he would react.

"Jesus Christ, you did this in church?" He laughed, lifting up the hospital photo of Natasha. *I should have just killed her.*

"I was told you saw her for breakfast," I stated, and he looked up to me, eyes wide, before turning to Fedel.

His jaw set as he threw the photo back on the table. "You had me followed?" he hissed.

"The morning you were being an ass," I paused and, grabbing the brandy, added, "the morning you were being a *giant* ass, I had you followed and your ex-girlf—"

"She was a bitch I fucked in the past, not my ex-girlfriend," he snapped.

Leaning in, I made sure he could see my eyes. "I'm not sorry, not even a little bit, and I don't care who she was. She wanted to be a part of your future, and I made sure she knew what would happen if she crossed that line again."

His nose flared but he simply glared at Fedel. "Why are you showing this to us?"

"Ms. Briar filed a police report to Sam, claiming, ma'am, that you were the one who attacked her. Brooks is waiting for your directions," Fedel replied.

"Kill her," he demanded. "I warned her when she ambushed me before."

"That would look bad." I sighed because I really did want the bitch dead. "If she were to be killed, it would be too obvious. She has family. They would realize it, and that is just too many loose ends for one whore."

I just wasn't sure what to do with her.

Liam pinched the bridge of his nose before lifting up the photo again. *"A broken nose and jaw, large abrasions across the forehead, with trace amount of bleach in her throat.*

"Bleach in her throat?"

I shrugged. "They must have used bleach in the toilet bowl I stuck her head in."

He tried not to smile, but I could see his lips twitch up. Shaking his head, he placed the file back down.

"Ninety percent of those wounds could have been self-inflicted. After all she is a very unstable woman with a history of stalking and violent acts in a fit of jealously," he said, seriously, looking over to Declan, who looked much better than he did earlier in the week. He was lucky I had only used my small knife.

"Declan, make sure all records of Natasha Briar list her as mentally unbalanced. Fedel, have Brooks flag her as mentally ill as well by whatever doctor she visited—pay him well enough to make sure he stresses the need to get her 'help'—and by the end of the week, make sure she should be in West Ridge."

"West Ridge is the worst mental hospital in the state, if not the country." I smiled. If Natasha wasn't crazy now, she would be.

"I know. We can kill her after the dust settles." He smiled back.

"How romantic. I hate blondes." I laughed along with him. However, I stopped when I heard a snicker.

"Poor Olivia." Liam turned to Neal. I didn't bother giving him a glance.

"I don't give a shit," I replied, looking out the window. "She should be happy I took it easy on him."

Liam shook his head. "You broke his nose—something I'm starting to see you're good at—and damn well choked the life out of him, then tasered him."

"Are you defending him? I did worse to Declan, and he didn't even shoot you." He was too calm about this, and it pissed me the fuck off.

"I second that," Declan muttered just loud enough so we could hear him.

Liam rolled his eyes. "We're going to war, remember. After tomorrow, hell is going to break loose. We are family, and we need to make sure our personal shit is together. Besides, you stabbed Declan with a knife the size of a dagger."

"Are we seriously discussing the type of weapon used to stab me in the chest?" Declan asked, and it was my turn to roll my eyes.

"It wasn't even really your chest. It was much closer to your shoulder-blade. The worse you needed was stitches, you big baby," I added, and Neal snickered until I glared at him again.

"I have a much bigger knife waiting for you," I snapped.

"If Neal ever shoots anything near me again, I will take off his head and mount it on the fucking wall." He seemed to mean it, but I wasn't sure.

"I still hate him," I replied, drinking.

"Looks like I'm not the only romantic one." He grinned, however, it was interrupted by a cellphone. Neal answered it quickly before handing it to Liam.

"Father." Sighing, Liam placed it on speaker before setting it on the table. "To what do I owe the pleasure?" Liam asked, sitting up straighter. I didn't understand why men always felt the need to prove something to their fathers.

"Liam, Melody, I'm sure you both took time out of your busy schedules to watch the news. The police commissioner is becoming a problem." Sedric's voice sounded hard, like he was trying to control his anger.

"Yes—"

"We are handling it, Sedric. Is that the only reason you called?" I asked before Liam could make a fool out of himself. He looked me dead in the eye, as if I'd lost my mind.

There wasn't a reply at first, just a deep breath. *Did I tick off Sedric? Too fucking bad.*

"Evelyn just received an invitation to a wedding being held here in Chicago for a Saige Rozhkov and Amory Valero."

Liam's eyes narrowed as we looked at each other. Nodding, he took a deep breath.

"We will be attending. If that is all, Father, we must be going," Liam replied, ending the call before he could get another word in.

Rising from our seats, we both walked into our private cabin at the back of the jet. The second the door closed, I began to speak.

"You are the head of this family, not your fucking father. You do not sit up straighter for him. You do not even give him all your fucking attention. And you sure as hell do not answer his questions like you are still second-in-command. The only person who gets that amount of respect is me. You are a leader, so lead. You share with him when you motherfucking feel like it. Not when he calls and barks. You may be his son, but you are not his child. You are *Ceann na Conairte*, and I am the Boss, even to our fathers. If you embarrass me or yourself like that again, I will rip out your throat."

LIAM

She's right. That was the very first thing that went through my mind after she left. I was the *Ceann na Conairte,* not my father. I had seen him as such for so long that it was almost second nature to show him that same respect. Stepping off the plane, Mel stood before none other than Coraline.

"What in Jesus fuck happened to my wife?" Declan asked from behind me.

"What happened to her hair?" Neal asked, staring at the shorthaired girl standing in front of Mel.

Without answering either of them, I walked to my wife only to be met with another shock.

Is that the ugly duckling? Adriana stood beside Coraline, her nest of a hair tamed, her glasses gone, and her face covered in light makeup. She wasn't drop-dead gorgeous, but she didn't deserve the ugly duckling title anymore.

"Adriana, ride with us," was all Mel said when I reached her. "Cora we will talk later."

Once we reached the car, the driver opened the door for us while Adriana took a seat up front.

"I'm guessing you had something to do with this?" I asked Mel once we were on our way home.

"She came to me. I had Adriana do what she could," she replied, not in the least bit worried about how this might turn out. Declan . . . well

Declan really couldn't do shit, and that's probably why she wasn't bothered.

Sighing, I turned to the woman up front. "Well, what can my sister-in-law do?"

"She was difficult the first day, frustrated with herself and the world on the second. The third day, she puked up half her weight, and then the rest of the week she got a lot of the basics down. She will need more practice, but she is getting used to carrying a knife. Mrs. Callahan was right about the gun. She tried it, and almost blew her hand off." I could hear the amusement in her voice. However, my mind couldn't picture Coraline doing any of those things.

"And her hair?" Mel asked.

"She got a little carried away with the whole becoming a warrior thing. She demanded to listen to *Rocky* during one of the morning sessions. Then at night, she wanted to listen to *Eye of the Tiger* on repeat. Eve—Mrs. Callahan found it fitting."

Mel sat up. "I thought I told you to keep this discrete."

"I tried, ma'am. The second and third days were the hardest for Coraline, and she was so sore she couldn't hide it during dinner. Mr. and Mrs. Callahan believe it is just self-defense. Olivia Callahan tried to tell Neal, so I had her phone jammed, ma'am."

Mel frowned but nodded, even though no one else would be able to see her but me.

"I see." I frowned as well. Family dinner tonight was going to be interesting.

"It's nothing to worry about. We have much bigger things on our plate like Saige and Amory," Mel said, hissing out their names as if they were poison.

"Which is why I think we should plan a small trip to Italy."

"Liam, we cannot take out Vance's cars now. It's probably at the bottom of our to-do list." She wasn't getting it though.

"We don't have to go, our men could go. After all, what better time to destroy cars and maybe a home or two while everyone is celebrating a wedding?" They would be so blindsided.

She smirked. "Guerrilla warfare."

"Exactly."

"Adriana, when is the wedding?"

"Three weeks from today, ma'am," she replied quickly, handing us a wedding invitation. Mel stared at it with just as much disgust as I did. Allowing it to drop to the floor, she turned back to me.

"Are you sure you don't mind not being able to physically destroy Vance's things?"

It was the only downside. "Yes, but seeing Vance's face during the wedding when he gets that call will surely make up for it." He wouldn't even be able to publicly display his anger. Instead, he would have to take it up the ass and just smile at me.

She shook her head at me and stared out at the city. I watched her eyes storm over and I wished more than anything I could read her mind. She turned to me with a smirk that I wanted to kiss off her fucking face.

"My father told me once that the world wanted Kate Middleton or the first lady, someone to kiss babies and write big checks on your behalf." She said it slowly, but I still didn't understand.

"You want to write a check?" Why would that get her so excited?

"Yes." She smirked, looking back outside. "To the men and women of the Chicago PD who were injured during those terrible fires. After all, how can they afford all those bills? I even think we should do it in person. I bet our favorite Superintendent and commissioner, Officer Patterson, will be there as well to console the families."

Dear God, I loved my wife.

"Take us to St. John's Medical Hospital." I smiled alongside her, reaching into my jacket for my checkbook.

"Should I make it rich or obnoxiously rich?" I asked, wondering how many zeros to put in the space.

"Obnoxiously rich, of course. Something only a Callahan can do." She grinned, looking toward Adriana. "Adriana, how fast can you leak it to the press?"

"Ten minutes. If you would like to change, I brought clothing. It's in the back," she answered, already dialing.

She had standby clothes?

Mel nodded, taking off her seatbelt as she climbed into trunk of the car.

"Seriously? How un-first-lady-like?" I grinned, looking back at her.

"Shut the fuck up, you Irish asshole and keep your eyes forward."

"Why? I've seen it all before?" She smirked. "We wouldn't want our driver peeking, would we?" My eyes narrowed at the man behind the steering wheel. At her words, he visibly tensed. She knew I would watch him like a hawk, which would stop me from staring at her.

I would have to make her pay later on tonight.

MELODY

"The Chicago Police Department is important to the wellbeing of this city. My husband and I do not want our men and women in uniform to worry about the medical bills or their livelihoods after protecting us. It is my great honor to present this check for nineteen million dollars to our commissioner and superintendent, Officer Patterson." I smiled into the cameras that stood in the ER wing of St. John's Hospital. Officer

Patterson glared at me with a mixture of hate, anger, and disgust. But he took the money anyway.

"Thank you so much, Mrs. Callahan," he said, practically sneering through his teeth. "I'm sure this will help the families who lost love ones and those injured, overwhelmingly so."

Liam smirked beside me. "It was such a tragedy. Those old factories should be checked. Aren't they also known for their crime? Are the police looking into this?"

Commissioner Patterson opened his mouth, but the reporters heard Liam's questions and jumped on him.

"Commissioner Patterson, is this going to be one of the things you plan on fixing in Chicago?"

"Commissioner, is there going to be an investigation?"

"Is it true your house was also destroyed?"

"Rumor has it that this was a terrorist attack?"

"Did this have anything to do with your investigation of Flight 735?" That caught my attention, and Liam's apparently because his jaw tightened.

"Ladies and gentlemen, this is a hospital, and we do not want to bother any of the patients that are here in need of medical attention," Commissioner Patterson told them all as politely as he could.

A doctor stepped forward as the reporters fanned out. She looked almost star struck as she stared into Liam's eyes.

Could she still be a doctor if I cut off her hands?

"Mr. Callahan, I'm Dr. Amy Lewis, thank you so much for the donation. Your family has been so kind to the patients of this hospital as well as the staff. It would be our honor to show you around. I'm sure the victims of this accident would love to meet you," she gushed, while I tried not to vomit in my mouth.

"I don't believe that would be a good idea," Commissioner Patterson stated, causing the whole staff to look at him like he was crazy . . . most likely because he was.

"It's been a *difficult* couple of days. They may need their rest."

"I assure you, we are doing or best for every patient her," Dr. Lewis replied, but only because she wanted to spend more time with my husband.

Stepping in front of Liam, I smiled like I was in a fucking Crest commercial. "Of course, I would love to meet them. Sweetheart, do you have time?"

Liam raised an eyebrow at me. "Anything you wish, my love."

Dr. Amy Lewis looked like she came in her scrubs at the sound of his voice. *I wonder if I can smash her head in?*

"Where are we going first?"

She seemed startled by my voice, as if she had forgotten I was still here. I felt my hand slide to the back of my pants toward my knife when Liam grabbed me, pulling me into his arms.

"Control yourself, love," he hissed into my ear.

Taking a deep breath, we followed the stupid bitch as she led us toward another part of the hospital.

"This is our burn unit where many of the officers are being treated," she replied, moving down the hall as if she were putting the men on display.

I wasn't sure what it was that made me stop in front of one of the officer's rooms. Maybe it was all the flowers, cards, and balloons. Or maybe it was the small girl who sat in her mother's lap, laughing with her burned father that did it. The side of his face was wrapped in bandages along with both of his arms, but he was still alert.

Stepping in, the family froze and looked to us.

"Officer Pope, this is Mr. and Mrs. Callahan. As of a few moments ago, they have paid off all your bills," Dr. Amy-what's-her-face stated, joyfully.

The woman in the chair broke out into sobs before running up and giving me a hug. I was not a hugger. However, I couldn't be myself.

"Thank you so very much. You have no idea how much this means to my family," she cried, stepping back to adjust herself and pick up her daughter.

"Anything to help. I can't imagine the life you live," I said softly. "Always worrying if your husband will get wounded, or even worse. It's the least we can do."

"Thank you. Really, thank you." She wiped her face, turning to her daughter. "Tell Mrs. Callahan, thank you, sweetheart."

The small girl hid behind her hair. "Thanks."

"Let's go tell Grandpapa the good news," she replied, looking back to her husband for a moment, who nodded slowly.

"There's that first lady," Liam whispered, kissing the back of my head and handing me a cup of coffee.

"Mr. and Mrs. Callahan," Dr. Amy, the whore, called out.

"Liam, I will stay," I told him. He gave me an odd look before exiting with the rest of them.

Officer Pope simply glared at me, and I knew he had an idea of who we really were underneath the public mask.

"I have no idea why people choose to become police officers." I frowned, looking over his burnt skin, half of his face was basically melted off.

"Someone has to put people like you away," he struggled to say.

Raising an eyebrow, I smiled. "That's never going to happen, and if it were, it wouldn't be you. I've seen better looking beef jerky."

"I could have a wire," he hissed out, and I rolled my eyes while reaching over to push on his wrapped skin. He cried out softly.

"You don't have a wire, and even if you did, I have a frequency jammer. If that didn't work, then I would kidnap your family until you confess to tampering evidence to falsely arrest me." I wasn't an idiot, and after all, we were in a hospital full of cops.

His eyes narrowed. "Aren't you ashamed of yourself? Don't you have guilt? Or are you all just heartless, cold-blooded snakes? Your drugs kill dozens of people in this city alone, just in one week. God knows how many people die in this country just so you can make a buck. You all are sick. How the hell do you sleep at night?"

"Who did you lose?" I asked him, taking a sip of my coffee. His words didn't bother me.

"You don't give a damn."

"Nope, not at all." I smiled. "You see, you're blaming me for something that isn't my fault. Do you blame a bartender for giving someone a drink? No, because he is supplying a demand. No one is forcing anyone to do or take anything. Whoever died, it was on them and their family. They should have gotten their shit together. Their family should have stood by them. Instead, you look for someone to blame."

"You must be fucked up in the head to think like that. There ain't any justification for what you people do," he snapped, looking away. "You insult us more by pretending you're good Catholic folk.

You don't care about God. I don't think you even believe in Him."

"I do. I care about God, and I do believe in Him." I really did. "However, I know why I was created. God needs me. What would happen if there weren't people like me? If the world were perfect, if everything was the way you wished it to be, then why would you pray? God needs me, because without us, you forget about Him. He is on my side, not yours."

"We will see about that. The commissioner has his eye on you all. He won't rest until you are all in jail!"

"Then I'll rip out his eyes and put him six feet under. You should thank God you are in here, because after tomorrow, Chicago will never be the same. You can tell the commissioner I said that," I replied, leaving the coffee cup with my lipstick imprint on the counter before turning to leave.

"By the way, I sleep perfectly fine at night. It's all about the thread count."

I smiled at him once more before leaving. Chicago would burn, and they would know it was their fault. Once the smoke cleared and the dust settled, we would rebuild. But we would own this motherfucking city.

Stepping into the corner, I placed a call.

"Put Officer Pope and his family on the list."

"Yes, ma'am."

TWENTY-THREE

"Courage is the power to let go of the familiar."

—Raymond Lindquist

SEDRIC

"I believe your son and his wife just dismissed me."
My nose flared as I clutched onto the phone in my
hands.

"Why is it whenever they do something wrong,
they magically become 'mine'?" my wife asked as
she dressed.

"Because . . ."

"Choose your words carefully, dear."

Walking up behind her, I grabbed her waist
pulling her to me. "I ruled once. I was king, and yet
my own children are dismissing me as if I were a
butler. When did I fall so far?"

She laughed, turning back to me. "My dear, you
were king, and when you were, no one could speak a
word to you. Your word was law, and those around
you listened. Neither your sons nor I could talk you
out of anything you wished. But you gave up your
crown because it no longer fit. In doing so, you

agreed to allow Liam and Mel to rule as they wished."

"They may bloody well destroy this family." I pouted as she kissed me.

"Then let them. We have more than enough independently to leave and never be found if we wish. However, you and I both know they aren't destroying this family." She was right, but I didn't like it.

"I just wish they would—"

"No. You promised me you would only get involved if they asked. They haven't, so stay the fuck out of it. You have done your part. I just want my husband."

Staring into her eyes, I nodded before grabbing hold of her shirt and ripping it from her body. Buttons popped off her like bullets.

"Then have him, because he definitely wants you," I whispered before ripping her bra off her as well. Her breasts jiggled free, and I smirked to myself before taking them into my mouth.

She moaned my name, and the last thing on my mind was my children, or their chaos.

TWENTY-FOUR

"We don't murder, we kill ... You don't murder animals, you kill them."

—Samuel Fuller

MELODY

Flipping on the television, I couldn't help but grin.

"Three weeks ago, Commissioner Patterson, you stood before us all and promised to make this city safe! You promised that you would put an end to the blood and corruption, but instead, all you have done is made it worse! For three weeks, it has been raining blood! The death count is up to twenty-seven that we know of. Most of them innocent people who just want to live their lives in peace. People are dying left and right! You did this!" A man yelled out in the crowd.

"My son was walking home for school. He walked that same path every day and then ..." A mother sobbed with a photo of her son in her hands.

"Twenty-seven in the suburbs, fifty-four in the city, two a day in the most poverty stricken parts of

the city. Commissioner Patterson, is this the new normal?" a reporter asked.

Commissioner Patterson looked old, tired, and stressed as he tried to find the words.

"The Chicago Police Department is . . ."

"The Chicago Police Department is no safer than we are! How many men and woman have we lost in the last three weeks?"

"We have lost at total of nineteen men in the line of duty." Commissioner Patterson sighed. I could feel the defeat coming through the screen.

"How can you keep us safe, if you can't even keep your own people safe?"

"Is the FBI going to get involved?"

"Nope," I said aloud and even if they did I had more than a few friends I could call on.

"Each one of these instances has been at the hands of multiple criminals, leaving them up to the Chicago Police Department to solve. However, they will be consulting on many of the cases involved." The Commissioner stood firm.

"Will the Governor call for a state emergency?"

"Not if he wants to lose his next election." I'm sure he was a friend of the families, Coraline held a function for him.

"We are not at that point yet. I understand how frightened you all are, but please don't lose faith in us. It is what the people who are responsible for this all want."

"Do you know who is responsible? Some have speculated this is because of the Irish Mob, others say there was a breakout at the county jail."

I wanted to listen to his reply. However, I was distracted by the man kissing my neck from behind. Leaning into him, I allowed myself to relax.

"Keeping an eye on our city?" he whispered when he came up for air. Wrapping his arms around me, he pulled me closer.

"The Commissioner seems stressed." I smirked, reaching up to run my hand through his hair.

"With all the murders, robberies and bad press, I would be stressed as well." He snickered. Turning me to him, his eyes went straight to my breasts, but that's what I got for standing in my underwear as I watched the news.

"Like what you see?" I whispered to him while pulling on his tie.

His eyes were coated with lust before he shook his head clear. "Yes, very much so, and as much as I would enjoy making you scream my name until your voice cracked, we have a very important wedding to get to."

"You're turning down sex for a wedding?"

"It's not just any wedding love." He pouted. "It's Saige and Amory's wedding, which means . . ."

"Which means you get to sit and eat their food and drink wine, while our men fuck them across the ocean."

"And I don't want to be late for a moment of it."

Stepping closer to him, I retied the bowtie around his neck. "Of course not. Who would like to have sex when they could watch Vance lose control? Who knows when that could happen again. You won't be having sex with anyone for a while either, but still."

I kissed him deeply, biting onto his lip before breaking away. His mouth dropped open as my words sunk in. "Sweetheart . . ."

"This body is now closed to you, husband." Stepping away from him, I turned to walk to my closet but he pulled me back.

"Let's not do anything rash," he replied lifting me up and throwing me on the bed, crawling on top of me as he brushed my hair back.

"We don't have time." I smiled as he kissed me.

"We're the guests of honor. We can make time," he whispered kissing from my lips to my cheek and then to my neck.

Pushing up against him, I was able to flip him onto his back. Sitting on his waist, I stared into his eyes.

"You made your choice, husband now deal with it." I smirked as I ground my hips into him before rising, and sure enough his hard-on was clear to the world.

"Wife."

"Husband." I smiled, and the moment I took off toward my closet, he leapt off the bed after me.

Sadly, he was too slow, and I was able to lock myself in my closet.

"Damn it!" He pounded on the door as I laughed.

"Calm the fuck down and finish getting dressed," I called out as I looked for the shoes I wanted to wear.

"Take off your underwear. You won't be needing them tonight!"

"The fuck I will! You aren't getting shit from me," I replied even though I couldn't stop grinning.

"Fine then, I will rip the bloody things off you." His voice was fading, and I rolled my eyes at him.

Hearing the door close, I smiled to myself. In the last three weeks, my relationship with Liam had changed drastically. We no longer fought with one about personal matters. Instead, most of our issues were with the job, and even those were few and far between. Sometimes our plan of attack didn't mesh well, and the only way we could settle it was to "fuck it out." Neither of us complained about that though, and I was sure he disagreed with me sometimes just so we could have sex afterward, the little prick. Yet, I found myself smiling more often because of him. I was happy, and that just seemed odd to me.

He insisted we have our "dates" at least once a week. The first week was awkward because I hated the word date and neither of us did anything really but work. The second week he brought me a snitch, a lower-level pawn who had been in the process of speaking with the police to get out of jail time. Too bad for him, we wire tapped all our men's phones. To make an example of him, I gave him embalming fluid to drink and when he died, we made sure to ship his tongue to the Commissioner.

After that, Liam and I didn't come out of our room for two days. The date we had this week consisted of Liam and I both naked on our bed watching the local news. We had scheduled a hit on three officers and their families.

"Ma'am, it's Adriana. I have your dress." Adriana knocked. Opening the door, I pulled the dress from the bag.

"Perfect." I smiled, touching the satin of the dress.

LIAM

Stepping out of our bedroom, I tried to wipe the grin off my face. However, it was damn near impossible. I hadn't known before that I would have no other choice than to say I was in love with Melody Nicci Callahan. I loved how she broke people's noses, how she smiled whenever we killed someone. I loved the way she moaned my name while we made love, only to slap me afterward. She was ruthless in everything she did, and yet she could still manage to be open with me. We had both changed. I felt like

I had known her for a lifetime and not just a few weeks.

"So I'm guessing by your smile that all is well in your bloody wonderland?" Sedric asked me as I reached the study.

He was decked to the nines like myself and seemed just as excited as I was, despite the fact that he didn't know any of our plans.

"Yes, father," I said stepping into the study. "All is well in our bloody wonderland. In fact, the adventure is just beginning."

He sighed, taking a seat in front of the desk. "Must you torture me boy, or will you tell me what is going on? Half the city is covered in blood and the other half is afraid of its shadow. Both you and Melody insisted that we attend this mockery of a wedding. However, neither Neal nor Declan are going to be in attendance."

"You always said I was impatient. If so, I see where I get it from," I replied pouring myself a glass of wine.

"I'm guessing you and Melody are no longer shooting at each other."

"For now. My wife's opinion of me changes more often than the tide. She may shoot me tomorrow if I tell her I dislike her gun collection."

"But at this moment—"

"Are you asking as my father or as a *Ceann na Conairte?*" I cut him off leaning into my chair because it was *my* chair and not his. Kicking my feet onto the desk I watched as his eyes narrowed at my shoes. He used to hate it when I placed my feet on his desk as a teen, but he couldn't say anything now.

"I'm asking as a father. Son, are you happy with your wife?"

"Yes, father, everything is bloody and well in fucking wonderland." I drank some more. "She is . . . she is Bloody Melody and perfect. God created her and then shattered the mold afterward, for the world could not handle two of her."

"Look who has become a poet."

"Hardly, it was a simple fact." My wife was a ruthless animal, and it only made her sexier.

"So then I could expect something to go terribly wrong at this wedding." He really wanted to know. It was almost sad.

"I hope when I have a child, I'm not in the predicament you are in." I laughed at him.

"Knowing you, I doubt you will allow your son or daughter to take the throne as easily as I did." He was joking. He had to be joking.

"Bullshit. The amount of hell you put me through—"

"I put you through hell so you could sit in that seat and call hell to you. In three weeks, you have brought this city to its knees." He almost sounded jealous, but I could also hear the pride.

"We, Melody and I, brought it to its knees. However, it's not bowing yet. The police commissioner is still holding out for hope to overcome the mess. A judge gave him the okay to place wiretaps on the house and our phones." I snickered. That was only after the first week.

"When was this?"

"It doesn't matter." I grinned drinking again. "We had jammers and frequency scramblers placed throughout the house, and then updated all the phones. Melody insisted that we make an example out of the judge."

I waited for it to click in, after all it had been all over the news that week. He shook his head as the realization hit him.

"Judge Randal. They found him hanging from the bridge. I figured, but I didn't understand why."

"I don't believe the commissioner has had any help with the courts since then." Because they were fucking smart.

"And you both don't want to end him?" Oh, how the tide had turned.

"And let another wannabe hero take his place? He is about to break, and when he does, his moral compass will either force him to take his life or he will just drink himself to death. Either way I don't give a flying two fucks." He picked a fight, and now he was going to lose.

"Bloody wonderland," he said again with a smile. There was a knock at the door, before I could reply.

"Enter," I called out and in walked my mother dressed in a beautiful long-sleeved, green dress.

"You look beautiful mother," I said, standing up to greet her.

She kissed my cheek. "Thank you, son. I came to tell you that there are two officers at our door. They're asking to speak with you. I thought I would let you know personally. This is the third time, Liam. I'm not pleased."

Rule Sixteen: Never displease your mother.

"Call my wife."

"No need." Melody stepped inside, making me want to drop to my knees and kiss her feet. She was an absolute vision in the long, strapless white dress she wore. She looked like a goddess or an angel, and I felt lucky to even stand before her.

"Father, Mother, thank you. However, my wife and I have some business to attend to. We shall meet you at the wedding."

"Please send the officers in," my Mel replied as she walked, more like glided, toward me.

Taking her hand, I kissed it once my parents were gone. "You look beyond beautiful."

"Save your flattery and tell me we are going to kill these sons of bitches for returning here." She glared as she fixed my hair.

There was another knock at the door, and I smirked at her.

"Let's find out." I grinned, walking to my desk. "Enter." Sadly it wasn't the commissioner, but his Smokey the Bear sidekick along with another broad-shouldered man with orange hair.

"No commissioner? I'm insulted." I turned to Mel who only glared at them.

"The city is a bit too chaotic for him to make it," Smokey said. "As you know I—"

"We don't care. What do you want?" Mel asked, looking at the younger man next to Smokey.

"We're here to wave the white flag," the orange-haired man declared.

I felt my brow rise and a smirk curl my lip. When I looked over to Mel, she frowned. Of course she would, white flags weren't her forte.

Stepping toward the man, I looked him over. "You're Irish."

"Yes, Mr. Callahan."

"Who the fuck forgot to recruit you?" I snickered. Most of all the Irish-born natives in the damn state worked for me in some form.

He glared at me. "I wanted to be the first of my family to do right by the law."

"Well then, as you can see, we are on our way out."

Mel replied stepping toward me. "We will speak to the commissioner at a later time. You both found your way in, I believe you know the way out. Please give Officer Pope and his family my regards."

They couldn't speak and that may have been due to the fact that she looked sinfully beautiful in white, or because Officer Pope and his family were no longer alive. They nodded with rage building in their eyes. The door slammed once they exited.

She turned to me and frowned, straightening my tie again. "You know they were lying right?"

"Yes, and what do we do with liars?" I asked my hands on her hips. She smiled as well, reaching into my tuxedo jacket to pull out my phone.

"Monte, two officers should be leaving the premises. Please make sure to escort them back to the station. You and I both know how tricky those high bridges can be." I watched her mouth as she spoke, and I wanted nothing more than to kiss the breath from her lips.

She noticed once she hung up and placed her finger on them.

"Candy store is still closed." She glared. "After all, you want to see Vance's face instead."

"Lov—" She didn't even allow me to finish speaking before she walked away. *Damn it all to hell. Vance better fucking cry and piss in his fucking pants.*

MELODY

"Shoot me, please." I groaned as I watched Amory and Saige kiss. It was like they were trying to suck the skin off each other's faces.

"Not before you shoot me," Liam whispered back. His eyebrows wouldn't stop twitching, and had it only been us, I would have laughed over it. However, it wasn't just us. We were surrounded by at least three hundred of Vance's closest "family and friends." The wedding was so boring that Liam and I spent most of our time texting Declan and Neal for updates.

But it was game time now. Taking our seat at table five, with the rest of the Callahans, we waited for the text message signaling it was done. However, the true fireworks didn't start until Vance got the call. I was tempted to tell them myself. However, Vance still thought I was some little lamb unaware of the world around me. He was a fucking idiot. From Saige's letters, he must have known I was the child who was spared on the plane. However, he still didn't see me as a threat.

"Black, Red, and White just doesn't seem right for this time of year." Coraline frowned as she looked around the wedding hall.

"Yes," I replied, looking Olivia up and down. "Adding red to the color scheme was a bad choice."

Olivia's blue eyes narrowed on me. "So is wearing white to another woman's wedding."

"There are very few people I consider to be 'women.' Saige is a snake," I said drinking water. "Don't ask what I consider you to be."

Evelyn sighed while Liam snickered. Sedric was too busy checking his watch. He was dying to see what was going to happen as well.

"There is no hope for you two is there?" Evelyn asked Olivia and me.

"Not if she keeps harming my husband and then forcing him on assignments when he should be by my side," Olivia said.

"Olivia, snap at me again and you won't have a husband. In fact, I would just as soon kill you and move on. You're not worth anything anyway, so do us all a favor and sit in the corner like a good little trophy." I rolled my eyes at her as Liam's phone went off.

Tilting it to me, I watched as a very expensive looking house, along with one too many cars went up in flames. The cameras caught every angle of the house, including two women banging on the door trying to free themselves.

"And they are?"

"Apparently Vance and Amory shared two special friends." Liam snickered, and I could see the reflection of fire in his green eyes.

"That's disgusting. Saige should be thanking me." The thought made me want to puke in my mouth.

"She's calling someone," Sedric said. Liam and I looked over at him and tried not to laugh. He had switched seats with Evelyn just to see the fucking phone. Evelyn looked to me and winked, drinking her wine.

"I think I know who," Coraline said, causing us all to follow her gaze to Vance who was in the middle of giving his son a speech. He glanced at his phone for a moment before going on.

"... it is for this reason I would like to welcome my daughter Saige Valero to the family. May she and my son make us all proud."

Everyone but us applauded loudly. When Vance gave the microphone to Jane, I believe her name was, Saige's maid of honor, he went to answer his phone. Sadly, it was too late, because Liam and I could see that the woman had passed out, probably due to the smoke. Putting his phone away, Liam took my hand and kissed it as we watched Vance listen to his messages. His back was turned to us but the moment he hung up after placing another call, he turned to us, his eyes were wide and deadly. All the "emotion" he had during the wedding was gone, and all that was left was this monster. It looked like he'd squeezed the phone so hard the screen cracked. Liam smirked and gave him a short nod as if they were friends.

"Do you think he is angry?"

"One can only hope, love."

"Entertaining indeed." Sedric smirked, leaning back into his chair.

"That was only the first course father." Liam grinned, and I couldn't wait for dessert.

LIAM

I didn't make a habit of smoking. However, this damn wedding had gone on for far too long. Amory was now fully aware, which had to mean his new wife was as well. The tension between us, as we pretended to be nothing more than guests, was boiling under the surface. Even the way Saige cut her steak, which was so rare it looked like it was dripping blood, seem to antagonize us. She glared at Mel with so much hatred even Olivia had to look away. My Mel smiled at her as if she hadn't noticed. I knew she had though. The clicking noise under the table as she loaded her gun with one hand was proof enough.

So I took a small smoking break inside the bathroom stall like I was still in high school. Neal and Declan had been my role models until the point my mother found them and beat their asses so badly that they couldn't sit. That was the last time either of them smoked. I, on the other hand, had never been caught.

Maybe Mel could beat it out of me?

"Did you see Callahan's bitch?" a voice called out from the other side of the stall.

"The Italian wench in white?" another replied, and I felt myself freeze.

"What I wouldn't give to fuck the shit out of her tight pussy. I would ride the fuck out of her until she broke down like a good little cunt whore. Then—" He didn't get to finish for the simple fact that I stepped out of the stall and put a bullet in the back of his friend's head.

The body fell onto the urinal he was pissing in. The man beside him—how dare he call my wife a whore, cunt, and bitch—stood with his pants down in shock. I knew him. He was Amory's best man, Alex.

He turned to me, opening his mouth to speak, but I took the liberty of grabbing him by his hair and smashing his head against the marble above the urinal.

"That Italian wench is my fucking wife!" I yelled, using his head as a hammer against the wall.

"You don't talk of her as you piss." *Slam.*

"You don't talk of her, period. You don't call her anything but fucking Mrs. Callahan." *Slam.*

"And you sure as fuck don't talk of her with your fucking hand on your dick." *Slam. Slam. Slam.*

Releasing his head, which was covered in blood and brain matter, I watched as his body fell to the ground. He most likely died after the first two hits into the wall, but all I could fucking see was red. I wanted his head to come off his fucking shoulders. Sighing, I turned to the mirror to find my suit covered in blood.

With a groan, I reached into my jacket and pulled out my phone. "Eric, I need a new suit as fast as possible," I told him as I washed the blood from my hands. Looking down, I noticed the blood spreading across the marble floor and onto my fucking shoes.

"Damn it. Get me new shoes as well."

Hanging up, I dried my hands and stared at the bodies around me, just as another fool stepped in. He froze, looking first at the blood and then to me.

"Anger issues," I said to him reaching for my gun. "Step into my office."

He tried to turn and run but I shot him right in the spine, and his legs gave out.

"Guess you won't be stepping anywhere, huh?" I asked him before blowing a hole through his face. Again, the blood splattered onto my hands, and I couldn't help but groan once more.

"See what you made me do?" I asked the dead man before locking the door and rewashing my hands.

The worst things happened when you smoked. But thank God for silencers, I thought to myself.

MELODY

When Liam sat back down, he kissed my cheek. I looked him over quickly and something didn't seem right.

"Did you change?" It looked like the same suit but only fresher, like he hadn't been wearing it all day.

"Why would I do that?" he asked me, but there was a glint in his eye.

"Don't play coy with me."

He smirked, kissing me once more and whispering, "Later, love."

"So what's next on the menu?" Sedric asked as he wiped the corners of his mouth.

Evelyn smacked on his chest. "Will you stop? You're like a child at Disneyland."

"Bloody Wonderland, actually." Liam smirked. I wasn't sure what that meant but Sedric did, and I guess that was all that mattered.

"Liam and I have to say hello before any more excitement occurs." I smiled as Liam and I stood.

Saige and Amory must have had the same idea because they were walking right to us.

We met them in the middle of the dining hall.

"Mr. and Mrs. Valero, congratulations. You and this wedding were beautiful." I smiled reaching out for Saige's hand.

"Thank you, Mrs. Callahan." Saige smiled back, shaking my hand. "And kudos to you for wearing white and not caring what people think of you."

"My family's opinion is all that matters to me." Which was bullshit because only my opinion, and sometimes Liam's, mattered to me.

"Yes, our apologies about your father then." Amory bit his lip at me with lust in his eyes. He reached over to shake my hand, but Liam grabbed his wrist and forced him to shake his.

"I'm quite possessive," he told him. "I'm sorry about your best man."

I looked to him confused for a quick moment before Amory and Saige scanned the room quickly.

"What did you—?"

"Thank you so much for the lovely evening. However, Liam and I aren't fireproof," I interrupted and Saige turned to me, confused once more.

"What?"

"Fire!" someone yelled behind us, and sure enough, flames were breaking out above us.

"What a shame, you should try to save your gifts. The big one is usually a blender." Liam grinned.

The room broke out in panic. The people looked like animals trying to leave a watering hole. They tripped, pushed, and pulled at one another to make it out the doors.

"You want war! I will fucking give your war!" Amory roared at us.

"It's always been war. Don't cry because you're losing." Liam grinned.

"I'm going to fucking kill you!" Saige yelled at us.

"We're looking forward to seeing you try." I smiled. "By the way I lied, your dress is hideous and this wedding . . . well it sucked so badly even a blind man couldn't stand to look at it."

"You little bitc—"

"Ma'am we have to go!" A guard of theirs yelled as she pulled them away. Liam and I stared around as the fire spread.

"Have you both lost your minds?" Olivia screamed over the chaos of the room. So many people, so few doors.

"Liam!" Evelyn and Coraline yelled while Sedric watched in glory. He knew we wouldn't be stupid enough to trap ourselves.

"Enough," Liam snapped at them, and I saw the flames in his eyes again. It turned me on. I couldn't deny that.

Taking my hand, we nodded at them to follow us. Everyone was so busy trying to run to the front door that they didn't even notice us. Liam pushed opened a small part of the wall we'd had installed after discovering the wedding location.

The moment it opened, Declan and Neal stepped through. Coraline and Olivia both ran into their husband's arms, and I felt tempted to roll my eyes. We had called them back just in time to pull this off correctly.

"Save it, let's go."

The men being . . . Callahan men . . . made sure we *girls* went through the new tunnel first, however I waited at the door for Liam. He was the last to exit, and as we closed the door, we met the eyes of Vance as his men tried to pull him away. I smiled at him before giving him the middle finger just as Liam shut it completely. Turning back to me, he grinned.

"So mature."

"You're jealous you didn't do it." I smirked as we walked through the underground tunnel.

"Next time. I really hope he doesn't die." He pouted looking back as we reached the lake. There was a boat waiting for us.

"No, he isn't going to die. He's too big of an ass to die so easily." I smirked as he helped me onto the boat.

"I swear you're both pyromaniacs." Declan laughed as he handed us a glass of champagne.

Looking back over at the mansion behind us, I couldn't help but agree.

"Where to sis?" Neal yelled from the steering wheel. Olivia hugged him as he moved us further and further away from the home.

"The city," Liam and I said together. Everyone broke off into their own private conversations giving me time to turn to Liam.

"It's later."

He rolled his eyes. "There was a little hiccup in the bathroom. It got messy, I killed two . . . three men and had to change. Nothing major."

"You need to control your temper." I leaned in to kiss him.

"One of these days I will . . . maybe." He kissed me back.

Motherfucking day made.

TWENTY-FIVE

"My husband and I have never considered divorce. Murder sometimes, but never divorce."

—Joyce Brothers

OLIVIA

"So you're okay with what just happened?" I wasn't even sure where to begin. Neal didn't respond but started to change out of his tuxedo.

"Neal!"

"What Olivia, *what!*" he yelled, throwing his tie onto the bed.

"Don't you 'what' me! We just set a mansion on fire—"

"You didn't do shit. Melody and Liam did," he interrupted me as he walked into the closet.

"Exactly, and it was wrong! How many people just died?" He was acting like he didn't care. But this had to have bothered him. I was so angry that I wanted to kill them all.

He looked at me like I was insane. "It's the job, Olivia. I don't give a shit about who died. I'm not paid to give a shit. This family is all I care about, and you know that, so save me your bull about the innocent."

Crossing my arms across my chest, I glared at him and bit my tongue to stop myself from saying what it was I really wanted to say.

"They are reckless and callous, which isn't a good combination! They have no idea what they are doing! You sell drugs! You are not murderers! How old is Melody? Twenty-four, twenty-five? She walks around like she owns the goddamn world!" I hated her the fucking most.

"Because she does!" he snapped, stomping out of the closet and into my face.

"No, she doesn't, and neither does Liam. He shouldn't even be *Ceann na Conairte*! You should be. This is all fucked up! They treat you as if you're a fucking dog. They treat us all like we are their fucking pets. She shot you twice! And each time you defend them! You are the oldest. You are the strongest. You should be *Ceann na Conairte*!" There, I fucking said it.

He shook his head at me and sighed before taking a seat on the bed. I fell to my knees in front of him and kissed his hands.

"You have always allowed Liam to hold the past over you. Now his wife is doing the same, and she isn't even—"

"Enough, Olivia," he replied so coldly I flinched. "Do you want to get a divorce?"

My jaw dropped open as I stared at him. "Neal you can't . . . What? No, I don't want a fucking divorce."

I got to my feet as he stared at me. He stood up, walking to my closet and started to pull out my things.

"Neal, what in seven hells are you doing? I don't want a divorce!" I yelled again trying to stop him.

"That's the only way I know how to protect you. We could get divorced, you would have to get a new identity, and I would leave you enough money that you wouldn't have to worry. Once Melody and Liam found out they would most likely have you killed. You speak French right? France could be good for you, the shopping, the—"

"Shut up you asshole! We have vows. I'm not divorcing you. I would rather have them kill me." His words stung, and I tried to fight the tears that were building up in my eyes as he pulled me in and kissed me hard, but it was only when he broke away from my lips did he finally truly look at me.

He kissed my forehead and I stayed in his embrace. I loved his arms. I felt protected, and loved, and special.

"I love you, Olivia, I truly do," he whispered. "But I love my family more. If it came down to Melody and Liam and this family, I have to choose them. It's in my blood to choose them. I want you at my side, but you need to understand that we are family and we are pawns. Melody and Liam rule, which means when they call, you answer. They tell you to jump and you try to reach the sky."

"Neal—"

He pulled back so I could stare into his eyes "No. Listen to me Olivia. Just because I am firstborn does not give me any right to be *Ceann na Conairte*. I don't want to be *Ceann na Conairte*. Melody and Liam were born on the dark side of the moon. They enjoy this life. They watch people burn in their beds. When they aren't doing that, they are making sure needles stay in people's arms and coke in their noses. That is all they do all the time. It's what you do when you're the *Ceann na Conairte*. I watched our father go half-mad because of what he was forced to do. I've watched my mother dip herself in cement just so she could stand beside him and not break. She wasn't always so tough. This life changes us. It forces us to become cold-blooded and not to care for anyone but the family. I handle being a sidekick, because I don't want to walk so deeply in the dark. I do not want *us* to walk so deeply in the dark."

"So what am I supposed to do?" I hissed, breaking out of his hands. "Bow down to them as though they are King and Queen."

He looked at the clothes on the ground and then at me. "You have three options—bow, hide, or die, Olivia. So yes, you will bow down and kiss the ring like we all do. You will jump when they ask, come when they call, and anything else. Or, you can be packed by the time I get back."

He walked past me and toward the door before turning again. "I knew when you married me that you loved the idea of power just as much as you did me. I knew you wanted all the things that came with being a Callahan. I've tried to give it all to you, but you need to understand Olivia, you are not the queen, you are the princess. You will always be the princess. You may wear a tiara, but it will never be as big or as shiny as Melody's. Hopefully you love me enough to be just Princess."

"Neal—" He slammed the door.

"I do love you," I whispered to myself. Falling to my knees, I gathered my things and put them back into the closet.

Tracing my tattoo on my wrist, I sighed. He was right. I did love the idea of power when we got married. I was so excited to be marrying a Callahan, and Neal Callahan at that. I thought all my pain would go away. But in the back of my mind, I could still hear his voice sometimes. He was like this never-ending part of me that wouldn't go away. No matter how many times I tried to wash him off me, he was still there. I married Neal for a lot of reasons. First because I really did love him, and second, because I knew he wouldn't dare come after me as a Callahan. I thought I could have it all—the fame, the husband, and the protection. Neal thought it was his fault we couldn't have children, but the truth was it was mine. It was because of what that monster and his friends did to me. They broke me.

Even after all this time, I still couldn't speak about it. I felt disgusted with myself, and at first I thought Neal would be, too. I knew better now. I knew he loved me, which is why I knew he would hunt him down. I just didn't know if I was ready to face that darkness yet. Melody had taken the seat I wanted, but I had Neal. I still hated her, but I had Neal and I wasn't ready to lose him yet either. So I would bow and kiss the fucking ring.

TWENTY-SIX

"Truth will come to sight; murder cannot be hid long."

—William Shakespeare

MELODY

"I hate you," I hissed again as I ate my French toast.

Liam rolled his eyes, flipping the files in front of him. "We're in public, sweetheart."

"They can all fuck themselves with these dull knives for all I bloody care." I looked around his favorite restaurant to find at least ten pairs of eyes staring at us as if we were some kind of movie stars. Well, we *were* some kind of stars, but it was still annoying as fuck.

"Careful, they may stop seeing you as America's darling." He smirked, drinking his coffee in disdain. I knew he would prefer brandy and right now, so would I.

"They can have their fake darling back after we dump Amory and Saige's bodies in one of the Great Lakes," I said in Irish.

351

"Patience, love."

Gripping the knife in my hands, I felt my nostrils flare. "To hell with patience. It's been four months since their wedding. Since then, they have burned half our fields in Mexico, killed seven of our men in Italy, and cut off thirty percent of our weed from the east. Which you should know costs us about a hundred million every week. I want their heads on a stake, and I want it fucking yesterday. But somehow, you fucking convinced me to wait. So fuck you and fuck them and fuck this goddamn hat I have to fucking wear!"

I wanted to take off the giant yellow sun hat and throw it at him, but that would bring too much attention to myself. Pinching the bridge of my nose, I tried to breathe. The past four months had been an all-out war. The Valero were coming at us with everything they had. We expected as much. However, with the cops now watching us more than ever, our actions were limited. The Valero were most likely behind that as well, but right now, I was ready to bomb the police station, kill the Valero, and move on. But instead, I was in a stupid five star restaurant, waiting on the motherfucking real housewives of Chicago for some charity shit.

"First, that is a lot of fucks. Second, your hat is nice." He smirked as I glared. "And we will find an opening soon. However, right now the plan we came up with last night is the one we're sticking with."

"I was high off sex and couldn't think straight," I snapped, drinking the sorry excuse for tea they offered me.

"But that is where all our master plans are created."

"Really? Isn't that where you came up with the plan to pump more heroin into Boston? Now the mayor is involved."

He leaned back in his chair with no care in the world. "That's only because his idiot daughter went and overdosed. He's busy blaming dealers as if we held the needle to her arm. His bad parenting is apparently our fault. Mayor or no mayor, it was a good idea. The demand is growing."

"Liam." I sighed, pinching the bridge of my nose. "We keep going like this, we are going to be stretched too thin. We can't fight Chicago and Boston with Valero still screwing us. The mayor is going to be doubling down his efforts to trace it."

"Fine," he hissed, leaning in. "We stay neutral for now. We have a shipment coming in tonight that I will redirect and hold. But the moment the Valero are out of the picture, we are pushing hard."

"Deal. In the meantime, we can up the weed. The shit is almost legal anyway, and both coasts are addicted." Weed was as good as gold now. We sold to medical pharmacies where it was legal, and small street gangs where it wasn't.

"Then it's settled . . ." He paused causing me to look over at the door where Commissioner Andrew fucking Patterson made his way toward us.

"Who do you call when it's the police who are stalking you?" I sighed, looking over to Liam, who glared at the man approaching.

"Us."

Commissioner Andrew fucking Patterson placed two sliver badges on the table, causing Liam and me to share a quick glance.

"Shiny." Liam snickered, taking a sip of his coffee. "Is there a reason why you are putting that filth on my table?"

Patterson looked like he had aged at least ten years in the last four months. "The officers your men killed today were fresh out of the academy."

"You should be careful of what you accuse people of Commissioner," I hissed, looking around the room once more. No one could hear us, but he was being fucking stupid.

"You even had their families killed, didn't you?" He laughed bitterly, ignoring me completely.

"Commissioner—"

"A six year old girl now has no family, thanks to you! I know you're the ones behind Pope and Jeffery! You people are sick! You will burn in hell!"

"Commissioner! Have you lost your mind?" Liam yelled, standing up as two guards walked toward us.

"Maybe I have!" the man yelled as the guards held him back. "But you won't remain untouchable forever! One day, someone is going to make you all pay for your crimes."

"Get this man out of here, he is upsetting my wife!" Liam screamed as the guards pulled him away.

Upsetting me? Fuck that, this shit was funny as hell but I could play the damsel in distress. I guess.

"Fuckin' Callahans wouldn't be in power forever! Just wait, someone is gonna pay you back tenfold, and I will laugh, you monsters!" he said, like the joker was on 'shrooms.

"Get him *out!*" Liam roared again, while I placed my hand to my heart like a good damsel in distress.

When he was gone, the manager ran toward us, bowing so low you would think he was trying to kiss Liam's cock . . . jeez. Since when did we live in Japan?

"I am so sorry, Mr. Callahan, please . . ."

"It's not a problem. Please, just keep that man away from our family," Liam said before taking a seat back down. He waited for the room to return to order before staring at me with hard eyes.

"You were the one who ordered it?" he asked me in Irish.

"Yes," I replied back, unsure about why he looked like I was the one he wanted to kill.

He pinched the bridge of his nose. "You let the girl live."

Sitting up straighter, I glared back. "She wasn't home, and I wasn't going to hunt her down. She is six fucking years old."

"Then you should have waited until she was home," he hissed, moving to the edge of his chair. "I don't care if she was six or twenty-six. She is his family and therefore should be dead—"

"You make it seem like that one girl has any power," I snapped back at him. He needed to calm the fuck down before I stabbed him here and now.

He stared at me as if I had lost my mind. "She is the daughter of a cop, a blue blood. She isn't a threat now, but what about in twenty years when she is out of the academy? She will be like a bloodhound looking for revenge. Children grow up, and unless you know something I don't, we are going to be around in twenty years. I will not have the past bite us in the ass. After all, look at you. You were six once, and what happened to you then changed your life forever. You are the last person I thought I would ever have to explain who we are or what we do."

He stood up and kissed me on the side of the check harshly for those who might still be watching, before whispering in Irish, "Stay here, my mother has arrived. I will take care of it."

He fucking sounded disappointed in me. Who does this motherfucking bitch think he is? Did he just sit me? I was the fucking Boss, and I sure as hell didn't take orders. Coraline, Olivia, and Evelyn walked in with a whole group of other charity woman before I could beat his head in. Each one of them smiled and laughed as though they were breathing a different sort of air.

"Ladies, isn't my youngest, handsome?" Evelyn said, giving Liam a big hug.

Liam laughed but it was his fake laugh, the one he did for crowds. "The most handsome, some say."

They all laughed at him while I eyed his skin, wondering where would be the best place to impale him.

"The cockiest as well." Evelyn grinned.

"I shall take that compliment." He winked at a few of the older ladies, forcing me to act like an embarrassed wife and smack him in the chest. I was not in the mood to play this stupid game.

"We've had our breakfast. Honey, don't you have business to take care off?" I dug my nails into his skin but the bitch didn't even flinch.

"You all had breakfast already?" Coraline asked us, looking to our table as waiters cleared it and added a new table to make room.

"Sorry, ladies, only God knows when I would see her again after she disappears with you all. I had to at least start my morning with her." Liam charmed is way into the cougars' arms. They eyed him like he was a god himself. Both their facial expressions and his words made me want to puke.

"Young love." Olivia laughed, causing me to glare at her.

"Goodbye, Liam."

"It's already begun." Liam laughed, kissing my hand. "I know when I'm not wanted."

The women aww-ed as he left, and I tried my best to actually look flattered, but my face just wouldn't have it. Evelyn, Olivia, and Coraline all seemed to notice. Smiling at them, I took a seat as the other women all took theirs.

"Ladies, welcome to the Seventeenth Annual W.E.W.—Women Empowering Women," a peppy blonde announced once the ladies were seated. "I would like to thank Mrs. Coraline Callahan for once again hosting us all here. Thank you so much for everything you do."

I glanced at her, but she didn't meet my gaze. *Two steps forward, six steps back, for Cora.*

"How often do they hold these meetings?" I whispered to Evelyn as everyone clapped.

"First Saturday of every month. You've missed quite a few," Olivia replied before Evelyn could speak, and right on cue the peppy blonde turned to me.

"Please give a W.E.W. welcome to the newest member, Mrs. Melody Callahan. We all know how that first year of marriage is." They turned to me, and I forced myself to smile and blush at the plastic army in front of me.

"Be happy you missed so many," Evelyn whispered, causing Olivia and Coraline to snicker.

It took a while, but finally, all the women were so caught up in their conversations that I no longer had to force myself pay attention. They had to be the saddest and most desperate women I had ever met. None of them cared about the charity. They only cared about upstaging each other in who had more money to give, just to prove how rich they are. None of them could hold a candle to any wife of a Callahan. However, they all wanted to come in second place. So if they had to feed the starving villages to be thought highly of, they would do it.

Coraline shifted for the nineteenth time since she sat down, causing me to look her over quickly. I could tell a lot had changed in her. Her arms and legs were more toned, and she seemed much more alert and capable now. She had even cut her hair down some more, but despite all that, she still looked beautiful, almost had a movie star kind of beauty.

"Are you ready to be working with me next, Coraline?" I asked her softly. Her eyes went wide and grinned.

"Are you serious?" she asked, because she obviously didn't know who I was. I didn't joke around with things like that. I rarely joked at all, in fact.

"Adriana said you are getting too used to her. So, yes, I am serious."

"Yeah, first I would have to talk to Declan—"

"What?"

"Declan," she said again with a frown. "When I told him, he kind of laughed it off, and we haven't talked about it much. But I think that's because he doesn't see Adriana as anything to worry about. You, on the other hand—"

"I'm something to worry about," I added, placing Declan on my Callahan ass-kicking list. "Have you tried making him listen?"

She looked at me like I was crazy.

"You do know you are a woman, correct?" I smirked. "Grab handcuffs, make him hard, tell him what you want to tell him, and then leave him there to think about it."

"I could never do that, Declan would be so—"

"Horny, which you can use to your advantage. You are a motherfucking Callahan woman. You do what you want. If you want to train with me, you train with me, and if Declan doesn't like it, remind him of the days when all he had was his hand." I was dead serious, even though Olivia was laughing beside me. For all the improvement Coraline was enjoying, I was shocked she was still hiding behind this shell.

"Mel, I'm not like you—"

"No one is like me, but that's not the point," I interrupted, and I would keep interrupting until she found the balls to stop me.

"It's just that I don't know how to be this strong person. Declan means the world to me, and I don't want to hurt him or lose him," she whispered, and I was tempted to drown myself in my soup.

"If you keep focusing on how lucky you are to have Declan, then you're going to forget how lucky he is to have you. Imagine you're a princess and then demand to be treated like one," Olivia replied, and I was a little confused. Since when did I get on the same page as the blow-up doll?

"All my sons need to be knocked upside their heads every once in a while." Evelyn gave one of her motherly smiles.

"Or shot." I smiled, causing Evelyn to glare at me, and I simply shrugged, it was true. Bullets spoke louder than words.

"Melody, do you mind if we speak in private?" Olivia asked me, oddly polite. I glanced over at Coraline and Evelyn who seemed just as shocked. Nodding, I stood, waiting for her to follow as I headed to the women's bathroom.

Taking off the stupid hat, I placed it on the counter before turning back to her. "Speak."

"I wanted to apologize for my hostility and for being—"

"A rude, immature bitch?" I asked, crossing my hands.

Her eyes narrowed at me, and it looked like she was trying her best to bite her tongue. "Yeah, for that, too."

"I won't accept your apology until I know why you're offering it." I turned back to the mirror trying to fix my hat hair.

"Because that is what grown people do? We apologize when we are wrong," she snapped before taking a deep breath.

"Well, I'm calling bullshit." I smiled. "You see, when people apologize and mean it, they don't need privacy. So I'm guessing Neal put you up to this. What did he say to make you try and humble yourself?"

"He—"

"Don't lie to me, Olivia. I'm much better at it than you, and I have no problem breaking your head against this mirror. You can take a little drive to West Ridge and ask Natasha if you don't believe me." I couldn't kill her, but I hated liars and would make that clear.

She stared at me wide-eyed and nodded. "Fine. A few months ago, Neal and I talked about it. I've been trying to stay out of your way, but I know we are going to have to speak sometime. I just . . . Neal wants me to make peace. I love Neal, so I will do it."

"What is with you all and bending to what your husbands want?" They really were Stepford wives.

"It's called love, Melody," she snapped at me once again. "When you love someone, all you want is for them to be happy. That doesn't make you weak, and that doesn't make you an idiot. Liam is head over heels in love with you, he would die for you, and yet you cringe at the thought of it. Coraline and I are not G.I. Janes, and we can't walk on the dark side of the moon and come back okay. But at least neither of us are scared of love. So I'm saying sorry once again. I have to go home to my husband, have amazing sex, and see him smile."

She said nothing else before walking out. When she did, I turned to the mirror and stared at myself. I remembered a time when my life was so much easier.

LIAM

Most people—a lot of people—would be disgusted with what I did tonight. They would call me a monster, tell me I was heartless or cruel. But none of them knew the life I lived or walk down the same dimly lit streets as me. I was head of the family. I was the *Ceann na Conairte*. Which meant it fell on my shoulders to protect this family from past, present, and future nuisances. All you had to do was watch an old mafia movie to see how one loose end brought down some of the greatest empires there ever was.

Rule Two: Take no prisoners and have no regrets about it.

Anyone we captured were either killed or flipped to our side and used for intel. But after we got what we needed, they were killed anyway. Any man who can flip on his boss once can do it again. What made the Callahans successful is that we had evolved past all the mistakes that had brought other greats down. We didn't cheat on our wives, and we didn't do any of the smack or drugs we sold. Those two things alone were things the mafia world was known for. However, it was also the first thing that brought them down. Everyone stayed clean, even the men closest to us. The men of our family had worked too hard to become what they were today for some junkie to snitch to the police to save his skin. Wives were key, because if you treated them right, they would live and die for you. I had no regrets for what I did. I didn't kill because I was a sick twisted motherfucker. Everything was for the betterment of the family.

Sighing, I played away on my piano. I came back late and I didn't feel like dealing with Mel or anyone else for that matter. I thought she understood, but she just wrote it off like it was nothing. She was too focused on Amory and Saige. Yes, they were a huge problem, but we needed to cover all our bases. Vance would just love it if we hung ourselves. He was trying to spread us out all over the globe. The more areas to cover, the more room for mistakes. I just needed to find an opening.

"You're going to wear out the keys," my wife called out behind me, but I couldn't bring myself to look at her. I knew whatever she was wearing tonight would leave me smitten . . . fuck that . . . it would leave me fucking hungry for her.

I just kept playing. I wasn't even sure what it was. I just played. However, with each step she took, I could feel her like a wave of warmth behind me. I knew when her hand was hovering right over my head, and I leaned into it without thinking. She ran her fingers through my hair before stepping onto the seat next me. From there, she climbed onto the front of the piano, placing her legs on either side of me and forcing me to play while staring right at her. Damn her to hell.

"Mel . . ."

"Do you love me?" she whispered, looking me dead in the eye. I froze. What could I say to that? If I lied, she would know. If I told her the truth, she would push me away. So I just played.

She slid down, the keys chiming as she hit them, until she was in my lap. Kissing me, she wrapped her legs around my waist.

"Do you love me?"

"Yes, I love you. You don't have to say it back. I can wait."

She took a deep breath and dropped her head down.

"Mel, I'm serious, you don't have to say it back now. I can wait." I tried to lift her chin, but she ripped her head from my hand.

"Mel . . ."

"I'm not good at love," she whispered.

"I know, that's why I was waiting." I rubbed her thighs, not for anything sexual, but so she could feel me and know I was here holding her.

She ran her hand through her hair and sighed. "I've been working on it."

"I know that, too." I've watched as she peeled back layers of herself for me to see day by day.

Rising from my lap, she walked over to the window, and I missed her warmth.

"I've always been the strong one, Liam. I'm good at being the strong one. I don't want anyone to ever see me as weak or—"

"There is not a person alive who truly knows you that doesn't fear you or think you're weak," I whispered, stepping behind her. "What is wrong with you?"

"What if I was pregnant?" She turned to me quickly. "No one sees a pregnant woman and thinks, 'holy shit, this woman could kill me with her bare hands.' All they see is this . . . this *incubator* who stuffs her face and waddles like a penguin."

I laughed. "I would say like a duck, but a penguin works."

She hit my arm hard, and I laughed some more. She always made me truly laugh.

"Sweetheart, we still have a while before you're waddling like anything."

"Yeah, a little under seven months." She frowned, lifting up her shirt for me to see a tiny bump that was almost unnoticeable. I had seen her naked so many times I could tell.

I felt the words leave my throat as my mouth dropped open. My hand went to her stomach before I met her gaze. Each time I tried to form a word, it was lost by the time I opened my mouth again.

"You're pregnant," I whispered.

She nodded. "Ten weeks."

My legs gave out under me, and I found myself on my knees, my head on her stomach. I couldn't hear anything, but I felt so humbled, in love, and overjoyed. Her hands found their way into my hair again as I kissed her stomach.

"I love you, too, Liam. I just don't know if I can say it often," she whispered. "So you're going to have to say it to him or her a lot."

I laughed and nodded. She bent down in front of me, and I gripped the sides of her face.

"Holy shit, I'm fucking pregnant," she whispered.

"Holy shit, indeed," I whispered back before taking her lips. Pulling her body to mine, I lifted her up bridal style and walked over to the bed.

"No sex on the piano?" she asked in my arms.

"I don't want sex. I want to make love to you."

Dropping her in the center of the bed, she raised an eyebrow at me. "You are so cheesy, Liam."

"Shut up and enjoy it." If I was going to die of something, it was going to be of happiness.

She pulled me by my belt onto the bed and hopped on my waist. "You cannot treat me differently."

"The fuck I am." Everything was different now.

"Liam, I'm serious." She glared at me.

Sitting up, I grabbed her sides to hold her in place. "So am I, you're pregnant."

"That doesn't make me handicapped or made out of glass," she snapped, and I would have to prepare for a few months of it. But that thought only brought a smile to my lips.

"Melody, if you would let me, I would wrap you in bubble wrap and make sure you were surrounded by at least four men on the ground and two in the fucking sky."

"And I would use the motherfuckers' heads as target practice. Until I start to fucking waddle, no one is to treat me any fucking differently. If they do, I'll chain them to the back of your stupid Audi and rip them apart. Pregnant or not, I'm still fucking Bloody Melody," she yelled in my face.

There had to be something fucked up with me if I found her threatening to kill people while pregnant sexy. Kissing her, I made sure to leave a mental note of where our argument had left off before flipping her onto her back. I could feel her small hands ripping at my clothes, trying her best to pull them off me as I was trying to do with her.

"Say it again," I whispered, kissing down her chest.

"What?" she gasped out in pleasure as I made it to the promise land, the land of milk and honey right between her thighs.

"Tell me you love me." I kissed her other lips, before placing three fingers inside her.

She didn't speak as I quickened my fingers in and out of her. She moaned out loudly as I slowed down.

"Liam . . ."

"Tell me," I whispered, moving so slow she rocked against me in hopes of forcing me to move faster.

"I fucking hate you!"

"And?" I asked, smirking. I loved watching her this wild because of me.

"That's it." She smiled, and I bit her thigh gently.

"I wanted to drink all of you," I muttered against her skin toward my fingers. "I wanted to make you come with my tongue."

Pulling out, she whimpered.

"But since you once again want to be difficult"—I smiled, releasing my throbbing cock out of my pants—"I'm going to have to fuck it out of you."

Before she could respond, I slammed into her and her body jerked off the bed.

"Fucking Christ, Liam," she hissed out in pleasure, locking her legs around me. However, I pulled them apart.

"This will be all about my pleasure and not yours if you don't say it, love." I grinned as she fought against me, but I always won this fight.

"I fucking hate you."

"And?"

"I kind of love you, too, you asshole," she mumbled, and I would take it.

Capturing her lips in mine for only a moment before I sucked her breast, she rocked against me while I stroked within her. Each movement was painfully slow, but I didn't want to rush this. I wanted us to ride each wave of pleasure with her. But my wife rarely did what I wanted. Wrapping her legs around me once again, she pulled me even closer to her before flipping me on the bed. Her head rocked back while she rode me, and I had to hold on to the headboard. My grip was so tight, I was shocked that it didn't break.

"Jesus, Mel." I groaned. I couldn't hold it anymore. Grabbing her waist, I held on, watching through half-closed eyes as she brought me the greatest pleasure.

"I love you," I cried as I came along with her. She fell on top of me, and my first instinct was to wrap her in my arms.

All I could smell was sex, and all I could hear was her deep breaths mixed in with mine. We stayed there, wrapped in each other's arms for what seemed liked hours before she looked up at me. She didn't say anything just stared, and once again, I wished I could read her mind.

"What?" I asked as she rolled beside me. My hand went to her stomach protectively. The next fucking Callahan, my kid, was less than seven months away. It made me want to make love to her all over again.

"We should have used condoms," she whispered, placing her hand over mine.

"Not today. Not fucking ever." I didn't want anything between us. "You don't want a child?"

"Kids are smelly and loud. You never know what they want because they can't talk. Their heads are way too big for their bodies, which means if you drop them, they're going headfirst. They're like little aliens." She sighed, and I tried not to smile. She was scared and worried about being a mother, and because she was my Mel, she would never just come out and say it.

"Only in the beginning—"

"Yeah, because they transform from aliens into monsters. First, little monsters who cry and throw tantrums, then to sex-crazed teenagers who think they are smarter than everyone else. That's going to be the next eighteen years, Liam. I'm not like your mom. My patience will run out, and I am going to say or do something—"

I kissed her. "There were days my mom was even scarier than my father . . . a lot of days, actually. However, my parents made it work, and we turned out fine."

"You're a sex-crazed, closet smoker, who sells dope, crack, and smack for a living. Not to mention a murderer." She rolled her eyes at me before laughing.

"Like I said, I turned out fine." Honestly, the worst thing was the murder, but that wasn't my fault. People thought they could steal from us, threaten us, and I made sure that wasn't tolerated.

"I'm a planner Liam," she said, sighing. "I like to know how I'm going to approach things, or kill them. This, our kid, isn't part of my plan. We have Saige and Amory to deal . . ."

"Don't stress, love. I can handle—"She pulled a knife from under the pillow and held it to my throat. Pushing me back, she took a seat on my waist once again.

"If you try to put me on the bench, Liam, so help me I will start cutting body parts off. I may be pregnant, but I am still Bloody Motherfucking Melody. I can destroy anyone I want. I'll chalk it up to hormones." She glared, and I could see the same woman who shot me in the thigh.

I felt my dick rise at her words and her position on top of me.

"Bloody Motherfucking Melody, indeed." I snickered, rubbing against her. I watched her eyes glaze over as she let the knife drop to the floor and kissed me.

When our phones rang and she pulled away, I felt the need to snap whichever fool thought to call us at two in the morning.

"Speak," she said into the phone as I kissed her legs. "We will be right there."

No, we'll be right here! My mind begged.

Hanging up, Mel jumped out of bed, leaving me hard as a fucking rock in bed.

"Amory and Saige burned down my fucking house," she snapped angrily as she stomped into the closet.

I groaned to myself. "Damn them all to hell."

"Liam, get your horny fucking ass out of bed and help me kill a bitch!" she yelled.

Oh, I was going to kill them all right.

MELODY

I leaned against the car, watching as the Giovanni Villa burned to the ground. The fire department was trying their best to control the fire, but a deadlier one was burning inside me.

Fedel ran up to me. "There was a note on the gate, ma'am."

I saw Liam reaching for it, but I snatched it before he could and glared at him. He was not going to treat me differently. I wouldn't have it.

You burn my shit, I burn yours. All is fair in war. Congrats on the baby. Such a happy time for you both.
XOXO
A&S

Liam grabbed the letter, his nose flaring with just as much rage as mine was.

There was only one other person who knew I was pregnant.

I roared into Fedel's face. "Find Dr. Anderson, now!"

Liam turned to me, his eyes still hard. "Everything is different now."

I nodded, opening the car door and taking a seat. Everything was different. I was now a bigger target. I was always a target, but now so was my child—the next leader of our empire—and because of that, I was going to have to change. Not into Evelyn or Coraline, but a different type of leader. I was going to have to figure out how to be ruthless *and* pregnant. Amory and Saige picked the wrong motherfucking family to mess with.

TWENTY-SEVEN

"He pulls a knife, you pull a gun, he sends one of yours to the hospital, you send one of his to the morgue . . ."

—Al Capone

LIAM

"What's a five letter word for mortality?" I asked the man in the hospital cast in front of me.

He said nothing, but that had to be due to all the morphine. Smirking, I snapped my fingers and filled in the spaces of the newspaper crossword.

"That's right, death," I said to him. "It seems even God is mocking you Commissioner . . . ex-Commissioner now, right? People don't like suicidal cops."

He just glared as I continued with my game.

"Seven letter word for ineffective. Don't tell me, failure. Seriously, this is today's crossword. Can you believe it? It's like they made it about your life."

"Is that why you're here, Callahan, to kick a man when he is down? I'm not shocked," he hissed out, but I wasn't sure if that was due to the pain or because he was ticked off.

"I don't kick a man when he is down. I put a bullet in his skull. You should know that." I sighed, placing the paper down.

"Then kill me already," he yelled, making me want to roll my eyes.

"Not until you answer a few of my questions," I replied, rising to my feet. I reached over and grabbed his oxygen mask.

Taking it off his bruised face, he took a deep breath before it turned into short gasps for air. He reached over for the nurse call button so I pushed it for him. Once, then twice, and then a few more times for the heck of it.

"This side of the hospital has been cleared, so let's chat." I grinned, giving him a few seconds of air before pulling the mask from his face again.

"Go to hell," he breathed out.

"My wife is a raging homicidal hormonal pregnant woman. I sleep with hell." I sighed, giving him air again.

"Give me a second to shit bricks of sadness."

And I laughed, too, before grabbing the pillow from behind his head, pressing it against his face.

"I'm not in the mood for a smartass," I snapped at him. When I took the pillow off his face, he coughed like a dying chain smoker.

He held on to my hand as I fed him his air. "Let's start with something simple. Why did you jump out of your hotel room? That could kill, you know."

He tried to hold on to the air but I simply ripped it from him.

"You burned down my house."

"I wasn't charged, tried, or arrested for anything."

"I know it was you! You Callahans destroy everything." His voice broke, and again, I rolled my eyes. "But you warned me and I should have . . . you warned me and so it's my fault they died. That little girl, you sick mother! I told you about her! It was me. I-I—"

"Please don't get emotional, that was only my first question." I needed him alive right now.

"No games, what do you want from me? You have taken *everything*." He coughed, leaning back on his bed.

"I want to know everything you have on the Valero." He laughed liked a mad man, and when he did, I held the pillow to his face again. He struggled until he was too weak, and it was then that I let him go.

"Let's do this again." I held on to his face. "Tell me about Amory, Saige, and Vance or so help me God, I will make you wish you had died. I will make sure you are alive and well, trapped in your own fucking body like a jail cell. Each day, I will make sure someone personally gives me a patch of your skin until you are nothing but an open wound. What . . . do . . . you . . . know?"

He smiled. "They want you dead, your wife, your child, and every last Callahan. They tried bringing you down the legal way, but I'm a failure remember? They are just as ruthless as you are. Word on the street is that your wife's personal doctor was tortured and then dismembered."

"Word on the street? Did you hear that when your body collided with it?" I wanted to rip the smiled from his lips.

"Doesn't change the fact that they are coming for you," he said, and when he did, I pulled away, grabbed the morphine drip and replaced the liquid.

"This is adrenaline in small doses. It blocks out pain. In large doses, it does the opposite. You feel everything." I tapped the bag. "You're not going to ride to the afterlife in sweet painless bliss. You're going to feel it all, and right as your heart gives out, think about how big of an idiot you were to step into my house. The very day this city was born, people like me have run Chicago. You thought you were the next somebody who did shit. But all you will be remembered as will be the motherfucker who failed at his marriage, failed at his job, and failed to even kill himself."

Grabbing my newspaper, I walked back to the door.

"This isn't over Callahan. It doesn't just end with me. You won't always be untouchable. You're only human!" he yelled at me.

"All men are touchable, Andrew, those who touch me simply lose their hands. So let them come. I'm only just beginning. What I've done to you is not even the beginning." A second later the adrenaline must have kicked in because he shook and screamed like a fish out of water . . . much to my ears' enjoyment.

Stepping out into the hall, Declan, Neal, Monte, and Fedel all stood waiting for me. Declan walked over, handing me a phone as we walked out of the hospital.

"Hello, sweetheart." I smirked.

"You no good motherfucking bitch!" she yelled at me.

"Sweetheart, we don't want our kid coming out swearing like a sailor." I laughed as Fedel opened the car door for me.

"The life-form who is fucking with my emotions, draining my energy, and stealing half of all my food is certainly in a sac of fluid and can't hear a word I'm saying. You went to see the commissioner without me!" she screeched as I flipped through the files in front of me.

"Love, you were knocked out cold this morning . . ."

"Then use your motherfucking hands and wake me the fuck up. You benched me!" Little did she know, I tried to wake her up but she was no longer in the land of the living then.

"Love—"

"You left me here with your mother, who is now calling every motherfucking asshole with a drop of Irish in their veins to the house. I will kill someone, cut off their head and put it on the dashboard of your car if you do not fix this shit. I'm eleven and a half weeks and barely showing!" Her hormones were going to cost me my life . . . or a relative.

"Mel, sweetheart . . ."

"Call me 'love' or 'sweetheart' one more time, sweetheart, and I will bust your teeth in," she said sweetly.

"I got nothing from him. Antonio and Eric told me they caught one of the Valero men, Cross, in Mexico. They should be in the house, and you can handle that when I get back." There was silence on the line, which I prayed meant she was okay.

"I hate this," she whispered into the phone. "I hate how I have no control of how I'm feeling. I feel like a ticking time bomb, Liam. It's pissing me off."

"I'm good at defusing bombs, lov—" I stopped. I could almost feel her rolling her eyes. "I get it. One step at a time, and I will try my best to help to not tick you off. Would you like a smoothie?"

"That ticks me off!" she snapped. "Since when could you bribe me with treats like a fucking child."

I groaned, pinching the bridge of my nose. "So no smoothie, then?"

"Mango, banana, orange and extra kiwi," she replied before hanging up, and I fought back a laugh.

"Take me to Smoothie Hut," I told the driver up front. Neither he nor Fedel said a word. But what could they really say? I had a pregnant and dangerous wife waiting for me back home.

MELODY

Taking a deep breath, I rolled into a ball on my bed.

"How are you feeling?" Evelyn said, literally sounding like a bird from a Disney movie, before taking a seat beside me.

I'm tired, hungry, or annoyed every ten minutes. I spent the first weeks puking in Adriana's bathroom just to hide it from Liam, and now you're treating me like I'm an infant.

"I'm fine, Evelyn," I said coldly, sitting up.

"Cut the bullshit, Mel. I'm serious, I get that you want to remain 'Boss,' but you're also about to be a mother. That supersedes anything else. So drop the act and speak to me as if I were Liam." If I spoke to her like I spoke to Liam, I would lose it.

"I shouldn't be pregnant, Evelyn. I did everything but take my uterus out not to become pregnant. Yet here I am. This kid is taking all my energy, and I'm tired all the damn time," I said, leaning against the pillows.

Damn him and his Irish swimmers.

"You're still in your first trimester. Fatigue is normal. Give it three more weeks, and it will fade." She smiled, taking my hand into hers. "Mel, you don't understand how happy this makes me. How happy this has made our whole family. I'm going to be a grandmamma."

"Yeah," I said with no emotion, because I wasn't excited.

"You don't want a child?" I could tell she was trying not to judge me, but I could see the worry in her eyes.

"I kill people, Evelyn. It's part of the job, and have no regrets about it because I'm good. I'm one of the best there ever was. History will put me right up there with Al Capone and Charles "Lucky" Luciano. I'll be the second woman on that list next to Xie Caiping. That was my baby. That's the kid I've been taking care of for the last seven and a half years. I don't know how to take care of that child, while taking care of this one."

There, I said it. I took a deep breath as Evelyn processed.

"You do know the reason for family right?" She smiled. "You are good at delegating everything but your power."

"That's because power shouldn't be delegated." It's what made me stronger. Why share that? I was already splitting half of it with Liam.

"Maybe not. Maybe you could do it all by yourself. The only downside would be losing your mind, Liam's heart, or your child." I don't know why my hand went to my stomach but the smirk on her face annoyed me. I had Saige and Amory already aiming for its life.

"I don't have to tell you to be yourself. But do use us if needed. Liam realizes he needs you, and I doubt he would side-step you. Do less, but when you do something, make it lasting. Leave a mark. Your men and the rest of the world will see you as you are—Bloody Melody." She winked at me as Liam walked in. He looked confused and slightly worried. I guess he thought if I was talking to his mother, something had to be wrong.

"I will leave you and the Mad Hatter alone, for now." She gave me a small hug, which I didn't return. I was not a hugger, but I patted her on the back.

"Darling." Evelyn hugged him and smirked at the smoothie in his hands. "That's a small cup."

"What?" Liam replied, looking at it. Evelyn winked at me before leaving, even though I had no idea what it meant.

"Are you all right?" he asked, handing me the smoothie.

I rolled my eyes, slurping down the drink. "I can't have alcohol. How would you feel? And this is a small cup."

"Touché." He laughed, falling next me. He had this annoying new habit of rubbing my stomach as if it were a fucking crystal ball. It seemed to make him happy, so I didn't say a word. Someone should be excited for this kid.

"What did the commissioner have to say?" I asked, shaking my drink—stupid fruit kept getting stuck at the bottom.

"We ruined his life, we killed his men, we are evil . . . same old, same old." He sighed. "I didn't get anything new out of him."

"Please tell me you ended him then. I'm done with the Chicago PD." If not, I can always go back to the hospital myself.

"It's done. He died painfully and slowly. Monte stayed behind to make sure." He kissed my stomach before looking to me.

"This Cross person, how far up the chain is he?" The closer the guy was to the boss, the harder it was to make him talk.

"Personal guard to Vance's favorite mistress, Hera." He smirked, taking a sip of my smoothie. I glared but said nothing about it. He handed me his tablet and I flipped through some of the files.

"Have Declan look for this Hera. She has to have a money trail." Being his favorite meant she was paid off well enough to keep her happy.

"I already have," he told me, and I almost wanted to pout, stupid hormones. I was not a pouter.

"Why don't you just get me caught up since you're the reason why I'm behind," I snapped at him. He was so cocky, and I was torn between jumping him and beating his face in.

"I killed Patterson. Antonio and Eric have Cross in the basement. Hera hasn't left Vance's side from what Declan could tell, and I wasn't able to get the extra kiwi—"

"What the fuck do you mean you couldn't get extra kiwi!" I yelled, opening the lid to my drink. "You can fucking destroy Chicago, make it rain blood, but you can't get a fruit in my drink?"

"I was just joking." He laughed at me, and I punched him right in his fucking nose.

"Fuck, Jesus Christ, Mel!"

"Jesus Christ wouldn't mess with a pregnant woman, you idiot."

He shook his head wiping off his nose. "One of these motherfucking days—"

"Careful, Liam, you don't want your child to hear you threatening his mother."

He glared at me before smirking. He always smirked, or smiled, or laughed when I mentioned I was carrying his kid. It was like he was on drugs. Leaving him on the bed, I walked into the closet and grabbed my white heels along with a new dress shirt.

"Your breasts are bigger," Liam said from behind me. I could feel the lust rolling off him in waves.

"I know, it's how I figured out I was pregnant to begin with." All my bras were custom made for me and me alone. When they no longer fit correctly, I knew. I had been the same size since I was sixteen.

"I should have noticed," he whispered, closing the distance between us.

"Liam, don't. We have to go." I wanted him, but I also wanted to get back to my job and his dick was the reason why I was in this situation.

His eyes were glazed over when he ripped open the shirt I just buttoned. He stared at my breasts for a moment before pulling me into his chest. With one hand, he lifted me up, holding my ass.

"He's a prisoner, he isn't going anywhere."

Grabbing his hair, I bit his lip. "Cork your cock. Put me down, and you will live to have sex another day. I have a job to do."

Forcing myself out of his arms, I picked a random shirt and walked out. But not before hearing him curse and it was my turn to smirk. Pregnant or not, I ran shit.

LIAM

She left me so hard I had to take a quick shower so I wouldn't have to face our men with a hard-on. When I walked down the stairs to the basement, I was met with a crowd of our men waiting for something. In the interrogation room sat one of

Valero's men chained to his chair. However, my wife was nowhere to be found. It took me a total of eleven minutes to take a shower and dressed. She should have been here already.

He didn't even need for me to ask, he nodded to second door in the room, where Eric stood in front of and he opened it upon my gaze. Stepping inside, I found my Mel sitting in front of a severed hand with a rod through its middle finger. Fedel and Neal stood beside her as she just stared at it.

"It's Dr. Anderson's hand," she told me without looking away. "They left another note."

Fedel handed me the letter.

We planned to send his whole body, however, we got a little carried away. All we could save was his hand. But that's all a doctor needs right? So sad he won't help you like he helped your mother when she was pregnant . . . you're going to need all the help you can get.

XOXO

A&S

"When did this arrive?" I hissed to Fedel and Neal.

"The men at the gate checked it a few minutes before you got here," Neal said.

Pinching the bridge of my nose, I took a deep breath. "Leave us."

"Don't," she snapped at them, and they froze. "We're done here. I've gotten all that I needed."

She said nothing more before rising from her chair calmly. She was so calm it was eerie. The moment we stepped out, Declan handed her another smoothie.

"From mother," he said quickly. She glared at him, taking it from his hand before walking into the interrogation room.

When Fedel walked in, he placed a chair out for her. My mind went straight to the first time I ever laid eyes on her. She had changed so much since then and yet was alike in so many ways. We both had changed.

"So this is the Italian bitch who managed to piss off not only Vance, but also Amory and Saige," Cross said, and I felt my hand twitch. I wanted to rip his motherfucking tongue out.

To make it worse, Mel did nothing. She didn't even speak. She just sucked on that damn straw.

"What? Do you plan to strike me down with your eyes? Where is that big bad bitch who set fire to the bosses' wedding? Or are you just an Irish bitch now? Did Callahan fuck all the fight out you?" he asked her, and my eyes were clouding over. I was going to rip his throat out of his neck.

"Speak, you bitch!" he yelled, fighting against the chains. "You think I will just talk? You think I'm afraid of you? I fucking ran all the prisoners for the Valero. I was the one who cut off your motherfucking doctor's hands. He begged and begged for mercy. He didn't talk until I started cutting. So call the motherfucker really in charge, bitch, so we can get this over with. I'm no rat."

Before I knew it, I already had my gun in my hands. Had she not spoken, I would have gone in there my fucking self.

"Monte," was all she said, and he came out of the fucking shadows of the room like he was a damn ninja with a sword in his hands.

"What the fuck?" Declan, Neal, and I all said at the same time.

Placing her cup on the ground, Mel stood up as calm as I had ever seen her.

"My father taught me a lot of things growing up," she began as she circled him. "He had this weird thing for swords . . . iron swords, though. He told me I should get martial arts training and shipped me off to Japan, because they knew their swords. I thought I would come back a motherfucking ninja, but I got my ass kicked."

"Is there a point to this trip down memory lane sweethea—"

Before he could finish, Mel's sword came down, slicing through his wrist.

"Holy Shit," Declan, Neal, and I said together once again as we stared at the hand on the ground.

They spoke out in shock while I was kind of turned on. My wife was fucking bold, beautiful, and deadly. She never failed to amaze me.

Cross screamed loudly, even though Fedel stuffed something in his mouth.

"The point is, I have a sword, motherfucker." She grinned, only an inch from his face as he huffed and puffed, trying to fight the pain.

"You're going to answer my questions or you lose limbs. That"—she pointed to his bloody hand—"was for your comments before. I'm so in charge I could be the fucking Energizer bunny."

He muffled something that sound liked fuck you, and Mel's grin widened.

"Do you know why we call people rats?" she asked him as Antonio walked in with a cage full of the beady-eyed creatures.

Mel, with no reservation, grabbed one of them.

Note to self—ask doctor about shots for her and the baby.

"Because they are self-preservation creatures. They have no honor, no loyalty. It's all about doing what they can to save themselves. In fact"—she smirked throwing the rat into a small jar—"they will eat anything if it means their survival."

"She wouldn't," Neal whispered.

"I'm done doubting Melody. It's unhealthy to be proven wrong so many times," Declan whispered back.

Cross struggled as Antonio fit the jar and the rat on the end of his decapitated wrist. But she wasn't done. Despite her calm appearance, she was seething. Pulling out a lighter, she held it to the jar, and the rat ran toward his wrist to get away from the flame. Cross screamed against the sock.

"So many limbs, so many rats. You called me a bitch . . . twice, insulted not only my intelligence, but also my abilities, and then killed my doctor. How ticked do you think I am?" she asked him.

"First question and I'll make it easy. What is the Valero's next move?" He only screamed in pain.

"Take your time. I can wait for you to stop screaming," she added, drinking her damn smoothie.

MELODY

"He's unconscious," Fedel informed me, putting his hand to Cross's neck. I was surprised he was still alive, he lasted two hours.

Sighing, I stood up and rolled my neck. "Make sure he doesn't die."

Cross had only given bits and pieces of information, most of which didn't make any sense. It had to be the blood loss. However, I would get an answer, and I would put an end to them all.

"It's you who should be worried about dying." Cross spoke out in a daze. His eyes were barely open, and he was so pale he could have been mistaken for a corpse.

"I still have my hands and foot." Who the fuck did this idiot think he was?

He smiled and laughed like a mad man. Fedel punched the side of his face, but Cross only laughed harder. Then the house shook so violently I had to hold on to Antonio for a moment. It took me only a second later to realize what caused it.

Liam busted in. "The east wing was just bombed, we need to move."

"See you all in hell motherfuckers. Tell the Boss I said hello." Cross laughed and passed out.

There was another explosion and the look in Liam's eyes as he pulled out not only one but two guns was the deadliest I had ever seen.

We were under attack.

TWENTY-EIGHT

"Any of you fuckin' pricks move, and I'll execute every mother fuckin' last one of ya."

—Honey Bunny, Pulp Fiction

MELODY

"Monte," I hissed through my teeth, and a second later, he placed a machine pistol and two extra mags in my hands.

"Your orders are to shoot to kill everyone but Amory or Saige," Liam snapped at him. Fedel and Monte didn't even waste a second before they were out the door. Placing the magazines in the back of my pants, I could feel the bloodlust kicking in.

"Where is the family?"

"The safe room . . . where you should be," he said to me, grabbing hold of my arm before I could leave.

"Liam, I don't want to waste bullets, but so help me God if you think for a second that I'm going to sit behind walls and wait for the storm to settle, I will end you myself," I snapped at him holding my gun to his nose.

His green eyes narrowed. "You're pregnant. Get the fuck behind the wall, Melody."

"Fuck you." I glared back before walking out. The moment I did, all I saw was destruction. It was like . . . it was like we were bombed. Lights flickered, wires dangled from the ceiling, and all I could hear was gunfire.

Leaning against the wall, I held my gun to my chest as Liam came up right next to me.

"Done treating me like a bitch and not your wife?" I asked, trying to see where the gunfire was coming from.

"You better not get hurt or I will kill you myself, love." Liam smirked, kissing my cheek before stepping forward, shooting blindly into the hall and yet somehow, hitting the motherfuckers.

Stepping out from behind the wall, I glared at him as he smirked. "I hate you."

"You love me . . ." He was cut off as I shot into the hall at one asshole hiding behind a broken door.

"You forgot one." I smirked before running down the hall and I could feel him right behind me.

The moment we reached the east wing, it looked like an all-out war between our men, who used every part of themselves, including teeth and fists, and broken glass to kill if they were without a weapon. From the corner of my eye, I saw Neal almost rip the arm off a Russian. The air was clogged with the scent of blood, and I was going deaf from all the noise around me. Out of nowhere, a blade sliced up my leg, and the second I looked down, I met the eyes of the fool who thought it was a good idea to cut me with glass.

Stomping my heel into his face, I screamed as his blood went everywhere. Wiping my face with my arms, I turned to see Liam slit a man's throat. When he looked over again, he wasn't looking at me. I followed his gaze, in time to see Amory put a bullet in Eric's forehead.

Liam roared so loudly I would have thought it was him who made the house shake. "*Amory!*"

Amory appeared shocked at first, as if he had forgotten whose house he had attacked. But the shock soon gave way to fear as Liam stalked toward him like the devil himself. The moment anyone blocked his path, they were struck down so quickly I didn't even have time to blink. I wanted to watch him rain fire and brimstone on the fool, but I wasn't sure what they knew our how much they were after. There were only a few of them left. I needed to make sure that all our files and information weren't being stolen right from under us.

"Neal!" I yelled for him but he was too far gone in his thirst for blood, and was busy shooting down the motherfuckers in his way. He looked almost giddy, like he was in some video game and invincible.

Glancing back at Liam one last time, I watched as his fist collided with Amory's face before running down the hall. The further I went, jumping over rubble and exposed wires, the louder the screams. At first, I wasn't sure what it was. Between the sparks, smoke, and the flames, I could barely see a few feet in front of me. As I peered around the corner, I heard someone scream.

"Let go of me!"

It was Olivia, yelling as three large men surrounded her like wolves around a sheep.

"You're pretty," one of the men said, "but you would be prettier on my cock."

They all laughed as he grabbed at her, and in that second I put a bullet in his head, causing the blood to spatter all over her face. She stood there, shaken, while the other two men spun around, releasing a hail of bullets.

Jumping behind what was left of a broken wall, I yelled out, "You have two seconds to run before I place a bullet in your brains."

"Fuck you, bitch, you're outnumbered," one said in a heavy accent.

"Come out like a good bitch and we'll be gentle with ya," the other said, laughing, and all I could hear was Olivia's scream. She was annoying as fuck. Why couldn't she have just gone to the safe room like a good little damsel in distress?

Taking a deep breath, I stood up slowly, hands up.

Guns pointed in my face, the men smirked. The one holding Olivia smiled. "Drop the gun, sweetheart."

"I warned you," was all I said to him, smirking as Fedel came up behind the other one. I shot through the hand the motherfucker was holding Olivia with, and when he backed up, I shot him right in his eye.

Rushing over to Olivia as she screamed, I grabbed her bloody arm. Ripping my shirt, I wrapped it quickly and forced her to look me in the eyes.

"Why the fuck aren't you in the safe room?"

"N-Neal . . ." she stammered in shock. "I–I-Neal."

Slapping her across the face, I glared into her eyes. "Get your shit together and move, or I will kill you myself. Fedel, get her to safety. She fights, knock her out."

He nodded and I left her in his care before running down the hall. This had to be a distraction. They wanted something. The east wing was nothing but bedrooms, and if they were smart, they had gotten blueprints of the house, which meant they knew what was in the west wing. Some of our most important documents, cash, and codes were kept in west wing.

Running up broken stairs, the heat of a bullet seared me as it pierced my shoulder with so much force, I landed on my back and rolled down the stairs.

It was the woman I remembered seeing at Amory and Saige's wedding smiled as she looked down at me. "Oops, did I hurt you?"

I tried reaching for my gun, but she stomped on my hand.

"Do you even know who I am?" she hissed down at me, her gun pointed in my face. "Your people killed my brother."

"Sweetheart, we've killed a lot of people. I don't give a fuck about your brother, lady." I said into the barrel of the gun.

"You bitch!" she screamed, but I would give her something to scream about. Grabbing on to a nearby electrical wire, I pressed the exposed wires against her leg, turning away as they sparked and shook her as though she was having a seizure.

Crawling away from her, I held my shoulder and tried to keep calm. I felt the urge to grab my stomach, but I couldn't. I couldn't stop, and I couldn't allow myself to panic. But even knowing all that, I still found myself rubbing circles over my stomach for a moment before I got back up and headed up the stairs.

When I entered the secret room, I found no one there. Pulling up our files, I began to send them to other computers before deleting everything. I heard what sounded like glass cracking and turned around, pointing my gun at the face of the devil's mistress. But the gun slipped from my hand as I glanced down at the blade in my stomach.

"I warned you," Saige Valero said, laughing. It was the last thing I remembered before everything went dark.

LIAM

"Hold him still," I told Declan and Neal as they brought Amory to his knees in front of me. The fucker thought he could out run me. The moment I had my hands on him, he knew his life was over and the prick ran. I caught up to him in what was left of my half-a-million-dollar garage.

Placing my brass knuckles on, I pounded his face.

"You thought you could come into my house," I yelled as I broke his jaw. "You thought you could destroy me?" I loved the sound of the bones in his face breaking with only his skin to hold it together. "You thought you could burn my fucking house down!" I couldn't even see his face through all the blood.

"You thought you could hurt my family? You reckless"—his teeth burst out of his mouth like popped corn—"idiotic"—*punch*—"motherfucking cunt!" *Punch.*

The moment I stopped, the flesh of his nose was kissing his lips and one eye was out of its socket.

"You? The great big piece of shit who no mother could love and no father could even respect. But worst of all, the man-whore who just had to fuck up my motherfucking day," I sighed, wiping my nose before grabbing the chains.

"I saw this on a movie once," I told him as Neal and Declan bound his feet and hands to the ends of two different cars. "I always wanted to know if the human body would actually rip apart."

Amory coughed up more teeth as they bound him. "How's your wife, Liam?"

It was only then did something click in my mind, and I felt my heart drop into my stomach. However, I couldn't let it play on my face. Instead, I nodded to the two drivers and they begin to drive away from each other as Amory's body rose from the ground and his screams increased.

"I'll be sure to mail this to your father," I told him, nodding once more at the drivers, and pushing it to full speed. I reveled in the sound of his cries as his body ripped open. But looking up, his words still haunted me.

"Where the fuck is my wife?" I yelled over the roars of the engines, and as I did, Olivia rushed in covered in blood. Neal didn't even waste a moment, rushing to her side, but she just pushed out of his arm and ran to me.

"Melody—she saved me, but ..." She stammered, and stopped speaking the moment she saw the two halves of Amory's body.

"Olivia!" I yelled, grabbing her arms. "Where is my wife?"

Shaking, her eyes went wide. "She left me with Fedel, and he put me in one of the safe rooms. But I saw on the camera, Saige . . . some room full of computers . . . everything was . . . Melody didn't see her . . . she . . . Saige . . ."

I never thought I would have to raise a hand to any woman in my family but in that moment, I slapped her so hard she fell on the ground. Neal stepped forward, but Declan held him back.

"Olivia, one last time . . . *Where. Is. My. Wife?*"

"Saige stabbed her in the stomach. Then Patrick came and helped Saige escape with some documents. Sedric is with Melody now," she sobbed.

I never ran so fast in my life. I felt as though I was possessed. I couldn't see anything. I couldn't hear. And by God, I didn't want to feel anything. The only room Melody would go to would be in the west wing. She would have tried to protect our files. Files they could have gotten with Patrick. I trusted him. I brought him into this family. And he fucked me over. He had balls, but not for long. I stopped when my feet could take me no further, and stared at the river of blood that led to my wife's body. My father hovered above her, his shirt off and wrapped around her body.

"Your mother has called an ambulance. I've stopped the bleeding for now, but . . ." Falling to my knees, I wasn't sure what to do. She looked so pale, so sick, and so different from the woman I saw only a few hours ago.

"Liam," my father snapped at me, trying to pull me from my despair. "Your wife will live. Right now, you need to stay calm. Do you understand me?"

I nodded. All I could do was nod as though I was a fucking bobble head. "Patrick Darragh. Patrick betrayed us. I—"

"Son, you have done your duty. The house is secure. Take care of your wife," he said, and I felt the pressure building up in the back of my throat. I wanted to hold her, but I couldn't, not without possibly causing any more damage. Kissing her forehead, nose, and lips, it took all my willpower to back away as the paramedics came in.

MELODY

Everything hurt. Everything was darkness. But in that darkness, one voice rang out louder and stronger than all the rest.

"Melody. My beautiful Melody. I'm right here." He sounded so sad.

"Liam . . ." was all I could say before I drifted back into the darkness.

LIAM

"Mr. Callahan, don't worry. We have the best doctors operating on your wife. If there is anything—and I mean *anything*—" Grabbing her by the neck, I slammed her body against the wall.

"Are you flirting with me, Dr. Lewis?" Her eyes widened in fear, as she tried her best to pull my hand away from her very narrow throat. I only squeezed tighter. "Are you flirting with me while some idiot is sewing my wife back together? Tell me you aren't so I don't have to rip your head from your shoulders, you classless, low-life, idiotic bitch!"

"Please," she cried, kicking her feet wildly.

"Liam, we are in public," my mother whispered behind me.

"So? Who are you going to call?" I turned to the rest of the hospital staff. "I own this motherfucking hospital, and I own this fucking city. If you didn't know it before, you know it now!"

Turning to the bitch as she turned blue, I glared into her eyes. "Never come near me again or I swear on the head of your mother and father, I will kill you."

Dropping her on the ground, I took my seat again, pulling out a cigarette as my father handed me a lighter while mother frowned. It was the only thing that could calm me down now. Neal held on to Olivia for dear life. Declan kept staring at Coraline as if she could disappear at any moment. I knew they were still fighting or whatever the fuck they were doing, but they would be fine. Despite the fact that she wasn't looking at him, she did allow him to hold her hand. The only ones who truly seemed calm were my parents, but I knew it was simply due to the fact that they had done this before. It wasn't the first time we had lost a child because of the Valero, but it would be the last. I would make sure of it. I did my best not to think about it. But it left a burn in my chest and made my blood boil.

The moment the surgeon came out, we were all on our feet.

"Don't waste words. How is she?"

"Mr. Callahan, your wife is fine and is now in her room. We did everything we could for the child, but . . ."

Turning away from him, I nodded at Declan and Neal who already knew no one but family and her doctors were to enter that room.

"Thank you, doctor."

"Blake, sir, Dr. Nickolas Blake," he said quickly, shaking my hand. I tried to leave but my mother held on to me.

"Everyone go. We need a moment." She said it in such a way that none of us could even bring ourselves to argue. I had never heard so much anger roll off her tongue. She and my father shared a quick glance before she pulled me off to the side.

"Mother, whatever it—"

"Right now, this very moment, will define you and your marriage forever," she said. In her eyes, all I saw was pain. "The wife you once knew is not going to be the same woman you see when you walk into the room. Imagine that Melody 'the Boss' is simply asleep and how you react will define how long she remains so. She needs to mourn."

She doesn't know my wife. She didn't even shed a tear after her father died.

"Mel isn't the crying type."

My mother slapped the back of my head, something only she could do. "You're not listening to me. Your wife was attacked. Her child was stolen from her. She isn't the same 'type' you remember. At least not now. You have two choices—pull away or hold on to her even when her words and actions hurt you. Because they will, believe me they will. Do not make the same mistakes your father and I made."

"You came through it," I whispered. Here they were, so many years later, as in love as ever.

She smiled, but it didn't make her eyes shine like usual. "I asked for a divorce. I had the papers drawn up and even called my cousin in Canada. Your father agreed. Had you not gone to the hospital, we wouldn't have made it. He couldn't handle my mood swings or all the names I called him. I couldn't stop myself from blaming him. We made it. But we made it through the hard way. So this, son, is your defining hour, and how you react now will either break or make your future. Whatever pain and anger you are holding on to let it go before you see her or you may just lose her."

She kissed me on the cheek before leaving me standing there, unable to even speak. I couldn't even breathe. Walking into a nearby supply room, I let the tears fall for the child I would never get to meet—who I would never get to know—and I tried to not let myself grow angry with her. What was fucked up was the fact that my anger at Mel overshadowed my anger at Saige. I told her not go. I told her to get in the fucking safe room, but she didn't listen. She never listened.

Slapping my cheeks, I took a deep breath before walking back out again. No one made eye contact with me until I stood right outside her door. Neal and Declan were smart enough to look away.

It felt like hours before I found the will to walk in, and to my surprise, Mel was sitting up. She looked so dazed, like she had gone to war and come back, but nothing was the same as it once was. Evelyn kissed her forehead, while Coraline gave her a small hug. Olivia stayed back. She stood next to Sedric with her head hung low as if she were some servant, and the sight of it pissed me off.

"Out," was all I had to say before they left, and it was in that same moment that I knew my mother was right. Never in all our months together had I ever see Mel jump at my voice.

Taking a seat beside her, she shook her head at me as she fought the tears building in her eyes.

"Say it," she whispered.

"Say what?" Anything she wanted me to say I would say.

"Say it was my fault. Say I killed our child. Say it was for the greater good, because I would have been a horrible mother anyway."

Anything but that. Taking off my jacket, I laid next her, pulling her into my arms.

"This was not your fault, and you did not kill our child. You would, and will, be a great mother," I whispered, kissing for forehead.

"Then why do I feel this way?" She held on to my shirt as she fought back her sobs.

I couldn't answer, mostly because I couldn't think of what to say. I felt so guilty for thinking that this was her fault just moments ago. This was Saige. This was the Valero, and they would pay dearly.

After Mel had gone to sleep, I let go of her and stepped out into the hallway.

Neal, Declan, Monte, Fedel, and my father all stood waiting. I didn't trust any of them. That's what Patrick had done. He had broken the band of trust that we kept in our innermost circles.

"How did this happen?"

"Patrick was the one who found the lead on Cross, the man Melody was interrogating." Declan stated. "He had a CS-5 jammer implanted inside of him. With that, it blocked half of our defense codes and sensors. From there, Patrick opened the gate from the inside. He's been working for them for mouths. We have no idea why he betrayed us. All they needed was a person willing to die, and Cross was that person. With the botched surgery he had to get the jammer inside of him he did not have long anyway. It was simple."

"Getting into our home should never be simple," I said, pinching the bridge of my nose. "I want him found and I want to know how no one else knew. Then I want you to call every Irish or Italian man in the damn country able to build our house. We aren't moving."

"Liam we can stay in the summer home—"

"We are not moving!" I yelled, breathing through my nose before taking a step back. "I will not be chased out of my home like a poverty stricken street rat. There is plenty of house left. Pick a room and deal with it, Father."

He raised an eyebrow at me, grinning before he nodded.

"As for Vance and Saige, take photos of Amory's body and send it to them. When you're done, throw Amory's body anywhere you fucking please. Ship him to the moon for all I fucking care. Just make sure Vance knows those pictures are all that he will ever have left of his son." Part of me wished I hadn't killed Amory outright and used him for some leverage to bring down his father.

"When are we hitting back, boss?" Fedel asked me, and I do believe that was the first time he had ever called me his boss.

"We start now." I glanced over to them all. "Declan, gather every motherfucking hacker and suck him dry. Anything you can destroy, do it. The rest of you, your orders are the same. Shoot to kill. I don't care if they're in the street or their damn beds. We're ending this if I have to bomb all of Russia to do it."

TWENTY-NINE

"The family that mourns together survives forever."

—J.J. McAvoy

SEDRIC

It was déjà vu. No father ever wanted to watch his son suffer as he had. Our sons and daughters were supposed to move forward. Make new mistakes. Forge new paths and conquer new mountains. Yet Liam was fighting my battle. I should have killed off Vance years ago. I should have prevented all this, but I failed.

Allowing the smoke to fill my lungs, I stared up at the sky.

"Sedric." Jumping at the sound of my wife's voice, I looked back to find her glaring at the joint in my hands.

"Sorry," I whispered, preparing to throw it out, when she simply took it from my hands and took a long drag.

Smirking, she handed it back to me. "Only tonight. After today, it should be allowed."

410

"This reminds me of college." Smoking on the roof after a long, hard day of sex. There was some studying every once in a while also, but still.

"I was pregnant, remember? I couldn't smoke."

"Oh, right." I laughed as she hit me, but I just held on to her.

"Will they be okay? Can they get through this?" she whispered.

"I don't know. It's only the first day."

CORALINE

I really didn't know how I got to the maternity ward. I was simply walking and next thing I knew, there were babies as far as the eye could see. They were all enchanting and peaceful. Looking at them almost made me forget that the world sometimes sucked.

"They are cute, aren't they?" Declan whispered next to me.

"Shouldn't you be guarding Mel?"

He smiled. "Neal, Fedel, and Monte are all standing watch."

I said nothing, and he looked at the babies.

"I keep trying to wonder what ours will look like. Liam was so happy. He was kind of high all time."

Again, I said nothing.

"Cora—"

"What Declan?" I snapped. "You want me to give you the time of day because you sat outside my door and played music? But you wouldn't give me the time of day even after I let you fuck me any way you pleased."

He took my hand and kissed it before taking a step back, not speaking any longer. When I looked through the glass, a few of the babies were crying.

"See what you did?"

DECLAN

I couldn't help but smile at her. Even now as she cursed me out, as she should have, I smiled. She had killed someone. She was in the east wing when the bombs went off, and she fought her way to the safe room. A knife right in the motherfucker's throat. If I didn't know better, I would say I was falling in love with her all over again. But the truth was, I had never stopped loving her. I never could. I could wait her out. I could take every jab as long as I got her in the end.

OLIVIA

Staring at my phone, I read Neal's text message over again. It was all that was keeping me together right now.

I love you and the moment I can, I will be at your side. I'm so sorry I wasn't before.

I tried to breathe. I tried to think. But all I could feel were the hands of those men. I almost fell out of my seat when Adriana took a seat beside me.

"You were raped once weren't you?" she asked me, and I did, in fact, stop breathing.

"What? Why would you say—"

"Don't insult me by lying." She smiled sadly. "I know what a rape victim looks like, and I also know what it feels like when Melody saves you from it. She takes you and she makes you unstoppable. She gives you your power back. She brings you back to life. So the next time a guy thinks he can ever lay a hand on you, you can show him what it feels like to piss off God himself."

With that, she left me wondering who her Harvey was and what had she done to him.

THIRTY

"I want to see your face when I kill you! I want to see the light leave your eyes!"

—Voldemort,
Harry Potter and the Goblet of Fire film,
J.K. Rowling

MELODY

Day 5

"Liam can be such an ass sometimes," Coraline said as she fluffed my pillow. "You should be resting in the summer house drinking a Sex on the Beach and watching the *Young and the Restless*. But instead, he has us all on lockdown. Can you believe that? We're on house arrest!"

I said nothing.

Sighing, Coraline fell onto the bed next to me. "I killed someone."

I said nothing.

"Right, that's probably not a big deal to you," she whispered. "But for me it's a huge deal. He came out of nowhere and I just reacted. Adriana told me to always carry at least two knives on me at all times, so I did. I still do. And that day I just pulled them out . . . and killed. But you know the most fucked up part?"

Again, I said nothing.

"I didn't care," she said. "The prick came into my home and tried to hurt me. And when I threw the blade right into his jugular, blood went everywhere. But all I could think was, '*fuck this asshole better not have AIDS.*' That's fucked up right? I'm a good person. I was a good person. Before, I would be freaking out, praying over him or something, and yet all I wanted to do was kick his ass because he might have just given me AIDS."

Nothing. I said nothing.

"Mel, please speak to us. It's been five days. At least say something. Anything," Coraline begged me, but I couldn't.

Shifting onto my side, I tried to go back to sleep. I just wanted the darkness. I just wanted to sleep. It was the only time I felt anything.

"We love you, Mel." It was the last thing I heard before the darkness returned . . . thankfully.

LIAM

"Where are Vance and Saige?" Neal yelled. The prisoner he was speaking to dangled from the ceiling in front of us as I cut into my steak.

"Go fuck yourselves," the fool choked out.

Neal looked to me, and I simply nodded while taking a bite of the bloody beef in front of me.

Taking the drill from Declan, Neal held the point to the man's collarbone.

"Last chance. Where are Vance and Saige?" Neal asked again.

Before the fool could get out his insult, Neal drilled, ripping through skin, muscle, tissue, and bone. He screamed like a pig on its way to the slaughterhouse . . . mostly because he was. Neal stopped only when we could see the drill head on the other end of the man's body, then he pulled it out and moved to the other shoulder.

"Where are Vance and Saige?" Neal shouted into his face. "I swear to God I will drill through your penis next if you don't start speaking."

The fool spit up all over himself as he gasped out for air. "They're in hiding."

"No fucking duh!" I snapped, wiping the corners of my mouth. "I want to know where they're hiding. I have people burning your crops, bombing your labs, and killing your brothers. There will be more blood. There will be retribution. It can end with your bosses, or it can end with your whole family. Choose carefully, there are many more of you, and we have a lot of drills."

Handing me a glass of brandy, Antonio walked past me and held up another drill to the man's belly button.

"Where are Vance and Saige?" Neal asked one last time.

All eyes in the room were on him. "I swear to God—"

"God doesn't come to this part of the house, so swear to me," I told him, leaning back in my chair.

"I swear . . ."

"Kill him." He was wasting words and didn't know anything.

Drowning out his screams, I closed my eyes and took in the hum of the drills. They, for some reason, relaxed me. But sadly, it ended all too soon.

Antonio checked his pulse, then turned to me splattered in the man's blood. "He's gone, sir."

I sighed. "When I said kill him, I meant do it slowly."

It just went to show if you wanted someone killed right, you had to do it yourself. Declan handed me a file, I looked through it quickly before rising.

"What number is he?"

"He's the seventh we've lost during questioning. Weak-ass bitches," Declan answered, opening the door for me.

Frowning, I nodded. "Find me more. I want them all dead. I want Vance, Saige, and all the damn Valero to know I'm coming for them."

As I left, they dragged the fool's body away. Neal's forte was not torture, and neither was Declan's really. That had always been left to my father and me. We were good at it, and in a sick, fucked up way, we enjoyed it. But after what happened, something changed within them both. Neal was fueled by the rage of knowing what could have become of his wife. Declan had lost Coraline in a way. Gone was the shopaholic woman who never seemed to understand the world around her, and in her place was a murderer. She had gone through that and still didn't want to speak with him. He took her punches, and then unleashed it on whichever poor fuck came against us. But I understood. Walking through the construction site that was now my home, I knew what would await me when I opened the door to my room.

Coraline looked at me shaking her head in sadness before leaving. Taking off my shirt, I threw it next to the clothes Adriana had laid out for Melody. None of them seemed to have been touched since this morning.

Kneeling next to her, I brushed back her hair. "Have you eaten?"

She said nothing. She didn't even look at me. Five days of this and I feared it was just the beginning.

"Adriana, I need food. Anything Mel would like, now." I snapped the phone shut before sitting on the floor in front of her.

At least she's breathing. That was the only comfort I had. Flipping through the file in my hand, I just started reading, I didn't want her to feel like I was cutting her out, or that I didn't need her. Because I did, I needed her badly.

"Declan and Monte have been trying to get through the Valeros' firewalls. Their system isn't as strong as ours, so instead they created a freakin' hundred different firewalls. They can hack it, but it will take time. Right now they haven't had any luck. They are working through the eleventh firewall now." I waited to see if she would say anything but again, there was nothing.

"So far we've spoken to seven Valero members, and they have all said the same thing. Vance and his family have gone into hiding like some fecking caffler. The two bit arsewipe took his manky whores . . ." I paused for a moment and groaned. "I'm so pissed off I'm sounding like my grandfather on St. Patrick's Day."

MELODY

He made me smile. I didn't know if he could see it, but he made me smile. I did wonder why he tensed just slightly when mentioning his grandfather.

"Anyway," he said without less of an accent. "They're in hiding. We have all their bank accounts being monitored. The moment we break through the firewalls, we will drain them dry. For now, if any of them withdraw even a penny, we'll know about it. We've already burned all their known crops on both hemispheres and bombed twenty-nine meth labs. If there are more, we will find them. They aren't getting away from us. They have no other choice but to die."

He stood up when Adriana came in with a bowl of something. I couldn't really hear what they were saying, and I didn't care. I wanted to go back to sleep, but my body wouldn't let me.

"Love," he whispered above me, but I didn't reply.

Sighing, he lifted me up with ease and placed me on his lap, as if I were some chi . . . child.

"Love, eat. It's just soup," he said as he started rubbing his thumb against my bottom lip. "Mel, love, I'm begging you. Open your mouth, or I will force it open."

I listened and he looked disappointed, like he wanted me to fight him. But I was tired. All I wanted to do was go back to sleep. The only way I could do that was to listen and allow him to feed me, one spoonful at a time.

DAY 9

"It's morning, Melody," Olivia said as she opened my curtains so wide the sun blinded me. I didn't want the sun. It was too happy. Too full of joy and life, it didn't know when not to shine. It should know that it was a dark day. It should know not to come my way. I wanted the moon. I wanted the night. I wanted the darkness.

But I was too tired to yell at her. Instead, I simply rolled away from the sun.

"You know I was jealous of you," Olivia said, taking a seat on the edge of the bed. "I'm still kind of jealous. I'm always jealous. I don't try to be. It comes from having divorced parents I guess. You're always fighting for attention, and they're always giving it to you because they feel guilty. But with you it was a different type of jealously."

Go away Olivia, I thought but didn't speak.

So she went on. "When I first heard that Liam was getting married, I was kind of hoping she, you, would be like Coraline, the old Coraline, willing to let me have the spotlight and come to me for advice. I think I wanted to be Evelyn in away. I wanted to be the heart of the family. But you weren't like Coraline, or even Evelyn. You were a mafia boss. You, a female, ruled the Italian mafia. When Neal first told me, I thought he was joking. It should have been impossible. No way would any man, true mafia gangster bow down to a woman, and yet there you were. And the men were bowing so low they were almost kissing your white shoes. Do you know that's a thing on Twitter?"

Please go away Olivia, I thought to myself once again, and again I failed to say it out loud. So she went on . . . again.

"Hashtag, Melody Callahan," she whispered. "You're trending. You're always trending, and you don't even know it.

"Anytime we step out in public, you're on Fashion Police, or some other random magazine, being praised. But you don't care because you're a fucking Boss. So of course, I was jealous. The stunningly beautiful, always fashionable, deadly frightening Melody Callahan? How the fuck are any of us supposed to stand next to that?"

Why won't you go away?

"I shouldn't care right?" She sighed. "But I do care. You're everything I wanted to be and then some. The object of every man's desire, and yet never a person. I was born beautiful, and I don't mean that in a cocky, 'I love myself' sort of way. I was born beautiful, and guys always liked me for it. But there was one guy who liked it a little too much. I was a freshman in college. I was actually saving myself for the one, and I knew he wasn't it. So instead of paying attention in school to those stupid flyers and posters that all read '*No means No*,' he . . ."

She sobbed, and I just wanted to sleep.

"He pulled me into his dorm room, and no one did anything because I was the pretty girl who most likely did get around. His friends were there and they all—" She stopped, staring at her tattoo, running her finger over it so many times I stopped counting. "When they finished, they laughed at the fact that I was the loosest virgin they had ever had. When I got home, I had never cried or scrubbed myself so hard. The next day I pulled out of all my classes and finished the rest of my college career from the safety of my bedroom."

I wasn't sure what she wanted from me, but I enjoyed the silence as she lost herself in her thoughts. Sadly, it was short-lived.

"I got this tattoo a month before I found Neal. A Dara knot, I wanted to be strong again and it made me feel that. I think that's why I found Neal, I wasn't broken anymore."

If you are in this family you are broken, don't kid yourself.

"He made me feel safe again, happy again. But there is still this part of me that I can't fix. I hate people. I hate men ... *all* men outside of this family."

That is the very definition of broken!

"And I hate women in some ways, because I hate myself. So when I saw you walking as if you were on water, I hated you the most. Neal tried to knock some sense into me. He said you're the queen and I'm the princess. After that, I was able to handle it until Evelyn told me you were pregnant." She laughed bitterly.

You are insane Olivia. Leave me alone.

"I wanted a child of my own. Neal and I tried over and over again, and here you, the woman dripping in blood and sin, were going to have a child. So I cursed God. I told Him that He was an egotistical, bigoted asshole. Where was the justice? All the shit I had gone through and I just wanted a child. You kill, you steal, you lie, and yet, He gave one to you. But here I am regretting it so badly, Melody," she whispered the last part.

"I never ever meant to hurt you, and I swear from this day forward I will always love you like I should have from the very beginning." If she knew me at all, she should have known I didn't want or ask for her love and that I knew it was bullshit. She wanted to make herself feel better not me.

I was tired of listening to her. So I just slept.

LIAM

"What's your name dear?" my father asked the young crackhead before us as I drank my brandy.

"Whatever you want it to be." She winked, and I almost puked.

My father on the other hand just leered. "I think Julia Roberts is the only one who can do that line."

"Redheads your thing?" She pouted, which was also sickening, as she twirled her brown hair.

"My wife's my thing," he replied, taking a seat before her. "And your life should be your thing. You see, the only thing that is keeping you alive right now is the thought that you may know something. If you don't, well . . ."

He just stopped, and the whore began to shake. "I need something to get the edge off."

Rolling my eyes, I forced myself not to snap her neck.

"What's your poison?" Sedric said, walking over to the tray of drugs Fedel laid out for him.

That got the girl to perk up like a bitch in heat. "Heroin and Cocaine."

"Somebody's a rock star," my father said. "But let's not get greedy. Pick one."

She pouted once again, and once again, I was torn between puking and ripping her lips off.

"Heroin," she said, and my father grabbed the injection before handing it to her.

"Do you need help?" he asked.

But the girl just shook her head untying her halter-top and using it as a tourniquet with no shame that her breasts were exposed to the world. Moaning out as though she was at the peak of a climax, she rode the wave of poison in her veins.

"Druggies man," Monte whispered in disgust. This was a constant reminder why none of them were allowed to do any shit.

"Where's your boss, dear?" Sedric asked her softly.

"I don't know." She smiled, and I felt myself losing control. "They said they were going to Finland. No one ever checks Finland."

"Did they tell you this?" Sedric questioned looking back at me.

She shook her head like a child "Nope. Vance had just finished fucking me. He's an ass. He left me high and dry. I was almost begging. But nope, he was done and wanted me out. So I went in the shower and heard him talking to some redheaded bitch. Ha-ha, you both like redheads."

"Do you know anything else?" Sedric asked her. "This could save your life."

"I'm horny. Can I get a last fuck instead of a last meal?" She grinned reaching for my father's crotch.

I was tired of her. Nodding over to him, he held a gun to her skull. "This isn't jail. You don't even get a last prayer."

Her body slumped over the table with the fucking needle still in her arm. Sedric just looked at her in disgust—the mask of kind smiles was gone—the man who stood in front of me was the same man who made me who I was today. Shaking his head, he put another two in her before handing the gun over to Fedel.

"Such a fucking idiot." He frowned, pulling out his electric cigarette. It was the only compromise my mother would allow him.

"So Finland then?" Declan asked me.

"No, not until we know for sure. I don't believe we have any men there but double-check and pull them out. I don't want them catching on. Besides I still need to talk it over with my wife," I replied as I opened the door.

"Is she speaking yet?" my father asked, but he knew the answer.

"No, no she isn't, but she will." I had to believe she would snap out of it.

"Don't give up hope, son."

Easier said than done.

MELODY

Day 14

"I had a crush on you," Declan whispered from his spot at the foot of the bed. "Crush is such a stupid word. It was more like lust. I shouldn't be telling you about it, but I'm hoping you will get pissed and kick my ass. You know, like Bloody Melody would. I know Liam would skin me alive. No seriously, he actually had us skin one of the Valero. It's like he is going through a historical Roman torture manual and just picking shit. I wouldn't be shocked if we crucified someone next."

I need to put a "do not disturb" sign on the door.

"Yeah, so please don't tell him. Maybe one day when we are old and gray . . . no not even then. He would be senile and probably worse. He acts just like our grandfather sometimes, and our grandfather is an insane, perverted arse of the highest degree. He lives in Ireland and prefers to stay there, which is good. He would understand why I lusted after you. It's hard not to. I think every man with a working dick does. But I'm the only one foolish or stupid enough to stay it out loud." He laughed because he was stupid.

Very stupid. No wonder Coraline is pissed at him.

"It's gone now. Not that you're not attractive because you are, but I think ... I *know* ... I'm lusting after my wife a whole lot more. You had something to do with that. I don't know how you did it. Maybe it's just for the fact that you exist. But you did it. You took my lamb and made her a tiger. She isn't a lioness like you, but she is deadly in her own right. Plus the new hair style gets sexier with each passing day," he said.

Closing my eyes, I went back to sleep, trying my best to drown him out.

LIAM

Day 18

"I thought I said no one was to enter Finland?" I asked them as I drank straight from the bottle.

Antonio nodded. "You did, sir, but she spotted one of our men in the airport before they had a chance to leave. They had no choice but to bring her along."

Sighing, I stared at the blonde woman known as Vance's favorite mistress, Hera Pompilio. There was nothing I could do about it now. She wasn't the big fish I wanted but I could use her as bait.

"May I?" Declan asked, stepping up to the mirror.

"Knock yourself out." Maybe he could use his gentlemanly shit on her.

When he walked in, her dead eyes stared right through him.

"Are you the man who killed my son?" she questioned softly.

Declan simply raised an eyebrow. "I've killed many sons, ma'am. You're going to have to be more specific."

"Amory Pompilio Valero. Age twenty-seven. Six feet, two inches tall. Blond hair, blue eyes, he—"

"No, I did not kill him," Declan said. "That honor was left to my brother and two cars. I was under the impression Amory's mother died when he was young."

"That's what you get for being under everything." She smirked. "I was always made to be Vance's wife. No other woman could carry his child, not even his stupid wife. I told him he should kill her and marry me, but he told me he couldn't. That he made some deal, but I knew it was lie. He took Amory from me and gave him to her. She was so beyond herself with happiness. Every day taking care of my son, I hated her. The day Amory called her Mother, I rammed an ice pick through her heart. Vance was pissed so he broke four of my ribs and my jaw. But he loved me too much to kill me." She laughed so effortlessly, I wondered if Natasha could use a roommate in the asylum.

"Sad," Declan said, but I knew he didn't give a fuck. "Why were you in the airport in Finland?"

She didn't answer. Instead, she just checked her nails.

"Hera, what you tell me could be the difference between a painfully slow death, or a quick one. One where you could be with your son, again," Declan told her.

"So my options are death or death? Fuck you and fuck my son. I wanted to get him out of this life before, and he told me he could handle it. Now he's . . ."

"Now he's in pieces somewhere in the Great Lakes." Declan smirked. "I'll take credit for putting him there."

"You are all so damn proud of yourselves. A bunch of murderers, liars, thieves, and cheats." She frowned. "Your women hate you, you know. They hate you, and they hate what you do. They don't want this life. They wanted the money and the fame, but they didn't want the drugs, blood, and the horror."

Declan grinned, looking evil. "You don't know my wife. If you did, you wouldn't be so quick to speak. And you sure as hell don't know the Boss. So sweetheart, tell me what I need to know and we can move on?"

She leaned in. "Fuck y—"

Rising from his seat, Declan walked around the table until he was right in front of her face. Hera did her best not to look like she was going to piss in her pants, but she failed.

"Do your worst. But believe me, Vance has done worse."

Declan grinned, holding a knife to the side of her face. "Everything he did was healable. After all, in the end, all you have is your looks. Imagine what Vance will think when he sees his favorite toy cut and sewn back together like Frankenstein. My stitches aren't that great with live patients."

"What could you possibly need to know, huh?" she yelled. "We went to Finland to hide. Amory fucked up. Vance spent months, if not years working on different ways to raid this fucking place. He had everything planned to a *T*, even the day. But Amory couldn't wait. He didn't want to listen, and because of that, he was killed. Is that what you want to hear? Or do you want to know that Vance is losing his mind? Amory was the last straw. Vance killed one of his brothers because he thought he had betrayed him. The other brother is in the wind. Everything is fucked. He's going to know you have me, and he's going to hide again."

Declan turned to me and smirked. It was almost sad how quickly she talked.

"You were in the airport. He'll just think you abandoned him." Declan ran the knife against her cheek.

"I would never leave him," she whispered. "He knows that. He knows that no matter how many times I say I'm leaving, I always come back."

"You're a fool. He doesn't love you, and because of that you will die alone," was all Declan said before he slit her throat, her body stilled for one moment before falling to the ground.

"Have every flight in and out of Finland monitored," I said before leaving. It was getting late, and I was going to miss my favorite moment of the evening.

I tried not to run, but this was the only spec of hope I would have all day. It was what got me through the day. Rushing into our bedroom, I smiled when I saw the bed was empty. I entered the bathroom, and smiled at the sight of my Mel bathing herself.

It was only four days ago she had found the will to bathe herself at all. It was a small step, but it was something. Taking a seat by the foot of the tub, I just watched her.

"Would you like me to do your back?" I whispered, and she froze like she hadn't realized I was in the room with her.

She looked up at me through her hair and handed me the loofah. It was another small step. She was on her road back. As she leaned on my free arm, I felt my heart leap. Slowly I rubbed her back, and smiled because I had hope; the dark nights were ending.

MELODY

Day 23

"So I have a confession to make," Neal said pacing in front of me.

Great another one, I thought as I cut into my steak.

"Liam wanted me to take this to my grave, but you won't speak. We've tried everything so maybe you will be so pissed at him and me that you will snap out of it." He stopped and looked me dead in the eyes, but I just ate slowly.

"I shot Liam because he asked me to." He waited for me to react, but I couldn't muster the emotion.

He frowned. "Seriously? You tasered me, you stabbed Declan, and all you can do now is stare at me? This isn't you, Melody. In fact, this surpassed creepy after the first week. I get you're sad, but Liam is going through hell for you. He is not stopping until he kills them all. I know the ruthless woman we all love and fear is still inside there, so can you please come out here and kick my ass or at least shoot Liam again?"

I just ate. It was the only thing I could bring myself to do.

LIAM

I made it to our bed just as Neal was walking out. He looked at me and frowned before leaving.

"We have to go to church, love," I said to her as I entered.

At least she's eating.

She didn't respond. She never responded, and it was starting to send me off the deep end. But I couldn't lose my temper.

"We've already missed three masses. A forth one and people might think I killed you." I smiled.

Grabbing the remote, she flipped the television on and sure enough, she went to Sunday morning mass. It was kind of funny and cute. Shaking my head at her, I took off my shoes and jacket before jumping onto the bed. She handed me the bottle of wine, but still didn't speak. Kissing her hand, I took it and drank.

"Do you have bread?" I asked, and there it was, a small smirk. It made my heart leap for joy, it brought water to my eyes, and it was my own personal Sunday miracle.

She didn't say anything, but a smirk was enough to get me through the rest of the day.

MELODY

DAY 25

"I don't know what to say to you," Sedric said.

I mentally groaned. *How about nothing at all?*

"So I will make this short."

Thank Jesus.

"Melody Nicci Giovanni-Callahan, get your fucking ass out of bed. This has gone long enough," he snapped at me.

Raising an eyebrow at him, I flipped on the television as Evelyn laughed.

"I told you it wouldn't work."

"Had to try, but apparently my daughter doesn't like to listen to me," he said kissing my head, before leaving Evelyn and me alone.

She sat on the bedside me. "I understand. They don't get it. How it feels to have a child living within you one moment and then taken from you the next. I understand not being able to move, speak, or even breathe because of the hole burning inside your heart. No else gets it. But I do, so stay in bed as long as you need, Melody. Grieve, and when you're ready, you will get up again."

I watched her as she got up before turning to leave. She was the only one who understood. Wiping the water that poured from my eyes, I held on to myself.

Go to sleep, Melody. Just sleep. I would get up in the morning, but now I just needed to sleep.

LIAM

"And just like that, the rat is back," I hissed at the man before me.

His nose was busted, eyes bruised, teeth were knocked out, and any exposed part of his skin was either burnt or cut. Patrick looked like he had been to hell and back.

"Sir," he said quickly, fighting against his chains. "I did this for you, to help you"

"You betrayed me to help me?" I said, slowly turning back to the rest of our men. So many of them wanted to watch this that we had to go outside.

"Sir, I swear, I never betrayed you. I've known you since college. We've been—"

"Get to the part where you stabbed me in the back," I said, pouring the gasoline over his head. "Remember the part where you left my wife bleeding-out on the ground as you escaped with the Russian slut."

"Sir—"

"Don't waste words. I can only hold this match for so long," I said, lifting the small flame in my grasp.

"Liam, I knew they were planning something. The only way to find out was to make them think I'd jumped ship. I had no idea what Saige had in store for your wife. I just knew the Valero had to come to an end. The information I've gathered can help you bring them down. They aren't in Finland anymore. They went to Tanzania. It was the only place they thought you couldn't reach. You have people in all of Europe, but not in Africa. I'm telling you, I wasn't betraying you." He cried out in panic.

Shaking my head, I let the flame drop but sadly it was already out.

"So you became a spy without my knowledge?" I laughed. "You're lying—"

"No—"

Punching him in his broken nose, I held his face. "Never interrupt me, or have you forgotten your manners while with the dogs?" I squeezed his face. "You're lying to me, Patrick. You should know better than that. You betrayed me before, and now that the walls are closing in on Vance, you're trying to save yourself. You're a rat through and through. I think my wife gave a good definition of that word before."

"Liam—"

"Don't speak my name," I said, taking a step back. "I don't care why you betrayed me. The simple fact is that you did, and by definition, that means you are against me."

Striking the match, I didn't even hesitate as I threw it into the trail of gas. It took only a second before his whole body was up in flames. He screamed and flailed violently, while the men just cheered and sang into the night. Turning away, I just happened to look up to find my wife staring down at the burning man.

When our eyes finally met, I saw . . . I saw my lioness stirring.

MELODY

DAY 26

Drinking, I waited for them to come aboard. If Adriana had done her job, they should have known where I was.

"It's nice to see you, ma'am," Jinx said, giving me a brand new bottle of wine.

I nodded but did not speak. I didn't want my first words to be to him. A second later, Nelson opened the door to the jet, allowing Liam to come through, dressed for war. He looked me over quickly. His eyes shined like green diamonds in the sun and grin spread across his face. He looked like he was trying to contain himself.

"What the fuck are you looking at? We're heading to the jungle and plan on people hunting with guns not arrows," I said with no real edge in my voice at all.

"You could kill them with your shoes if you want, I'm happy you're here," he said sitting in front of me. He squeezed my hand. "Real happy."

"Speaking of killing, Neal told me something very interesting." I grinned as I sipped. His eyes went wide before he turned to Neal, who froze like he had forgotten his confession. I missed my old self. I hated that bed and I didn't want to think about it. I needed to be me.

"I can explain—"

"Don't bother. I've thought about it, and I've partially forgiven you." I understood what he did, but that didn't mean I liked being manipulated.

"Partially?" Liam asked with a smile.

He couldn't stop smiling at me, and it was pissing me the fuck off. *Yeah, I was talking. He needed to stop looking at me as if he wanted to fuck me over the table.*

Part of me knew I was just being this way because I wasn't sure how to explain my feelings. I understood how he felt because I felt it to. I wasn't part of the living dead anymore.

"I'm Melody Nicci Giovanni-Callahan, which means I have to seek vengeance, even with you, husband."

"I look forward to it."

As Jinx took us into the sky, I stared at the sun through the clouds. Liam would enjoy my revenge, but not until I made Saige pay dearly. An eye for an eye, and life for life.

THIRTY-ONE

"I guess I've played a lot of victims, but that's what a lot of the history of women is about."

—Jodie Foster

ADRIANA

She didn't have to say anything, all she did was hold out a plane ticket. She wouldn't force me to go. She wouldn't even ask, it was my choice, and I simply took it from her and left her bedroom. Of all the men in Mel's crew, I was the only one she would ever let leave if I wanted to. Before Liam, I was the only one allowed to see her when she as down, when she had her dark days.

They were never like this, where she couldn't even get out of bed, but they were dark enough to make normal people cringe. What she did to those who crossed her during her dark days was borderline insane. I, on the other hand, wasn't normal. Once upon a time, I was. I was bubbly, preppy, and most likely annoying, like every other teenager. But that all changed the day my father went into debt.

Walking into my bedroom, I pulled out my knife and makeup set trying my best to hide those memories, but they would never go away. Nothing could ever make you forget your father selling you like a piece of cattle. I didn't even know shit like that happened to people in America.

It was almost ironic really that *Taken* was the last movie I saw before I myself was taken right out of my room. But my father wasn't an ocean away. No, he stood in the doorway with his head down as they came for me. I kicked, I screamed, I called out to him and my mother, but they turned away. If I hadn't been speaking to Mel on the phone, there really wouldn't have been any hope for me.

We were both freshmen in college, and everyone just stayed away from her. It was like she was the moon, and they gawked at her from afar. And just like the moon, she was cold, distant, and downright scary. There was no reason for either of us to have spoken if it hadn't been for some school project. She never really talked to me when we worked, and I was a rambler then, so it worked out fine.

That night I screamed for my parents and when they looked away, I screamed as loud as I could into the phone that was left on my bed. They shoved me in the back of their car and gave me a cocktail of drugs that took the fight right out of me.

The first night was the worst. They all took turns with the less pretty ones, I fell into that category. I cried, I puked, I begged for death, and it was only the first day. The girls who had been there longer were just wasting away in beds, so high they couldn't even pick themselves up.

I knew I wasn't going to end up like them. I swore I wasn't going to end up like them. I planned on killing myself the moment I had a chance. When my next round of guests came on the second day, they laughed at me as I struggled against the chains. They liked fighters, they liked breaking them, and just as they dropped their pants, bullets were flying everywhere.

They seemed like angels of death, shooting down the pigs who dared to call themselves men. It happened so fast that I wasn't even sure if I was still sane. I thought my mind was just trying to protect me. That was until I saw her. She walked in, looked around until she met my gaze, and I had never felt so disgusted with myself. I cried, and she simply walked over to me and gave me her white jacket.

She told me, "As long as I live, this will never happen to you ever again."

That was the start. She took me in and forced me into therapy while she personally kicked my ass in training day in and day out for a year and a half. It felt like only weeks then. When I was better, in the sense that I was no longer weeping during the day and puking during the night, she told me I could go. But where could I go? I begged her to let me stay. I promised to stay loyal to her as long as I lived. It was then that she told me about who she was and what she did.

After a year and a half of seeing bloody walls, drugs, and guns everywhere, it wasn't too hard to figure out. She told me the only way I could stay was to prove myself. I wasn't sure how, but I would do anything.

So she drove me back to my old house on the corner of 54th and Adam Street, gave me a gun, and told me to get my justice. My heart was beating so fast I could hear it my ears, and I didn't want to let her down. I didn't want to let myself down. I wanted to kill them for what they did to me. Parents like that shouldn't get to live. So I rang the doorbell, and when my father opened the door, he nearly pissed himself.

"Hi, Daddy." It was the last thing I remembered saying before I lost myself. When it was over, I walked into the kitchen to find Mel eating the dinner my mother would never get to eat. She looked me over before sliding me a glass of wine.

"From this day forward, Adriana, I'm your Boss," she said to me. "You will treat me with respect. I will treat you with a lesser form of that respect. But if you ever betray me, I will kill you, and I like you. But I will still kill you."

"Yes, ma'am," I said, sucking down the wine.

"Do you need anything?" she asked once she stood up.

"There is nothing for me here, ma'am."

"Then burn it to the ground," she said, before walking out the door.

Any part of the old Adriana died in that fire. From those ashes, I came out a Phoenix. Mel had always reminded me that we all had the capacity to be ruthless, that all we needed was the right push.

"Whoa." Antonio smirked from my doorway at the transformed woman staring back at me. Kissing my neck, he met my gaze in the mirror. "Sexy, but this isn't my Phoenix. Where are you going?"

"The Boss," I said, and he didn't ask any more questions, he knew not to. He kissed my neck before walking to the door.

"Be safe, baby," he said as the door shut.

Antonio and I . . . well it was new, complicated, and fun. I hadn't dated since joining Mel, however, Antonio and I always found ourselves in these situations with our clothes off. I had to tell Mel, and when I did, she said that as long as our loyalty to her outranked our lust for each other, she didn't give a fuck who we screwed.

Grabbing my stuff, I walked out of the house basically unnoticed, and it was only when I was about to board my flight, I sent a text to Liam. Mel would be right behind me. She wanted blood. She would get her revenge.

THIRTY-TWO

"There was a murdered corpse, in secret land and violent death in thousand shapes displayed."
—Geoffrey Chaucer

LIAM

I couldn't help but watch her as I drank my brandy. The way she cleaned her gun over and over again had to be one of the sexiest things I had ever seen her do. She was mesmerizing, from her long ponytail, to her sleek tank top and camo pants, everything about her was memorizing.

"I feel you staring at my breasts," she said not bothering to look at me. But her voice alone was enough to give me a hard-on.

"If it bothers you, love, stand up and let me stare at your ass instead." I grinned, finishing the rest of my drink before standing up.

"Liam, we need to focus," she hissed as I ran my fingers against her neck.

Kissing the base of her throat, I grabbed her breasts. "I am focusing."

"Liam stop," she said, pushing me away.

Backing away from her, I pinched the bridge of my nose, trying to calm myself down. What the fuck was wrong with me? She had just started to speak less than twelve hours ago, and I was trying not to jump her. Being in the plane with her so close didn't help. Never had I been happier to take her bitching.

"Mel . . ."

"Liam . . ."

We both stopped when there was a knock on the door. Sighing, Mel stood up and opened the lodge door, allowing both Neal and Declan to walk in. Declan immediately gave me a look as if he knew what had just happened. However, with the thin walls I wouldn't be that surprised.

Vance was right in coming to Tanzania. Neither Mel nor I had ever been here before, but luckily the American dollar was as good as gold. It only cost us five hundred dollars to buy this wooden lodge in the middle of the fucking jungle. It wasn't the Ritz, but it would do for now.

"Can we come in?" Neal asked.

"She opened the fucking door didn't she?" I stated, pouring myself more brandy. *Thank God that Nelson kid kept the plane well stocked.*

Walking over to me, Mel capped the brandy bottle, glaring at me before looking back at them. "What do you have?"

Declan pulled out a map and opened it over the table. "So were in Seronera, here." He pointed. "From what we've gathered speaking to some of the locals, a group of men with *Vs* on their arms came through here two weeks ago."

"We think they are hiding out in Lobo, about forty-five miles from here. If we leave now, we can make it before daybreak. I've already bought a helicopter from one of the townsfolk, Jinx is fixing it up the best he can now," Neal added, pulling on the strap of his sniper rifle.

"You, Antonio, and Jinx along with the rest of the snipers will stay back ten miles. I'm guessing the helicopter you bought isn't going to hold all twelve of us, so look for another one and have Adriana fly it," Mel stated looking over the map. "Declan, you and Monte, along with the rest of the men, will back the twenty-five mile mark."

We stared at her as though she had just lost her fucking mind.

"So you and I are supposed to raid their hideout by ourselves?" I asked her slowly. Maybe she wasn't quite ready to come back yet.

"Ma'am, Adriana didn't even come with us." Declan eyed her carefully before shooting me a look. This was too important to fuck up, and we only had a small window.

"Maybe you should rest," Neal started, but was cut off by Mel cocking her gun.

"Please finish that sentence, motherfucker. I'm begging you to finish that sentence, so when I tell Olivia why her husband came home with a bullet, I can say he forgot who the fuck I am . . . a deadly mistake. Especially since I haven't liked your bitch-ass from the get-go. So go ahead and tell me I need some rest."

Neal made the wisest choice of his life and kept silent, Declan on the other hand . . .

"Ma'am . . ."

"And you," Mel snapped, turning her gun on him. "You keep your mouth shut or I will be forced to tell Liam all the naughty things you've been dreaming of doing to me."

"What the fuck!" Before he could even blink, I had a gun to his skull. I never thought I would have to shoot my best friend, but I'd been wrong on many occasions lately.

"Drop your gun, Liam."

I just glared at the bitch-ass motherfucking cunt that dared to call himself my right-hand man. "Fuck no. I'd rather kill him slowly. Maybe set him on fire."

Pushing Declan back, Mel stepped in front of my gun. "I wasn't asking. Put the gun down now."

"We will have words later, cousin." I glared over at him before doing as she asked. I would deal with her later as well.

"Now that all your blood is pumping to the right places," she hissed at me. "Adriana, come in."

And sure enough, a blond-haired woman with green eyes stepped in. She was sexy, in a whorish type of way, and could definitely not be ugly duckling, Adriana. However, she walked over to Mel with her head held high and pulled a cell phone out of her bra.

"Is there anything else you needed, ma'am?"

Holy mother of fuck. Sure enough, that voice belonged to Adriana.

Nodding, Mel placed the phone in her back pocket. "Thank you, Adriana, feel free to change. I hope that wasn't too much for you."

"Never, ma'am," Adriana replied, taking off the blond wig. "I placed the bombs throughout the compound like you asked. They sweep the place every morning though, so tonight is the only chance you have."

"He didn't touch you did he?" she asked with no emotion whatsoever. Anyone who knew her was aware that emotionless Mel was as ruthless as they come.

"No, ma'am. I was too European for him. He wanted to taste the native culture." She frowned, blinking rapidly as she pulled off her fake nose.

"Thank you, Adriana."

Adriana nodded before leaving, and I could feel my blood begin to boil over.

Why the fuck am I clueless right now? I thought to myself as I cracked my jaw. Walking in front of her, I leaned in on the other side of the table.

"Speak, now," I said, afraid of losing my temper with her. One moment I wanted to fuck her brains out, the next, I wanted to snap her neck. Why did she torture me so much?

She leaned in and whispered, "I think I should rest."

"Mel . . ."

"After Adriana let you know I was on the plane, I had her follow along on a commercial flight. We've cut off most of Vance's drug supply, but the money he makes from trafficking is a lot higher—"

"You let Adriana get abducted?" That was the most reckless thing I had ever heard from her. Trafficking wasn't a joke. Adriana was most likely drugged within seconds of being taken. They could've done God knows what during that time, and worst of all, Adriana could have been blown . . .

"I see the wheels of hell turning in your eyes, and you need to breathe," she snapped at me. "Yes, I let Adriana get abducted, but she knew what she needed to do. After all, it wasn't the first time the Valero had taken her. This time she didn't go in as a victim, but as a motherfucking liberator. So as I was saying before you grew a heart, Mr. Grinch, Adriana was taken from the airport. What she did, and how she got out, I'm not aware of because it just fucking happened. All that matters is that their hideout is laced with Cyanide bombs."

"You want to smoke them out." Declan smirked stepping closer, and the moment he did, I stabbed the table right next to his hand. He looked up at me with eyes wide before taking a step back.

"We smoke them out like rats, and we shoot them down one by one while they're blinded." Neal grinned, circling the area around Valero's hideout. "They will come running as fast as possible, but they will be too fucked up to even pull the trigger."

"You planned this all out in a few hours." I didn't even bother trying to hide how impressed I was.

Turning to Neal and Declan, I signaled for them to leave. Declan was out the door faster than I had ever seen him move.

She poured herself a glass of brandy, but neither of us spoke. We both were too hardheaded for that. Knocking back the rest of my drink, I licked my lips.

"I missed you," I whispered. She was the only one who could take all the fight right out of me and put it back in at the same time. "I missed you, and us, and who we were for that short moment in between hating each other and losing . . ."

I didn't think I would ever be able to say it out loud. It hurt too much, and no matter how far down I pushed, the pain it came back again.

I was so lost in my thoughts, I hadn't even noticed she'd moved beside me until I felt her hand in mine. Lifting it to her lips, she kissed my knuckles, and I couldn't help but moan at the softness of her lips. How long had it been since I kissed her. As if she could read my mind, she cupped the side of my face before kissing my lips. She tasted like honey and I almost came in my pants when she bit my lip.

"I've missed you as well," she whispered. "I-I needed time. I didn't know how much, but I just knew I needed a moment to be—"

"To be sad," I finished for her, wanting nothing more than to close the distance between our lips.

"Yeah." She smiled sadly, and I wanted to wipe it from her face. "I never meant . . . I knew I couldn't be any help in the mindset I was in. I hope you didn't get used to ruling without me."

"Never." I cupped her check running my finger across her bottom lip. "I could never rule without you. I need you, physically, spiritually, and emotionally."

"I need you, too, but I need to take care of Saige. I can't—"

"Shh," I murmured as I unbuckled her pants.

She moaned as I cupped her ass lifting her onto the table. "Liam we don't have time . . ."

"I know." I sighed. "I just need a taste to tide me over."

Before she could speak, I pulled her pants and underwear down, kissing her forehead, then her lips, before kissing the top of her breasts. I even bit one, causing her to gasp as I played with her pussy.

"Liam . . ."

"Shut up, Mel," I said, falling to my knees and allowing my tongue the pleasure of tasting her.

She moaned as my tongue went deeper inside her, I could feel her rocking against my face, begging for release. Her wetness dripped all over my fingers as I thrust them into her.

"Fuck me, Liam . . ." She grabbed ahold of her breasts, pinching her nipples, while riding me.

"What happened to not having time?"

"Make time." She grabbed a fistful of my hair, pulling me up to her face. Kissing her made my dick beg for release. Knowing that she was tasting herself on my lips was almost too much.

"You've had enough control for one day, love," I whispered grabbing ahold of her breasts. I wanted her to be my bitch, because she was my bitch. She pulled at my pants until they finally dropped, allowing me the freedom I desired.

I pulled her off the table and flipped her around, falling to my knees again as I kissed her ass before biting it and rising back up.

"Li . . . oww . . . ohh!" She screamed as I shoved my dick right into her ass.

"You've ticked me off," I told her grabbing onto her hair as I slammed into her so hard her ass jiggled, begging for me to slap it, which I had no other choice but to do.

"You've captured my heart." I pulled her up lifting her shirt and bra in order to squeeze the fuck out of her breasts with my left hand. My right hand traveled down her stomach to cup her wetness.

"Fuck, Liam . . ." She wrapped her arm around my neck.

"You've driven me half mad," I said, biting her ear before pushing her back down onto the table.

"You've made me fall in love with you." Grabbing her waist, I slowed my thrusts only for a second before I rammed into her again making her moan random words.

"You've made me into a monster." I held on to her sides while I fucked her so hard and fast, everything that was once on the table fell to the ground.

I fucked her over the map of the damn country, and she loved it so much she couldn't even speak. I fucked the words straight from her lips. She came not once, not twice, not even three times, but four. Reaching back, she grabbed a fistful of my hair and hoisted herself onto her knees, pressing into my chest. Her face was so close to mine each time she came, her eyes would glaze over like she was reaching a new high. And the look on her face, the look of a woman fucked beautifully was too much for me to handle.

I pulled out of her, and she all but collapsed back onto the table as I came all over her back and her ass. It was the most glorious thing I had ever seen.

"You fucking prick . . ." she said through gasps. She always pretended like she hated when I came on her, but she secretly loved it. I had claimed her, and she loved when it was my turn to dominate her almost as much as she loved making me her bitch.

Rising from the table, she did her best to stand straight, and I just smirked, running my hand through my sweaty hair.

"Ten minutes . . . you could have done better." She grinned, stripping her shirt and using it as a towel.

"We're on a time crunch, the faster we kill these mother fuckers the more time I will have to make love to you later. I had to fuck you one more time for good measure." I snickered, pulling up my pants.

Walking into the bathroom, she shook her head at me. "You've had enough control for the night. Next time, you're my bitch."

I couldn't wait. I just had to make it through tonight. If the money, territory, and revenge weren't reason enough to kill Vance and his people, the thought of my Mel controlling me was enough push me to kill anyone. This war would come to an end. I would see to it, for the sake of her, and our future family.

MELODY

I had been waiting for this ever since I got out of the hospital. As Liam drove through the plains of the African continent, I took in the night air. I had never felt so alive in all my life. My moment with Liam was animalistic, lustful, and downright pornographic, and yet it was just what I needed to breathe again. He made me feel things that no other man ever could. I knew that no matter what happened, I was in love with him.

He understood me. He loved me. And was everything I needed. I'm not sure if I could ever show him how much. Truthfully, I wasn't even sure if we were going to live. Yes, we had it all planned out, and the ideas Liam added after our little fuck fest were genius, but there was always a chance that things could go wrong. It was the truth we all understood . . . sometimes you plan and still end up dying. There was nothing you could do about things you didn't know.

Liam never let go of my hand as we drove forward. To anyone else we had to be batshit crazy. But for us, this was the only way this could end. We couldn't wait hours on end to strike back, this wasn't some CIA mission. This was a battle—a war between Mafia houses—and this time, Romeo and Juliet were on the right side.

Each passing moment as he drove felt like an hour, and by the time he put the car into park under the tree and kissed my knuckles, I was all but jumping out of my skin. I needed to get this over with. I needed to be me again, and the only way I knew how to do that was to make them pay.

He reached into the backseat and pulled out two machine guns along with three different sized clips before handing me one.

"Are you ready?" he asked, and it was a stupid question, because he knew the answer already.

Flipping open the phone, I dialed quickly before snapping it in half. Neither of us had to wait long before the small village shook so violently that we could feel it in the car. Birds flew in the opposite direction along with anything else that lived. Even the clouds covered the full moon as if God himself was trying not to look at the hell we were unleashing. It took everything I had not to think about the day our home shook that way. The white smoke spread around the building like a disease crawling into every part of the home until a few men came running out guns drawn. The doses were on the lower end of the scale. I didn't want them to die. I wanted them to be confused, dazed, and helpless.

Liam didn't even hesitate, stepping out of the car with his gun clenched in his hands. I jumped out as well, and we waited until more of them had no choice but to come stumbling out before we unleashed a hail of gunfire.

Through a flash in the air, the dirt below us kicked into the air as Antonio, Neal, and Jinx all hovered overhead. Handing me a gas mask, we walked forward with all the ease in the world, as we were given cover. I could hear them cough trying to hack out the poison in their lungs so I did them a favor by shooting them on sight.

We didn't really give two fucks who it was. The moment something moved, we shot it down. Vance and Saige would be in the safe room so there was no need to be careful. After all, we wanted them to die slowly. Those bitches were hoping we would just forget about them? Fuck no. Naked women screamed at the top of their lungs as they tried to make their escape, well at least some of them did, the rest of them just sat down and wept. The further we went down the hall, the hole that used to be my heart seemed to beat against my chest.

It was only when we reached the double doors did Liam and I glance at each other before kicking it in. There, naked and chained to the bed, was a man and a woman both panicking and breathing in the toxins slowly. Vance disgusted me. Shooting at their chains the man looked me dead in the eye before looking back at the wall.

"Run, you idiot," Liam snapped, and they did, they ran as far as their naked legs could take them.

Walking toward the end of the wall, Liam knocked. "Vance, are you alive back there?" he asked, and when he got no answer, I placed a brick of C4 against the wall before we both put the pillow against it. Falling back behind the dresser, we both grinned at the sound of metal tearing against metal. We couldn't move as a hail of bullets came at us like a swarm of bees.

"Come out, come out, wherever you are," she sang, and I wanted nothing more than to rip her throat from her neck. But Liam held me back, gripping my thigh.

"You came looking for us?" She laughed. "Is this because I killed your poor *baby*? I'm not sorry. I would do it again!"

All I could see was red, and before Liam or even God himself could stop me, I jumped out from behind the desk. She didn't even hesitate before shooting, one bullet hit me right in the chest, and had it not been for the bulletproof vest, I would have been gone.

Ignoring the pain, I jumped up running forward before jump-kicking her right in the face. Her body flew back into the mirror before sliding down. Grabbing the shard of the mirror, she ran toward me, but Liam, the fucking controlling ass bitch, shot her through the wrist.

"No!" I yelled at him. The redhead was mine.

He looked me over quickly before running into the safe room.

Saige, however, didn't even take a second before she came at me with the large shard of glass.

Dropping my gun, I punched her right in the nose, elbowed her in the neck, and power-kicked her in the knees, sending her down. It was only when she was on her knees, did I draw my own knee back and bring it full-force into her face.

She fell back, and just as I was about to grab onto her hair, a rope tied around my neck, choking the life out of me.

"I've been waiting to do this since the first day I saw you," Ryan hissed into my ear as I struggled for air. The prick grabbed onto my breast. "I think I'll only leave you unconscious so that way you can wake up to me in you."

Just as everything was going black, his grip on me was gone as his body fell back to the ground a bullet through his skull. Liam stood in front of me, nose flaring like a bull. Hell was once again reflected in his eyes. It was then that Saige thought it would be a good idea to try to stab him, but before she could, I grabbed her arm and twisted it until I heard a sickening pop and her arm went limp.

"Vance had a motorcycle, he's gone," Liam said, but I knew he was pissed. He wanted this done yesterday.

"And you'll never catch him," Saige said, from her place beneath us . . . as she fucking should be.

"You're going to die soon, so I'm going to let you know this little fun fact." I bent down, looking into her eyes. "This is going to hurt, you're going to cry, and right as your soul leaves your body, you will cry out to God, and not even He will show you mercy."

With that, I punched her right in the face and her eyes rolled back.

Glancing up at Liam, he smirked throwing me his phone.

Guess who's driving toward us, the text read. I hated guessing, but just this once I would enjoy playing along.

LIAM

"Vance, Vance, Vance." I smiled at the bonded and gagged man in front of me. He looked so weak, so . . . not worth my time. How there was ever a time where I dared worry about him was beyond me. He was a sexually perverted old man with Russian friends.

"I've dreamt of killing you since I was child," I told him, pulling the gag from his mouth. "I thought about how many ways I could destroy you, and I have to say, this was one of those ways."

"You think this is over?" Vance asked, and Mel punched him in the jaw.

"Love, he's mine to beat the shit out of." I frowned at her. Rolling her eyes, she held up her hands before leaning against the tree with Saige kneeling in front of her.

Our men gathered around us, all watching with joy, pride, and most of all excitement. They had grown to either enjoy my method of torture or hate it in silence. Either way, this has been long overdue.

"What were you saying?" I asked him pulling out a knife. "Something about this not being over?"

Vance grinned. "You stupid Irish bastard. You thought I was something to worry about? You don't even know what's coming. I was your buffer, without me she will come after you next."

"You're not making sense, Vance," I sighed running the blade against his cheek. "And you don't have a lot of time to explain."

Again, Vance grinned, looking over to my Mel. "Ruthless isn't she? Just like her mother."

At that, Mel's eyes narrowed.

"Oh is that rage?" he asked her, and I punched him right in the face, sending him onto his back, but he just laughed.

"Correction, that was rage." He grinned before coughing up blood along with a few teeth. "But poor little *Melody*, the little girl who lost her mother so tragically at my hands. But wait?"

He laughed on like a mad man. "She isn't even dead!"

"What are you talking about, Vance?" Mel replied shooting him in the ankle.

But Vance was so mental, he didn't even flinch.

"I mean, my sweet girl, your mother is alive, your mother and grandfather are both alive actually. Ruling in secret. They have just been waiting for us to kill each other and pick up the pieces." He sighed shaking his head.

"You're lying," I hissed, shooting him though his other ankle.

"Maybe," he said, falling onto his back. "Or maybe all those years married to Orlando 'Iron Hands' Giovanni changed her, made her into something dark and ruthless. After all, the apple can't fall so far from the tree. But you'll see soon.

You can't touch her. She's untouchable, they are all untouchable."

Mel and I both unloaded our weapons into him, not stopping until every last bullet was in his body.

Grabbing Saige by the hair, Mel forced her to stand right beside Vance's fallen body. Pulling the ripped shirt from her mouth, Mel glared into her eyes.

"Was he telling the truth?"

Saige just smiled. "Fuck you, fuck your mother, and fuck every last one of your men."

Taking a deep breath, Mel took a step back.

"Strip her."

Saige's eyes widened as the men closed in on her. "You're going to let them rape me?" She tried not to look scared. The men all cringed at the thought.

"No one wants you, whore," Fedel said from behind her, causing the men to laugh as they approached. Without a second thought, they ripped all her clothes off, leaving her standing there bloody and dirty.

"You get to leave this world the same way you came in," Mel said holding her hand out as Adriana handed her a pair of scissors.

"First, bald." Kicking her bad knee, Mel grabbed a fistful of hair and cut. She pulled and cut until all Saige had were clumps of red hair. When she was done, she grabbed the handcuffs Saige was in and cuffed her to the back of the Jeep.

"Second, screaming."

The rage, the fire, the pain in Mel's eyes made it clear to everyone that they should not stop her until Saige suffered, and this was the only way. Mel was going to drag her body for God knows how many miles until Saige either died from the shock or the loss of blood. The animals would do the rest.

"Please . . . please . . . don't do this. I—" Mel just stuffed a sock in her mouth.

"A life for a life," Mel whispered to her. "You crossed the wrong family."

Monte held open the car for her, and she smiled at me through the mirror.

"This is going to hurt you way more than it's going to hurt us," I said to her before stepping in through the passenger side door.

Starting up the engine, Mel hit the gas hard, and screams filled the morning sky, but I just turned up the music. We were finally on top of the world.

"When did you take out my fucking CD?" Mel snapped at me as she drove faster.

"Your taste in music is shit, love."

"Just because I don't like that fucking classic and old school hip hop crap, doesn't make it shit."

"All those artists are auto-tuned anyway. I like real music," I said, turning it up just a little bit louder to drown out the screams.

"What the fuck is this?" She glared at the radio.

"MC Ren," I said, and she just stared at me. Smirking, I began to rap along with it, causing her eyes to widen before she broke out in a fit of laughter.

"You are a pale-ass white kid from Chicago Elite. You are not allowed to try to rap this."

"Hater." I winked and as she smiled. For the first time in forever, we both felt like we could just relax.

Looking out at the lions as they rose for another day, I wondered if we were any different. After all— I killed, ate, slept, and fucked just as they did. I was the king of the jungle, and the woman beside me was my queen.

EPILOGUE

"Like Alexander the Great and Caesar, I'm out to conquer the world."

—Jarod Kintz

MELODY

"Five." I kissed his nose

"Four." He kissed my forehead

"Three." I kissed his cheek.

"Two." He kissed my chin.

"One," we said at the same time before kissing each other deeply.

"Happy New Year," I whispered into the darkness of our room.

"Happy New Year, love," he whispered back.

Hearing the fireworks go off pulled me away from him, much to his protests, but I did want to see all the effort Evelyn had put in. Grabbing my robe, I stood at the window taking in the sight of all those celebrating like drunken fools.

"You know they say the first year of marriage is the hardest," Liam said, kissing my shoulder.

Groaning, I leaned into him. "We're still in the first year."

"Really? I swear it's been longer than that." He laughed, trying to untie my robe, but I slapped his hands away.

"Control yourself. We have a meeting, remember?" Despite the fact that I wanted him as well, this was important.

"You're starting the year off wrong."

"You'll forgive me, now put on pants." He was such a pain sometimes.

"You put on pants." He glared at my bare legs.

Rolling my eyes at him, I threw him his pajama bottoms. "I can wear whatever I want! So let's go, the family is waiting."

He frowned but wore his stupid pants, following me out of the room and into the study. There sat the whole family, along with Senator Colemen, Olivia's Father, who looked very confused about why he was here.

His whole demeanor changed when Liam took a seat in his chair while I sat on the desk.

"Thank you all for coming," Liam said to them coldly. "As you all know, it's been a stressful year. However, that's what happens when you take over a state."

"And now that we have the state eating out of our hand, we want the country." I smiled at them all.

"How do you plan on doing that?" Sedric asked, leaning into his chair.

Liam and I grinned before Liam spoke. "You run for the highest office in the land."

Declan coughed up his drink. "You want to run for President?"

"Hell fucking no," Liam replied. "Senator Colemen does, and we're going to support him one hundred percent."

Senator Colemen's eyes widened as he gaped at us. "You want me to run for President? Have you lost your mind? Is this a joke?"

I glared at the idiot. "No, this is an order, or did you forget who has been funding all your other campaign events?"

"You're going to run for office, and you're going to win," Liam said as fact. "And then you're going to work for us."

Senator Colemen shook his head. "That isn't possible. Not only am I part of an unpopular party right now, but I'm divorced and have only been in the Senate for a few years."

"Why are you under the impression that we're asking?" I stood, turning to face him. "You're running for President, you will be the President of the United States of America, and you will also work toward our best interests."

"As for your wife," Liam said, paging Adriana who opened the door to reveal the ex-Mrs. Coleman.

"Mom?" Olivia gasped quickly, rising to give her a large hug.

"There, look, a wife. And by coming back together, you will prove you can work with both parties, blah blah blah . . . you have a ready-made family with a lot of connections and deep pockets. When we say you're going to be President, we mean you are the next Commander and Chief. "

"We want the country and the world. Truthfully we wanted it yesterday so don't try to get in our way," I told him.

"It took even God six days to create the world, Mel. Let's not get ahead of ourselves." Neal acted like this was a joke.

"We may be all powerful, but we are not God. We do not want to create the world, we want to own it." Liam rose from his chair. With the end of the fighting, and wars, we could finally do what we did best—make money. We had a whole shipment of drugs pouring in, and we needed to focus on the business.

By the end, we would be untouchable, and what better way to do it than having the President of the United States in your back pocket?

LIAM

When they all left, only Declan and I remained in the study as the sunlight slowly started to creep in through the blinds as it rose over the forest. A new year, a whole new brand of problems, and I wasn't sure how to even begin to tell Melody.

"Check it again, Declan," I commanded pouring the brown liquid in to the crystal glass, this was just . . . *fuck.*

"Liam, I've checked more than ten dozen times in the last two weeks. Nothing is going to change the fact that—"

"Don't you dare fucking say," I snapped, squeezing the glass. "If you say it with that much conviction then it's true. And if it's true, I'm going to be the one who has to explain it. I do not want to fucking explain it."

"Liam, it's time we face this head on. You know it. I know it. It's time Melody knows it."

Easier said than done. I pinched the bridge of my nose and cracked my knuckles trying to ease the tension through my body.

"We've been so happy, Declan," I whispered, staring at the sun as I drank slowly. "She's been happy. How do I tell her that everything she knows is a lie?"

He paused, taking a deep breath as he walked up beside me at the mirror. "It's better that she hears it from you, than finds out on her own."

He handed me the folder once again, and I stared at the woman with short black hair and warm olive skin. Standing tall and proud with her sunglasses on.

"They look so much alike."

"They *are* alike Liam, and all the evidence shows Vance was right. There is much more to this than we knew. Not only that Aviela Giovanni, Melody's mother, isn't dead, but that she's been behind it all. She wants to kill not only you, but her own daughter."

"And Orlando knew?"

"He did what you're trying to do now and protect her. But I doubt that's going to work much longer. Aviela Giovanni just entered the States."

And just like that, I could feel the floodgates of hell beginning to open.

"May God have mercy on all our souls when Mel finds out."

THE END

Children of Vice Sneak Peek

Children of Vice

is the first spin-off novel from the bestselling *Ruthless People* series, and will follow the lives of Liam and Melody Callahan's children. You do not have to start with *Ruthless People*. If you are joining the Callahan family just now, all you need to know is that Liam and Melody had three children. Twins, Donatella and Wyatt. And Ethan, who is their oldest and first child

...this is his story.

PROLOGUE

"Monsters make choices.

Monsters shape the world.

Monsters force us to become stronger, smarter, better.

They sift the weak from the strong and provide a forge for the steeling of souls.

Even as we curse monsters, we admire them.

Seek to become them, in some ways.

There are far, far worse things to be than a monster."

—Jim Butcher

ETHAN

I'm not sure when it happened...

When it began to crack and alter shape...

Looking back, there are so many moments that could be the one, the origin.

If you asked anyone who wasn't family, they'd say it happened the day I was born.

That the moment I came into this world as a Callahan, the innocence, the morality, and the virtues that are normally common to everyone else, were defective. Like a house with fractured windows. If you asked anyone within my family they'd say the windows were not fractured but frosted and bulletproof because that is how it should be. After all, the people who were pointing at my windows were the same people who used blinds. That was my family all right...stupidly rich, dangerously powerful, unspeakably ruthless, and obsessed with extended metaphors. But the thing was...I didn't care if I was a house with fractured or frosted or bulletproof windows. If people were curious to know the type of man I was, they were free to find out at their own peril.

What I cared about was when.

When did it happen?

When did I understand what it meant to be a Callahan?

To be Ethan Antonio Giovanni Callahan.

Staring up at the waters above me until my eyes drifted closed, one memory, one moment came forward...

ETHAN - AGE ELEVEN

He looked like what everyone said Santa Claus was supposed to look like...with everything but the long white beard, though, which made his red-faced, white-skinned, fat body, cloaked in red robes disturbing to see.

"Why is there a screen here if I can still see you?"

He laughed. "Is this your first confession, boy?"

I don't like him. I thought immediately and for three good reasons too.

One, he laughed, when I was being serious.

Two, he didn't answer my question.

Three, he called me "boy."

"Yes," I answered anyway but only because Mom told me to be respectful in church.

"By your seat there is a card. It will tell you what you have to say."

I really don't like him.

Why would you put a card in a dark stall? It was stupid.

Reaching around me, I got the small little card and lifted it up, reading.

"Forgive me, Father, for I have sinned...but no, I haven't." I looked back up at him.

"Really now?" he said, his voice going up. "You haven't done anything wrong?"

"Nope."

"Sometimes we may think things aren't wrong or are so small that they aren't sins, but God cares about them all," he replied.

"Okay, when I have something I'll come back," I told him, putting the card down.

"So you've never said anything to hurt someone? Maybe pushed your little sister—"

"Why would I push my sister?"

"Or hit your brother?"

"Didn't do that either."

"Yelled or fought with your parents?"

"No. My parents would kill me and then bring me back to kick my ass to Ireland so every Callahan there could kill me again." I laughed at that. I liked Ireland. Everyone was kinda like Uncle Neal.

"Callahan?"

The way he said the name made me pay attention to him. He said it like...like it was shocking or scary even. No. When I looked into his blue eyes they were wide-open and shaking. I didn't know that was possible. Maybe his whole head was shaking and I could only really see his eyes.

"Yea." I nodded, adding, "I'm Ethan Antonio Giovanni Callahan, first son of Liam Alec Callahan and Melody Nicci Giovanni Callahan. Are you new to this church?"

He didn't reply, so I knocked on the screen.

"Why are you scared?"

When I said it he sat up more and focused in on me. "I'm not scared."

"You're lying...you should confess that."

His whole jolly priest thing went away when he spoke again. "Understanding who your parents are, I now see why you are so ill-mannered and pompous at such a young age."

Hurt him!

I wanted to, but I kept talking instead. "Who do you think my parents are? I'm sure—"

"It's not who I think they are. It's who they are. Murderers."

"So?" I asked him.

"So? So?"

I nodded. "Moses was a murderer. King David was a murderer. Actually almost everyone in the Bible is a murderer...expect Jesus. But since he's part of God, doesn't that make him a murderer by connection? Because God tells people to kill people too and—"

His voice started to rise. "You are twisting God's words."

"No, it's there. I'm sure."

"You..." He took a deep breath. "In the Bible, boy, God is seeking justice, a righteousness for the whole world, in a world in which there are bad people who hurt people, because back then there were no jails. There was no way to stop people from continuing to hurt and cheat others. The church teaches us every life is precious and in a modern world jails do exist. As such murder is a sin."

"What about the army?"

"It is for the overall well-being of the country and only approved by the church if it is absolutely necessary."

Are all adults dumb like this?

"So then being a murderer is okay. You just need permission. And you can only get permission if it is necessary. My parents only do things if it is necessary—"

"Nothing your parents do, boy—"

"Stop interrupting me!" I snapped, glaring at him as I stood up in the booth. "Stop calling me 'boy.' I told you my name is Ethan Antonio Giovanni Callahan. I haven't interrupted you once. I've allowed you to speak your mind. And you're the one being rude. I told you they are my parents and you still want to talk bad about them to me. If gossiping isn't a sin it should be and you should confess to it. My parents only do things if it is necessary. People attack us all the time, and we defend ourselves, our families, and our people. If my parents weren't murderers...if I wasn't a murderer. We'd be dead!"

He gasped. "What did you just say?"

I didn't reply. The more I looked at him, the angrier I got.

"You've killed someone?"

"Yes, but I'm not asking for forgiveness."

Again, he made another huffy sound.

"What have they done to you? How old are you that they turned you into a monster?"

"Thanks be to God." I said the last line from the confession card he'd told me to pick up before, which meant we were done. Opening the door, I blinked a few times, adjusting to the light.

"Ethan, what took so long?" Dona popped up right in my face. Her dark brown hair was curled up a lot and it made her look funny, but she still liked it. She was grinning like she knew something I didn't. Dona's smile always made me smile no matter what, though.

But before I could say anything, she was already heading toward the booth I'd walked out of.

Grabbing her arm, I pulled her back. "Don't go to him."

She looked at me for a long time before nodding and stepping back next to me. "All the other ones are full. Daddy, Mommy, and Wyatt went in."

I looked around the cathedral and in the wooden rows were all of Mom and Dad's people. Two were directly behind Dona, speaking to each other, and a few others moved through the crowd to be closer to one of the stalls where I guessed Dad, Mom, or Wyatt were.

"Just wait for another one."

"Okay," she agreed, sliding into one of the rows, her green dress puffing up when she did.

Just when I sat next to her to wait, another person moved to the stall, but jerk face Santa Claus came out. He didn't look at me. Well, I think he couldn't see me over all the other people. He apologized to the guy trying to go in next before going back. For some reason, I couldn't look away. I had this feeling in me and I didn't know what it was.

"Where are you going?"

I didn't realize I was standing and moving until she said something.

"To the bathroom," I lied and started to walk through the crowd.

"Ethan!" one of my dad's guards called out to me.

"Bathroom!" I lifted my phone for him to see. I knew he was still following me, but I didn't care. I wasn't doing anything bad. Plus, all the people made it hard for him to catch up.

When I made it out of the main chapel, I looked to my left and right, but the fatso was gone. I went right because...well, why would he go to the church shop place? The farther down the hall I went the darker it became, and the light coming in from the blue stained glass made it look like the sky before it rained. I walked and walked until I got to a hall with a sign that said 'Priests Only.' Ignoring it, I walked down the hall. Most of the doors were closed and one cracked open the tiniest bit. I heard his voice.

"What do you mean the audio did not work?"

Tilting my head and looking through the slit, I saw Fatso near the glass window, trying to look out at someone, gripping the phone in his hard.

"Fine. Fine. That doesn't matter. The boy confessed it. I heard him say with his own mouth that he and his parents were murderers."

What?

It was only then that I noticed the wires on his desk.

It clicked.

Him being new.

Him being new and coming to this church, my parents' church, and hating my parents.

"So you're saying even if I testify it's not enough? What do you want me to do? Catch them in the act?" he yelled so loudly I guessed he didn't hear the door as I came in.

But then again it was even more quiet than I thought it was.

"Look, the deal was...no, you listen to me! The deal was I do this and no one finds out about Ohio. I will not—ugh—ahh!"

"—ugh—ahh!" Those were the sounds he made as my knife went into his back.

Thump.

The phone slipped out of his hands as he tried to turn. Pulling the knife out, I watched as his red robe got darker and darker as the blood came out.

"What...what...what did you...?"

"This." I stabbed him over and over again, anywhere I could, his huge body fell backward, trying to grab onto the desk but falling to the floor.

"Aww, man!" I groaned at my now broken knife. "I just got this one too!"

Sighing, annoyed, I picked up the phone, which was already disconnected. Stepping over him, I grabbed the wires and pulled and cut them.

"Mon...mon..."

"Monday?" I turned back to him.

He was trying to crawl, but to where I didn't know. "Mon…"

"Monkey?"

His belly rose and fell, rose and fell. He was in shock, I think. He was staring at me in shock. His blue eyes shone with tears, not sad tears. Or forgive me tears. Just another liquid coming out of his body.

"Monster," I said to him. "That's what you want to call me, right? This week in school they made us read Frankenstein. It was cool. I liked it. I like books that make me think. That's why I'm in the advanced class. My favorite part is when the monster looks at Dr. Frankenstein and tells him it's his fault. It kinda reminds me of now. You called me a monster. I walked way. Then you threatened the monster. And so if it comes down to you or me, I have to pick me."

"Go to—"

Taking out my second knife…well, Wyatt's knife, I stabbed him in the throat and pulled it out. When I did, blood went everywhere. Wiping my face, I moved to the window that was stained glass too, trying to see what he was looking at before.

"Ethan?"

Turning around, it was my dad's guard. He looked between me and the guy in red…I wasn't sure if he was cop or priest. Pulling out his phone, he dialed one number before speaking.

"Dozen Lilies delivered to my location," he said, walking closer to us.

"From Ethan," I added.

He just stared at me, and so I stared back.

"Yes, that's right. A dozen lilies from...the second. Let the boss know."

"Let them all know," I whispered mostly to myself, staring at both of the knives in my hands.

Rule 103: always have a knife.

ONE

"Begin, be bold, and venture to be wise."

—Horace

ETHAN

It was only when my lungs began to burn, begging for air, did my eyes open again. When I did, I could see figures walking up to the edges. Sitting up from the bottom and swimming till my head broke the surface, I brushed my hair back, inhaling the cold air through my nose.

"Good mornin', boss," all four said.

Two to my left and two to my right.

Replying to none of them, already at the edge, I lifted myself out of the water, walking over to the shower to wash off. A maid, who was trying her hardest not to look at my cock as I rinsed off, dropped sandals at my feet once I stepped out. However, before I could reach for the towel, she made a move to dry me. Toby, saving her life, reached out and grabbed her wrist, gripping tightly as I took the towel for myself and tied it around my waist. When I looked up again I scanned her and then behind her, at the chair where my breakfast was waiting.

"Where is the second towel?" Toby demanded her, releasing her arm.

"Second...what?" She stared wide-eyed and back at me as I moved to my chair. "I'm sorry, sir. I only brought one."

Ignoring her, I sat down, lifting the cover from my food only to wish I hadn't. Annoyed, I dropped the cover back onto the plate.

"I'll get another one—"

"Get out," I spoke under my breath, speaking up for the first time, reaching for my phone and rising back from the chair.

"Sir?" She leaned in.

Scrolling through my messages, I started walking toward the elevator. "Toby, tell the head maid that if she ever tests my patience with halfwit maids again, it will be her who will be seeking new employment."

"Noted." He nodded for her to leave, which she did as if she'd seen the devil himself, forgetting the bloody tray she'd brought in, the idiot.

"Today there is another Chicago City Honorary Brunch. Your grandmother wanted to remind you your sister will not arrive until tomorrow, so you'll have to do the speech," Greyson, the second in line of my men behind Toby, informed me as we entered the elevator. "The speech has been emailed."

I'd already begun to read it before he spoke.

"Next." I waited.

"Mr. Downey...he's here." I gazed up from my phone. He nodded, adding, "It's starting just like you said it would."

"Brilliant." I couldn't help the smirk that spread across my lips. "Let's not keep the traitors waiting."

Exiting the elevator on my floor of the family mansion, there were only two doors on opposite ends of the hall, and neither of them followed me as I reached my own. Pausing, I glanced back at them. Both of them stood shoulder to shoulder, as positive as either of them could be. Grey's short orange Irish hair and large frame, and Toby's shoulder-length brown hair and slimmer build.

"Sir?" Toby stepped up.

"The bodies are about to start piling," were words I shouldn't have had to tell them but did anyway. "And anyone who tries to stop me will find themselves buried alongside their families under that pile."

They did not speak. However, there was nothing they could say...their actions would speak for themselves as would mine. Entering my master room, I took off the towel around my waist, tossing it onto the couch before my bed...a gift of my aunt's, who'd done the whole remodeling of the mansion after my father's death per my request and to the annoyance of both my siblings. By the time they'd finished breaking down walls, putting up new ones, and recreating the whole floor plan, the room looked unrecognizable. Gone was my parents' modern classic bedroom, and in its place, my rustic one, double in size with dark mahogany from floor to ceiling.

There were no doors, except a single one to enter and leave. Walking to my closet, the lights brightened in a row as I passed my suits, heading straight to the middle tabletop, and scanned my finger. The lid slipped back, allowing me to lift the very last gift my mother had gotten me before her death, a silver Diamond Back Colt revolver 38

Special, the words *Che sarà, sarà* engraved on the wooden butt of it.

Loading a single inside, as I did every morning, I put it to the side as I reached for a suit. It did not matter which; I'd be burning it at the end of the day.

Ringgg.

"Is she here?"

"Yes, sir," Toby stated.

Not replying, I hung up.

Not even a second later, I could hear her voice from behind the door.

"Ethan?"

"Here," I said as I buttoned up my navy shirt.

She entered, wearing a bright yellow tailored suit and black heels. Her hair was dyed a copper-blond and cut right above her shoulders.

"Nana, we've spoken about this. You're seventy-three. You can't go around upstaging twenty-year-olds like this."

"Flattery." She pursed her lips and crossed her arms. "I can testify all Callahan men have mastered it. Unfortunately for you, years of exposure have made me immune."

"Should I switch to insults?"

"Would you like to die?"

I smirked at that. "Are you threatening the Ceann na Conairte?"

"Is that what you've become now?"

My jaw clenched as I reached for my tie. *"Grandmother*, I haven't had breakfast yet. I'd advise you to take heed and stop."

"Oh well..." She gasped, taking a seat on the leather bench against the wall separating suits from the rest of my clothing. "Only because you've *advised* me."

"I turn twenty-eight on Saturday."

"I am aware."

Was she? "That's a year older than my father when he'd gotten married to my mother."

She laughed. "Is that why you've been agitated...well, more agitated...than normal lately? Had your grandfather not forced him, he would have waited till he was—"

"Thirty." No matter what, for him to be respected as head of the pack, the Ceann na Conairte, the rules, yes, rules set by my senile, also dead great-grandfather, and passed down from father to son, demanded we marry.

"You still have two years."

"Aren't grandmothers supposed to be worried they'll die before seeing their great-grandchildren?"

She sucked her teeth angrily. "Are you saying I'll die before you get married? Me, who's lived to see your great-grandfather, your grandfather, great uncle, and father murdered? I'll somehow have a shorter life than you?"

Turning around toward her, her eyes narrowed and eyebrows arched.

And it was funny to see her act so gentle and relaxed... "After almost twenty-eight years, you'd think you'd understand my sense of humor by now?"

"You'd think after almost twenty-eight years someone would have told you that you aren't funny in any sense."

To appease her as best I could, I tried self-deprecating. "As if a Callahan man would listen to the opinions of others."

She didn't want to, but she smiled anyway. "Why have you called me here?"

"I've found a wife—"

"Come again?" Her eyes went wide as she stared at me.

"A wife," I said very slowly. "I've found one...well, her."

"Ethan, a woman isn't a cat! What do you mean you found her?"

"It's a long story. Nevertheless, she's going to need your help. She's not exactly Callahan material—and before you ask, I do not know her. She is a tool in a very important game, a tool I need you to secure without a doubt so she'll be ready by my birthday."

She stared at me shocked, confused, annoyed until she finally snapped. "Ethan! I swear to God, if you do not stop being so cryptic—"

"You are aware that someone of the Irish in Boston isn't pleased with this family, correct?"

She grinned, rising to her feet. "Jealously must be hard."

"I would not know," I replied, and she merely made a face as I continued. "*Nana*, that is all I can say for now."

Sighing, she stood in front of me and reached out to place her hand on my cheek, but I backed away. Unfazed, she dropped her hand and spoke again, "You do realize marriage in this family is undoable, correct? You know nothing other than she isn't Callahan material, which is the most important thing for her to be, and yet are willing to sacrifice the rest of your life, privacy, and peace, simply so your grand plan can come together?"

"If it means protecting this family's name and legacy, I'd set myself on fire." I felt my whole body tensing as I spoke. "I will not be the son who inherited the kingdom only to let it crumble at my feet. That is not my fate."

"You do know this is why your cousins are scared of you, correct?" She pouted. "They think you'd kill even me in order to win...let alone them."

I stared at her a long time. She was testing me, wanting to hear what I'd say, and so I didn't answer. Reaching over, I grabbed the gun and placed it in the concealed shoulder holster under my arm before grabbing my coat and offering her my arm.

"Would you like to join me for brunch, Nana?"

"Fine, you can tell me all about where to find this girl," she replied, walking toward the double doors to exit.

"Ethan..." Her voice trailed off as she eyed me dangerously, when again I didn't answer.

"Ricker Hill."

"PRISON?"

"Didn't I mention that?" I paused by my door, hand on the handle.

"NO, you fucking did not!" She cursed, and I couldn't help but smirk.

"And here I thought you didn't judge, Grandmamma—"

"Well, you were wrong for once."

"Once out of a million is hardly a bad record. Shall we go?" I held the door open for her.

Her nose flared and she looked as though she wanted to smack me. However, she maintained her composure upon seeing both Toby and Greyson standing in wait.

"This isn't over."

How could it be? It hadn't even begun.

Dear Reader

I would like to thank all the ruthless people who made this book possible. From my Internet readers to my best friends.
You all are absolutely amazing.
I know if it weren't for you, I would have never made it to this point.
All of you have made me feel incredibly special!

Ruthlessly Yours,
J.J. McAvoy
Just a 20 something year-old-girl
screaming from behind a computer screen.

Discover More by J.J. McAvoy

The Ruthless People Series
Ruthless People
The Untouchables
American Savages
Declan + Coraline (prequel novella)
A Bloody Kingdom

Single Title Romances
Black Rainbow
Sugar Baby Beautiful
That Thing Between Eli and Gwen

Serialized Novels
Child Star

About the Author

J. J. McAvoy first started working on *Ruthless People* during a Morality and Ethics lecture her freshman year of college. If you ask her why she began writing, she will simply tell you "They wanted to get their story out."

She is the oldest of three and has loved writing for years. Her works are inspired by everything from Shakespearean tragedies to modern pop culture. Her first novel, Ruthless People, was a runaway bestseller. Currently she's traveling all across the world, writing, looking for inspiration, and meeting fans. To get in touch, please stay contact via her social media pages, which she updates regularly.

Acknowledgments

It takes one person to actually write a book.
However, it takes an army to keep that person sane.
So to the
FIVE amazing teachers who let me paint the sky
red,
FOUR insane friends who told me to listen to the
voices in my head,
THREE nosey brothers—Jodd, Justin, and yes you
Alex—who brought me Oreos,
TWO awe-inspiring parents who always told me
just do it, and really believed I could,
ONE publishing company, TWCS, that took a
diamond in the rough and made it "reflect,"
Thank you all so much.

Notes

1. We are lagging behind.
2. Oh, my sweet girl.
3. Goodbye.
4. Welcome to the family, Callahans.
5. Sweet little girl.
6. Without respect.
7. Hello my little pretties.
8. Welcome aboard, ma'am.
9. Who are you fuckers? Drop the guns.
10. I am Liam Callahan. This is my fiancée, and you two are dead.
11. All the fucking drugs are gone. Damn those cunts to hell. Vance is going to kill us.
12. My lovely, Mel.
13. Hello, my sweet child.
14. Hello, my sweet father.
15. You look so beautiful, Melody. I'm sorry I was not strong enough for you.
16. You are, and will always be strong enough.
17. Be good to her, Liam.
18. Be good to him, Mel.
19. I will,
20. You all make me sick.

Printed in the USA
CPSIA information can be obtained
at www.ICGtesting.com
LVHW012207030424
776388LV00008B/181